TRIAL & ERROR

By

Alan Sears

xulon
PRESS

Trial & Error
by Alan Sears

Printed in the United States of America

ISBN 9781619042384

Cover design by Bruce Ellefson

www.xulonpress.com

www.telladf.org

DEDICATION

———⟩◆⟨———

This book is dedicated to the entire ADF team and its allies around the globe who work tirelessly to defend our most precious, God-given liberty: Religious Freedom.

*"No enactment of man can be considered law
unless it conforms to the law of God."*

Sir William Blackstone

Prologue

—◆—

G reg Mayer stood ankle deep in wreckage. He was saddened not only by the loss of life, the still unsolved mystery, but most of all by the fact that he had grown used to seeing the remnants of disaster.

Mangled and burned sheets of aluminum, ripped by ferocious stress, littered the floor of the large, open space of the hanger.

No, littered was the wrong word. To the untrained eye, the twisted struts, the bundles of wires, the bent hydraulic lines, the deformed seats that had once provided comfortable resting for the passengers of the Gulfstream G550 might look like nothing more than refuse piled up and waiting for a dump truck to cart it all off to a landfill. To Mayer, it was much more.

He had overseen the process of laying out every recoverable piece of the business jet that took the lives of two associate justices of the United States Supreme Court, two pilots, a deputy U.S. Marshall, and an aide. All told, six barely recognizable corpses, torn and burned. It had taken DNA testing to tell which limb went with which torso.

As best as could be done with the remains of a craft that had plummeted nearly twenty thousand feet, pieces were set on the hanger floor in a manner that roughly corresponded to their location before the crash. Reconstruction was part of what a National Transportation Safety Board investigator did. Reconstruct the aircraft as much as possible and look for the cause of the crash.

Mayer strolled the cluttered floor looking at bits and pieces he had studied countless times before. As the Go Team's Investigator-in-Charge,

Greg Mayer was responsible for the investigation. He had a great team of experts, each were experienced and specialists in their field.

He raised his gaze from the fractured remains of what had once been a beautiful business jet and looked through the clear skylights overhead. A half moon pressed its light through the darkness of the 2:00 a.m. morning. He should be back in his Houston hotel, fast asleep and dreaming of less stressful jobs, but sleep eluded him. The passing of time made him more anxious. His team had a good idea of why the jet came down, and it wasn't good. Associate Justices Collins and Grouling were assassinated in a most unusual way. The weapon had been a series of ones and zeros, the code to a program that took over the aircraft's computer system. That much he knew. He knew very little else.

He redirected his gaze to a pair of seats, the one's in which the crushed and shredded bodies of Collins and Grouling had been found. Even in the dim light,—Mayer had turned on only half of the overhead lights—he could see the stains of blood and other body fluids on the leather surfaces of the seats.

The country waited for answers, as did the President of the United States, the Chief Justice of the Supreme Court, the Attorney General, as well as the head of the National Transportation Safety Board. His boss had selected him to be the IIC on this case because Mayer was the best investigator at the NTSB. At the moment, he felt like the rawest, untested rookie.

Although he would never admit it publicly, Mayer, there in the dim hanger surrounded by a Stygian Texas night, began to believe the perpetrator would get away with it. The eyes of the FAA, the FBI, and the rest of Homeland Security were on him. He had never failed to solve a case yet and although technically he had solved the case, he knew his work wasn't done.

He moved to one of the windows and stared into the still night. Looking back was the reflection of a man in his mid-fifties, short, curly brown hair cut close to the scalp, a dominate nose, and weary blue eyes. He studied the reflection and felt a moment of disdain.

He was failing in his mission.

Mayer spoke to his reflection. "We're not finished yet. No, sir. Not yet."

Chapter 1

"24-601"

⟹◆⟸

The Hague, Netherlands, May 30, 2018

Noise pressed into the small space and Pat Preston did his best not to listen. In the early weeks he often resorted to pressing his index fingers into his ears so deeply they hurt. The pain was more tolerable than the relentless buzzing. He would hum, hoping to drown out the incessant sound burrowing into his brain.

The screams were the worst. The sudden outbursts of manic laughter were unsettling; the moans heartrending, the weeping soul-shredding, but the screams — they came in the middle of the night, or shortly before dawn. Piercing and powerful, the screams had fought through every barricade of courage, pressed through barriers of resolve, dissolved with acid-like efficiency whatever remained of the man's dignity. Like a hill saturated with rain, pride and determination lost its tenacious hold on reality and slid away, leaving men little more than bags of mindless flesh capable of only fear and despair.

Pat Preston knew the feeling. It took three nights before he could sleep; five days before he could eat what he was served; two weeks to exorcize the occasional thoughts of suicide; and three weeks before he stopped telling himself he was dreaming.

He wasn't dreaming. He was a man alone in a small gray cell. No windows. One bed: a raised bier of concrete with a worn four-inch mattress resting on the flat surface, covered in worn, coarse military style blankets. Just two. No pillow. He wondered about the men who had the mattress before him. Where were they now? Had they become screamers as well? Were they wasting away in some prison worse than this one?

Could a place be worse? Pat knew there were worse places, but he had trouble imagining them. Perhaps in Turkey or a Russian gulag. Such places were expected there, but not here. This was one of the most civilized cities in one of the most civilized countries. The people who designed this prison were erudite folk, educated, highly regarded.

Pat paced the space: four strides from left to right (he thought of it as north to south, but he couldn't be certain if he was correct); three strides east to west. About nine by twelve, give or take a few inches. One hundred and eight square feet. His children had bigger bedrooms.

He touched the west wall. Maybe it was the southwestern wall. It was late afternoon. With no window, he couldn't see sun nor sky, but he could tell by the wall's growing warmth it was sunny outside and past noon. It also meant the world was just on the other side of the reinforced concrete. How thick was the wall? Four inches? Six? Two feet? It didn't matter; it might as well be a mile.

He had everything a body needed but nothing the mind desired. He had the bed. There was a seat-less, metal toilet fastened to the floor with thick bolts, a steel sink protruded from the gray surface of the wall. Next to the toilet and in front of the lavatory, set in the floor, were foot buttons that activated water for the devices. The amount of water was limited. In the floor, next to the sink, was a two-inch diameter drain. No shower. Just a drain. A small wash cloth was provided every day so Pat could wash his body with water from the sink.

When he arrived two months ago, they stripped him of his clothing, his possessions, and his dignity. There was no privacy. His living room was his bedroom; his bedroom his bathroom. A single video camera kept track of his every move, an unblinking, ever vigilant eye. When he slept, they watched; when he sat on the toilet, they watched; when he ate; they watched. Watched every hour of the day; watched every minute of the night.

No windows, no bars, just a heavy steel door mounted on exterior facing hinges. The door reached from floor to the ceiling just seven feet above the floor. The door had a wire-reinforced window, mirrored on his side. If someone were at the window watching him now, he wouldn't be able to tell. Near the bottom of the door was a small slot with a flap. Three times a day someone would push a metal tray of food through it. No plates, just food on the tray and a plastic spoon. The spoon had to be returned or annoyed men would enter and search for it.

Over head a single low-voltage light protected by a steel and glass enclosure cast dim illumination through the cell. The light never went off. It glowed twenty-four hours a day. Pat had not experienced darkness since they brought him to this place.

This was Hell.

Through the years of his ministry, Pastor Pat had preached a number of sermons on Hell. It was his least favorite topic and brought more sorrow to his soul than anything else that crossed his pulpit to the congregation of thousands of worshipers at Rogers Memorial Church in Nashville. Still, Hell was a doctrine of Scripture and he felt obligated to teach that truth along with the rest of the Bible—a conviction that started all his troubles.

Nashville: so far away, home to his family; his kids; his wife. So many miles distant in time and space. The image of Becky rose to his mind. He could see her playing with Luke and Phoebe. He always pictured them at the ages they were during his early days as pastor of the 10,000 member church: a year old for Phoebe; two years old for Luke. They were older now. He had watched with pride as Luke started school and Phoebe adjusted to preschool.

He missed them. Every second of recollection cored out a little more of his sanity. But he would not give up. He took his stand and he would not allow his children to see him crumble. Not that they could see him now separated by thousands of miles and a wide, unforgiving ocean.

He felt a chill. The temperature in his cell was controlled by others, deliberately designed to keep him uncomfortable. It was never too cold or too hot, but always just a little too warm or a little too cool to be comfortable, all engineered to limit his resistance and physical strength. Even his food was regulated to follow a prescription designed by a physician. He received exactly enough calories, carbohydrates, proteins, and other foods to keep him alive and healthy, if not satisfied. He was allowed only water. No coffee. No tea. No soda. Water and water alone. In his more paranoid moments, he wondered what they put in the water. The drinks were served in sealed mugs that made Pat feel like a toddler learning to drink from a sipper cup because he couldn't be trusted not to spill.

Near the bed, recessed into the wall, was a small nook that held two books, the most he was allowed, both worn paperbacks. One was a compilation of the writings of C.S. Lewis, Pat's favorite Christian thinker. He had written his doctoral dissertation on the man. The second volume was a New Testament. He had asked for a complete Bible but that was, they told him, unacceptable since such a large book could be thrown at one of the guards. Perhaps they spoke from experience. Pat couldn't imagine hurling a Bible at another man.

Pat sat on the edge of the bed, his bare feet resting on the cold concrete and ran a hand on the stubble of hair on his head. His hair was kept short by two guards who arrived every Monday with an electric razor and ran it over his head for sixty-seconds. "For health reasons," they had told him during his first shearing, but he was pretty sure it was meant to strip away a little more of his identity. Every other day he was allowed the use of a heavy duty electric razor to shave his face. They allowed him four minutes to do so. The razor always arrived dirty and clogged with the hair of the men who had used it before him. So much for "health reasons."

Everything was timed. The meals arrived, best he could tell, at the same time every day. Each morning he was allowed one hour of exercise: 100 walking laps. It was the only time he saw a human not in a guard's uniform. Several prisoners shared the time, but were not permitted to walk together or speak. Still, seeing others reminded him he was not alone. He wondered about the men. Some were older, several younger. Each looked thin, worn, and desperate. Pat relied on his faith to keep him going. He often wondered what they relied upon. It was then that Pat committed to praying for the other

14

men. He did so three times a day, after every meal. He didn't know their names so he assigned monikers: Fred who looked American; Benny who looked Danish; Jason for the black man; and Theodore for the man with the wire-rimmed glasses.

Pat lay on the pillow-less bed and tried to imagine himself somewhere other than the gray holding-cell awaiting trial by the judges who should not have authority over him or any American. Pat had committed no crime and he certainly hadn't done so in Europe, yet he had spent two months as the guest of the International Court of Justice and his government; a government that had signed a treaty vastly expanding the court's reach and jurisdiction.

His crime? Preaching. He, like tens of thousands of ministers before him, preached a simple Gospel that portrayed Jesus as the only means of eternal salvation—a message that was broadcast over television, radio, and the Internet. That sermon and others like it claiming Jesus was not *a* way, but *the* way . . . not *a* truth, but *the* truth had landed him here.

He felt it coming: the onslaught of self-pity. It came several times a day and, no matter how many times he told himself he wouldn't play the game again, he did. First he blamed his old college friend, John Knox Smith, Assistant US Attorney General and head of DTED: Diversity and Tolerance Enforcement Division, of the Department of Justice. From friends to adversaries in a process Pat had yet to understand. He did understand that he was in a drab cell and Knox was sitting comfortably in his home.

The sense of despair washed over him like a tidal flood, but he fought against it. Pat was determined to remain strong. He refused to let others see a Christian despair. He would follow the course before him, even if the path was no longer than the width of his cell.

"Attention Prisoner 24-601. Attention Prisoner 24-601."

Pat didn't move.

"Attention Prison 24-601!" The volume was twice as loud and pounded Pat's ears.

"Listening. I'm listening."

"Prisoner 24-601. You will remove your uniform and stand at attention for visual inspection." The disembodied voice bore a heavy Dutch accent.

"Now? Why? What's going on?"

The volume increased another dozen decibels. Violence through sound. "Prisoner 24-601, you will stand, remove your uniform and stand for inspection."

Pat stood. "Uniform. It's the same surgical style pants and top I've been wearing since I got here." He raised a hand. "Never mind. I will do as I'm told."

Pat stripped, folding his garb and underwear, setting them on the bed. Then stepping to the center of the cell, he faced the door.

"Prisoner 24-601, take two steps back."

Pat did and waited. His stomach twisted into a knot, but he struck a casual, nonthreatening pose: hands to his sides, head raised so his eyes focused on the door, and his bare feet flat on the cement.

A buzz echoed in the small room and the heavy steel door swung outward. Six men—Pat expected the usual four—entered. Each looked like they could play frontline on any NFL team in the States.

"Gentlemen," Pat said with a nod.

The only weapons they carried were rubber truncheons. As far as Pat was concern, the most deadly weapons in the room were the guards. *Let my demeanor be a witness, O Lord. Give me control of my mind and my mouth.*

"You know the position," one of the guards shouted. "Why aren't you in the position?"

"I apologize." Pat spoke softly. "I wasn't expecting visitors—" Two of the uniformed men spun Pat around and forced him to the wall, pressing his nude body to the cold surface. One of them cursed. "Hands on the wall. Spread your feet." He smacked a truncheon across Pat's lower back. Pain scorched his spine. Still, the man showed restraint. He hit Pat just hard enough to hurt but not so hard as to leave marks or strike him in such a way that the other men couldn't conceal the act from the ever-present video camera. Prisoner abuse wasn't allowed in such a civilized prison, or so he was told when he arrived.

The smallest of the men stepped to Pat's side while two guards ran their hands over Pat's naked body as if he had pockets of skin in which to hide a machine gun. He had long ago given up the attempt to find logic in the actions of the guards. He knew it was meant to embarrass him, to make him even more uncomfortable.

The thin man smiled. "I hope you are enjoying your vacation, Preacher. The next place they send you will not be nearly so nice as these fine accommodations."

"I hope you'll visit. I'd hate to see our new friendship end."

The thin man lost his smile and Pat immediately regretted the glib comment. He had learned the best course of action was to keep silent and show no emotion.

"You should mind your tongue, Preacher. You are still in my care."

The thin man waved the others off. Each took a step back but remained within arm's reach. Pat turned his face to the wall and tried to focus on a small cavity in the concrete's surface. "Look at me, Preacher."

Pat turned his head and stared at the man. He had trouble sensing a soul behind those eyes.

"You have a face-to-face meeting today, Preacher Man."

The news stunned Pat. The few meetings he was allowed with his attorneys and the one time his wife was allowed to see him had been conducted by video. No personal contact. At one time, in the US, that would have been considered cruel and unusual punishment; not here. Here it was standard operating procedure.

"Ah, see, we have something in common," Thin Man said. "You are surprised by the news and so am I."

"I don't understand—"

"Nor do I, but no one asked my opinion, which is a good thing for you. Such a meeting is a . . . a *hassle* . . . is that the American word?"

"Yes. Hassle."

"You see, your meeting is causing me to miss my lunch break, and poor Jacques here was supposed to leave early for his forty-day holiday. Now he must be late to his own holiday. This has made his family unhappy, but you probably don't care about that, do you?"

I've seen my wife once in months and my children not at all. I can't feel sorry for a man starting a five week vacation a little late.

"Nothing to say, Prisoner 24-601?"

17

"I'm just as confused as you, sir."

"Interrupting breaks and holidays is another violation of our international human rights. I hope they charge you with that crime as well."

Pat chose silence as his response. Anything more he said could only make things worse.

Thin Man seemed disappointed that no response came. "Get dressed and be quick about it. I am told we are not to keep your guest waiting. For some reason, my superior was very emphatic about that."

The comment puzzled Pat even more, as did the clothing one of the guards had set on the bed next to the simple, monochrome garb he was forced to wear each day. These clothes included a shirt with buttons, something he hadn't seen since being stripped of his own shirt two months before. There was also a pair of black trousers and loafers.

Pat dressed quickly beneath the unflinching gaze of the six guards. The shirt was a size too big, or maybe he had lost more weight than he realized. The pants had an elastic waist and fit nicely. The slip-on shoes were a little cramped but Pat didn't mind. It beat being barefoot.

"Out the door and to the left."

Pat nodded but said nothing as he shuffled from the cell, three guards in front of him and three behind. He moved down the hallway to another steel door, this one of standard height and had been painted white. The thin man opened the door and stepped to the side. Pat was ushered in. He expected a divided room and a Plexiglas window to separate him from the visitor. Instead, he found a simple metal table bolted to the floor. At the side of the table closest to him was a gray metal chair, also bolted to the floor. Opposite that were a pair of empty chairs.

"Sit," the thin man ordered. Pat did. "Jacques."

One of the other guards knelt by Pat and roughly slapped a stainless steel shackle around Pat's ankle. The cold of the metal pressed through his pants leg. The shackle was tethered to the floor by three feet of chain. Pat could stand and move, but not very far.

The six guards stepped away from the table and positioned themselves around the room, their backs to the wall.

Across the room was another door. Pat heard the electronic lock slide and the door opened.A man walked in, followed by a woman.

Pat's jaw dropped. A moment later, he shot to his feet.

Chapter 2

The Man in the Red Shoes

━━▷◈◁━━

Pat's first thought was: *I've fallen in my cell and hit my head. Concussion. That explains it. A concussion.*

Several people entered the room. One was a middle-aged, handsome man dressed in black and wearing a clerical collar. Next to him were two men in gray suits; the suits, although well-tailored, seemed a tad too small. Then Pat realized the suits weren't too small, the men were too big. Although dressed like businessmen, these two didn't seem the kind to sit behind a desk and worry about actuary tables, stock prices, or the prime rate. A glance at the prison guards told Pat they had taken notice of the men.

Next to the man in the clerical collar was a dark-haired young woman with Mediterranean features, ebony eyes that first scanned the room, then Pat. She wore an expensive looking, tailored pant suit in charcoal gray, a white blouse, and the kind of pumps his wife Becky always called "sensible shoes." She had a quiet, confident beauty.

The others moved to the side, their heads lowered slightly as the black-skinned man neared the table. On his head rested a white skullcap called a *zucchetto*. Pat knew the name only because he had taught a comparative religion study at his church. He spent several sessions on Roman Catholicism. To prepare, he learned everything he could about the Roman church's hierarchy and that included the vestments worn by popes, cardinals, and bishops. Some of the facts he learned buzzed in his brain: bishops wore purple zucchettos, cardinals red, priests wore black. Only the Pope wore a white skullcap.

The black man moved to the side of one of the chairs. His white robe and hooded cape were clean and pressed as if just delivered by the papal tailor. A gold pectoral cross rested against his chest. Pat's eyes drifted to the Pope's hand and saw the gold Fisherman's Ring on one finger. His studies came back to him. The ring represented St. Peter the Fisherman, the man Roman Catholics considered the first Pope. Each ring was unique to each Pope. It was customary to kiss the ring during a papal audience, but physical contact was forbidden in the prison. Not being Catholic, Pat wondered if he would have kissed the ring anyway. He had no idea about the theology of such an act.

"I am Monsignor Ramone Erik," the priest said. "I am pleased to present you the Holy Father, his Holiness, Pope John Paul Benedict."

Pat's mouth went dry. He waited for words to come, but for the first time in his life, he was speechless. He tried to swallow but failed.

The black man smiled, revealing a row of perfect, white teeth. He leaned forward and spoke softly. "Do you think we should sit?"

Pat blinked several times, then returned the smile. "Yes, I think we should." He waited for the leader of 1.5 billion Catholics to sit first, then lowered himself into the metal chair. The woman sat next to Benedict and Pat noticed a thin, leather folder containing a legal pad. When she opened it, he could see several typewritten pages held together with a plastic paperclip.

Benedict leaned forward, setting his elbows on the table and folding his hands. "Are you well, my son?" His voice was deep and smooth.

Pat wanted the man to define what he meant by well. "I am not ill."

"That is good to hear." Benedict stared deep into Pat's eyes as if sucking the truth from his brain. He then smiled broadly. "I have had many rules broken to see you, Reverend Preston. Many have told me that insisting on a personal visit might not be prudent. It seems my presence causes a disturbance wherever I go." He paused.

"Sometimes I long for the days of the simple priesthood when I served a small congregation in Nigeria."

The comment made Pat smile. "My first church peaked at one-hundred-and-fifty—on Easter. There is something to be said for small congregations."

"Yes, but God has different plans for us." Benedict leaned back. "Through the kind favors of some friends in the diplomatic corps, arrangements were made for me to be here—at my request, you understand. Still, there are rules to be observed. I am told I cannot shake your hand, and we must remain seated at all times. Apparently, two men of the cloth like ourselves frighten these people."

Pat tried not to grin. He had no idea the Pope had a sense of humor. "They are a cautious bunch."

Benedict nodded. "I am also told I may not pass anything to you directly. I do not like such rules, but I thank God I can be here to visit with you." He rubbed his chin. "Although we differ on some things, Reverend Preston, we have much in common. Our faith in the one, true God and His Son, the Savior Jesus Christ."

"You know, it's that kind of language that landed me in here in the first place."

The Pope grinned. "If they wish to arrest me, they are welcome to . . . try." He leaned on the table again. "My time is short, so I must say what I've come to say quickly. First, I have come to tell you that you are not alone. No matter how lonely you may feel, millions care about your situation. It is not you alone that is on trial, but all of us who feel God's call to spread the Gospel to the world. When I send out my intentions for worldwide prayer in a few days, every Catholic priest and religious order across the globe will be asked to pray for you, by name, each day until this all ends in victory for the Kingdom of God."

"Thank you. That means a great deal to me."

"I pray for you daily and will not cease as long as this matter remains unresolved. I have watched several hours of your sermons on video. I have read your dissertation on C.S. Lewis. You may not know this, but while working on one of my three doctorates and before becoming archbishop in my homeland Nigeria, I studied under some of the same professors at Oxford as you. Years apart, of course. I, too, wrote about Mr. Lewis. I remain a fan of his Narnia books as well as his nonfiction work."

For reasons Pat couldn't fully fathom, he felt comfortable in the man's presence. His emotions ricocheted between amazement, confusion, excitement and even hope. He wondered how many hours they could spend talking about the symbolism Lewis used in his fiction, but he knew that would not happen.

"I have also come to pray for you, Reverend Preston." Benedict reached across the table and touched Pat's arm.

"No touching!" Jacques snapped the words and started toward the men. Before he could take his second step, one of the men in suits stepped in his way. He placed a hand on the guard's chest. Jacques grabbed the wrist, but seemed unable to move it.

"I wouldn't do that." It was the first words the woman said. Her words were firm but unthreatening. They also traveled on a pleasant accent. "I don't know how much you know about the Swiss Guard, but no matter how much training you've had, it isn't enough to do what you're thinking."

Jacques backed away one step, his hand on the truncheon. The Pope's security man gave no sign of being intimidated.

"My apologies." Benedict removed his hand from Pat's arm. "The mistake is mine. Please forgive me." He made eye contact with Pat who, for a moment, saw a glint of mischievousness in the man's eyes. "I will be more careful."

Apparently, Jacques and the others knew better than to speak. Pat Preston didn't consider them the sharpest crayons in the box, but he knew they weren't fools either. The Pope was, after all, the Pope.

"I appreciate all the prayers I can get. Thank you."

"I have also brought you a gift of sorts. Reverend Preston, please meet Countess Isabella San Philippa. She is a layperson who was been of great service to the Church. She is a gifted lawyer."

Pat and the countess exchanged nods. "Countess?"

Isabella smiled. "Yes, a real countess. I work for the Holy See through the Office of the Secretariat of State. For time's sake, I will simplify. The department I work for runs the Holy Father's office and his day-to-day affairs, as well as overseeing the international relationships the church has with countries worldwide.

"I am the chief troubleshooter. I solve legal problems related to the Church and its activities. I know you have attorneys on your side and they have done a good job so far, but you need someone with more international expertise to work with them. The Holy Father has asked me to do so. On his behalf, I have approached your attorneys from the Alliance and they have approved this meeting."

"I'm not sure what to say."

The Pope raised a finger. "If I may, Dr. Preston, I would like you to hear a little more from Countess San Philippa." He turned to Isabella. "I believe a man like Dr. Preston would appreciate a few words about your background."

"Yes, Holy Father." She turned her gaze back to Pat. "I was born in Switzerland to diplomat parents. We traveled the world. During my childhood, I visited more countries than most people can name. As Catholics, we attended Mass in whatever country we found ourselves in, but it meant little to me, at the time.

"I attended law school in both Europe and in the United States, earning an advanced degree in International Law from New York University. After graduation, I clerked in the Supreme Court of Europe in Luxembourg. I served there for three years until I was asked to clerk for the chief justice of the International Court of Human Rights in Strasbourg. I oversaw the training of all staff lawyers for the court and, eventually, even the newly appointed justices. I have no desire to sound immodest, but my program was well received, so much so, that the court here in The Hague asked me revise their training programs, which I did. Because of that work, I know the machinery of the court and every justice very well—all except the most recent appointments."

She paused.

"Countess," the Pope said. "Dr. Preston is a spiritual man. I'm sure he will be equally interested in your spiritual journey."

She smiled. "I mentioned I had very little interest in the Church or spiritual things as a child. While working here in The Hague, I met my husband whose family holds the title from ancient nobility. He is a wealthy man whose family made its fortune in international shipping. This allows us to do a lot of things for the Lord others are not free to do. More importantly, my then boyfriend, now husband and father of my two children, re-introduced me to the Lord. I believe you would say, 'he led me to the Lord.' As an adult, I made a spiritual commitment. Of all my journeys, that has been and remains my greatest adventure."

One of the guards snickered, but no one at the small table acknowledged him.

"Together we read the Scriptures. I left the court and spent a year of spiritual sabbatical. When His Holiness took the Chair of Peter, a mutual friend suggested me for the Secretariat to address some legal matters. I have been doing such work every since."

"I don't know what to say. This is all so sudden and overwhelming. I am not a wealthy man—"

Benedict raised a finger and Pat stopped mid-word. "Dr. Preston, Peter the Apostle told the crippled man at the Gate Beautiful, 'Silver and gold have I not, but what I do have I give unto you. Take up thy bed and walk.' Things have changed. The church may not have cash laying about, but it has many resources. What I have is yours. In addition to the prayers, the friendship which I now offer, and the help of the countess, I will, through her, if and when it is appropriate, offer other support on your behalf." He leaned closer. "They may have silenced you for awhile; they will not silence the Church."

Tears flowed down Pat's cheeks. Emotion choked him.

Pope Benedict rose from the chair. "Thank you for meeting with us. I hope we provided a little encouragement."

Pat struggled to his feet and spoke softly. "Your Holiness, as a Protestant, I've . . . What I meant to say is . . ."

"I know you do not hold the Holy See with the same affection and respect we do. I also know you have been critical of the papal system. As I said, I've read your works and listened to your sermons, but you should know this: In my position, I am called to work with many whom I disagree with and who disagree with me. I am not asking you to become a Catholic. I am asking that you let one brother in the Lord help another, as you have helped others during your ministry. Do you know what death is, Dr. Preston?"

"Yes, of course."

"Death is merely that act by which we finally get our doctrine straightened out."

The comment made Pat smile.

"I was orphaned by rioters who killed my parents before my eyes. My sisters also saw the slaughter. A group of nuns took us in, saving our lives and teaching us about Christ and opening the Scripture to us. In my country, as in so much of Africa, we know there is no hope for mankind outside of Christ. Protestants and Catholics there have many disagreements, but we all agree on the Lordship of Jesus and the battle for religious liberty, life, and marriage."

He lowered his head for a moment as if looking for his next words on the floor. "I, too, have many disagreements with you about a segment of the church that has gone without direction for so many centuries, but for now we must face this present darkness together. You are not alone in this fight. Soon other priests and pastors will be forced to walk through the fires you have. We must extinguish those flames. Do you agree?"

"Yes. I agree." A new sense of hope percolated through him.

"Good. I can straighten out your doctrine once this is all over."

For the first time in several months, Pat Preston laughed.

"Let us pray," the Pope said.

"I'm sorry, sir. Time is up." It was the thin guard.

Pope Benedict's eyes swept over the man. "I shall pray." It wasn't a request.

The Pope crossed himself as did the monsignor and the countess. The two Swiss guards kept their heads up and their eyes on the uniformed men in the room.

Preston lowered his head and for the next few minutes listened as the orphan from Nigeria, now the leader of the Roman Catholic Church, prayed. He prayed for Pat, the case, the Body of Christ, even for those guarding and prosecuting Pat. Pat also prayed aloud, calling to mind his family and asking God for the strength and wisdom to be a witness to all around him.

When he had finished praying, Pat looked up and said, "You know, Your Holiness prays like a Baptist."

"And you, Reverend, almost pray like a Catholic."

"One thing remains, Your Holiness," Isabella said. She turned to Pat. "Dr. Preston, may I join your defense team?"

"Only if you call me Pat, Countess."

Chapter 3

Two Wives

"I brought cookies." Wilma Benson stood at the door with a turquoise Melmac platter of chocolate chip goodies. The platter reminded Becky Preston of the dish-ware her mother owned. Melmac occupied many kitchen shelves in the sixties and seventies.

"You shouldn't have." Becky stepped aside so the elderly woman could enter the small bungalow house in the east part of Nashville. "I still have cookies left over from last week."

Wilma seemed stunned. "I thought the children would have eaten them all by now."

Becky took the platter and shut the door. "I limit their cookie consumption. They'd eat cookies for breakfast if I'd let them. Especially *your* cookies."

"That's sweet of you to say, dear. Baking keeps me busy. It's important to keep the mind occupied."

Although somewhat bent by age and osteoporosis, the seventy-four year old woman moved with a practiced grace. A few times Becky had seen a hitch in her step, but today she walked easily to the dining room table. At times Becky thought the woman was in better shape than she, even though there was nearly four decades between their ages.

Becky set the platter on the table as Wilma took one of the seats. "Where are the children?"

"At a neighbor's. Play date."

"It's good for them to have friends, even at their young age."

"Coffee or tea this time?"

"Coffee would be nice." She sighed as she sat as if the trek across the room had been a mile long.

"It'll be coffee for me as well. I need it." Becky poured two mugs and delivered them.

Anticipating Wilma's arrival, she had already set cream and sugar at the center of the table. Both used cream but neither used the sugar or sweetener. Still Becky set the items out just as her mother had taught her so many years before.

"Need it?" Wilma studied Becky as if pertinent information had been printed on her skin. Didn't sleep well?"

Becky shook her head. "No. Phoebe had a nightmare and woke Luke up. They both slept in my bed the rest of the night. I'm one of those people who has trouble going back to sleep after being awakened." She immersed her attention in the coffee. Wilma was looking at her. The older woman could read her thoughts. She didn't know how Wilma did it, but it was unsettling. Perhaps having been a pastor's wife for five decades gave her a supernatural skill at discovering truth buried in mounds of lies.

"Poor thing. How many does that make this week?"

"Three for Phoebe and two for Luke." Becky brushed a strand of reddish-brown hair over her ear. The red was new, an effort to change her mindset by changing her hair color. It hadn't worked. The small house that replaced the spacious parsonage provided by her husband's former church was no larger, no newer, no better appointed. She was still a virtual-widow with two small children, no income, and living on savings and the help of family and friends.

"And you?"

Becky looked up. "Sorry?"

"Your nightmares, dear. How many have you had since we met last week?"

Becky shrugged. "It's been a good week. Only two."

Tears filled Wilma's eyes. Wilma did more than sympathize; she empathized. Pat had explained the difference in a sermon the previous year: "Sympathy and empathy are similar. Both words come from the Greek, but there is a big difference. Sympathy means to feel sorry for someone; empathy means to feel the same thing as someone." The sound of Pat's voice played in her ears as if he were sitting at the table with them. It had been a long time since she and her husband shared something so mundane as drinking coffee and chatting about how the previous night's sleep went.

A hand, soft, wrinkled, and covered in nearly translucent skin, touched her forearm. The act communicated more than all the sermons ever preached. Wilma was a walking, breathing, poster of Christian compassion. Not the kind of compassion put on by the wife of a preacher because it came with the job. Wilma oozed compassion: genuine, heart-centered love. To Becky, Wilma was the poster-child of Christian charity.

And she knew why.

Their paths had crossed many months before, after government agents invaded her husband's church while he worked late. Suspecting that criminals had forced their way into the building, the frightened seventy-six year old pastor retrieved a pistol left in his office by a worried deacon who felt protection was needed for the church tellers who counted the sparse offering each Sunday. After all, the church "isn't in the best part of town." Wilma's husband, Pastor Teddy, thought it easier to ignore the weapon than argue the point.

Terrified that thugs meant to harm him, Pastor Teddy raised the weapon, hoping to frighten off the thieves. The door to his office sprung open and the pastor saw several men dressed in black. Armed men. The gun he held went off. One of the men fell, a bullet hole in his head. The other men opened fire. How was the old man to know the black clad assailants were government agents?

An overzealous team leader and a terrified minister became an unfortunate concoction of death. Pat had explained it all to Becky after Wilma came to his office seeking someone brave enough to perform a funeral service for a preacher who, no matter how unintentionally, killed a lawman. Pat said yes in a heartbeat. That's the way he was. People first; self later.

Becky stood by Wilma as they lowered the old man's casket into the cold ground. Now Wilma stood by Becky as she grieved the imprisonment of her husband in a distant land, and the effects it had on her and the children.

"I think you have it worse." Wilma drew back her hand and cradled the coffee cup, absorbing the warmth. The woman's hands were always cold. Poor circulation. Not unusual in a woman of her years and health. Still, no matter how cold her hands, the widow's heart remained warm.

"Worse? How do you mean?"

"I lost my husband in a moment's time. Oh, the pain is still there. I'm sure it will stay with me until I walk the streets of glory." She gazed at the table as if seeing something only her eyes could perceive. "I remember the police coming by my house to say Teddy had been shot and killed, and that . . ." She swallowed, "that he had killed that poor man."

"Poor man? Wilma, the man charged into Pastor Teddy's office, waving a gun. And why? Because people in the neighborhood complained he had been passing out Gospel tracts."

"I know, dear, I know. It's just that . . ." She didn't finish the sentence.

"I'm sorry, Wilma. I'm still very bitter about everything."

Again, Wilma touched Becky's forearm. "No need to apologize to me, dear. I have my moments of anger, too. More than moments, really. When I think of the things they said about Teddy . . . The words they used: intolerant, moral terrorist, murderer . . ." Tears flowed down wrinkled cheeks. "Anyway, it all happened so quickly. Your ordeal is so slow. Still, I believe you and your husband will be reunited and that all this madness will end."

Becky wanted to share Wilma's optimism, but she had been unable to believe everything would be put right. True, Pat was still alive, but he might not be released for a very long time. And would he still be the same loving husband and father? He had been through so much, fought such deep depression. The church he had poured his time and his life into had turned its back on him. Wilma's tiny church of elderly parishioners had been her only support in town. The small band of worshippers had pooled their limited resources to send Becky to The Hague to visit Pat while Becky's mother took care of the children. It nearly broke the church.

"I hope you're right, Wilma. I really do. It's just so hard to remain positive and . . . Christ-like through all of this. I'm filled with hate toward so many people who fabricated all of this. They don't care that they're destroying other lives in an effort to make themselves look good and push their stupid agenda."

Wilma nodded, then sipped her coffee. "And God?"

"What about God?"

"Are you still angry with Him?"

Becky studied the woman. She was mind-reading again. "I never said I was angry with God."

Wilma smiled. "I was. I had a good, long talk with God about His willingness to let a servant who served him faithfully for fifty years be killed and his reputation ruined. I held nothing back. I wondered how God could let such a thing happen to a man who surrendered so much to serve a small church be murdered in the church office."

"Did you get an answer?"

"How do you argue with Someone who gave His own Son to redeem your soul?" She reached for a cookie and set it on a napkin. "When I was young, I thought being a Christian meant being exempt from trouble. It took a long time for me to realize that suffering was part of the package. The mark of the Christian isn't that we are exempt from trouble, but how we deal with it when it comes our way." She paused. "Of course, you already know this."

"Knowing it and living it are two different things."

"Very true, dear."

"So you're no longer angry with God?"

Wilma shrugged. "I'm still angry and hurt, but not with Him—well, most days. I'd be a liar to say that I still don't let my feelings be known. Of course, He already knows." She took another napkin and dabbed at her eyes. "I think being honest with God is one of the things that has kept me sane. It's not like I'm telling something that has escaped His attention. One thing I know is that God walks with us no matter how tough the journey. I also know it is better to have His company than try to go forward without it."

"I wish I had your strength."

Wilma chuckled. "Odd, I was thinking on the way over how much I wished I had yours."

Chapter 4

Papers Served

=>◇<=

The wall behind him bore his name on a score of plaques, diplomas, and certificates. Intermingled among the finely framed diplomas from Princeton and Harvard Law School were photos of him with Supreme Court associate justices, Supreme Court Justice Isaiah Williams, Attorney General Alton Stamper, Vice President Angela Baxter-Brown, and President William Blaine. There were a dozen other photos of the six-foot-two, blond-haired, blue-eyed man glad-handing Senators and Congressmen, as well as most of the country's sitting governors. All of them bore: "John Knox Smith."

He took great pride in each diploma, every award, and the certificates and photos that reminded him that he was one of the most powerful men in the country. He had the ear of every major policy maker, nearly every dean of the major law schools, and called news media moguls by first name. He needed praise and achievement like most men needed air. Over the last few years, he learned to tolerate opposition, a slow legal system, threats, and sixteen hour workdays. The only thing he couldn't tolerate was failure. He couldn't stand it in himself and had no patience for it in anyone else. As assistant attorney general for the United States, he had forged an image of a man slow to hire and quick to fire.

Yet, tolerance was his mainstay, the blood that coursed through his veins. He had built a fledgling Department of Justice into a force gaining recognition throughout the Western world. His goal was to make the world safe for those whom others considered immoral. He had in just a couple of years made intolerance a crime. Hate speech could now be prosecuted, and prosecuting was what he did best. In most cases, he was a success. In one, he stumbled. More accurately, his team stumbled: The Reverend Dr. Pat Preston, mega-church pastor and former college friend was his thorn in the flesh. Because of a blunder made by one of the DTED teams, the man almost got off on elementary evidence issues. Had the pending trial remained in the United States, his team's incompetence would have been revealed, Preston would be a free man and John's reputation would be tarnished.

That problem was enough to cost him some sleep, even though he was certain of victory once Preston was tried at the Peace Palace in The Hague.

At the moment, his attention was fixed on another failure. Every week, legal papers that numbered in the hundreds of pages crossed his desk, but none bothered him so much as what he held in his hands. Unlike the large, professionally framed photos of famous and powerful people hanging on the wall, a different photo drew his attention. It was a small photo set in a cheap drugstore faux silver frame, the same frame he had bought several years ago. The image was of a smiling woman with dark hair and eyes that squinted when she smiled. Sitting on her lap was a toddler holding a toy police car. He seemed uncertain about having his photo taken.

His wife and son. Jack, the toddler, was nine now—no, wait. He was older. Maybe ten. "How can you not know the age of your own son?" he whispered. He waited for the flood of guilt. It never came. *That's right; he had a birthday last month. I wonder if Andrea remembered to send him something.* He made a mental note to ask his personal assistant if her memory was better than his.

He moved his gaze back to the divorce papers. Their arrival didn't surprise him, but the reality of it was unsettling. John couldn't remember the number of times he had used a legal service to deliver a summons or some legal document. Being served was embarrassing.

Now he had choice to make: agree to the divorce or contest it. His impulse was to fight. It was part of his nature, but he saw no sense in it. Cathy had left many months ago and he had yet to feel remorse or loneliness. Jack, his son, was living in Colorado with his grandfather. *Cathy never could handle the boy. She was a failure as a mother and a wife, unable to think beyond herself and her wants.*

"Good riddance." He mumbled the words, expecting relief from the niggling sense he had failed at something. But had he? Maybe he was looking at this all wrong. He wasn't losing a wife; he was being freed from an entanglement. Having the Silver Springs home to himself had been a joy. A divorce would make it even better. Of course, she was asking for child support. He'd yield to that. He had his career to think of. She also wanted half of his earnings and half of the value of the house. That he would fight. Cathy had always been weak. He felt certain she would choose custody of Jack over the house. It would be a delicate matter, but he should be able to keep it all under control.

The intercom on his desk phone sounded. "Mr. Smith. You have a DTED meeting in five minutes. Is there anything I can get for you before you go to the conference room?"

"No thanks, Andrea. Place a call to Eddie Goodall at Goodall, Crowe, and Banks. See if he has time in his schedule to stop by for a few minutes this afternoon." A second later he added, "I have an open slot after four."

"May I ask what this is regarding? For Mr. Goodall, I mean."

"No. I'll tell you what; see if he's free for drinks. That would be better."

"Yes, sir. Drinks. If he is available, then where do you want to meet?"

He thought for a moment. He wanted a place with some privacy; a bar with booths. "Redman's. I haven't been there for awhile."

"Yes, sir. Redman's on Whitehurst?"

"That's the one."

John gathered his notes and immediately switched from his marital woes to the gem of his career: the Diversity and Tolerance Enforcement Division. DTED had changed the country and put the fear of law in the hearts of the haters.

John began to feel warm inside.

***

"Divorce? You're kidding, right?" Eddie Goodall, Esq. sat across the table from John and studied the inside of his glass of Scotch as if trying to see his reflection in the bar's dim light.

Redman's on Whitehurst was a bar. A high-end, bar that catered to men and women with titles in front of their names. On the way in, John shook hands with three senators, two congressmen, and two presidential aides and made eye contact with department directors from Treasury, OMB, and a few other government agencies. Patrons consider Redman's a safe place. Here the Speaker of the House could knock back drinks with the minority whip and not see the event in the next morning's *Washington Post*.

"I'm not much of a kidder, Eddie. You know that."

Eddie chuckled in an octave more fit to a man half his two-hundred-and-sixty-pound size. Eddie stood six-three and in college had been a mass of muscle. Years behind a legal desk had robbed his physique of the firmness that once turned the heads of the female law students at Harvard Law. It was there John met Eddie who was third year when John was starting and trying to wrap his mind around tort law. "Yeah, I know you're not much of a kidder, John. Everyone knows that. You never did learn to party. It was always the books with you. For the longest time, I thought you lived in the library at Langdell Hall."

The comment made him smile. "I slept in an apartment; I lived in the library." John turned the bottle of Sam Adams before him until the label faced him. The portrait of the founding father made drinking beer seem patriotic.

"You've come a long way. Assistant U.S. Attorney General. I figured you for a big law firm."

"Like you?"

"Hey, that's where the money is. Wanna compare your government salary to my income?"

The words stung. "I went into law for different reasons, Eddie. I want to make a difference."

Eddie raised a bushy, brown eyebrow. The eyebrow color matched the man's perfectly styled hair. John guessed he was looking at a $200 haircut. "You don't think I make a difference?"

"Come on, Eddie, you know what I mean. Some of us are destined for public service; some of us go the corporate route or . . ."

"Divorce? You can say it. I'm not ashamed of what I do. I made my money on the unhappy marriages of others. Just don't forget, I do all forms of family law. Besides, the divorce rate is up to sixty percent of first-time married couples."

"I wasn't being critical, Eddie. You seem a little sensitive this evening." John lifted the beer to his lips.

Eddie rubbed his eyes. "Yeah, I guess I am. This business can kill a man's soul."

"We're lawyers, Eddie. We don't have souls."

"Cute." The high priced attorney ran his finger along the rim of the glass accumulating a drop of golden liquid and then stuck the finger in his mouth. A moment passed. "Okay, enough of this. So who is divorcing whom here?"

"It takes two to divorce."

"Don't get cute with me, John. I had other plans for the evening and this little get together is making me late."

"Sorry. I'm avoiding the unpleasantries." John took another long hit off the bottle. "I got papers today."

"Easier to send them than get them, isn't it?"

John nodded but didn't look up from the bottle. Drinking alcohol—a depressant—might not be as good an idea as it first seemed.

Eddie sounded distant. "I've been through two divorces. That's ironic, isn't it? Divorce attorney gets a divorce, not once but twice. Somehow seems wrong." He let slip a defensive chortle. "Did I ever tell you about the first divorce I litigated?"

John shook his head.

"I guess not. Why would I? It was even more ironic. I represented a man whose wife filed against him. He was a marriage counselor. What's the old joke about the psychic who gets hit by a bus? She shoulda seen it coming." Another sip of the golden liquid, then he leaned over the table. "Did you bring them?"

John reached inside the coat pocket of his suit and removed a few pages. "Just the pertinent stuff. I'll messenger the full package tomorrow . . . if you take my case, that is."

"Of course I'll take your case. We got history."

Eddie tended to revert to his Jersey speech after a couple of drinks. Most of the time he kept his middle class upbringing a secret. He studied the papers. "Pretty typical. I take it you two are living apart."

"Have been for several months."

"She got your boy?" Eddie flipped through the pages.

"He's living with my father in Colorado. He's too much for her to handle."

"Too much for you, too?" Eddie lifted a hand. "Forget that. Sorry. It's the Scotch talking." He glanced at the paperwork again. "Still, she's asking for custody. Do you think that's a ploy for child support?"

"I already pay for his support." John thought for a moment. "No, I don't think it's a ploy. She's not the type."

"No, but divorce lawyers like me are the type. Ask for more than is fair and you might get it, but if you don't, you still get more than is deserved." He lifted his drink and studied John over the rim. Then, in one motion, downed the contents. He grimaced, then smiled. After a short shudder, he raised the glass, signaling the cocktail waitress for a refill. Returning his gaze to John, he winked and then asked, "So how hard do you want me to hit her?"

"Eddie, I want this thing to go away. I don't want to hurt her, I just want it gone."

"You sure? 'Cuz I can show she's a poor mother. After all, she took your son from you and fled to . . . Where did she go?"

"Her parents. They live in Connecticut."

"Okay, so we say she packed the boy up and sent him off to granddad, depriving you of visitation rights. I can build an abandonment case and throw in a little child negligence to boot. Her attorney . . ." He looked at the papers. "Cynthia Peters. I know her. A real scrapper. She's good, but not to worry, I'm better. Interesting. Your wife chose counsel from the D.C. area."

"Look, Eddie, I have to be careful here. I'm a public figure. If we don't do this correctly, then I'll be painted in a bad light and if I get mud on me, so does the Attorney General and that wouldn't be good for anyone."

"Really? Gee, buddy, I thought the whole Department of Justice was filled with warm, fuzzy, tolerant people. Isn't that what you've been fighting for all these months?"

A waitress with short, black hair and an even shorter dress delivered another tumbler of Scotch. She looked at John. "Another Sam Adams?"

His mind screamed, "Yes," but his mouth said. "No, thanks. I'm driving."

Eddie laughed. "So am I." He sipped the Scotch.

The waitress left to serve a half-drunk congressional aide.

"Look, Eddie, lawyer to lawyer, I wasn't a good husband and a mediocre father at best. I know it. I'm married to my work. My children are the new laws we've managed to get placed over the last couple of years. So all I want is to give her the divorce. I will continue to pay child support until my boy is eighteen. I don't make a ton of money, especially for living in D.C. but I do all right. Figure out some amount for the alimony and I'll pay it. Let's just keep everything on the down-low."

Leaning back, Eddie rubbed his chin. "I expected more fight out of you. I mean with you being you and all."

"What does that mean?"

"You have a reputation in the legal community. You know that, right?"

"I don't care what others think."

Eddie laughed loud enough to draw the attention of the other patrons. John pretended to laugh as if he had just told a knee-slapper of a joke. "You just told me to keep this on the down-low. Come on, John, everything I've seen about you tells me you spend a lot of brain fuel figuring out how to draw attention to yourself."

"You have an odd way of dealing with clients, Eddie. It's a wonder you keep any of them."

His friend's smile flattened. "They pay me for my work, John. I have to be nice to them. I'm assuming my work for you is *pro bono publico*, professional courtesy and all that, or are you going to pay my steep fees?"

"I'd prefer to go the professional courtesy route."

"Then you'll have live with my social awkwardness." He examined his glass. "I should lay off this stuff. It fogs my situational awareness."

"Ya think?" John wondered if he had made a mistake. He dismissed the idea. Eddie was tipsy now, but he wouldn't be during work hours. Eddie was the best at what he did. John retrieved a business card from his pocket and scribbled on the back. "Here. That's my private cell number. I don't want you calling me through the DOJ phone system or having to pass through my administrative assistant. This is personal."

"Understood. You know how to get hold of me."

"Eddie, let's do this quickly and quietly."

"One last question, John. How goes the Matt Branson investigation?"

"I can't talk about that."

"Can't or won't?"

"What difference does it make?" John leaned over the table, leaning closer to his attorney. "It's an ongoing investigation, Eddie. I can tell you it has the highest priority at the AG's office. No one gets away with killing one of our own. No one."

"Good. I heard he was a good man. You were friends in law school, right?"

"At Princeton. He went to law school in Michigan. We used to be close. We worked in the same building, but work being what it is, saw each other only occasionally." John retrieved his cell phone. "You need a cab?"

"Nah, I can drive."

"Sure you can, but you can't handle my divorce from jail. I'm calling a cab."

"In that case, I'm having another drink. I might as well be truly drunk."

Chapter 5

Fall Down Go Boom

———⟫•◇•⟪———

G reg Mayer stood in the newly remodeled laboratory staring at a large, white box with smooth, sleek edges that stood on a half-dozen hydraulic legs. It rested in the center of a stark white room. The letters NTSB decorated the side as did the insignia of the government agency. Three stripes—red, white, blue—ran horizontally along the exterior. A set of aluminum stairs led to a single door. The multi-million dollar device never ceased to amaze Mayer who had only been in the flight simulator a few times. Unlike many earlier versions of commercial flight simulators used by Boeing, Airbus, and NASA, this one could be tuned to act like almost any aircraft flying. Less than a year old, it had already been helpful in solving the mystery of three downed airliners—one Russian, one Canadian, and one US— and four domestic private aircraft.

"Greg?"

Mayer turned to see a tanned man in a charcoal gray suit enter the space. Neil Rice was a five-foot-six man trying to look six-foot-three. His shoulders were narrow but wide enough to carry several chips. His tanned skin made him look like someone who spent his off time surfing, but there wasn't much surfing in Washington, D.C. "Hello, Assistant Director."

"Thanks for meeting with me, Greg."

Mayer conjured an unfeeling smile. "How could I resist such a politely worded summons?"

"I didn't mean it to sound like a summons. I hope I haven't put you out." He extended his hand and Mayer shook it.

"I flew in early this morning."

"From the crash site? Houston?"

No, from Club Med. "Not the crash site. I was examining the wreckage again."

"How many times have you gone over all that twisted metal?"

Mayer shrugged. "It's not something I count."

"Sorry to be a pain, but my director is going to meet with the directors of the DOJ, the FBI, the FAA, and just about anything else with initials. They're getting impatient, so tell me you found something new." Rice tilted his head back to look up at the two story structure.

"Not from the wreckage. I just got word they've been able to pull enough info from the black box to recreate a simulation."

"Why do they call them black boxes when they're really orange?"

"Tradition."

"I guess . . . wait. Simulation? We're going to ride in that thing?" Rice pointed to the simulator, his face almost as white as the device's skin.

"You wanted an update on the investigation. If you're a little nervous, I can do it alone and tell you all about it later."

"Nervous? Me? No. I'm fine. Really. No problem."

"All right, let's see what our computer guys have pulled together." He started for the stairway that led to the simulator's door. Rice hesitated, then followed at a slower pace.

Although a good fifteen years older than Rice, Mayer jogged up the treads, leaving the Homeland Security man behind. He opened "the hatch," entered the cockpit, and sat in the pilot's seat. "You sit over there."

A dim light from an overhead bulb held darkness at bay, aided by the glow of the instrument panel.

"Wow, this looks like the real thing."

"In many ways, it is. We don't get off the ground, but the controls are largely the same. Fasten your seat and shoulder belt."

"Why? It's just a simulator."

"It's the latest in simulator technology. We can emulate most contemporary aircraft, although we're pushing our luck with a private jet like the Gulfstream 550. Some of the gauges and controls are in different locations, but we'll get an idea of what the pilots went through." He put on a headset and motioned for Rice to do the same. He spoke into the boom mic by his face. "You got a copy, Ricky?'

A voice poured from the headset. "Yeah, I got you, Greg. I still need a few minutes."

"No problem." Mayer pulled a pair of shaded glasses from a space near the pilot's seat. "Put these on."

"Not very stylish." Rice took them and pulled the arms back. "They look like 3-D glasses."

"That's because they are 3-D glasses. Most simulators work on a simple projection system. They're good, but nothing says reality like 3-D." He donned his pair, then activated a switch. A concrete runway appeared and the sound of jet engines purring filled the space. "Okay, let's review what little we know. The Gulfstream 550 was a new craft and had less than five hundred air hours on her. The pilots were well seasoned contract fliers. They worked for a service that provided pilots to high-end clients. The FBI has done full background checks on them. Both were former air force pilots. One had been a flight instructor and the other served as captain on Air Force One. Both left the service with honorable discharges. Both had served with distinction. Both left families behind."

The last comment made Mayer pause. The sight of grieving families haunted him at night. It was one of the few areas of his life where he had grown no calluses.

"They left George Bush International in Houston. It took seven minutes steering through traffic to reach 20,000 feet. Eight minutes in, a problem arose. And minutes later, they hit the dirt at speed."

"I thought you were unable to recover the flight data." Rice gazed out the "window" at the realistic scene playing in front of him.

"That's true. All the electronics were knocked out, and when I say knocked out, I mean shut off completely."

"What would cause that?"

"A full electric shut down which is highly unlikely under normal conditions, but these conditions aren't even close to normal."

"The flash drive was recovered in the airport restroom."

Mayer nodded. "We lucked out with that. Without that discovery, we'd really be blind. The college kid trying to pay his tuition by working as a janitor did us an enormous favor. He saw technical files about the Gulfstream and realized it might have something to do with the crash. At first, we thought it contained nothing but basic information on the 550 but we found something else: a digital virus."

"Like those that attack computers. I know this stuff already."

"Okay, you want to talk sports?"

"No. I get it; you're making sure I'm on the same page as you."

"I assume you have other things on your plate."

Rice huffed. "You have no idea."

"This is the only thing I'm focused on. I think about this day and night."

"Okay. I get it. Carry on."

"We're working on the assumption the virus overrode and then knocked out the computer. The 550 is as close to a commercial airliner as you can get, at least as far as onboard tech goes. In some ways, it's superior. Still, we were able to recover everything up to the computer shut down. A few seconds after that, all electrical systems failed. At that point, we lose flight data and cockpit voice recording. We're guessing from that moment on."

"So you're telling me we'll never know what really happened."

"I'm not saying that at all. I'm saying we'll have to extrapolate from what we do have. That's what we are about to do."

A voice came over the headset. "Ready on my end, Greg."

"Hit it, Ricky." Mayer turned to Rice. "You don't suffer from motion sickness, do you?"

"Why?" There was fear in his voice.

The simulator lurched and Rice let loose a tiny scream.

Gulfstream five-five-zero, runway three-three-left, cleared for takeoff.

The pilot echoed, *Cleared for takeoff, runway three-three left, Gulfstream five-five-zero.*

Through the 3-D glasses, Mayer watched the runway begin to scroll beneath them. His seat began to vibrate and he could hear the roar of the twin engines producing 16,000 pounds of thrust. His seat tilted back a few degrees simulating acceleration. The throttle levers moved forward on their own.

"And rotate," Mayer said. The pilot's yoke pulled back and the nose came up.

"How are you doing this without touching the controls?"

Mayer glanced at Rice. "The computer is repeating the data we were able to retrieve. We're not flying the simulator; we're watching it repeat Gulfstream 550's last flight."

"I'm not a pilot, so school me. What am I seeing?"

Gulfstream five-five-zero, contact Houston Departure on one-two-eight-point-two-five. There was a short pause.

Ah, roger. . . Departure on one-two-eight-point-two-five, so long. Houston Departure, Gulfstream five-five-zero is with you leaving four thousand for seven thousand.

Gulfstream five-five-zero Houston Departure, radar contact, turn right heading zero-four-five, climb and maintain eight thousand.

Roger, Houston, heading zero-four-five, climbing to eight-thousand, Gulfstream five-five-zero. There was a short pause.

Gulfstream five-five-zero, traffic in your turn at two o'clock, one-zero miles, southbound, a Boeing 7-3-7 out of one-two thousand descending to niner thousand.

Gulfstream five-five-zero, roger, looking.

"Air Traffic Control just directed the craft to the east and told them there was traffic ahead and above them."

The nose of the simulator dipped.

"This is amazing." Rice leaned forward but kept his hands to himself. "I can see Houston below. Look, the Gulf of Mexico." He pointed to the south. "This is incredibly real."

"You like the reality, do you?"

"Oh, yeah. I'm stunned by the detail."

In any other situation, Mayer might have felt happy for the man. Instead, he felt sadness. *So, you think the Nationals have a chance at their division this year?* The voice was deep and smooth.

Baseball is an old man's sport. I'm a hockey guy myself. A younger but still mature voice.

Hockey? Isn't that a girl's sport?"

Clearly, you know nothing about hockey.

There was a laugh.

"CVR," Mayer explained. "Cockpit voice recording." He had heard scores of such conversations as part of his training and part of his many investigations. One of the things that struck him about fatal air crashes was how normal everything seemed before the end came.

Gulfstream five-five-zero, climb and maintain flight level two-eight-zero, contact Houston Center on one-three-four-point-two-five.

Roger, climb to flight level two-eight-zero and contact Center on one-three-four-point-two-five, Gulfstream five-five-zero. Have a good one.

A moment later, the nose of the simulator rose. There was a bounce as if they were passing through some clear air turbulence.

Baseball is a metaphor of life. Don't recall anyone saying that about hockey. Maybe they don't know what a metaphor is.

I see how it is, pick on the hockey fan. Just a word of warning: Don't repeat that at a hockey game. A pause. *Passing 15,000.*

The pilots continued to chit chat. Rice spent his time looking at the simulated ground below through his 3-D glasses. "Man, I thought 3-D television was cool."

Twenty-eight thousand feet. The simulator lowered its nose until only a tiny pitch remained.

Autopilot on. The pilot sounded relaxed. *You see, baseball is not only a physical game, but an intellectual one—*

A claxon sounded.

"What's that?" Rice had tried to jump out of his chair.

"Listen. And tighten your seatbelt."

"You know we're not really flying, right?"

Pilot: *Inconsistent air speed indication.*

Copilot: *That's a new one on me. Shall I reset?*

Pilot: *Yes.*

Copilot: *Resetting now.*

A pause.

Copilot: *That seems to have done the trick—*

A digital klaxon sounded. *Inconsistent airspeed indication again.* The pilot's voice was smooth, calm, sounding more annoyed than alarmed.

"What's inconsistent air speed?"

Mayer pointed to a small display on the instrument panel. "They're on autopilot. This monitor shows information the pilots need. When something is wrong, the computer displays this warning. He pushed his finger closer to the screen. "On a car, the speedometer gives information about speed based on how fast the wheels are turning. An aircraft uses Pitot tubes. They're small, hollow projections on the outside of the craft. Passing air exerts pressure on a sensor in the Pitot tube and the computer calculates the air speed from the data. If the sensor fails or something happens to the Pitot tube, then the computer can't do its work."

"So all that means is they don't know how fast they're traveling."

"It's much more than that—"

The simulator shuddered and the nose dipped.

Pilot: *Autopilot disengage. Resetting.* Only the sound of the aircraft slicing through the air and the consistent roar of engines came over the headsets. *Reset fail. I'm not liking this much.*

Copilot: *You and me both. Good thing we're pilots, eh? Otherwise, we'd be up the creek.*

A second later the ambient engine noise ceased. A warning chimed loud enough to hurt Mayer's ears. His heart fluttered as if he were 28,000 feet above the ground clipping along at several hundred knots per hour instead of safe in a simulator bolted to the ground. The simulator dipped forward.

Swearing filled his ears. The pilot's voice was calm, but Mayer could hear the raspy tension of fear. *Engine number one is out— strike that. Both engines are out.*

The simulator shuddered and tipped forward another ten degrees. "Keep your eyes on the instruments, Rice. Watch the altitude and airspeed."

"Where?"

Mayer pointed at them. "Here and here."

"I don't understand. What's happened?"

"The engines quit. Keep watching."

The angle of descent increased and the airspeed, which had been slowing, began to increase.

Increasing flaps five degrees. Restart the engines. Restart the engines.

The nose came up a few degrees, then dipped again.

"Without power," Mayer said, "the pilot can't keep the craft's attitude or altitude. As the inertia of forward movement bleeds off, the jet becomes more brick than aircraft."

Mayday, mayday, mayday. This is Gulfstream five-five-zero and we are declaring an emergency." The pilot grunted, indicating to Mayer that he was struggling with the controls. The business jet was becoming hard to handle.

A different voice: *Gulfstream five-five-zero, Houston Center, what is the nature of your emergency?*

Houston, five-five-zero, we have lost all power to our engines. We also have . . . gauges . . .

"I didn't hear that," Rice said.

"I know."

Gulfstream five-five-zero, say your intentions. Do you want to go back to Houston?

Pilot: *Roger that . . . run . . .*

Your transmission is breaking up, five-five-zero. Turn right heading one-eight-zero, vector to Houston, descend and maintain one-six-thousand.

Understo...

Rice was gripping the arm rest. Even in the dim light, Mayer could see white knuckles. He wanted to find pleasure in the man's discomfort, but he was too ill at ease himself. He had read the transcripts and imagined this scene over and over, but until now it had all taken place in his mind. Feeling the shuddering, the sharp attitude change, the sudden decrease in airspeed, then increase as the craft nosed over was too real. He fought the urge to remove the 3-D glasses and hit the emergency end button on the panel before him. He also had to resist the urge to grab the yoke in an attempt to fly the plane.

"Why, um, why can we hear air traffic control and—" The simulator bounced and Rice groaned.

"Our tech's have the ATC recordings and have edited them into the simulation. That couldn't be done with communications from the Gulfstream."

Mayday, mayday . . . The pilot trailed off as if realizing the mayday had already been established. Mayer could imagine the difficulty the man faced. The amount of physical and digital input was enormous and the pilots couldn't trust the latter. *We are in a steep dive. Steep . . . unable to regain . . . instruments blinking . . . out . . .*

The instrument panel in the simulator went dark.

Gulfstream five-five-zero . . . Gulfstream five-five-zero?

The simulator tipped sixty degrees down, then jerked right with whiplash intensity. Rice groaned again. So did Mayer. Five eternally long seconds later, everything snapped left. Mayer felt the seat's arm rest dig into his ribs. There was rattling. The sound of wind whipping around the metal fuselage filled the space. The bouncing began.

Shudder.

Bounce.

Shake.

Jerk.

Twist.

"Make it stop, Mayer. Make it stop."

Mayer didn't. He was determined to follow the simulation to the ground.

Gulfstream five-five-zero, Houston, Gulfstream five-five-zero, Houston.

The voice of a female pilot broke in: *Houston Center, Cactus fourteen-twenty-five heavy, descending to flight level one eight zero, direct to Cordis.*

Roger, Cactus fourteen-twenty-five heavy, descend and maintain one-six thousand.

Cactus fourteen-twenty-five-heavy roger, down to one-six-thousand. We have visual on the Gulfstream. She's nose down. Steep dive and over banked left.

Thank you, fourteen-twenty-five. Can you maintain visual?

The simulator banked to the left more. Mayer felt himself slipping, held in place by the safety harness. He dug his fingers into the arm rest.

Through the simulated windows, the projection of the fast approaching ground flipped over.

Roger that . . . dear God . . . the Gulfstream . . . its upside down.

Copy that, fourteen-twenty-five. Upside down. We have the position. Five-five-zero, do you copy? Five-five zero?

The simulation stopped. The lights went out. Slowly, the cabin righted itself.

The female pilot's voice, soft and saturated with emotion came over the headset. *Cactus fourteen-twenty-five. Impact. He's down.*

A long pause followed her announcement. *Roger, Cactus fourteen-twenty-five-heavy, cleared direct to Alpine, descend and maintain one-five-thousand, contact Houston Approach on one-two-one-point-seven-five.*

Roger, descend to one-five-thousand, Approach on one-two-one-point-seven-five, Cactus fourteen-twenty-five-heavy. Her voice broke.

The lights in the cabin came up. Mayer was sweating; Rice had his hands over his face. They sat in the silence, stewing in the stink of fear, knowing they had heard the last words of two brave pilots. Mayer drew the back of his hand across his forehead. "If it's any comfort, Assistant Director, you felt what the pilots experienced. It could have been worse.

Rice snapped his head around to face Mayer. "Worse? Really? Worse than being almost turned on my head?"

"The simulator can't turn upside down like the Gulfstream did, so yeah, the simulation could have been more grueling. Just so you know, since you came for the latest information, neither associate justice was strapped in. Both had removed their lap belts."

"You mean . . ."

"Like ping-pong balls."

Rice undid his harness. "I've got to get out of here." He stood. "Where's the bathroom?"

Chapter 6

Hopeless Optimism

⋘─◆─⋙

"Found you."

Isabella looked up from the white metal patio table. The table was situated next to a large, classic square pool with a cobalt blue tile bottom, and an inlay image of leaping dolphins crafted from hand set mosaic tile. Submerged lights played on the gently moving surface, making the water inviting, a place to escape. And Countess Isabella San Philippa wanted to escape. Normally a woman of persistent confidence, her unflagging determination and focus were flagging.

"Ciao, Fredrico. You have come home to me." She rose and kissed him on the cheek. As she pulled away, her husband drew her close and pressed his lips to hers. She started to resist, but his warmth and the tenderness of his lips captured her. She let him hold her, his firm arms around her shoulders. For the moment, everything disappeared, withdrew into a different world. The pool, the colonnade bracketing three sides of the pool, the tile and hand worked concrete walks and plaza, the plants and trees imported from northern Italy, and the forty room, two story mansion designed in the early fifties by Fredrico's father. All that remained was Fredrico: the strength of him and the certain knowledge of their love.

He released her and she was as dizzy as a teenage girl after her first kiss. Married twelve years, each day remained new, fresh, and exciting.

"How did you know I needed that?"

"I'm your husband; you are *tesoro mio*."

"And you, husband, are my treasure as well." She sat again and he joined her. "It is late. I thought you ran off with another woman."

"I did. Several really, but I had to come back to you. You are my addiction."

He noticed the bottle of red wine and her half-empty glass. A clean, empty glass rested near the center of the table. He refilled her glass, then his. "I was kept late at the shipyard. Our newest ship has a few insects in it."

Isabella laughed. "Bugs, my sweet. The American expression is bugs, not insects. Are the problems big?"

"No, but enough to delay the launch a few weeks. What are a few weeks to us? The ocean was here when my grandfather started this business; it will be here long after I trade this world for the next." He shrugged. *"Cosí é la vita."*

She nodded and returned her eyes to the files and papers before her.

"Why do you work so late? Legal work is meant for the daytime."

She took a sip of the wine. "If only that were true. Your ships sail the oceans day and night to get from one port to another. Sometimes my work requires extra hours."

"Is this the case you were talking about all week?" He settled back and gazed at a near full, ivory moon.

"The Reverend Dr. Pat Preston. I told you of my meeting with him at The Hague."

"Yes, you did. In fact, it's all you've talked about for two days. I was beginning to feel insecure."

She set her hand on his. "Sorry, my dear, you're stuck with me."

He brought her hand to his lips and kissed it. "I never tire of hearing that." She let her eyes trace his face: olive complexion; rugged, sun weathered skin; thick, dark, arched brows; brown eyes; and hair the color of anthracite. His shoulders were broad and his arms thick; no forty year old man had a right to look this handsome.

"I don't know why God blessed me with you: rich, witty, and moderately good looking."

"Thank you . . . moderately?"

"Just testing your hearing."

He was every woman's idea of a prized husband: born into a multimillionaire family, he had helped his father take the shipping business higher and higher until it was one of the top grossing shipping enterprises in the world. He was worth billions, but the money was secondary. Few knew how he gave his annual salary away to charities and to the needy. He had once told her that on the day he was born, he was wealthier than most millionaires. He had no need for more money. He did, however, have a need for purpose, something that came to the forefront during his early twenties.

Like many Italians, he was born into the Roman Catholic church and attended Mass because it was required of him. Somewhere along his journey into manhood, he found a hunger and need for Christ. She had asked him about it many times and he had yet been able to explain it, but every time the subject came up, a new light came to his eyes. The best answer he could give was to tell of how the founder of the Methodist church, John Wesley, although already a minister, had a life-changing experience while traveling to America to do missionary work. "He wrote that he felt a strange warming in his heart. That is what I felt and I have never been cold again."

She took his hand. It was large and firm, made strong by working in the ship yards when he was young. His father insisted his son learn the business from the dry docks up. Being a billionaire's son provided no protection from hard work. He learned the shipping business from his father; he learned about business from the London School of Economics.

Fredrico gave her had a gentle squeeze. "What's bothering you?"

"I never said I was bothered." She looked away.

"I hear more than your words, love; I hear your heart. We've been married too long not to know when the other is uneasy." He tilted his head. "Is it the case?"

She nodded. "I've been pouring over the details. If ever a man was misjudged and falsely held, it is Pat Preston. He has committed no crimes in his country or anyplace else."

"You went to The Hague to visit him?"

"I accompanied His Holiness—"

"His Holiness went with you?"

Isabella grinned. "No, dear, the Pope doesn't go with others, others go with him, but yes, we traveled to The Hague along with his support staff. It caused a bit of a stir. He is committed to helping Preston and so am I."

"But you don't think you can. Is that it? It's not like you to doubt."

"The world is changing, Fredrico. It's changing at a rate I never thought possible. I've reviewed most of Preston's files. His American defense team did an admirable job. In fact, the Alliance—that's the name of an organization that represents ministers and others in matters of free speech—would probably have succeeded in getting Preston's case dismissed, albeit on evidence issues. It appears that's why the American prosecutor arranged for the trial to take place in Europe as a test of the expanded powers of the International Court of Justice."

"He can do that? Never mind. Of course he can. He did. I just thought Americans preferred to try their own."

"That appears to be changing. More and more, they and other countries are moving to a world court. In some ways that makes sense when the International Criminal Court tries some key leader of war crimes or crimes against humanity. Now the International Court of Justice is taking criminal cases. I believe the change is made to please the Americans. They have not been as supportive as countries in Europe." She inhaled deeply and then released it as if expelling her frustration. "Dr. Preston has done nothing more than preach from the Bible. He has committed no crime."

Fredrico studied the sky for a moment as if giving God time to chime in. "The Bible is a divisive book, Isabella. It always has been. Didn't the Apostle Paul say the word of the cross was foolishness to some and the power of salvation to others? The first chapter of First Corinthians."

Her husband's ability to recall Scripture never failed to impress Isabella.

"Yes, and I know Jesus said His message would pit father against son, mother against daughter.."

"Do not suppose I have come to bring peace to the earth: it is not peace I have come to bring, but a sword."

"Now you're just showing off."

"Maybe, but just a little. Do you know what surprises me, love? Your surprise surprises me. I have never understood why we Christians are so taken aback by unbelievers acting like unbelievers. Unbelievers cannot think like Christians. History proves the point. It is why there is persecution. Jesus told us persecution would come. It has been present from the first days of the church. Persecution takes different forms." He motioned to the distant glow of city lights. "Roma. Today people see it as the seat of the Church. Even Protestants acknowledge Peter ministered here and so did Paul. Much of Christian history happened just a few miles from us. Tourists come from all over the world to visit the Vatican in all its splendor, but before there was splendor, there was the blood of martyrs shed by Roman emperors. Less than two thousand years ago, the streets of Roma were lined with Christians on crosses. We are fortunate, my dear. We live in a time where physical persecution is rare in the Western world. Christians like us can live in security. I can be a believer and lead a multibillion dollar industry. It is different today than it was."

Isabella pursed her lips. She understood his point, but he was missing something. "What you say is true. I should not be surprised that persecution exists, even if it is legal persecution, but it represents more." She pulled her wine glass close and turned it slowly, the light of a table candle illuminated the dark red fluid. "Persecution takes many forms. Yes, we are blessed to live as we do, to have several homes across the continent, but we cannot assume persecution has ended."

"There are lands where Christians are killed for their faith. I have not forgotten them."

"I know. You have been generous with your riches." She pushed the glass aside and took Fredrico's hand again. "I'm afraid, Fredrico."

"Afraid? Of what? You are safe here. We have the best in security—"

She squeezed his hand. "I do not mean I am afraid for my safety. I am afraid for all Christians across the world. A new kind of persecution is rising, a legal persecution that is making martyrs of men like Pat Preston. He incited no riots; showed no prejudice; called no names. He just preached from the Bible. I've listened to the offending tapes. That's what the prosecution calls them: 'the offending tapes.' Of course, no audio tapes are involved, it's all digital."

"Old terms are hard to shake—"

"Listen to me, Fredrico."

He studied her for a moment, remorse in his eyes. "I'm sorry. I shouldn't interrupt."

She rubbed his finger with her thumb. "I listened to the sermons the prosecution used as cause for his arrest. They accuse him of hate speech, but I heard no hatred. I watched the videos. His sermons were recorded and aired over the Internet and television. There is no hatred in the man's eyes, in his words, or in his mannerisms. All he has done is preach from biblical texts. Some of those texts deal with the biblical view of homosexual behavior. Other times, he taught about doctrinal issues, even challenging our beloved Church and His Holiness. Being a Baptist, his doctrine is the same on core issues such as the nature of Jesus and the world's need of salvation through him, but others are very different. In every case, he spoke with dignity and restraint. There are many Catholic haters in the world, but he is not one. He does not agree with the Holy Doctrine, but I sensed no hatred. He even joked with the Holy Father. When he taught from New Testament passages dealing with sexual sins, he treated all the sins with proper weight."

"It sounds like the Americans want to prosecute the Bible."

"That's exactly what they want to do. Well, that's what the prosecutors want to do."

"And this is what frightens you?"

She nodded. "Already we have seen the church—all Christian churches—lose their footing in Europe and many other countries. The United States government is now prosecuting people who hold to the same faith many of its founders clung to so tightly. I'm afraid if we lose this case, it will be more than a loss for Pat Preston; it will be a loss for Christianity and its ability to tell the world who Jesus is."

He wrapped both hands around hers. "He has the best person on his defense: you."

She shook her head. "That's not going to be enough. I can assemble the best legal defense team possible. The Alliance who defended him in the early weeks after his arrest are very able. They have some brilliant attorneys. I have checked on them and their years of incredible, God-given success."

"You've been busy while I've been gone."

"And I will be busier still. I'm on the case because I know the ICJ and how it operates, but I'm not sure that's going to be enough and if I fail . . . if *we* fail, then more will be lost than one man's freedom. Much more."

"Where is that hopeless optimism you are so famous for?" He smiled.

She didn't. "I feel more hopeless than optimistic."

Chapter 7

Cardinal Injustice

——◇——

It was more than a knife: long, rusty, and dripping with blood. Light reflected off what little untarnished metal remained.

It hesitated high above his bed, held in a black hand with narrow fingers.

His eyes drifted from the hovering blade to the face of the man who held it: black with wide, dead eyes; a face split with a grimace of white teeth seemed to glow in the blackness of the small hut.

He heard a curse. He saw the machete rise.

It started down and he waited for the sting of metal in his flesh.

A thud. A grunt. A crash. The nub of candle resting on the rickety chair by his bed fell to the dirt floor.

"Run! Judah, RUN!"

His father's voice; words pressed through grunts and the sound of wrestling, punching, swearing.

"Judah, get out! Now. Now! NOW!"

Judah Chweng rolled from his bed and fled into the night, a pair of shorts his only clothing. More noises. Shouts. Cries. Screams. The sounds battered his ears and his soul like fists. People ran through the dirt streets of the village. He saw a woman being chased by two men, each with long knives. She fell. They pounced. Judah stopped watching.

He wanted to call for help, but no help could be seen. Mayhem poured into and out of every mud hut. He heard a woman pleading for mercy. Then a scream, followed by wailing. More pleading. He recognized the voice of Elizabeth Jeremiah, the neighbor woman and the village teacher. She begged for her life. She pleaded for the life of her young daughter. Whoever was in the house with her answered with a laugh.

"Don't hurt me. Don't cut me anymore."

Elizabeth's voice was soaked in tears, pitiful. "Oh God, show mercy—" She fell silent. Then Judah heard the screams of the woman's daughter.

More shrieks and pleading. They came from houses; from the street; dear God, from everywhere. Curses, condemnations of those who did not "follow Allah".

Judah heard struggling coming from his own house. He turned. He wanted to go back, but what could a six year old do. His father told him to run, but didn't tell him where.

He glanced at the woman and the street and saw what he didn't understand, turned and sprinted for the only place of safety he could think of: the tree at the side of his home.

Judah raced across the ground, his bare feet pounding the tamped ground, then leapt for the lowest branch. He scrambled up and up and up until the tree top swayed from his added weight. He had put distance between him and the mayhem below, but it wasn't enough to mute the cries of children and adults, the wailing of the dying, the pleading unanswered prayers of the desperate victims. Judah settled in the joint formed by limb and trunk, wrapped his legs around the limb and locked his ankles. He leaned forward, placing his shoulder against the trunk to steady himself. Then he pressed his fingers into his ears and struggled to keep his weeping silent.

Smoke rose with noises of death. He could smell the burning of wood and bodies.

Seconds passed like years. Minutes folded into hours. Judah dug his fingers deeper into his ear canals. Deeper. Deeper.

When the sun rose pushing back the blackness of night, it illuminated the darkness of the human heart. Smoke hung in the cool air, diffusing the sun's light. Reluctantly, Judah removed his fingers from his ears. Birds, oblivious to the massacre, sang in the distance. He forced himself to look down, to peer through the branches and leaves. Most of the village was obscured by leafy branches, but he could see bodies lying in the street. Blood poured from some. Others had been burned. A stray dog, its ribs showing through a mangy hide, walked through village, sniffing corpses and pausing to lap at a small pool of blood.

No one shooed the dog. The best he could tell, the marauders were gone, returned to whatever dark abyss they had slithered from. Or so he hoped.

Branch by branch, foot by foot, Judah descended from the sanctuary of his perch, pausing every few steps to listen for voices and to scan the area for signs of the killers. His heart pounded as fast as a hummingbird's wings. He would have stayed in the tree forever, had concern for his family not compelled him back to the ground.

He waited ten minutes near the lowest branches, straining his ears and scanning the area, trying to avoid the sight of human carnage. Somewhere about halfway down the tree, Judah's mind turned off: too battered by apocalypse to do more than the most basic thinking—keeping heart beating and lungs drawing air. With only sounds of wind in the leaves, Judah decided to complete his descent. He dropped to the ground and waited for someone to shout an alarm. No voice pierced the near silent village. Yesterday at this time, narrow columns of smoke from cook fires rose into the brightening sky. Today smoke rose, not in columns, but curtains; not from cook fires but from smoldering huts and bodies.

The half-starved dog Judah had seen earlier pawed at the tiny body of a young girl. Judah picked up a stone and threw it with a fear-laced fury. The rock struck the dog on the hindquarter and it yelped. The sound of its pain rolled down the dead street. Judah sprinted behind the tree, fearing the noise would conjure up the demons who tried to kill him last night.

No demons came.

Judah walked to the front door of his home, one of the few huts still standing, its tin roof keeping the sky from seeing what lay inside. He pushed back the flimsy door and looked into the dim space where he, his father, mother, and sister lived. His entire family was there. All had had their throats cut. His mother lay on her back, naked and staring through open but empty eyes. The crucifix she had never failed to wear was lying beside her, its leather necklace torn. His father lay near Judah's bed, the place where he had sacrificed his own life to save Judah's.

Scorching tears ran down the boy's face. He made no attempt to wipe them away. Instead, he pocketed his mother's cross and moved to the center of the one room hut, sat on the dirt for a moment. He lay back, then rolled to his side.

The sobs came.

Alone. The last of a village of two hundred.

Alone. The last of his family.

Alone.

Tears ran.

Pope John Paul Benedict I snapped upright in his bed, tears on his face, a sob caught in his throat. He raised his hands to his face and wept as he had repeatedly done for decades.

***

A short but firm knock drew Benedict's attention from the window overlooking the *cortile de Sisto V.* The sun had risen and bathed the Courtyard of Sixtus V in its light, reflecting off the light colored stone. He didn't bother to invite the visitor in. Monsignor Ramone Erik had instant access to the one often called the Supreme Pontiff. The Papal apartments were located on the third floor of the Apostolic Palace, a grouping of rooms that included a bedroom, a vestibule, a small office for Benedict's secretary, and a living room. The complex also included a private study, a nearby kitchen, a dining room and a medical suite for emergency medical attention or dentistry. The room most important to Benedict was the private chapel.

The recurring dream had kept him from going back to sleep. He had gone to bed at 10:00 as was his custom and fallen asleep a moment later. At 2:00 his sleep ended with the bloody reminder of his childhood.

"I am told you did not sleep well again, Holy Father. Are the dreams troubling you again?"

Benedict turned the corner windows of his bedroom to face his longtime aide. "Who told you we did not sleep well?"

"Your steward was worried and . . ."

"And what, Monsignor?"

"You looked weary at morning Mass and at breakfast."

Benedict's life was scheduled and regimented. On a good day, he would rise at 5:00 praying from the liturgy of the hours. Meeting with bishops and cardinals filled much of the day as did the writing of sermons. In the evening, he would pray the Night Prayer and spend a few hours reading. This morning, he had more time to focus on the prayers.

"Yes, the dreams have recurred. We will not be free from them in this life."

"Your Holiness knows I am available to him anytime, day or night."

"You are very kind, Monsignor, but the dreams are part of our cross." He turned his attention back to the window. "We have a full day, do we not?" By "we," the pontiff did not mean he and Erik. As the head of the world's largest church he, like those who had come before, spoke with the majestic plural.

"Yes, Holy Father. Mostly audiences. The French president is scheduled today. He wishes to pay his best wishes."

"Is he not the man who told his people there was no God?"

"Yes, Your Holiness."

Benedict smiled. "Should we remind him of his statement?"

"It would be impolite . . . but satisfying." The response made the pontiff grin.

Benedict turned and moved from the bedroom to the door that led to his small office and then into a massive library. He preferred to discuss church business surrounded by books. He moved to a set of deeply padded, ornate chairs crafted in the early 1800s by Italian artisans. Most of the rooms in the collection of spaces that formed the papal apartment were too ornate for Benedict's taste. His earliest home was a mud hut with a sheet metal roof that stood next to a large tree. After that, he lived in a Nigerian orphanage run by Benedictine nuns. Simplicity had been the rule of his life but, although every Pope could redecorate his quarters, he couldn't bring himself to remove what others had built.

"Despite the obligations of the day, Monsignor, we would like to finalize the wording on our priestly call to prayer for Dr. Preston."

Erik stiffened. "Yes, Your Holiness."

"Does something bother you, Monsignor?"

"I am uncertain about the wisd—the *choice* to call for such prayer."

"You were about to say, 'wisdom'?"

"Forgive me, Holy Father. It was a poor choice of words."

"You have concerns?"

Erik lowered his head. "I do. As do others. Several have approached me about the matter and have asked me to once again ask Your Holiness to reconsider."

"Do these 'others' have names?"

"Of course, Your Holiness, but they are all names you've heard before." Erik paused. "Well, there is a new one."

"Who?"

"Cardinal Mahoney."

The name sent a wave of warmth through Benedict. Michael Mahoney was a long time friend. Though nearly a decade separated them in age, they had attended seminary together and it was Mahoney who helped Benedict through the rigors of advanced Latin; and Benedict who helped Mahoney get a handle on broader church history. "His Eminence believes we are being unwise?"

A steward entered the library with two cups of tea and set them on a small table between the chairs. Two jellied pastries rested on a silver platter. Both men ignored them but did accept the tea. "He would not put it so rudely. None in the service to the Church would. He did ask for an audience."

"Grant it."

"I'm afraid the schedule is rather full."

"Then change the schedule. Our Lord taught us we are not to be slaves to the Sabbath; we should likewise not be slaves to a schedule."

Erik fidgeted. He was a man of detail and order, a cleric of unflinching discipline. Sudden changes bothered him. "Yes, Holy Father."

"Make time for him this morning. He is in Rome?"

"Yes, Holy Father. He arrived last night from Ireland where he lives and spends his retirement."

The pontiff chuckled. "Still trying to convert the Irish. Our own St. Patrick. I remember when he asked to be assigned to his family's home country. The man has a passion for the land and the people."

"He does good work. The churches have increased in attendance and he has been able to start two new schools."

"Please see to it we have an hour of interrupted time. We wish to reminisce before hearing about the folly of my ways."

"I am sure he will be available."

The pontiff rose. "We shall meet in the rooftop garden."

Erik stood. "As you wish."

***

Michael Mahoney was sixty-five going on fifty. He seemed ageless, no doubt helped by daily jogs and a nearly vegetarian diet. Benedict sat at a simple patio table, under a red umbrella, shielded from the late morning sun. Before him was a glass of ice water, and a snack of cucumber sandwiches. Monsignor Erik escorted the man through a pair of double doors. His platinum white hair made his red skull cap seem larger and brighter. For a man deep into his sixties, Mahoney moved with the ease of someone half his age. The grueling schedule of the priestly life, made more intense by years of service as a cardinal, had no affect on the man.

Benedict rose to meet his friend and extended his hand. Mahoney took the hand, then bent and kissed the Pope's ring. "Your Holiness."

"Your Eminence."

When Mahoney straightened, there was a broad smile on his face. As students, they often poked fun at the formality that had become the norm in the Roman Catholic Church. Much of it was like in the world's militaries to foster a sense of service and obedience, but to the two young men, it had seemed overworked. Now they were the keepers of formality. Mahoney's grin said everything words could not.

Benedict looked at Erik. "Thank you, Monsignor. We will call if we have need of anything."

"Very well, Holy Father."

"Thank you for making time to see me."

"I miss you, old friend." The majesty plural became a victim to a lifetime of familiarity. "Shall we sit? I have taken the liberty of having some sandwiches made."

"Cucumber! You remembered." Mahoney took a seat on the one of the padded metal chairs.

"I have grown a bit older, but my memory is as sharp as ever, my friend." Benedict sat. "You look well."

"I am well. God has been good to me. Especially after I gave up drinking."

Mahoney was an alcoholic. Although not common, the stress of a cleric's life drove some, as in any profession, to succumb to alcohol. Mahoney had been one such priest until he was unable to offer last rites to a dying parishioner because he was too inebriated to make it to the hospital. It was a sin he confessed many times over the years and the catalyst for a life change. Part of his ministry now was counseling priests with the same problem.

"I hear good things of your work in Ireland."

"God is good. The work flourishes, but at a slower rate than I would like." The Irish in the accent was like music to Benedict's ears.

"Ministry's greatest tool is patience. We do what we can; the rest we leave in God's hands."

"Well said, my friend, but men of our age may run out of years of life before we run out of patience."

"That is the course of life." Benedict paused. "I was sorry to hear of your sister's passing. What has it been?"

"Six months, Holy Father. You were very kind to send condolences."

"I only wish I could have been at her funeral Mass, but . . ." He motioned to buildings that made up Vatican City.

"You were there in spirit and your concern ministered to me more than words can say."

Benedict took one of the small sandwiches, freeing Mahoney to do the same. "I am told you have concerns about the prayer decree I will be sending to our priests around the world."

Mahoney chewed slowly as if trying to buy time. He was in an awkward spot. Before him sat the most powerful religious man on the planet, the shepherd to over a billion Roman Catholics; he was also facing one of his closest friends. "I do have concerns about the request, Your Holiness. I am unable to find a peace about the matter."

The corners of Benedict's mouth ticked up. "You know, old friend, it is I who must have a peace about such decisions."

"Of course, of course. I only mean to say . . . I am a servant of God and His appointed shepherd here on Earth. I will follow whatever mandate you issue. That being said, there is some . . . consternation . . . about asking prayer for such a prisoner and a non-Catholic at that."

"A non-Catholic, Michael? Do we only pray for Catholics? I was under the impression prayers should be offered on the behalf of all people."

"Of course, Holy Father. I'm afraid I worded that badly. What I mean to say is that such a request might be considered interference with the power of governments to exercise their God-given right to enforce laws which are meant for the good of all people. After all, the Apostle Paul taught us to submit to the governments of the world so we may focus on caring for the flock he has placed in our charge."

"I am well aware of Romans 13, Michael, but you know there is more to that passage than what you describe." Benedict set his sandwich down and wiped his mouth with a linen napkin. "The Redeemer made it clear we should visit those in prison. 'If you have done this to the least of my brethren, you have done it to me.' It is true Dr. Preston is not a Catholic, but he is a man of God. While he dismisses some of our doctrine and has no use for my office, his core beliefs about Jesus are the same."

"Forgive me, Holy Father, but he does more than dismiss some of our doctrine; he has taught against it. He seems to dismiss the teachings of the Book of James and he taught against the authority of His Holiness to speak *ex cathedra*."

Benedict nodded. "Yes, he has. I have studied those recordings. Still, though we disagree on many important things, I am not willing to let the man suffer at the hands of secular lawmakers who wish to overlap their authority with the teaching of Christ. What has history taught us, Michael? The evil in the world will rise wherever it is not challenged. We battle evil by presenting the Good News. What happens if we once again lose the freedom to speak the truth in love without government limits or censorship?"

"I do not believe that such can happen."

"No? It has in the past. Beneath the streets of Roma are the catacombs where our brothers in the early church hid to save their lives and the lives of their wives and children. There, many were buried with hand etched Christian symbols over their resting places. True martyrdom is limited to just a few countries these days but it can return, and if does, it will come swiftly."

"Your Holiness, as always, is as eloquent as he is concise, but there will be a reaction to this call to prayer. Our priests in the United States are already suffering from declining membership, battling the rise of the New Atheism, and, of course, reeling from reaction to sexual abuse claims from a generation of rebellion. The Church in Europe is on life support. We face dark days. I fear the proposed call to prayer will only add fuel to the fire."

"I pray it does, my friend. Let the fire fall." Benedict's eyes narrowed. "Surely you realize what is at stake here. This is not about an American Baptist minister being tried in The Hague. It is about the rapidly changing landscape of religious freedom and the freedom of speech. Michael, my old friend, there are forces afoot who wish to rip your Bible from your hand and they're doing so by positioning themselves as the arbitrators of morality; as if a government can decide what it is God demands. They offer a secular religion to substitute for the true faith. They wish to take God's Word from our hands, our hearts, and our minds and replace it with canon for laws. They do so by preaching the Gospel of Tolerance which is no gospel at all, and which is—in every respect—intolerant of everyone who refuses to accept it."

Benedict leaned back in the chair and bore his gaze into the eyes of his friend. "Jesus died for the church. Its foundation contains his blood. It is our obligation to live for He who made such a sacrifice."

When Mahoney didn't respond, Benedict continued: "You have read C.S. Lewis?"

"No, Holy Father. I do know one of your dissertations was on the man. An Anglican, I believe."

"Yes. A professor of medieval literature. His close friend was J.R.R. Tolkien. In one of Lewis' children's novels, he portrayed Christ as a Lion and rightly so. After all, He is the Lion of Judah. Do you follow me?"

"I'm not sure I do."

"The Savior was humble in every way and so He taught us to be, but he was also a Lion who could not be intimidated by religious leaders or political powers." Benedict snapped forward as if an invisible hand pushed him. "It is time for the church to learn to roar again."

"I hope Your Holiness has taken no offense by my concerns. I was asked—"

Benedict cut him off with an upraised hand. "You always have access to my ear, my friend. Beneath these robes is the same awkward Nigerian student you met so many decades ago. Just not as thin." Benedict laughed and Mahoney joined him.

A moment later, Benedict said softly, "The call to prayer will go out. It is not my goal to create trouble, but I will not shy away from it. If we do not become part of the solution, then we will be part of the problem. I do not wish to tell God I found comfort and safety more important than truth."

Mahoney lowered his head. "I understand, Holy Father."

"Michael, just once, call me by my name."

"Yes, Holy Fath—" He grinned. "Yes, Judah."

He had hoped hearing his given name again would remind him that he once wore the clothes of a poor man. Instead, it brought the dream back to mind.

"I will hear your confession now, Cardinal Mahoney."

"Yes, Your Holiness." Mahoney crossed himself. "Bless me, Father, for I have sinned. It has been two weeks since my last confession . . .

Chapter 8

JKS and Andrea

A ndrea Covington moved through the well lit interior of the National Gallery of the Arts, her heels clicking on the smooth, shiny floor. Tourists meandered through the east building. Magnificent works filled this building and the large west structure. A person could spend a week gazing at art created by the world's geniuses: Alexander Calder, Matisse, and others, but she paid them no attention, nor did she watch the crowds gazing at centuries old art and speaking in library tones.

He would be here. Her boss, John Knox Smith, came to the Gallery at least twice a week. More often if he were stressed. Considering his recent meeting with a non Department of Justice attorney indicated something aside from the grueling business of being an Assistant Attorney General was going on and Andrea prided herself on knowing everything.

She found him standing near a bronze statue of a naked man with a pitchfork standing on the ugliest dog Andrea had ever seen.

"I found you."

He turned his gaze to her. "I didn't know I was lost."

"You know what I mean." He looked drawn and worn. "I was worried."

"Why? Because I left early?" He returned his gaze to the statue.

"No, although you usually work later than everyone else."

"I needed a mental break; needed to focus on something other than law . . . stuff."

"Is he helping?" She nodded at the statue, her blond hair bouncing from the motion.

"Severo da Ravenna."

"The statue has a name?"

He frowned. "I've worked with you long enough to know you're not that dim. Severo da Ravenna is the name of the artist. The piece is called 'Neptune on a Sea Monster.' Ravenna created the piece five hundred years ago."

"Neptune. So that's not a pitchfork?"

"It's a trident. You're having fun with me, aren't you?"

"I'm trying to get you to smile. You have a great smile and the world seems brighter when you're happy."

"Really? If you say so."

She studied the small work of art. "So why this sculpture? Why a man with a trident standing on a really ugly sea monster?"

He didn't answer right away, choosing to allow his eyes to trace the eighteen inch high bronze form. She stepped closer, close enough their shoulders nearly touched.

"Victory."

She cocked her head.

He noticed. "Tell me what you see."

"I still see a naked man with his foot on a really ugly beast."

He frowned and she decided it was time to stop being glib. Clearly he was in a mood. "Try again."

"Okay. Sorry. I see Neptune, god of the sea, lording it over a sea monster. Presumably, he has been victorious over the creature."

"Good, keep going."

She studied the figure. Art was not her strength. She liked a pretty picture, but one pretty picture was much the same as another. Her art of choice was organization. No one was better at keeping track of information, organizing meetings, and making certain nothing interrupted her boss. "The serpent is still alive. It has its head up and its mouth open, but it's not trying to bite the leg that pins him down. It's looking at its attacker. Neptune hasn't killed it."

"Now you're getting it. Is Neptune going to kill the beast?"

"It's a statue. I'm pretty sure it's not going to move." This time John scowled. "Sorry again. I forget how important art is to you." It was. This place was John's refuge, his temple, the place he came to meditate. "No. Neptune isn't going to kill the beast."

"How do you know that?"

"Because he's holding the trident with the points up, not at the animal. He seems . . . satisfied with the situation."

"You should come here more often, Andrea. You see more than most do. So why did the artist choose to pose his subject this way?"

"I'd only be guessing."

"That's all right. Much of art is interpretation. Why do *you* think Ravenna made this choice of positioning?"

She inhaled deeply and let it out. Had she known there was going to be an art exam, she might have just gone home after work. "I'm probably wrong, but it seems to me Neptune is being shown as powerful—I mean, look at that six-pack he's sporting, and the other parts of his, um, anatomy." Her boss didn't respond. "He has controlled the situation, shown he is king of the sea, and the serpent is, what, contrite. Is that the right word?"

"I get the idea. Again, you're spot on. If Ravenna had Neptune killing the animal, then he would be making the Roman god appear cruel, someone who is abusing his power. For Neptune, the win is enough. The beast is subdued and won't be a problem again."

"You see a whole lot more than I do."

"I see many things more." He didn't move his eyes from the art-work. "You asked why I'm studying this sculpture. Let me tell you what else I see. I see our work with DTED."

The comment made Andrea's brain seize. "You see the DOJ and DTED in this five-hundred year old statue? She struggled to imagine how the piece could be associated with the Diversity and Tolerance Enforcement Division, the Justice department her boss created and led.

"Neptune ruled the seas. We are working hard to rule the legal world's view of intolerance, especially where it rears its ugly head against the targets of haters, those people who suppress the rights of our homosexual, bisexual, gender-crossing citizens, not to mention atheists, New Age adherents, pagan worshippers and anyone else.

As Neptune defended the sea, we must defend our country from those who use prejudice to rip it from its roots of freedom and liberty for all. But we have to be careful. Ravenna struck a balance here: power, total dominance, but not cruelty. This piece reminds me to be strong, engage and destroy the evil, but not abuse our power."

"Like so many have said we have."

He stiffened. "I suppose even Neptune had his critics. During the Civil Rights movement, the Ku Klux Klan complained the government was interfering with their right to free speech and the unbridled use of their liberty. We fight the same battle today, not only with those racist bigots who hate people of color, but those Christian bigots who believe their religious views are the only right way of thinking. They stand in their pulpits, protected too long by outdated views of laws, and condemn anyone who's not like them."

"Like Pat Preston."

"My former classmate went too far. And to think a screw up almost let him get away." He straightened his spine. "He is our sea serpent and we have him underfoot. Now we must move forward with everything we've got, but still appear like the fair and just people we are."

"That brings up one of the reasons I'm here."

He turned and raised an eyebrow.

"I tried to call you, but you have a habit of turning off your cell phone when you come here."

"This is a place for contemplation. Not just for me, but for other lovers of art. I don't want my phone disrupting them."

"You could put it on silent."

"I can silence the phone, but I can't have a silent conversation, and I refuse to get into a ping pong texting dialog."

"Of course. You have a right to some private time. Anyway, I received a message a short time ago. There's been a development in the Preston case."

"I don't like the way you said 'development'." His gaze bored into her. "Tell me."

"Perhaps we should go back to the office—"

"Andrea, I'm in no mood to play games. My day has been bad enough. Spill it."

"We just got word Preston had a visitor."

"Who?"

"You're not going to believe this."

"Andrea!"

"Okay, okay." She took a breath and considered taking a step back. "The Pope."

"The Pope? *The* Pope?"

"I believe there is only one."

Curses ricocheted off the art museum's walls. People turned and stared. "Come on." He took her by the elbow.

"Where are we going?"

"Dinner."

"This isn't a date, is it?"

Chapter 9

DTED Concerns

J ohn Knox Smith didn't enter the conference room, he plunged into it, slamming the door closed behind him and marched to the head of the conference table. Seated around the table were eight loyal members of the Diversity and Tolerance Enforcement Division team. Each a specialist; each determined to end intolerance as they saw it—more importantly, as their leader saw it. Smart, educated, driven as they were, none looked up from the table. When their boss was angry, it was best to stay quiet.

John looked around the table, making eye contact with the few willing to look in his direction. These were not people easily intimidated. He had chosen each, based on a strict list of criteria. Some were there as advisors on special issues, others led teams of investigators and prosecutors.

Donna Lewis served as the DTED chief of staff. While Andrea served as John's personal assistant, it was Donna who made sure the gears of operation and communication worked smoothly.

Joel Thevis sat next to her. As lead attorney, it was his job to oversee the DOJ attorneys who worked in the field and made the court cases.

Special Agent Paul Atoms headed the DTED enforcement unit and liaison to the FBI and Homeland Security. Postal Inspector Sandra Evans, from the Prohibited Mailings Section of the Postal Inspection Service, was the quiet one, at least in meetings, but she

73

had been a catalyst in stemming the inappropriate use of the US Mail to promote hatred by scores of organizations, especially organizations of the religious right. Or as she called them, "the religious wrongs."

Bob Maas had come over from the Criminal Investigation Division and Public Policy Enforcement Exempt Organization of the Internal Revenue Service.

Renee X was a "civilian" from outside government circles, head of OneAmerika. President William Blaine had made it known that the woman, who had raised a great deal of money and delivered votes from the sexual minority sector, would be a wise addition to the team. As former chief counsel for the ACLU, she had a sound legal background. That, coupled with her attack-dog attitude, made her someone to respect and, at times, fear.

The Reverend Lynn Barrett was a nationally recognized lesbian activist and founding pastor of the Metropolitan Urban Church. She was also a nongovernmental advisor, representing religious minorities that ran the gamut of goddess worshippers to a modern movement of druids and everything in between.

The junior member of the team was Mike Alden, a gifted attorney with the occasional legal insight, but a little too timid for John's taste. John hoped to change him.

He glanced over the small assembly. John had handpicked each one and Attorney General Alton Stamper had approved of each. Some of the team had worked with John on the national Hate Speech Task Force. The work of the task force had brought the issue of hate speech to the United States Supreme Court. The case, *Liberty Free Church v. United States of America* split the court 5-4 with the five coming down on John's side. That was several years ago. John had achieved every trial lawyer's dream: to argue and win a nation-shaping case before SCOTUS. John had done it at the age of thirty. That victory sent his star to the top and he became the youngest Assistant Attorney General in US history.

That was a great victory, but it was also the past. While he allowed himself moments of revelry about past accomplishments, he preferred to think about the next achievement. It was great to prove the use of publicly owned airwaves to promote bigoted religious broadcasting was illegal and tarnished the value of people who held themselves to a different moral standard or no standard at all. The FCC had issued a cease and desist order against the reading of any Bible passage or sermon that could be construed as hate speech as Reverend Jeremiah Helton was wont to do from time to time. That victory had changed everything. The world was changing, in part because of the people in this room.

"I'm sorry to bring you in on such short notice," John said, but he felt no remorse. "Late yesterday I was made aware of a development in the Preston case. Our man in The Hague says Preston had a visitor a few days ago."

"It can't be his wife," Paul Atoms said. "We would know if she left the country."

"No, not his wife," John said. "I doubt they have the money for her to make another trip. Word is Preston's church has abandoned her. She's living off a small savings and the help of family and friends."

"So much for Christian love." Renee X seemed amused by the news. "Who was the visitor?"

"The Pope."

Silence, as if the air had been sucked from the room leaving too little oxygen. Finally, Joel Thevis spoke: "Pope John Paul Benedict?"

"Do you know of another Pope? I'm talking about the guy in Rome. He made a special visit to the prison and spent some time talking to Preston."

"Wait, I'm confused," Lynn Barrett, said. "The head of the Roman Catholic church took time out of his schedule to travel from Rome to the Netherlands to visit a Baptist preacher?"

"I had trouble believing it, too." John sat down. "Somehow he called in favors or threatened to remove the warden's salvation, or perhaps something else, but he was given access to the prisoner and not in the usual fashion. They met in a small conference room, not through the dividers that keep prisoner from visitor."

"Isn't that a violation of protocol?" Bob Maas asked. The IRS man seemed perplexed.

"It's a huge violation. I guess it's hard to say no to the Pope."

Renee X laughed. "I wouldn't have a problem. In fact, I'd like a few minutes alone with the little weasel. I have a few questions about why he and his peers have stood by while his priests molest young boys."

John started to correct her by mentioning the small percentage of priests, smaller than what is found in the general public, who had been shown to be child molesters, but that was off track and he had no desire to be seen as a defender of the Roman Church, or any church. Instead: "Not everyone has your sensibility, Renee. And that's beside the point, isn't it? Let's go with what we know: The most powerful religious figure in the world has been chatting it up with the defendant. Why?"

Again silence. The news had stunned the team as much as it had John when he first heard of it.

"I don't like this," Joel Thevis said. Since he had been the lead prosecutor in Preston's arrest. No one, other than John, wanted to see Preston tried and convicted as much as Joel did. To win a case in the world's international court with its newly expanded jurisdiction would be a feather in both men's caps. It would also go a long way to redeeming Joel from the oversight of his legal team that had forced John to move the trial overseas. "You knew Preston in college. Was he Catholic back then?"

"No," John said. "I've never known him to be anything other than a protestant. In fact, he was anti-Catholic back then and even when he was pastor of his mega-church. You know the case as well as I do. He taught a series on confused world religions and included Roman Catholicism. He wasn't that kind to them."

"To be fair, Mr. Smith, he wasn't unfair, either." Lynn Barrett was not a Preston fan, but she did have a love for her own sense of balance.

Joel snapped at her. "He tore down the basis for their doctrine, taught that the position of the Pope is not based in the Bible, that there was no need for the confessional, that their Mary was just another woman—"

"Careful with the attitude, Joel. I might be a minister, but I have no problem putting my pretty spectator pump where the sun don't shine."

"And you be careful with threats—"

"Joel?" John stared at the man.

"What? I mean, yes, sir."

"Back off. I understand her point. He ridiculed the church, but he did so in a kind and loving way. Perhaps some of his best friends are idiots and Catholics." The group chuckled, all except Joel and Lynn. "We can agree Preston is not a fan of the Roman church. So why does the leader of 1.2 billion Catholics pick up and travel to The Hague to talk to our man?"

"Do we know what happened during the meeting?"

"Gerald Gower, our researcher in The Hague, was allowed to interview the guards who were in the room. He also obtained the security video of the event. I didn't ask how." John looked to his Chief of Staff. "Go ahead with your presentation, Donna."

She stood, turned to the laptop in front of her, tapped a key and the light in the room dimmed. She tapped another key and the large flat screen monitor mounted on the rear wall of the conference room began to glow. "What we are about to see was sent to us over secure Internet. I've done some editing to remove unimportant parts." A key click later, a full color video played. "This first shot is from the security camera covering the parking lot. The three vehicles belong to the Pope's entourage."

John saw one white limo bracketed by two large SUVs. The limo looked heavier than it should, causing John to assume it was bullet and bomb proof. The three-vehicle motorcade stopped at the curb in front of the administration building. Several men in suits exited and looked around. John had no doubt they were the pontiff's security. Several moments passed, then a woman with dark hair, a narrow waist, and a regal bearing exited the back of the limo. A black man John had seen in the media a number of times eased out of the car.

"That is Pope John Paul Benedict I. He has been Pope for a little over three years now and follows another Pope named Benedict. It's a popular name among the Popes. He's only 57 years old."

They watched as several of the suited-men took positions around Benedict as he and the woman started toward the front door. The woman was captivating, beautiful enough to make John's feelings that he so carefully hid from others stir.

The scene cut to the interior lobby. Donna said, "This is them checking in. Watch the female guard."

A uniformed woman looked up from a desk behind an enclosure of security glass. She froze, then stood. A second later, she raised her hands to her mouth. There was enough detail on the security footage for John to see the Pope smile and motion with his hand. The woman began to shake.

"I take it she's a Catholic," Renee said.

"Apparently. She exits her position and joins them in the lobby, then kisses his ring. I don't think we need to see all that, but you will want to see this." The scene shifted to a small room where the Pope's men relinquish their side arms; then a guard started to search the Pope. Two of the guards stopped him. The Pope says something and the prison guard was allowed to conduct his search.

"I bet that doesn't happen every day," John said.

"Judging by the look on the faces of Benedict's men, the Pope just saved the guard from a bruising." Paul Atoms seemed amused.

They watched in silence as the Pope, the woman and two of the Pope's body guards were ushered into a small room. Video from a different camera showed Pat Preston cuffed and seated in a metal chair. He looked thin and drawn. When the Pope entered, he looked stunned.

The woman spoke with a lilting, Italian accent.

"Who's the woman?" Joel asked.

"Just listen." Donna entered a command that raised the volume.

John tried to remain stone-faced, but it took effort. Seeing the very dark skinned Pope in his pure white attire sitting across from Preston unnerved him. There was no way this could be a good thing. It played like a scene from some legal drama with the Pope expressing concern, a little chit-chat, and even a moment of tension when one of the prison guards approached the pontiff and two NFL-sized men stepped in his way. He had no idea the kind of training the body guards had, but he guessed if push came to knock-down, it would be the prison personnel unconscious and bleeding on the bare concrete floor. He couldn't imagine the men reaching this level without being the best in the world. In the midst of it all, he heard the woman identify herself as Countess Isabella San Philippa.

Donna paused the video. "I did a little research. She really is a countess. She comes from old money and married the head of a shipping company operating out of Italy and three other countries."

"I don't like where this is going," Joel said.

Donna ignored the interruption. "She's not a daddy's girl, living off millions of dollars in some trust. She's a real player—an attorney with a good pedigree. I've been able to create curriculum vita. You want to read it now, Boss?"

"Just give us the bottom line. We'll focus on the details later."

"She's got legs," Donna said, "and I don't mean those long things she stands on. Educated in Europe, clerked for a few judges, then the International Court of Justice. She knows almost everyone. Later, she was retained to train incoming justices in the court's protocol. Best I can tell, she schooled at least half of the now sitting justices."

Several in the room groaned. John wanted to.

Joel groaned the loudest. "Wouldn't that disqualify her to try the case? I'm mean, that's what she's talking about, right?"

John shook his head. "I don't see how. There's no conflict unless she's has some kind of financial ties to one of the justices or one of them defended her. Still, we should look into that."

"What about Preston's current bank of lawyers? The Alliance isn't going to bow out," Renee said. "They're too single-minded. This case is as important to their movement to spread hate as it is to ours to end it."

"There's no limit to the number of allied attorneys Preston can have. The Alliance has trained thousands and many in Europe. They're like mad dogs looking for a place to make a mess." John pinched the bridge of his nose. "They'll welcome her. She knows more about this court than they do. They've tried lots of cases in Europe before, but not before this body under the new jurisdiction. They'll smother her with hugs. . . the Alliance is good at that." He swore under his breath. "Carry on, Donna."

"The countess is not only well educated and well connected— and let's not forget well off—but she is deeply religious. I believe the phrase is 'born-again Catholic', whatever that is."

"It means she's more than Catholic in name," Lynn said. "Some people go to church because they were brought up that way—"

"Brainwashed as children, you mean." Renee spat the words as if they were bits of putrid food.

"Pretty much." Lynn rested her elbows on the table. "This is especially true in certain groups like Orthodox Judaism, orthodox churches tied to ethnic regions: Russian Orthodox, Eastern Orthodox, and the like. Most Roman Catholics grow up going to Mass and are indoctrinated through catechism training. I think what Donna is saying is that our new opponent is a fervent Catholic by choice and belief, not because it's the only thing she's ever known. Am I right, Donna?"

The chief-of-staff nodded, her shiny, dark hair reflecting the dimmed overhead lights. "She and her husband give to charities around the world. They give a lot of money. In the short time I've had to pull this together, I've been able to glean a few things about their charitable foundation. Last year, they gave over 14 million Euros to religious organizations, Catholic and others, as well as several nongovernmental organizations that combat world hunger. They have also partnered with several billionaires to investigate ways of eradicating malaria, dengue fever, and more."

"So she's squeaky clean?" Paul Atoms asked. "No skeletons in the closet yet? Granddad didn't support Mussolini?"

"I don't know. I've only had time to do the basics. You know, internet stuff and what our guy in The Hague shot my way. I'm an organizational genius, not a private investigator. I'll leave it to you to turn over the rocks."

"What do we know about her legal skills?" John asked.

"You mean courtroom finesse?" Joel said.

"Yes," John snapped. Then he lowered his tone. "That's exactly what I mean."

No one spoke.

"So she's a mystery in that regard."

"I doubt it, Boss." Donna's tone remained even. It was one of the things John admired about Donna; she never succumbed to his bluster. If he offended her, she never let on. "She left the ICJ to work for the Vatican. It seems the Holy See spends a lot of time responding to legal action."

"No doubt brought by sexually abused boys and their fractured families." Renee stewed. She could suck the light and warmth from any room.

"I imagine there's some of that still going on, but there must be other issues. The Roman Catholic Church operates from Vatican City, the world's smallest country, but its reach is global in scope and nearly timeless, reaching back to almost the first century. You can't count a fifth of the world's population as adherents and not be the target of a steady stream of lawsuits from scores of countries, each with its own legal system and judicial history. Most attorneys in our country have trouble keeping up with our system, let alone one hundred-sixty others. She must be good."

Joel Thevis drummed the table. "The name is ringing a bell with me."

"I thought you didn't know her," Atoms said.

"I don't, but the more I think about the name, the more I think I've heard it before—" He snapped his fingers. "I know. I was having drinks with an old law school buddy. It was maybe a year or so ago. I can't be sure. He mentioned the name. I didn't pay attention at the time. Why should I? The guy's a blow hard. A successful blowhard mind you, but a little self-absorbed."

"Talk to him," John said. "Paul, see if you can get some info on the countess."

"It's going to be difficult since she's half a world away."

"Everything we do is difficult, Paul. Work your magic."

Donna cleared her throat. "You need to hear the rest."

The recording played and a few moments later, John's blood ran cold. "The Pope is issuing a prayer decree?" He shook his head. "Should we be concerned about this?"

"Only if you believe prayer makes a difference," Renee chuckled. She was the only one.

"Oh, shut up, Renee," Lynn snapped. "If bitterness were manure, you could fertilize every farm in the country." She turned her attention to John. "As you know, I'm the pastor of a very free-thinking and loving church. Traditionalists have labeled us "liberal", but that's a moniker I'm more than happy to wear since it means I'm not in their camp. I'm not a Catholic, but I do know enough to understand what the Pope is saying."

"Which is?"

"He's directing every Roman Catholic priest in the world to pray for Preston and to do so every day. There are still hundreds of thousands of these priests."

"Still, it can't hurt us, right?" Joel said.

"It can if it gets in the media. The Pope won't alert the media, but it will get out. There's a whole phalanx of reporters from around the world assigned to cover the Vatican. I guarantee word will get out."

"And that can be bad?" Atoms shifted in his seat.

"Yeah," John said. "That can be bad."

Chapter 10

Man-Eater

John Knox Smith's stomach had soured since the morning meeting with the DTED team. The coffee he sipped was helping. He insisted on brewing strong African coffee which did him no good, especially when events upset him, events like an unexpected visit by the Pope to a man John had put behind bars. The only positive thing about it all was that news of the papal visit had not hit the airwaves. If that got out, then the media would have the world believing that an Assistant Attorney General was facing off with the Pope. There's no way that would be helpful. There were many Catholics in the United States: one in five to be exact. Though most were inactive, their numbers amounted to seventy million people and Catholics were known to vote. John was not an elected official; neither was his boss Alton Stamper; but the president was as were their many friends in the House and Senate. That could be a problem. Even nominal Catholics might rise up if they thought someone was unfairly attacking the Pope.

To make things worse, Pat Preston was a Baptist and Baptists made up the largest segment of Protestants in the country. John had been doing his homework: The Southern Baptist Convention churches, of which Preston was one, had over 16 million members. Add in the other flavors of Baptist and that number grew to something like 30 million people. Catholics and Baptists together numbered over 100 million. Even though few were active in politics, no politician could afford to tick off nearly one in every four citizens. And that was just in the US. By moving Preston's case to the ICJ, John had made the trial global. Who knows what would happen if Catholics around the world started making a fuss? He avoided factoring in other Orthodox churches and other denominations.

John pulled a plastic bottle of TUMS from his desk drawer and chewed four tablets. The intercom on his phone sounded. He punched a button. "Yes."

Andrea's voice came over the speaker. "Joel Thevis and a guest are here to see you."

"Show them in, Andrea." John tossed the bottle of antacids into the drawer before the door to his office opened. He stood.

"Mr. Smith, this is Tyler Boon." Joel smiled as he and a large man who tipped the scales near three hundred pounds which he carried on a six-foot-six frame approached John's desk. "I don't think you two have met."

"I know the name," John said. "Everyone in our business knows the name of Tyler Boon." He held out his hand which the visitor took. For a moment, John thought he was shaking hands with Bigfoot.

"I've heard your name too, Smith." His voice was just an octave higher than thunder.

Smith? Joel tensed. *So he likes things informal.* He suspected Boon was attempting to throw him off balance. Men like Boon did such things.

"Thank you for coming on such short notice . . . Tyler."

Boon looked like a man who just pulled off a successful prank. "People call me Boon."

"All right, Boon. Let's sit at the table." Before anyone could speak, John started for a four-foot diameter, round table in the center of the large office. He wanted to put Boon at ease, but wondered if he shouldn't have used the large desk to try to intimidate the lawyer—if he could be intimidated.

Once seated, John said, "Can I get you anything, Boon? Coffee?"

"Nah, what I want you can't serve in a government office. But thanks."

"Again I appreciate—"

"Can we cut to the chase, Smith? I bill north of $500 per hour for my even most impoverished clients and more than double that for my corporate clients. I know that busts the Laffey Matrix fee schedules to bits, but I don't much care. What does concern me is I'm burning cash sitting in your office instead of mine."

"Then why did you bother to come?"

"I'm an idealist, Smith. You are an Assistant Attorney General. I like to think if I do you a favor, then someday you might do one for me."

"I can't make a promise like that."

"I'm not asking for a commitment. I'm just answering your question. I went to school with your man here. I figure I owe him one for the ol' alma mater." He waited one moment, then plowed forward. I understand you want to know something about the Countess Isabella San Philippa."

"Yes. Mr. Thevis tells me you know her."

"I do. What of it?"

"What can you tell me about her?"

"She's beautiful."

John tried to seem unbothered by Boon's antics. "Yes, I've seen her photo."

"She's rich. Married richer."

"Have you ever worked a case with her?" John folded his hands on the table.

"What if I have?"

"You're not in trouble, Boon. I'm not investigating you."

"I know that. I've never worked a case with or against her, but I have seen her in court. I did part of my studies overseas. For awhile I thought I would practice international law. Spent a few summers working with various European law firms. Not much, you understand, just enough to see how that side of the world works. One of the firms I was dealing with brought suit against the Vatican. Apparently they had built a church on a busy street in the red light district. Having priests and nuns walking around apparently drove customers away. Europe has a different sensibility than we do. They sued. The countess defended."

"And?"

"She destroyed them. Broke their case to pieces, then ground the shards to dust, and they were using the best lawyers money could buy."

"She's that good?"

"Good? I don't know how good you imagine her to be, but she's ten times that. She's the only lawyer in the world I wouldn't want to face. I'd take ten of you on at one time rather than face off in court with her, and I'm the best defense attorney you'll ever meet."

"She can't be *that* good." John leaned back, appearing unbothered but inside his organs were blending into a single mass.

"I hope this case isn't important to you. If you're planning on going up against her, then reset your plans. The woman will cut your heart out and hand it to you in a brown paper bag."

John's jaw tightened. "I think you underestimate me, Boon. I'm not some shyster who got his law degree online—"

"Save it, Smith. I know all about your time at Princeton and Harvard and I'm not impressed. I'm impressed by what's done in the courtroom. Everything else is just paper hanging on the wall."

John's first instinct was to pummel the man, but he was twice the size of John and looked like he could intimidate a grizzly. The second impulse was to kick him out of the office, but he needed someone to help them prepare a viable approach to the countess and this man knew her and lived in the DC area. So John followed his third impulse: he smiled.

"I like a man who speaks his mind, so I'll speak mine. I want to hire you as a consultant. Help us deal with the countess. Tell us what you know of her techniques, how she's connected to the Alliance, and what gives her an edge—"

"Not gonna happen, Smith. You can ask until the world ends, but I'm not working for you."

"I pay a good consultation fee."

Boon guffawed. "I flush more money each month on trinkets for my family and friends than you make in a year, Smith. I'm good at what I do and my skill has earned me a very comfortable salary."

"I might be able to arrange more than you think."

"Again, no. First, you and the DOJ can't afford me; second, I've defended some real lowlifes in my day, people who deserve to be in jail, but this case is too dirty, even for me."

"You don't even know what the case is."

"It's Pastor Preston's case. Don't ever think I'm a fool. I know Joel here works for DTED. I know you've made your name by rousting religious leaders and stooped so low as to force perp walks in front of the media."

"You're a high price defense attorney, Boon. Don't act righteous around me."

"I defend people for two reasons." He held up a large finger. "One, the constitution grants them the right to a vigorous defense; two—" Another finger shot up. "It keeps guys like you in check." Boon stood. "You've had a lot of success prosecuting pulpit jockeys and television evangelists, but you went too far when you started forcing judges out who didn't agree with your new way of seeing things. Good officers are leaving the police force and the FBI because they can't do the evil you demand."

John was on his feet. "I don't need a lecture from the likes of you."

"Yes you do, Smith. You need that and much more, but as good as I am, I can't give you a soul."

"You can leave."

"I plan to, but I've got something else to say. I hope the countess kicks your butt all over Europe and when your little empire comes down on your head and you need the best defense attorney in the country, don't come to me. My door is closed to you."

"Get out."

"Lately, I've had this dream you'll prosecute someone I defend. Man, I'd give my left arm to face you in court. Greedy as I am, I'd take the case for free, you weasel."

"GET OUT!"

Boon grinned. "Thank you for your time, Mr. Assistant Attorney General. It's been a real pleasure."

Boon left. John looked at Joel but couldn't speak. He could feel the blood coursing through his veins at high pressure. Joel Thevis rose and quietly exited.

Before Joel had the door closed, Andrea's voice drifted in. "I saw your friend leave —"

"Don't go in there, Andrea."

"Why?"

"Just don't go in."

Joel closed the door, leaving John to stew alone.

Chapter 11

Mystery Man

———⟫◆⟪———

The Nashville night was cool for late spring. The official start of summer was only a month or so away. A ghostly white moon hung in a cloud free sky, kept company by the few stars bright enough to push through the glare of streetlights. Becky Preston stood by the window, letting the scent of flowers in full bloom work its way to her nose. Next door, an elderly widow spent her days keeping scores of roses trimmed, weeded, and watered. Becky and her neighbors were the beneficiaries of the gray-haired lady's dedication to plants that would long outlive her.

A car, older than most of the neighborhood residents, chugged down the street, its headlights pushing back the darkness in front of it like the bow of a ship splits waters in its path. A night bird of some sort made a pronouncement and in the distance, a dog barked a response.

Inside the house rested silence: no television, no radio; the only noise the occasional hum of the ten year old refrigerator. The house, a place made rent-free by one of the members of Wilma's church, was less than a third the size of the home she shared with Pat. The bungalow style home had been built in the post World War II construction boom, but had held up well through the decades of summer sun, winter cold, and high humidity. There had been a time when she would have turned up her nose at the "shack," but she was a different woman then. Safety, security, and comfort were her great desires; now she was happy to have a place to live.

She had moved back to Nashville after spending time with her mother in Louisville. Mom had been a great help and the children thrived under her attention. She missed her father, a man who had spent forty years as a pastor. She always regretted not spending more time with her mother after dad died. After Pat's first arrest, the news media fury, and the relentless attacks by the leaders of the church that he had pastored so faithfully, Becky left, taking the kids to protect them from what they were hearing in school. It took awhile for her level of self-honesty to rise to the point where she would admit she was leaving to protect herself.

Now she was back in Nashville, partly on principle, partly because this home was made available rent-free. Pat's church had given him a generous severance, but that would soon run out. Becky was doing everything she could to stem the cash flow. Finding work flexible enough to match the school schedule of two young children had proved impossible. Still she looked; still she prayed for something that would allow her to stay. The option of returning to her mother's home was still available, but Becky resisted it. The stress was beginning to show on Mom. She denied it, but the signs were obvious. Pat's parents in Owensboro weren't an option, at least not now. They had been cool toward her after she left Pat to face the problems alone. She had returned, but some wounds took longer to heal than others.

Becky turned from the window and heard the sound of another car drive by. It was close to midnight and the passing of two vehicles was a parade for this neighborhood. She should be in bed, she told herself. Tomorrow was a school day and the children would be up early—complaining, but up. Sleep held no interest for her. Every time she closed her eyes she saw Pat, dressed in prison garb and twenty-five pounds lighter. He looked almost skeletal. When she lay in the dark, darker thoughts invaded her mind and she was helpless to evict them. Where once bed had been a refuge, it was now a torture chamber. The emptiness of the bed mocked her situation, dug at her thoughts with animal claws. More nights than not, she slept in a worn easy chair, the television nearly muted and casting its flickering light through the tiny living room.

She closed the window, slowly, gently, so as not to awaken the children, turned on the television and found a late night talk show. She keyed the closed captioning so the sound wouldn't fill the house. She lowered herself into the chair and wondered who the first owner had been and how many hours he had logged on the faux leather upholstery.

Her eyes closed, then opened, then closed again, as if her lids were growing heavier by the second.

She dozed. For a moment, she dreamed.

A noise.

Her eyes snapped open. One of the kids? She strained her ears. She heard no cries, no rustling in the beds. Lowering the foot rest, Becky rose and started for the bedroom the children shared. Peeking through the door which she kept ajar so she could hear them if they called, she saw two beds, each occupied. The sound of gentle breathing filled the space. Light from a nearby streetlamp pressed through the thin drapes, allowing her to see toys scattered on the floor. She sighed. She would have to scold them about getting out of bed to retrieve toys instead of sleeping as they should—

A shadow passed in front of the window: man-shaped, tall, bulky. Paused at the window, its head moving as if studying the edges of the window.

Panic rose in her like magma in the throat of a volcano. Someone was standing at her children's window.

Her heart seized. Her breath caught. "Oh, dear God!"

What to do. She first thought of the rack of knives in the kitchen, but couldn't make herself step away from the bedroom door. Adrenaline flooded her veins. Her heart restarted, pounding in her chest as if trying to break her ribs.

Not a knife. Not yet. Instead, she turned the bedroom light on and woke the children, speaking loud enough to be heard outside. She pulled them from their beds and dragged them into the living room, letting go only long enough to turn on lights. She sped through the house, flipping every switch until the interior glowed.

"Mommy," Phoebe said. "What's wrong?"

"Hush, sweetheart."

"Ma, I was sleeping." Luke always woke up in a grumpy mood. Being snatched from bed hadn't helped.

Becky snapped up a wireless phone and dialed 9-1-1. She also retrieved a butcher knife from the kitchen. "Come with me, kids."

"Where are we going?" Phoebe said. "I'm still sleepy."

"Mommy's bedroom. Hurry."

"Why?"

"Do what I say."

Luke looked suspicious. "Why do you have a knife?"

"Please do as Mommy says." She pinned the phone between her ear and shoulder, taking Phoebe, her youngest, by the hand. "Hurry."

Luke followed, making it clear he didn't like been awakened in such a rude fashion. "I don't know why I have to get up."

On the third ring, Becky heard a woman's voice: "This is 9-1-1, what is the nature of your emergency?"

"There's someone prowling outside my house. He was at my children's window." She shut the bedroom door and locked it. "Into the bathroom, kids."

"I don't have to go." Phoebe looked more annoyed than scared. Good.

"Is he still there?"

"I don't know. I turned on all the lights. I may have scared him away, but I can't be sure."

"That's a good idea. Where are you in the house?"

"I've locked us in the master bath."

"Good thinking. We have your address on the screen. I'm sending a unit right now."

"Please hurry."

"I have a unit responding. You said it was a man?"

"I think so. I saw his shadow on the window shade. He was big. I think he was wearing a hat—a baseball cap, I mean."

"But you didn't actually see him."

"I saw enough." Her tone turned harsh.

"Okay, ma'am. I want you to stay where you are. I'm going to stay on the phone with you. You tell me everything that is happening. Okay?"

"Okay."

There was a pause. "Do you hear anything unusual?"

"No." Becky pushed the children to the back wall, then turned her eyes to the small window over toilet. She set the knife down and pointed to the shower stall of the three-quarter bath. "Get inside."

"I'm not showering with Phoebe. Ew. Gross."

"You're gross and stupid."

"Yeah? Well you're ugly."

"You're not going to shower. Just do as I say." Becky pulled the glass door and moved her children inside, then closed the door, retrieved the large knife, and pressed her back against the shower. Her eyes moved from the bathroom door to the window and back. She was pretty sure the man would be too big to get through the three-by-three foot window, only half of which could slide open, but that didn't mean he couldn't shoot through the glass.

"Ma'am?"

She might feel silly later, but better than feeling regret.

"Ma'am?"

"Mommy, I'm scared."

"I know, Sweetie. Just hush for now. Mommy needs to listen."

"Ma'am?"

She spoke into the phone. "I'm here."

"Please stay on the line with me."

"I'm juggling a knife, a phone, and two kids in a small bath. If you want to come over and help, it would be appreciated."

"I understand, ma'am. I just need to know everything that's going on. Did you say you have a knife?"

"Yes. From the kitchen. It was the only weapon I could think of."

"Okay, I will let you know when the officers arrive. Don't open any doors until I tell you they're on the premises. Understood?"

"Yes. I understand."

"One more thing." The dispatcher's voice was smooth and calm. "When the officers arrive, please don't greet them with the knife. They're touchy about such things."

The woman was trying to lift her spirits. Becky appreciated that but only for a second."

"Mommy, what's wrong?"

"Hush, Phoebe, I'll explain later. Let Mommy listen."

Again she pressed her ears to pick up any sounds. She heard the old refrigerator again but nothing else. She fixed her eyes on the door know, uncertain what she would do if the knob turned.

"Ma'am, the closest unit is one mile out. It will be there soon. Another unit will be right behind it."

"Okay. Good. Thank you."

"You're doing a super job; just stay calm and stay where you are. Okay?"

"Yeah. I'm not going anywhere."

"This will all be over in a minute . . . Stand by."

Becky could hear the woman talking on the radio. "10-4, 10-23." Then, "Ma'am, the first unit is on the scene. They're going to search the area around your home, so you will likely hear them."

"Okay. Okay. Good. Thanks." Becky's breathing was erratic and heart clawed around in her chest.

Minutes passed like years. Finally, "Ma'am. The officers report the area is clear. One unit is going to search the area. Two officers are at the front door. They need to speak with you."

"Um, okay. I'll . . . I'll go open the door." She was fighting tears.

"Ma'am, they've asked the children not to come to the door with you."

"Okay . . . why?"

"I don't know. That's a field decision. Since your property is safe now, maybe you can have them go back to bed or at least wait in their bedroom."

She started to question the reasoning again, but decided against it. She shuffled them into their rooms and went to the front door. She reached for the lock, then stopped, turned and returned the knife to the kitchen. There was a gentle knock and a deep voice. "Police."

Becky opened the door and two uniformed officers stood on the stoop. Both looked younger than thirty. One had two stripes on his sleeve. "Evening, ma'am, the children—"

"Are in the bedroom; thank you for coming so quickly."

"Glad to be of service . . ." His eyes drifted down. "I hate to ask, but do these belong to your children?"

Becky looked down and saw two dolls: one Raggedy Andy; one Raggedy Ann. On their clothing, someone had stitched the names Luke and Phoebe. Each doll was speckled with blood and knitting needles had been jammed through their eyes.

Chapter 12

Countess Conference

＞◦＜

"Will you excuse me for a moment?" The silver-haired man with a chiseled jaw and deep blue eyes said.

"Certainly." Isabella smiled and gave a short nod.

The video conference had lasted an hour and contained material only a lawyer could love. Isabella sat in the office in the corner of the house overlooking the pool and tennis court. It had been designed to be a den, but Isabella had taken over the room and hired an interior decorator to make it into a comfortable office. Law books lined two walls, art from little known artists hung on one wall. The fourth wall sported large, mullioned windows. The window shades were drawn to block the late evening sun from interfering with the twenty-seven inch computer monitor that, until just a few moments ago, showed the face of a half dozen attorneys working for the Alliance, her co-counsel nonprofit organization of lawyers and paralegals dedicated to defending religious freedom, especially where it involved Christian ministers.

During the early weeks and months of Pat Preston's legal difficulties and subsequent arrest, it was the Alliance that came to his aid. She had done her research, having read every report and court document the Alliance issued in an effort to keep an innocent minster from going to jail for preaching from the Bible. She was proud to now be one of the allied attorneys. John Knox Smith, the American

96

assistant attorney general, had out-maneuvered them in Round One by arranging to have Preston tried as a test case in a world court. She had no doubt, having read the charges against Preston and the evidence mistakes, that Alliance attorneys would have—what was the American expression?—handed him his lunch. It still astonished her that a country founded on the freedom of expression and religion could classify a sermon about Christ being the sole means of salvation as hate speech. Her client had done nothing more that teach what Jesus had said about Himself. How was that hate speech? She thought for a moment, then reminded herself that Jesus' comment was one of the reasons He was crucified.

As experienced as the Alliance was, they were also drawn extremely thin. The sudden changes in American law dealing with hate speech had stretched the Alliance's resources to the breaking point. Attacks on the organization had limited their fundraising, and the sheer number of cases had become overwhelming. What did not break was their spirit and their consistent winning record. Over the last two years, thanks to repeated IRS audits and harassment, they lost many of their large financial supporters. Then came the RTDA—the Respect for Diversity and Tolerance Act of 2014. That set the stage for the DOJ enforcement division that could make a federal case out of anything considered hate speech or intolerance directed at another, based on race, creed, and sexual orientation. Where once an individual or group could voice an opinion as long as it wasn't slanderous or false, they could now be prosecuted. While the Alliance agreed that those holding opinions opposite to theirs also had a right to free speech, they and other Christian organizations had been portrayed as purveyors of hatred and as people who foment violence against those who might not fit the mainstream. In just a few years, "free speech" was no longer free.

The Alliance continued the fight in the United States and in other countries as it had done since its inception. Although accused of defending hatred, they had become the victim. She had learned that the Alliance had taken to hiring security to protect their offices and staff. Still they carried the banner and were showing the bruises for doing so.

She had to admire the men and women of the ministry. They could be making a great deal more money practicing law in other arenas, but they chose to champion a side that had fewer and fewer friends.

Now she was one of them.

The man who just asked for a few moments away from the video conference had told Isabella that his office had been "tagged"—an American phrase for graffiti—with swastikas. The Christian lawyers were avidly portrayed as bigots. She could hear the pain in the man's voice, and his sad eyes reflected weariness of too many hours worked, too many criticisms endured. That being true, she had also detected no surrender in his words or manner.

"I'm back. Thank you. That was my wife on the phone."

"No problem, Mr. Jordan."

"Everyone calls me Larry, Countess."

"Everyone calls me . . . Countess." She grinned. "But please call me Isabella."

He returned the smile and in that moment appeared ten years younger. "We are overjoyed to have you working on this case. Did my colleagues answer your questions?"

She had spent the last hour staring at six bright lead attorneys in the video conference. Each was an Alliance director for some area of the country. They had covered the history of the case that wasn't covered in the legal documents Larry Jordan had sent and offered suggestions for how to proceed with the case. "Yes. You have a very talented team."

"I'm just part of the team. I run the DC office. Scott Freeman is the President and CEO of the Alliance. He couldn't be with us today. He's arguing a case in New York."

"I hope to meet him in person soon."

"You will." He paused, then took the lead. "I asked you to continue with me a little longer because I sense you still have some questions or gray areas. That and I have something else to tell you."

"You are perceptive. I've created a timeline of the case to date and a history. I notice you have had, perhaps, the most contact with John Knox Smith. Is that true?"

"We have knocked heads many times. He doesn't much like me."

She chuckled. "Sometimes not being liked is a compliment. What can you tell me about the man, I mean beyond his biography? I know about his Princeton and Harvard education. I know he is the youngest Assistant Attorney General ever appointed."

"That's the sad part. He's brilliant and driven. He is the smartest attorney I've ever met, present company excluded, of course. He lacks a moral center—no, I didn't say that right." Jordan paused. "He has an undefined morality. He's not amoral, just ambiguous. Does that make sense?"

"It does and it frightens me all the more. It is easy to know what to expect of a moral person. The same is true of an immoral one. Those in the middle are impossible to predict."

"We keep tabs on him the best we can and within legal limits. I know he loves the spotlight, but it is secondary to his mission. His mission matters more than anything to him."

"Even more than his family."

"His wife has left him. They've been apart for months. My guess is she will file for divorce someday. For all I know, she may already have done so. I don't know much about his personal life." He rubbed his chin. "Pat Preston went to school with him. They were friends in Princeton. There was a third musketeer: Matthew Branson. They grew apart after college. Pat went to seminary, Matt went to law school in Michigan, and JKS went to Harvard where he excelled in everything."

"Could Matthew Branson tell me more about, how did your refer to Mr. Smith?"

"JKS. His initials. I'm afraid Mr. Branson was gunned down a few months ago. His killer is still at large."

"I'm sorry to hear that. Did he have family?"

Jordan looked down. "Yes. I didn't know him. He worked at the DOJ."

"With JKS?" She raised an eyebrow.

"Different department. JKS runs the DTED team and Mr. Branson worked in the OPR: the Office of Professional Responsibility."

"Which is . . ."

"They investigate DOJ attorneys who might have used their authority illegally or in a manner not allowed by the DOJ code of conduct. In a sense, they police the police—except we're talking lawyers."

"Interesting. There are those in the DOJ who disagree with JKS?"

"I'm sure there are, but criticizing an Assistant Attorney General, one appointed with the blessing of the president, is career suicide." It was his turn to raise an eyebrow. "You're not suggesting JKS had anything to do with the man's death?"

"No. Of course not. I just find it interesting. To provide the best defense, I need to know who I'll be facing in court. He's argued the preliminary motions; should I assume he'll argue the case?"

"He's argued before the Supreme Court several times; he'll want to argue before the full ICJ panel. His ego won't let him give that honor to someone else."

"Good."

"Really? Good?"

"Sometimes smart people defeat themselves. Not to worry, I'm not counting on that. Help me understand the team JKS leads."

"Sure. It's rather unique in some ways. He has a group of twenty or so lead attorneys and almost unlimited juniors he can call on for any research or minor tasks and a few designated special agents. There is a smaller core team that keeps things flowing. This includes a chief-of-staff, a lead attorney, an IRS Agent, a former FBI agent who liaises with the Federal Bureau of Investigation. He also has several civilian—by which I mean non-government employees—who advise him in matters dealing with what we could call fringe religions, and those dealing with 'gay, lesbian, and transgendered people groups', his words, not mine. Ultimately, he calls all the shots and the DOJ employees carry out his wishes. The civilians just provide guidance."

"Are the civilians influential?"

"Only at DTED. Outside of his office, most have little authority. One is Renee X—"

"Wait, her last name is X? Like the letter? Is this the sixties all over?"

"That's right. She started off as a radical feminist and was married for awhile. She hated the idea of taking her husband's last name so she decided to have no last name at all. The marriage ended and she became a spokeswoman for alternative sexuality. That is her right, of course, but she's so bitter that she's lost more followers than she's gained over the last year. Another advisor is a

pastor of sorts. I'm not sure what to call her because she doesn't fit any standard. Her church is an earth worshipping group. She promotes the 'goddess within.'"

"Are there any Christians among the advisors?"

Jordan had to think for a moment. "The religious representation is provided by Lynn Barrett."

"She is the goddess worshipper?"

"Yes. She used to be a PC USA pastor, but denounced the denomination for its refusal to bless polygamy."

"So, no true Christian advisors at all." Isabella typed the information into a file she started at the beginning of the meeting. "Doesn't seem very open and accepting to me."

"You'll find that to be true for the whole DTED operations. They're intolerant of anyone who disagrees with them." He began tapping the keys on his keyboard. "I'm sending an e-mail with a list of DTED objectives. We got this through the Freedom of Information Act. I'm surprised they don't have it posted on the DOJ webpage."

A few moments later the e-mail arrived with an attachment. Isabella opened it and read.

Organizational Objectives:

All: Identify organizations and individuals in open and flagrant violation of the United States Respect for Diversity and Tolerance Act (RDTA) of 2014.

All: Create a national interdepartmental and agency database on organizations and individuals engaged or suspected of engaging in violations of RDTA. This list should include religious organizations where sexual and other bias is advocated. The list will be maintained by the Department of Justice with Department of Treasury, Postal Service, and Internal Revenue Service cross reference.

Agencies: Investigate and prepare criminal case prosecution reports against organizations and individuals engaged in serious violation of RDTA for DOJ prosecutors.

Justice: Prosecute violations of RDTA seeking penalties for organizations and individuals up to the maximum levels allowed by law.

Justice: Prepare civil lawsuits to obtain prohibitory orders to stop all use of the United States Postal Service by organizations or individuals engaged in violation of RDTA. Most hate-based sectarian organizations cannot function without direct mail solicitation. The United States Postal Service must put an end to all mail that promotes or enables hate.

Agencies and Justice: Supply non-grand jury investigative data to the Federal Communications Commission for actions including suspension or revocation of broadcast licenses for stations carrying content in violation of RDTA.

IRS: Prepare administrative cases, to be backed by civil litigation, to eliminate tax exemptions for—and the deductibility of charitable contributions—to all organizations engaged in violation of RDTA, especially Christian and Jewish schools that openly oppose Darwinian and other scientific truth.

Justice: Prepare civil Racketeering and Influenced Corrupt Organization Act (RICO) lawsuits to seize all of the property, especially homes, churches buildings, and commercial property, hate literature such as tracts, films, videos, electronic storage media, and other publications owned or controlled by organizations or individuals involved in violation of RDTA. As soon as we develop an RDTA case, we should move with RICO.

Justice: Work with the public news media to provide maximum publicity, within the bounds of legal ethics, to ensure awareness of and compliance with the law.

Justice, in liaison with Congressional leaders: Review all sections of the United States Code and identify inappropriate language for updating. Seek and remove all authorizations for bias from law specifically including, the misnamed "Equal Access Act," the illusory claim "In God we trust" from currency, any funding for education or backing of student loans where the institution allows unlawful public religious acknowledgment.

Justice and State Department liaison: Coordinate with international law enforcement community, the United Nations, and the International Court of Justice to ensure that the United States is in full compliance with worldwide efforts regarding tolerance and equality. Determine which international conferences and events may merit DTED's active participation.

"This is chilling," Isabella said after reading it for the second time. "Bone chilling."

"I agree. That's why the Pat Preston case is so important. Countries are more tied together than most people realize. If JKS wins in The Hague, the dominoes will begin falling everywhere. No one can legally proclaim Jesus is Lord."

"I can see that. Well then, we will have to pray we don't lose."

Jordan pressed his lips into a thin line. He stared into the web camera as if he were looking at her from across a table. "I need to ask you to do something unpleasant, Isabella."

"Oh?"

"Last night—well, about six or seven in the morning Rome time—someone went to the house where Pat's wife and children are staying—"

"No!"

"They're fine. Everyone is healthy." He told her of the trespasser and the mutilated dolls. "She called me the next morning. She didn't know where else to turn. I made some calls to the police to learn what I could. The blood on the dolls wasn't human. It was beef blood, probably squeezed from some raw meat."

"That's horrible. I can't imagine the terror she felt." Isabella placed a hand on her chest as if it would quiet her heart.

"Someone needs to tell Pat. Part of me wants to leave him ignorant about the whole thing. He's got enough problems. This will be tough for him to hear. Every man wants to protect his family and he can't."

"I'll tell him."

"Are you sure? As one of his attorneys, I can make a phone call."

"No, a phone call won't do. He needs to hear it face to face."

Jordan looked concerned. "Are you sure you can do this? If you want us to find someone else, we can."

"Like you, I'm Pat's attorney. I took the job knowing it would be difficult. If this is part of it, then I must do it."

"Just make sure he knows his family is fine."

"What about protection?"

"I'm not sure what we can do. The police said they'd drive by when they can, but they can't provide full time security, and they certainly can't afford it."

"Let me think about that."

"Okay, Isabella. Is there anything we can do here on the home front?"

She leaned toward the camera as if leaning close to the man. "I have an idea."

Chapter 13

The Edge of Insanity

—⇒∙◆∙⇐—

Countess Isabella San Philippa sat at the small metal shelf that served as a desk for visiting attorneys. He faced her from his side of the thick plastic window that kept Pat from the free world on the other side. Her eyes were orbs awash in pity and sorrow. The words she uttered burned as if each syllable was a drop of molten lead being trickled on his soul.

"First, you must know your family is unharmed."

"Unharmed? What happened?"

She had looked down, unable to maintain eye contact.

"Tell me!" His words were loud enough to draw the attention of three other prisoners on his side of the partition, prisoners listening to their lawyers.

Isabella told him about the trespasser and the mutilated dolls. Pat slumped in his metal chair, his handcuffed wrists resting in his lap. He struggled to breathe; struggled to make sense of what he was hearing. He wanted to ask why, but there was no answer to the question. Nothing made sense anymore. Never had he imagined he would one day be in a foreign prison waiting to be tried by a group that could never be called "peers."

"They're okay?"

"Yes."

"No one touched them?"

"No."

"They're safe?"

"Yes."

"They're okay?"

"Dr. Preston, listen to me. Dr. Preston. Pat, look at me." Pat raised his eyes and saw compassion on Isabella's face. "Your family is safe and well."

"For how long?" A pressure began to build in him.

"The Alliance and I have arranged for a security guard to be parked in front of the house. I've also made other plans that will take place soon."

"What kind of plans?"

"I don't want to talk about that here, Pat. I just need you to trust me."

"I don't think I can trust anyone anymore."

Isabella frowned. "Listen to me, Dr. Preston. You can trust me and all of your friends at the Alliance. You must not give in to despair."

"It's too late for that."

"Then find your courage again." She hesitated. "There are two types of prisons in the world, Pat: the kind others put us in; then there's the kind we put ourselves in. You can't control the first. At least, not now. But you can control the latter."

"I've got to get out of here. My family needs me."

"That's going to take some time—"

"I'm an innocent man bound in prison while a real criminal stalks my family. Where's the justice in that?"

"Justice doesn't exist, Pat; justice is recreated every moment of every day. It's not a thing; it's an achievement."

"I've got to get out of this place. My family needs me. I need to protect them."

He rose. "Pat, sit down. We're not finished."

"I've got to get out."

Two guards moved to his side as Pat stepped away from the chair bolted to the floor. "I have to leave."

One of the security men took Pat's arm. He snapped away. When the guard grabbed it again, Pat pushed him hard enough for the man to lose his footing. He landed hard on the concrete floor. A searing pain that originated near his right kidney fired through his body.

"Pat!"

A blow from a guard's truncheon caught Pat on the right thigh. His leg buckled. "On the ground!" The heavily-accented voice was harsh and burning with fury.

Another blow across his upper back.

"Stop it! Stop hitting him!"

Pat landed face down on the cold floor. Two guards piled on him. He couldn't breathe. He didn't struggle. Didn't fight. What they did to him didn't matter. His mind was flooded with dark images of his family murdered and his children dressed like Raggedy Ann and Andy dolls, knitting needles protruding from their eyes.

The world turned gray and distant, his awareness fogged by fear, grief, depression, and pain. With a uniformed man on each side of him, he was led to the door, the tiny voice of Isabella calling after him. "I'm not finished talking to my client. I need to know he's okay. Guard! Guard!"

Pat walked with his head down, shuffling as he moved, his injured right leg moved slower than his left.

"That was very foolish," one of guards said. "Have you lost your mind?"

"I'm not sure. I'm not sure of anything."

A few moments later, he was seated on one of the examination tables in the prison clinic. A nurse with a shot-putter's build cut off his pullover shirt, removed his slippers, and stripped off his pants, leaving Pat to sit in the cool room with nothing but his undershorts. A modest man by nature, he would normally be bothered by the exposure, but fear for his family and an overpowering sense of futility kept him from thinking of himself.

The doctor took less than three minutes to conduct his exam. "You are lucky, 24-601. The last man who attacked a guard ended up with a concussion and broken clavicle."

"You can't imagine how blessed I feel. And, for the record, I didn't attack the guard, I just pushed him away."

"In this place, that is assault and, your sarcasm notwithstanding, you are lucky. There is some swelling over your left kidney.

Everything else is just bruising. If you start urinating blood, let the guards know, but I don't think the kidney was damaged. I will see some pain relievers are delivered with your meal." He held out two ibuprofen. "Take these for now. I will check in on you later."

He stepped away and waved the guards to take him away. Pat, nearly nude, was escorted back to his cell and thrown in. "Next time you shove me," one of the guards said, "I will make sure you don't come out of the infirmary." He removed the handcuffs.

That sounded good to Pat.

The metal door clanked shut, the sound of it assaulting his ears. Pat crawled to the edge of the cell and pressed himself into the corner. He shook from adrenaline laced emotion.

"Phoebe, my golden-haired darling." Tears began to run. "Luke, my little man. Becky. . . .Becky" The tears grew to sobs. The trembling became convulsions. His mind raced out of control.

Didn't expect this to happen, did you?

He had no idea what part of his mind initiated the internal dialog.

All those hours in high school and college dreaming of being a great pastor proudly proclaiming the Gospel and now look at you.

He raised his hands to the side of his head and began to rock.

The REVEREND Dr. Pat Preston, B.A., M.Div, PhD. All those letters and now dying by degrees.

Tears dripped from his jaw; mucus ran from his nose.

The world goes on as it always has. All your preaching, all your pontification, all your teaching fell on deaf ears. Your church abandoned you. Your country has turned against you. Ha, even your wife left you.

"She came back."

And how has that worked out for her? Hmm? She sits in a small house alone with the kids. You're not even on the same continent.

"Shut up."

You can't tell me to shut up. I'm you. I'm the only honest part of your brain. I am the reasonable aspect of the mess you've become.

"Please, please, shut up. For God's sake, shut up."

For whose sake? God's sake did you say? Where is God now? Someone is stalking your family. Do you suppose He was there helping. Maybe He was just watching. He must be getting a kick out of all of this. Every day the world moves another step away from His Almightiness and you, the great defender of His word, take a beating and get tossed back into a cell of isolation. Admit it, no matter how often you think of God, He isn't thinking of you. You're not on His radar anymore. You are a nothing. All your work? Nothing. That great education? Nada. Zip. What a waste of life.

"That's not true. It's not true!"

Self-deception is the greatest sin of all. Look around, do you see God anywhere? Do you think you're making a difference in this place? You couldn't change the people in your church. You couldn't keep your family together. You're not changing a single mind in this place. You're just one more walking, talking piece of meat to these people. The only value you have now is to be an encouragement to those who love everything you hate.

"No. No! NO!"

Yes, yes, yes. And do you know what? You've lost your family, your church, your ideals, and now you're losing your mind. I'm proof of it. You're talking to a voice in your head, and while you do, someone is hanging around the windows and doors of your family, peeking in at night, watching the kids at school. The worst part? You can do nothing about it.

Pat sprang to his feet, filling the cell with his screams, the same screams he had heard other prisoners make when he first arrived. He beat his head with his fists as he marched around his cell. Fury built in him like steam in a pressure cooker. The cooker burst.

Another scream.

He searched for something to throw. He snatched the CS Lewis book from the ledge inset in the concrete wall and threw it at the surveillance camera. The paperback did no damage. He ripped the mattress from the stand it rested on and threw it across the room.

No satisfaction. No relief. No hope.

Returning to the shelf, he grabbed the New Testament, looked at the camera again, then cocked his arm. "My family needs me!" He took aim but couldn't move his arm. He couldn't throw the one thing that gave his life purpose. It might be the reason he was here, but it was also his only source of comfort.

Drawing the New Testament close to his chest, he dropped to his knees, bent over so his head touched the cement and sobbed in rolling convulsions.

"I'm sorry. I'm so sorry. I'm sorry, Becky. I'm sorry, Luke. I'm sorry, Phoebe. I'm so, so, sorry, God. So sorry . . . so, so sorry . . ."

Guards poured into his cell.

Chapter 14

Ruby Fay, FBI

―――⟫◈⟪―――

S he walked with determination and purpose, much like an M-1 tank. Those who worked in the DC office of the FBI knew to move to the side. Ruby Fay was not one to alter her course. If she had been young, if she were pretty, if she were petite, then she might be the one stepping aside, but Special Agent Ruby Fay was none of those things. She was a chain smoking, bulky woman, with a pair of gray streaks in her hair she liked to call racing stripes. As plain spoken as she was plain, she had more years in the Bureau than most of the assistant directors and she had no problem reminding others of that fact. Despite twenty years in the FBI and five years before that with the Secret Service, there still was no sign that read, Ruby Fay, Assistant Director on her door. She had no door. Her office was tucked away in one of the spaces of a cubicle forest that spread across one of the lower floors of J. Edgar Hoover Building. 935 Pennsylvania Avenue NW.

Ruby shared the 2.8 million square feet of space with over 7000 other employees, almost none of whom she liked or respected. She carried a white bag containing two donuts: one chocolate with chocolate icing and one glazed. In her other hand was a large black coffee, strong enough to peel paint from the hull of a battleship. From her lips dangled an unlit Marlboro.

The faces that looked at her as she moved through the busy office were all younger than she, a result of John Knox Smith and his cronies who made it a priority to push out older agents who were reluctant to adopt the new intimidation techniques adopted by DTED and other out of control political units. She had taken to calling the office "the nursery."

She kicked back the desk chair with one foot, dropped the bag of donuts on the desk, set the coffee on the stained surface and lowered herself into the chair that protested with loud squeaks. Pulling the cigarette from between her lips, she set it in an ashtray that contained no ashes. Smoking was not allowed in government buildings, though a passerby might be fooled by the odor clinging to Ruby's clothing.

Leaning forward, she grunted as she struggled to remove her dark blue blazer, an article of clothing she had owned for twenty years. When asked about it she would say, "Fashion is cyclic. The jacket will be in style again." Truth was, she hated wearing the thing and only did so to conceal the holstered handgun clipped to her belt. She removed the weapon and set it in the top drawer of her desk, then addressed the coffee and donuts. She was two bites and three sips into her meal when her phone buzzed. She frowned and punched the intercom button.

"Yeah?"

"This is Assistant Director Joel Sleeth. I think my position deserves more respect than 'yeah,' don't you agree?"

"I do agree. I apologize. Let me rephrase, 'What's up, Assistant Director?' Was that better?"

"You know, you are the most unprofessional agent in the FBI."

Ruby took another bite of donut. "How nice of you to notice. It's good to know my hard work isn't going to waste."

He sighed. "We've got a meeting with Assistant AG Smith. We leave in five minutes."

She swore in a manner worthy of seasoned sailors. "I hate being summoned. Doesn't he know we're busy investigating?"

"It sounds like you're busy eating again."

"I'm a growing girl."

"You're somewhere over fifty-five and barely able to pass the field agent physical exam. In fact, I'm pretty sure you intimidate the doctor into giving you a passing grade."

A sip of coffee, then "All I did was ask if he's ever had his finances audited. I didn't mean anything by it."

"Five minutes, Special Agent. Not six. Not five-and-a-half. Five. I'll meet you downstairs at the door on Pennsylvania Ave and we'll walk over. Five minutes." Sleeth hung up.

Ruby set the receiver back in the cradle. "Assistant Director Joel *Slither* has spoken." She looked at the small desk clock and made plans to be at the door seven minutes later.

***

Ruby and Sleeth were escorted to John Knox Smith's office by an attractive blonde in a skirt a tad too tight to be proper for office attire. *I guess when tolerance is your mission statement, you can get away with anything.* Ruby had been here before and met Andrea whom she sized up as a self-indulgent woman who loved men in power. It was a conclusion she drew in the first thirty seconds and hadn't changed since her first meeting with the woman's boss.

"Assistant Director Joel Sleeth and Special Agent Ruby Fay." Andrea's voice dripped with honey.

"Thanks, Andrea." John didn't look up, but he did motion to the two office chairs on the other side of his broad desk. Ruby once again took notice of the photos on the wall of John with senators, congressmen, Supreme Court associate justices, the Chief Justice, and the president. Of course, there was a photo of the man with the director of the FBI.

Ruby plopped down in the chair and crossed her legs. She watched as the Assistant AG and the head of DTED reviewed a legal document. Some said the man had more power than the Attorney General himself, but Ruby had trouble rousing any reason to care.

Several minutes passed in silence. Ruby turned to Sleeth. "It appears the effort we spent getting here on time was unneeded."

"That's enough, Special Agent." Sleeth was not happy.

"I'm just sayin'."

"I'll be with you in a few minutes," John said.

"I should've brought my other donut."

John looked up, his face hard as the surface of his desk. "Feeling impatient, are we, Special Agent Fay?"

"I can't speak for you, but I'm getting a little antsy."

"Has anyone defined insubordination to you, Agent Fay?" John turned the documents on his desk face down, a subtle insult that amused Ruby.

"I'm acquainted with the term. Has anyone defined rudeness to you, sir?"

Sleeth snapped his head around. "You're out of line, Fay. Try to show some respect."

"Are you looking to get fired, Agent Fay." John pushed back from the desk. "Because I can arrange it."

"That's mighty intolerant of you. Surely you don't mean to infringe on my freedom of speech. Or perhaps you're biased against me because I'm a woman, or because I'm unmarried, or because I'm . . . not young."

"I hold none of those against you, Agent."

"I think you do. In the few years you've been an AAG, you've tried to change the face of the FBI, forcing out the older for the younger agents who are inclined to jump when you bark."

Sleeth rubbed his eyes. "Ruby, do we have to go through this every time?"

"Some of those agents were my friends."

"First, any personnel changes came from your director. I don't have the power to hire and fire FBI agents, although I bet a few calls would get you tossed."

"No doubt."

"Perhaps you should consider retirement. You've got the years in." John smiled.

"Not until I'm done with the Matt Branson case. When that one is put to bed, then you can have my badge. I'll even help you place it somewhere where you won't lose it."

John scooted close to the desk and rested his arms on the top. "Agent Fay, I know you don't like me. I know you think I'm responsible for the exit of many good agents. Well, in a sense, I am. The world has changed. Some people can't deal with that. I know something else. You want me to fire you. You'd have quite a case against the DOJ. I'm also aware there is a move to reverse some of the advancements our team has brought about. It's a futile effort. There is no going back, so can we get down to the work at hand?"

"Fine with me."

Sleeth turned to her, his eyes ablaze. "Fine with me, sir."

"Tell me about your progress on the Matt Branson case."

No one spoke. Finally Sleeth mumbled, "If you don't mind, Agent."

Ruby took a dramatic breath. "Progress is slow, but we press on."

"Describe pressing," John said.

"Here's what we know: Matt Branson, who used to be DOJ in the OPR was killed and found by joggers at Founders Park in Old Town. He was shot in the back. The bullet was an out of issue jacketed, hollow point made especially for the Treasury Department. His pockets were emptied, and his body dumped in the Potomac. We have no surveillance of the park, at least not in the copse of trees near the riverbank, nor do we have witnesses."

"But you're still looking for witnesses, right?" John steepled his fingers and rested his chin on them.

"Yes. The Metro Police are doing the door to door and surveying people who come to the park in hopes of finding someone that was there that night. There were no ear-witnesses either. We're working under the assumption the killer used a suppressor."

"All old news."

"Just being thorough."

"Why are Metro Police doing the leg work?" John's eyes narrowed.

"Because technically, it's their case. We're involved because you asked the FBI to help."

"Matt was one of our own."

"With all due respect, sir, he might have been one of ours, but he quit the DOJ to defend Pat Preston."

John lowered his hands. "He spent a good number of years here and that earns him the right to the best investigation."

Ruby raised a finger. "You see there, that's one of the things that bother me, Mr. Smith. The moment he walked out of this building on his last day of work, he became your . . . oh, what word should we use? Opponent? Yes, opponent."

"And why does that bother you? Matt and Reverend Preston were friends in college."

Ruby let a few awkward moments pass. "*They* were friends?"

"Yes, they were friends."

"Interesting. I would have thought you would have said *we were friends*." She pushed back a lock of hair. "I believe you knew them in college. Am I wrong?"

"No, you're not wrong. This is why I leave you on the case. Your reputation for thinking out of the box serves you well."

"Does it? Most of my supervisors find it annoying."

"It's difficult to have skills others can't understand."

A wave of nausea rolled through her. "Being a mere mortal, I wouldn't know."

"Knock it off, Ruby," Sleeth snapped.

Ruby ignored him. "I've done a little research and couldn't help noticing you were well acquainted with Preston and Branson at Princeton. Is that false?"

"No, but we drifted apart after college. Matt went to law school in Michigan and Preston went to a religious school."

"They're called seminaries. Three years of study beyond college."

"You a religious person, Agent Fay?" John asked.

"Not at all. God and I don't talk much. But I talk to a lot of religious types, and let me tell you the Alliance has a great file on you, Mr. Assistant Attorney General" Less than a second passed before she sprung another question. "So you and Matt Branson didn't hang out?"

The Assistant Attorney General, taken aback by her mention of the Alliance, was slow to answer. "Define 'hang out.'"

"Pal around, catch a movie, share a meal, take in a Redskins' game."

"We would have lunch every once in awhile. Sometimes we would go to an art museum. I go there frequently. I was trying to broaden his artistic horizons."

"Is this why you've asked FBI HQ to investigate a matter normally handled by police or the Bureau's D.C. field office?"

"Ruby—" Sleeth began.

"It's all right." John raised a hand. "Yes, it's one of the reasons. We weren't close, but at one time we were pretty close."

"Can you say the same about Pat Preston?"

"Agent Fay, Pat Preston is not part of this investigation."

"He's connected to Branson. We've checked phone records. They exchanged phone calls. Mrs. Branson told us he felt the DOJ was persecuting Reverend Preston for his faith. Did you know Matt Branson was a practicing Christian?"

"Yes. He and Pat were always trying to get me involved in that nonsense."

"Nonsense?"

"Come on, agent. You just told me you're not religious; that you and God don't talk."

"I'm mad at God. How did you feel when you learned Branson was leaving DOJ to help defend Preston?"

"It's his right—"

"That's not what I asked. I asked how *you* felt."

John's face hardened. Ruby caught a glimpse of Sleeth and he looked ready to explode. "Are you interrogating me, Agent?"

"Not yet."

"That's it." Sleeth was on his feet. "I apologize, Mr. Smith. I'll get someone else on this case."

"Sit down, Assistant Director. You'll do no such thing. I'd be disappointed if you did." He turned his gaze to Ruby. "I was furious. I did my best to get Matt to talk to Preston and tell him to step away from the hate-speech. I owed him that much."

"Preston was your academic rival in college?"

"In some ways. We were on the debate team. He often faced off against me."

"Who won?" Ruby didn't let up. "I'm asking you."

"Watch your tone, Ruby." Sleeth shifted in his seat as if tacks were rising point first through the padding.

"Many, maybe most of the debates went his way. He's a natural speaker. My skills lay elsewhere."

Ruby drummed her fingers on the arm of the chair. Sleeth fidgeted again. "Mr. Smith," she said as smoothly as asking directions to the freeway, "do you have a handgun?"

He tipped his head back. "No."

"Have you ever used such a weapon to fire Smith & Wesson, jacketed hollow-point, Treasury load ammunition?"

"You mean the old rounds once designed for the Secret Service?"

"Yes."

"No one uses those any more. The federal government doesn't use them."

"Mr. Smith, have you used a weapon to fire Smith & Weapon, jacketed—"

"No. Let's just say it. I did not kill Matt Branson. If I did, why would I insist on the FBI's involvement in the investigation?"

She shrugged. "To make you look innocent."

Sleeth snapped. "Agent Fay! You cannot come to the office of the Assistant Attorney General at his request and then accuse him of murder."

"I haven't accused him of anything. I've just asked a few questions."

"The implication is clear and you are out of line."

John interrupted Sleeth. "Why not? I suppose someone could build a case that I had motive. Now she wants to know if I had the means. It's not bad thinking, really."

"I'm sorry, sir," Sleeth said.

"Don't be. I find Agent Fay's thinking refreshing. I also find her rude, insubordinate, self-absorbed, and bull headed. She would have made a good attorney."

"I'm just an old cop, sir. Not much more."

John leaned over the desk and smiled. "I did not kill Matt Branson. I did not cause him to be killed. While his decision to defend Pat Preston bothered me—"

"Infuriated. I believe you said infuriated."

"While Matt's decision to defend Reverend Preston *infuriated* me, I did not kill him. Matt was a good lawyer, but I would have cleaned his clock in the courtroom. It would be to DTED's advantage to have Matt leading the defense; he had far less experience than those zealots in the Alliance. Nice guy, a distant friend, but he was a pigmy in the court room. He was at his best processing bureaucratic complaints against other attorneys." He leaned back again. "Now, do you have any more information for me?"

Ruby shook her head. She had hoped to rattle him but had only managed to irritate the man. He was either innocent or a conscience-free, expert liar.

***

Sleeth didn't speak until they were back in the pool car. "I can't believe . . . I'm amazed—no stunned—no appalled . . . I should have you up for review. If this causes me any trouble, I will come down on your like a bag of wet cement."

"You know how to sweet talk a girl."

"I am serious, Ruby. That kind of behavior can get you canned."

"It's not the same. The FBI, I mean. Smith and his lapdogs have been pressing the old guard out of the bureau. He may win, but he will have to shoot me first."

"What was all that about the Treasury load hollow point?"

"Just what you heard. Ballistics show Branson was killed by a round of old ammunition no one should be able to get, and that's a major clue."

"You're going to need more than that. Just because Smith is government doesn't mean he has access to defunct ammo. There are tens of thousands of agents, marshals, military, treasury, capitol police and more that carry weapons."

"But not that load. Besides, there's more."

Sleeth slowed the car. "Like what?"

"Shortly after Branson's body was found, Smith was in the National Gallery of Art. I interviewed a lot of employees there. They know him. That day he came in and looked around. Not unusual, but . . . Did you notice how Smith dressed?"

"He's always dapper. He's one of those clothes horse types. What of it?"

"I spoke to some of the janitorial staff. One man remembered Smith's visit that night."

"How so?"

"He tracked some mud and grass into the lobby. The guy cleaned it up which is unfortunate."

"Because?"

"It hadn't rained that night. Maybe our illustrious Assistant Attorney General picked up a little something on his shoes while making a quick visit to Founder's park." She looked out the side window and shrugged. "I'm just sayin'."

Chapter 15

Pressed Down

When Pat Preston opened his eyes he saw the same gray ceiling that greeted him every morning. Except this wasn't morning. At least he didn't think so. The prison had sounds. Mornings sounded different than evenings. In the early morning there were almost no voices; in the afternoon the sound of guards moving prisoners or talking would creep into his cell. He was hearing the latter. It took all his concentration to come to that conclusion. His thinking was slow; his mind sludge.

He blinked but remained still. Slowly the gears in his brain began to turn. He next became aware of the camera's eye in the cell. He was always aware of the camera. A watched man seldom thought of anything else. He didn't want to move, fearful it would draw the attention of the guards, and for now he wanted to be alone.

The brain sludge thinned. For some reason, it seemed odd he lay on the thin mattress and didn't know why that would be odd—then the recollections surfaced. Mental images strobed in his mind: his loss of control, his fear for his family, his fury about being unable to help them or even talk to them; the image of his wife, Becky, daughter, Phoebe, and son, Luke blazed the brightest.

Sorrow, helplessness, and an overpowering sense of impotence filled him. Tears pooled in his eyes, blurring his vision, but he remained motionless.

His heart felt heavy, like lead.

His breathing came in short inhalations.

His ribs, back, and legs hurt. Flashes of memories starring a half-dozen guards splashed on his mind. He recalled the taser strike that set every nerve on fire, the punches to his sides, the truncheon strikes on his back and thighs. Unconsciousness was a blessing.

Hopelessness. He thought he had worked through the feelings of despair; felt he had come to the quiet courage that is the hallmark of martyrs. When he first arrived he had said, "Here I stand. I can do no other. God help me." Each day he recommitted himself to being the best witness for Christ he could be. He had just blown that. In many ways, he had ceased to be himself.

Sound bites from the hundreds of sermons he had preached percolated in his mind. How many times had he said the greatest Christian myth was the idea that Christians were exempt from trouble? He had even chastised a church member—a deacon at that—whom he overheard say to a visitor, "If you give your life to Christ, you will never be sick again." Nonsense. What God did for His followers was provided a sense of peace.

And that was the problem. Pat felt no peace. Where was the "peace that passes all understanding?" He had prayed for it, pleaded for it; begged for it, but it was slow coming. There had been moments when his courage flagged, when he hungered for a taste of emotional, spiritual peace. He was in the most civil prison in the world, or so it had been described to him, but he couldn't imagine a place more cruel or soul-sapping.

"God doesn't lead us to a desert," he had proclaimed from the pulpit, "but He will join us there." He had used that line time and time again. Now he stood on the hot sands of unjust incarceration, scanning the horizon for any indication of the presence of God but could see nothing but desolation.

He recalled holding the hand of an elderly lady in his church who had been diagnosed with inoperable cancer of the pancreas. The diagnosis was a death sentence and she knew it. Pat had comforted her as much as a man could and when he left, the pity began. What could be worse than that? Now he knew. If he were dying of cancer, he would still be able to see his family, feel the love of friends, and know what was coming. Here he had none of that.

The lock on his metal door sounded. Pat slammed his eyes shut and willed himself to be still. He didn't want to face whoever came through the door.

The door swung open, squeaking on hinges that struggled to bear the weight and motion of the massive slab.

"Reverend Preston?"

A strange voice. Male. Deep. New.

Preston remained still.

"I believe you are awake, Dr. Preston. I have brought your food."

Don't move. Let him think you're still unconscious.

A hand, big, rough, yet gentle touched his foot. A band of metal moved around just above the ankle. He hadn't noticed it before, but his leg was chained. The man removed the metal cuff. Pat remained motionless. The smell of cooked food graced his nostrils. For a change, it smelled good.

"Dr. Preston. Please look at me."

Giving up the pretense, Pat opened his eyes. At the foot of the bed stood a tall man with wide shoulders that tested the stitching of his uniform shirt. Dark hair, longer than he expected on a guard, hung over his ears in easy waves. Bright, blue eyes stared back at him. Then came the real shock: the man smiled.

"How do you feel?"

"Like a man who was beaten by a gang of guards."

"Understandable, since that is what happened."

Pat couldn't place the accent. He didn't sound Dutch or French. Pat wasn't sure what he sounded like. "You're new."

"No, I've been around a very long time . . . oh, you mean I'm new to you. Yes, this is our first meeting." He smiled again and it unnerved Pat. "Do you need to use the toilet?"

"Um, I'm good for the moment."

The man nodded. "You should know your outburst has changed things a little. The authorities have decided a guard be present while you eat and when you use the toilet."

"Really? I understand the eating part. They think I'll make a mess or throw the tray."

"That is true. Are you going to throw the tray?" He walked to the sink where the simple tray of food rested and walked back to the bed.

Pat swung his legs over the edge of the bed and sat up. "No. I think I'm done throwing things. It seems to bring undesired results."

The man chuckled. "I love understatement. It is the king of humor."

"King of humor, eh? Will I get beaten if I ask your name?"

"Of course not. Why would I beat you?"

Pat shrugged. "It seems to be a hobby for some of your friends."

"Friends? Oh, the other guards." He shrugged, but seemed to have to think about the action first.

"Some of the others lack restraint."

"Is that some of the understated humor?" Pat took the tray. The food looked freshly cooked and was still hot, something he hadn't experienced often since coming to the prison.

"Yes. Did I do it right?"

"I guess." He tasted the food. It was good. "So why do I have to have a guard if I want to use the toilet?"

"The warden wants you secured to the bed except during exercise, eating, and going to the bathroom. It's part of your punishment. They've taken away your freedom and your ability to communicate with others, your privacy and hope so you have very little else they can take."

Pat felt the guard's scrutiny. "You can relax. My throwing days are over."

"I am wondering if you need to see the doctor in the infirmary."

"Been there; done that. I'm sore, bruised, humiliated, but otherwise okay." Pat dipped a piece of dark bread in the brown gravy that covered what looked like Salisbury steak. It was thick and tasty. Unlike the watery substance he had been served before. Was this the way prison officials apologized?

"I asked the cooks to make the gravy for you. I assume you like gravy."

"I do. White gravy, brown gravy. It doesn't matter. How'd you know?"

"Are you not from the south regions of the United States? Gravy, potatoes, grits, fried chicken."

"Fried everything. You arranged for this food?"

"Yes. I watched them prepare it. Just to be sure."

"Sure about what?"

"Do you normally lose your temper like you did this morning?"

"No. I'm not a violent man." Pat looked away. "Truth be told, I'm ashamed."

"It is against prison policy to add any nonfood substances to a prisoner's food."

Pat blinked as he tried to process the statement. "Are you saying you put something in the food? A drug?"

"Of course not. I wouldn't do that. There are those who might."

He stopped eating and stared at the plate. The guard was telling him his food had been poisoned. No, not poisoned. The man asked if acting out was something he had done before. *They've been drugging my food? Why?*

"Are you saying they've been giving me drugs that alter my thinking?" He stopped and looked at the camera. "That might explain a few things."

"Explain what things?"

Pat looked away. "It doesn't matter."

"Everything matters, Dr. Preston. To what *things* do you refer?"

Pat regretted the comment. Still, Marcus was the first guard to show the slightest interest in him. "Since you drew the short straw, you might as well know. I haven't been myself. My emotional stability isn't what it used to be."

"How so?"

"My outburst is a good example. I . . . fluctuate."

The guard looked at Pat's food for a moment. "It is to be expected. This is a difficult environment."

"You can say that again."

"This is a difficult—"

Pat raised a hand. "I was joking."

The beefy guard grinned awkwardly. "So was I."

"Cute."

"What did you mean when you said I drew the 'short straw'?"

Why wasn't this guy concerned about those listening into the conversation?

"Someone has to bring me food and watch me while I relieve myself. A job no one wants. You got stuck with it."

"I asked for the privilege. I will be the one delivering your food and checking on your well being."

The Pope's visit. That must be it. Maybe they're afraid the Pope will hear about my beating and somehow make life miserable.

The man tipped his head to the side. "It is not wise to over think things, Dr. Preston."

"I have no idea what that means."

The guard moved back to the sink and retrieved the now familiar "sippy" cup and handed it to Pat.

"Why would you request this duty?"

"Why wouldn't I?"

"I'm sorry, but I'm still a little too foggy in the head for riddles."

"I understand." He let a few moments pass. "My name is Marcus Aster."

"That makes two names I know. Of the guards, I mean. I know Jacques and now yours."

"Many guards hide behind anonymity. They prefer not to be known. To know a person's name is to know something about them."

"Then why tell me yours?"

Again he shrugged, this time more smoothly. "It only seems right. I know yours."

"You are an odd man, Marcus."

"You're not the first to say so. You won't be the last."

Chapter 16

Beatrice

—————⟫◆⟪—————

B ecky approached the door to the house slowly and used the security peephole to stare at the visitor. Even through the small security device she could see the long shadows cast by a descending sun. She had kept the kids home from school and drawn all the curtains.

"Mrs. Preston?" The voice on the other side of the door came from a woman with shoulder length black hair. She had a rich Italian accent. "I am Beatrice. I believe Countess Isabella San Phillipa gave you my name as well as Mr. Larry Jordan."

Becky's heart raced. The accent was right. The names were right. The woman matched the description Isabella had given her. Still, she couldn't unlatch the door.

"Signora, your husband's attorney sent me. I believe they told you to expect me." She raised a small, leather folder revealing a badge. "I'm with the *Corpo della Gendarmeria dello Stato della Città del Vaticano.*"

"In English, please," Becky said through the door.

"Who is it, Mommy?"

"Hush, Phoebe. Let Mommy think."

"I am with the Gendarme Corps of Vatican City State. May I come in?"

Becky did her best to see past the woman. She appeared to be alone. She inhaled deeply, set her spine straight and unlocked the door. In took another two seconds before she had the courage to turn the knob and pull the door open.

The woman was even lovelier, now that Becky wasn't peering through a small lens hole in the door. The woman gave a two hundred watt smile. Becky judged her to be in her mid thirties, five-eight, slim and firm. She wore a woman's gray business suit with a mauve scarf. She held what looked like a book bag.

"Buona sera." The woman lowered the badge and folder. "The countess rang you, si?"

"Si . . . yes, she did. So did Mr. Jordan. I'm sorry to be so slow, I'm . . ."

"Cautious?"

Becky smiled. "Yes, cautious after what happened." She stepped to the side. "Please come in."

As soon as the woman crossed the threshold, Becky closed and locked the door. Checking the lock twice.

"Who are you?" Phoebe asked. She stood slightly behind her mother. Luke stood to one side, his arms crossed as if he was ready to protect the castle.

"Phoebe, be polite."

The guest bent forward until she was almost eye to eye with the little girl. "My name is Beatrice. I'm here to help you, your brother, and your mother."

"Beet-twist?"

Beatrice laughed. "Close. Bee-a-trice. My accent is confusing you. I'm from Italy. Do you know where Italy is?"

"I do," Luke said. "It's far, far away. They eat spaghetti and pizza."

"That's right and so much more." She lowered her voice. "Do you want to know a secret?"

"Yeah!"

"We Italians didn't invent spaghetti. People think we did, but we didn't. We learned to make noodles from the Chinese. A famous explorer sailed all over the world and ended up in China. His name was Marco Polo and when he came back to Italy, he brought spaghetti. We did, however, invent spaghetti sauce, and that's the really important part."

Phoebe's eyes brightened. "Mommy, can we have spaghetti for dinner?"

"We'll see, sweetheart. You and your brother go finish that puzzle, okay? I need to talk with our new friend."

The kids returned to the coffee table where they had been working on a jigsaw puzzle, Luke helping his younger sister.

"You made good time. I didn't expect someone from Italy to arrive so soon."

"I was not in Italy. I was in Atlanta. The Holy Father is visiting the United States in two months time. I am his liaison to the local police and Secret Service."

"I'm still a little confused about what you do." She led Beatrice to the dining room table and put a pot on for tea. "All I know is you're here to . . ." She looked at the kids. "To protect us."

"That is true, but not me alone." She situated herself on the seat and released the single button on her coat. Becky caught a glimpse of a holster. "I am part of the Vatican's diplomatic security force. Do you know much about the Vatican?"

"I'm afraid not. I've been a Baptist all my life."

"We have many people of other . . . persuasions visit the city-state. I've even arrested a Baptist." She paused a beat before grinning. "Vatican city is very small, less than half a square kilometer. A little over eight hundred people live there, but millions visit. It is a city and a country. It is where the Pope lives part of the year."

"So you are part of the police force for the Vatican?"

"Yes. It's a little more complicated than that. There are two agencies charged with protecting His Holiness, those around him and keeping peace in the city. The best known group is Pontifical Swiss Guard. When you visit the city, they are the ones in the eye-catching uniforms. They also provide personal security for the Pope. I am part of the Corp Della Gendarmeria dello Stato della citta del Vaticano. From 1970 to 1991, we were called the Corpo di Vigilanza dello Stato della Citte del Vaticano—Vigilanza for short. The word means to be vigilant or to watch. Some still call us Vigilanza. We are a small but dedicated group. A few of us also qualify as part of the extended diplomatic corps. One of our duties is close security for the pontiff. When he travels, so do I. Protection is my specialty."

Becky nodded as if understanding, but she wasn't sure she did. "Larry Jordan told me about the Pope's visit. I was surprised, to say the least, but grateful for his help and prayers."

"He is a man of action, Becky. May I call you Becky?"

"Please do. May I call you . . . I only know your first name."

"Beatrice is fine. Thank you."

Becky decided not to press the point. "I'm not sure how to say this. I don't want to offend—"

"Let me guess. You wonder how one woman can provide protection?"

"You are good."

"There will be more than just me. The countess has arranged for a private security team to help. Mr. Jordan of the Alliance . . . the Alliance, si?"

"Yes. They're part of Pat's defense team."

"Mr. Jordan asked for recommendations from people in Washington. I am told he knows many important people. They know of a company here in Nashville. I will oversee their work and stay with you and the family. Is this agreeable to you?"

Becky nodded.

"*Bene.* Becky, you must trust me, unconditionally trust me. Most likely there will not be a reoccurrence of the previous event, but it is my job to assume the worst. It is my job to be paranoid."

"Pat used to say those who are not paranoid are not paying attention. He meant it as a joke. It's not so funny now." She then added, "I trust you."

"This is good, very good. I will tell you what will happen next. I will do a quick study of your home, then I will make a call. One of the security men will bring a few items I'm sure we will need to make the home secure. These are small but effective measures. I will be part of your family until we are certain you and the children are safe again. That means I will be living with you. Do you agree?"

"Okay."

"I will sleep on the sofa."

"No need. I can move the children in with me and you can have their room."

Beatrice shook her head. "Thank you, but no. The sofa is in the center of the house. I can better hear noises at windows and doors if I am in the living room. But yes, I want the children to sleep in your room, at least at first. It must be this way."

"I understand."

"The children will stay with us for the next week. No school. It takes more personnel to protect children in different classes and protect you as well. We can make arrangements for a private tutor, if need be."

"Yeah! No school!" Luke was listening.

"I like school," Phoebe said.

"It's just temporary, sweetheart." Becky turned her attention back to Beatrice.

"You will not be house bound. In fact, it is best for you to get out from time to time. Change the schedule. We will travel together. I will drive at all times. There will be another car with us at all times."

"Isn't this terribly expensive?"

"Yes, Becky, it is, but I have been asked to tell you that expense is not your concern. The countess believes you are worth the cost, as is your husband's case. She and the Holy Father believe that much more is on trial than your husband. Much of the future of all churches and faith rest on this."

The teapot sounded and Becky retrieved it, setting out two china cups and an assortment of herbal tea. A few moments later, both women had steaming cups of tea. "You may have friends over, but I need to know about this well ahead of time. I'm afraid the children cannot invite friends over. It would be improper to expose minors to possible danger."

"This all scares me."

"Fear is a good motivator, Becky. It has kept me going for years." She sipped the tea and commented on how good it was. Becky was sure she was just being polite. "Do you have any questions?"

"Not at the moment, but if we all travel together, things are going to be cramped. After Pat was arrested, the bank repossessed our cars. I have an old clunker."

"I've selected and rented an SUV that is very comfortable—and fast." She grinned. "May I please look at your house?"

"Of course. I'll give you a tour. The house is tiny, so it won't take long."

***

Less than two hours later, two men had arrived at the house, identified themselves as employees of the private security firm in Nashville. The firm catered to executives and music and movie stars. One man who identified himself as "Chip" had the shoulders of a lumber jack and the hairstyle of a billiard ball. His eyes were dark and always moving. Becky had the idea he was straining his ears to hear every sound in the neighborhood. The other man was trim and short, with thick brown hair and kind, hazel eyes. His handshake told Becky all she needed to know about the man's strength. Bernice called him "Roloff." Last names weren't given. Both men did produce IDs, but Becky was sure Beatrice had already met them or she wouldn't have opened the door.

The men spoke softly and Chip patted the kids on the head. "I brought you something," he said and produced two handheld video games. He then looked at Becky. "I hope that is all right. They have educational programs on them, not just games. It will help them keep their minds off all the disruption."

Becky detected a slight accent which she took to be Scottish. "Thank you. I take it you have children."

"Yes, ma'am." He motioned to Roloff. "We both do." He offered no more information. "Time to get to work."

Chip and Roloff exited but returned a few minutes later with cardboard boxes of various sizes.

Roloff got right down to the business of organizing their moves. "I suggest the perimeter first."

"Agreed," Beatrice said.

Without a word, Chip took several of the boxes and exited the house; Roloff unpacked a wide computer monitor and two iPads. "Where do you want me to set up?"

"Coffee table." Beatrice pointed to the piece of furniture. "I'll be sleeping on the sofa."

"I usually have to offend the wife before I get to sleep on the sofa." Roloff winked at the kids. "Can I help you move the puzzle to the dining room table?"

"We want to play with the video games, Mommy," Phoebe said.

"I'll pick up the pieces. Why don't you go to Mommy's bedroom? You can sit on the bed and play."

The children scampered away as Becky and Beatrice gathered up the oversized pieces of the puzzle.

"Sorry to disrupt your home, ma'am." Roloff unpacked a laptop computer.

"You don't know what a great comfort this is."

Thirty minutes later, the widescreen computer monitor glowed with electronic life. Beatrice explained. "In a few minutes you will see images of your property. There are six wireless cameras. Four cover the perimeter of the house; one will show the street in front of the house; one will cover the backyard. Each camera sends a wireless signal to the computer which plays in on the monitor. Chip is setting up the cameras. We'll be able to see anyone who approaches the home."

"Will they be sleeping here as well?"

"No, they will be stationed in vans nearby. They have monitors in the van so they will see the same thing we see and can respond in moments. When they're off shift, others from their company will take over."

"I assume someone will replace you when you go off shift."

"I don't go off shift. Think of me as the aunt who never leaves."

"That's comforting."

"Wait until you taste my coffee." She picked up two small boxes and removed what looked like four keyless ignition fobs. "These are alert transmitters—panic buttons. If you see something I don't, hear something in the night that doesn't sound right, then press this button and it will alert me and the others."

She then retrieved what looked like Bluetooth earphones used with cellular phones. "Each of these is a transmitter good for about twenty meters. We have handheld radios should we need to broad-cast over greater distances."

"This has to cost a fortune," Becky said. "I feel guilty."

"Don't. I know the countess and when she wants to do some-thing, she does it without any thought to cost. Besides, she and her husband spend more on electricity for their homes than they're spending on this."

"You're joking."

She shook her head. "They have three mansions and a condo in New York and one in San Diego. And those are just the ones I know about."

Becky didn't know how to respond. The kindness of this stranger was beyond all her experiences.

It took less than two hours to set up the surveillance system and to add security locks to the doors and windows. Chip instructed Becky and the children how to release the locks if they needed to escape for any reason, such as a fire. Soon Chip and Roloff had left to their respective posts and Bernice had triple checked all the locks.

Only then did Becky allow herself to feel a moment of relief.

Chapter 17

Papal Prayer Decree

<figure>
⟫⟨
</figure>

"Thanks for coming, Lynn," John Knox Smith said. He had been waiting for her in the conference room which had a larger television screen than in his office.

"Glad to help." She took a seat to his right.

He glanced at her, then paused. Her blond hair was streaked with pink. "You change your hair color like I change socks."

"I'm not that bad. Beside, change is good." She moved a few strands over one of her ears. "Do you like it?"

"Um, sure. You look good in pink." He realized he was uncertain what her real hair color might be.

"Am I the first?" She looked around the room as she removed her laptop.

"It's just us this time, Lynn. The DTED is a great group, but they tend to talk over each other. I need you to help me understand what we're about to see."

"Okay, what are we about to see?"

"I got word the Pope is going to make a statement to the press about Preston."

She froze mid motion. "Are you sure you heard right?"

"I think so. Why?"

"The Pope doesn't hold press conferences. The press covers his sermons and his travels, but I doubt we'll see the Pope fielding questions from a bunch of reporters. It's just not done." She continued setting up the laptop.

"He's that arrogant?"

She shrugged. "I've never met the man, so I can't say if he's arrogant or not. The Roman Church is rooted in centuries of tradition. More than any other Christian group."

"But the word I got was he would announce this prayer thingy from Rome at ten our time." He looked at his Rolex. "That's five minutes from now."

"Prayer thingy? I love lawyer talk." She grinned. "I don't know who your source is, but he or she needs to be a little more specific. Is it going to be on television?"

"Yes. Andrea set it up. I guess the Vatican has its own television station."

"The Vatican has its own everything." The laptop came to life. "Most likely, someone will read a statement from the Pope. Even that is a bit odd. The prayer decree we learned about earlier would normally be sent out as an encyclical, maybe even a bull, but not likely."

"You're losing me."

Lynn moved the laptop to the side. "Sorry. Religions have a language all their own. Roman Catholics are the worst. There are a lot of terms that can be classified as 'inside baseball,' terms only the initiated use freely."

"But you have a handle on it?"

"I should. I was a nun for five years before I became a PC USA pastor."

He looked at her. "That didn't come up when we hired you."

"I don't talk about it much. I left the Church and its narrow views and controlling ways behind. I keep track of all things that deal with religions, but that part of my life I'd just as soon forget."

"Will this bother you?"

"No. I'm not that fragile. I just find the Catholic view—well, any backwards conservative Christian thinking—distasteful. Anyway, back to your question. The Pope can issue directives in a number of ways. The most formal and most important is the *constitutio apostolica*, the Apostolic constitution. These are generally addressed to the Church as a whole and have something to do with important doctrine. We won't be seeing that, I'm sure. The idea came from Roman law in which an emperor could institute some important law. The church adopted the practice back in the days of Rome. These are very formal and sometimes called a Papal bull."

"How apropos." John smiled at his own humor.

"Not that kind of bull, John. 'Bull' is short for bulla. A bulla was a clay seal with an imprint pressed into it. A cord would be tied around a scroll or book. The bulla sealed the cord. Over time, bulla came to refer to an official letter or document. A slightly lower document of importance is the Papal encyclical."

"Encyclical? Like encyclopedia?"

"Same root word. It comes from ancient Greek meaning to encircle. An encyclical is a letter sent to a group of bishops or all of the world's bishops. In the old days, letters circulated from town to town. Encyclicals are less formal than Papal bulls."

"Okay, well tell me if I should take notice of something." He turned on the television. "This is a feed from Rome. They're streaming it over the Internet."

"I figured as much."

"What about language? Will you be able to tell me what's being said if they speak in Italian or Latin?"

"Yes, but I'm sure this will be in English. English is close to being universal."

They stared at the image of a simple lectern centered on a low stage. There were no decorations. A small group of reporters sat in folding chairs. John could hear a low mumbling, as if a funeral were about to start. An elderly man entered dressed in a black cassock with scarlet piping and buttons. A scarlet sash encircled his waist. A red skull cap sat on his head.

"Interesting," Lynn said. "He has a cardinal reading the encyclical and he's in ordinary dress."

"I don't follow."

"There are different forms of dress for different situations. This guy is not wearing formal attire. Also, I would have expected someone like the Pope's general secretary to do the reading, not a cardinal."

A name appeared in the lower third: Cardinal Michael Mahoney. Lynn tapped the name into the search engine of her computer. "I know this name."

"From where?"

She shook her head. "I can't remember . . . wait. I think he served with Pope Benedict, before he was Pope Benedict." John heard the woman's fingers pounding the key. "They were at the same seminary at the same time. He's the former Primate of All Ireland."

"He's the what?"

"Primate, not the simian kind. It means he oversaw the church in Ireland. Primate is from the word primacy."

"You Catholics have your own language."

She stiffened. "I'm not Catholic, John. You know that. I *was* a nun. I'm not one now. I escaped when my sanity returned."

"My apologies. I didn't mean to be so general."

"No problem." She motioned to the screen. "Here we go."

"My name is Cardinal Michael Mahoney. I have been asked by His Holiness to read from an encyclical to all bishops. The encyclical I hold is written in the Holy Father's hand. Printed versions of the message will be made available to members of the media. I should say to those familiar with encyclicals, this one is quite short."

He straightened, cleared his throat and read aloud: "Encyclical Letter of the Supreme Pontiff Benedict XVII to the bishops, priests and deacons, men and women religious, the lay faithful, and all people of good will on prayer for respect of the Gospel of Jesus Christ and those who proclaim the holy message."

"Kinda full of himself, isn't he," John said.

"With them, it's not about ego but formality." Lynn typed as she listened.

Cardinal Mahoney continued: "The Gospel of love and forgiveness has through the centuries been hindered by those who wish to silence the announcement of God's love for all of humankind. Our Savior faced such attempts at censorship during his earthly ministry, and the soils of our planet are stained with the blood of good men and women who gave their lives so others could hear the message of hope.

"Intolerance of the Christian message has always been present, but in these last days has grown in intensity and come upon the faithful by those garbed in civil law. We have become aware of many of God's servants who are denied simple human rights because of the message of love they preach. One such man has become a symbol of such injustice, and he inspires people of faith around the world."

Mahoney kept his eyes glued to the document before him. "The Reverend Dr. Pat Preston of the United States sits this day in a European prison cell in what is to him a foreign country. He, like the Apostles Peter and Paul before, is incarcerated not for a crime against humanity, but an activity demanded of all God's servants; a command to go into the world with the Good News of Jesus the Christ. His imprisonment is our imprisonment and that of the generations to come.

"As our brother Paul taught the church in Rome: 'And how will there be preachers if they are not sent? As scripture says: How beautiful are the feet of the messenger of good news.' And, 'But it is in that way faith comes, from hearing, and that means hearing the word of Christ.'

"It is here directed that all people of faith, all cardinals, bishops, priests, deacons, and the religious seek God's face on behalf the Reverend Dr. Pat Preston, asking our Heavenly Father to free him from captivity and granting those who persecute him the vision to reconsider their current direction and repent from such a wayward act."

Mahoney paused at that as if having trouble getting all the words out. "Such prayers should be made daily and with all sincerity."

The cardinal looked up. "This completes the reading." He turned and walked from the room.

"He didn't take questions," John said.

"That wasn't a press conference, John. It was a public reading of the Pope's letter to the church and anyone else reading it."

"So that's it? All he did was ask people to pray?"

"John . . ." She stopped. "How strong is our professional relationship?"

The question made him uncomfortable. "I consider it sound. Why?"

"Because John, I need to be frank with you."

He tensed. "Go ahead."

"You're not getting the picture. You hold people of faith in such low regard you assume all of them are stupid and self serving. Now don't get me wrong, I have no use for the Pope or his bloated church, but I don't underestimate them."

"Neither do I."

"I think you are, John. I really do. You've just been served and you don't even know it. The Pope may be misguided, bound by centuries of useless tradition and a fiction gospel, but he's not stupid. The man speaks half a dozen languages, holds two PhDs—earned degrees mind you, not honorary—and leads an organization composed of billions. Billions, John. Not millions, billions."

"Okay, I get it, but praying for Preston can't help him any."

Lynn closed her eyes. "Prayer is a good form of meditation, although I don't for a minute believe there's anyone in heaven to hear it. That's beside the point. We moved Preston out of country because you couldn't win here, because of evidentiary mess up. That made this a case for the Western world. The Pope just made it global. He mentioned Preston's name. Pat Preston's name will be part of Church history forevermore. You're lucky he didn't mention you by name."

"What difference would that make? Why should I care if he mentions me by name or not?"

"I don't know if you can understand this, John, but he was doing you a favor. Trust me; you don't want a few billion people thinking you're persecuting them."

"I'm not."

"You say that like it matters. Lump together Roman Catholics with the Eastern and Greek Orthodox churches, toss in all the evangelicals, the Lutherans, the Pentecostals and every other flavor of Christian and you have a mass of opposition almost impossible to imagine. You do know what a tsunami is, don't you John?"

"Of course I do."

"There's one headed our way, and it's not made of water, it's made of people."

"It can't be that bad." He turned off the monitor.

Lynn closed her laptop. "For every action, there is an opposite but equal reaction. Who said that?"

John didn't have to think. "Isaac Newton. It's one of his laws of motion."

She stood. "Not only can you expect an action from the religious folk but a reaction from those who hate them. Do you realize what the Pope has just done?"

"He asked a bunch of priests to pray for Pat Preston."

"He has just issued to the faithful a call to arms. Not guns, but resistance. Our lives have just become a lot more complicated."

She walked from the conference room.

Chapter 18

Andrea's Move

<hr/>

The ladies room in the DOJ building was empty. Most of the employees on the DTED corridor had left for the evening. The exodus never failed to amaze Andrea. How quickly the buzzing of scores of lawyers, paralegals, investigators, and secretaries could be stilled by the silent movement of the clock's second hand as it swept past the "12", aligning for one second with the minute hand. With the hour hand already on the "5", the official end of day had arrived. Buzzing was replaced with soft sounds of relief and the sound of desks being locked. The elevator swallowed the workers and disgorged them on the first floor so they go do battle with DC rush hour traffic.

Not Andrea. Life in the DOJ building was far more interesting than the life she spent in her small apartment. She often worked late, although her boss, John Knox Smith, held the record for time logged in a desk chair.

Not tonight.

She removed a tube of lipstick from her purse and leaned close to the long mirror mounted on the wall above a series of sinks. The reflection returned the image of a slender but shapely woman with shoulder-length blond hair and deep blue eyes. She wore an Anne Klein stone gray, three-piece suit over a sky blue long-sleeve ruffle-neck blouse. She tipped forward on her black Christian Louboutin pumps and raised the lipstick to her face. A simple necklace sporting a single pearl dangled from her neck. She applied the lipstick with well practiced precision.

Andrea moved back from the glass and fiddled with her hair for a moment, satisfied it had endured the day well and still held enough bounce and wave to be eye catching. She pressed her lips together, then pushed them out in a provocative pout.

Clothing was important to Andrea. So much so, she had chosen to live in a smaller apartment to leave more money for shopping. There were many ambitious women in the world, but she was of an even rarer breed: she grew her self esteem from the success of others. More specifically, she loved powerful people and John Knox Smith was one such person. Helping him advance, helping him keep his balance on the pitching ship of Department of Justice work was what she lived for. That and the undying hope John would one day be hers.

That day may have come. Although she lacked the Ivy League, private school education many of those around her had, Andrea was no dummy. More than once she had proven to be capable of learning things she should not be privy to. Not being hindered by a conscience, she felt no hesitancy to open a file or do a little research of her own, which is what she did as soon as John left to meet with Eddie Goodall of Goodall, Crowe, and Banks. A quick review of their website revealed the focus of the law firm. They did corporate tax, something John didn't need; they did incorporations, something else John had no use for; and they did divorce. Especially Eddie Goodall. That fact coupled with the mysterious papers John had received a few days ago, his pensive mood which was only interrupted by outbursts of anger cinched it for Andrea. Cathy Knox had made her move. She was dumping her husband. Good for her. *Good for me.*

She smiled at her reflection.

One thing Andrea had learned was that most men could be swayed easily by charm and flirtation, but a few—like John—needed something more: a shock to the ego; something to knock him off center. Most wouldn't have sensed it, but Andrea saw deeper into her boss than anyone else. She thought of it as "reading his frequency," and his frequency had definitely changed over the last few days.

She straightened her coat, double-checked its single button, and satisfied that everything about her was perfect, strode from the restroom.

***

John rubbed his eyes. The words on the document before him seemed to crawl around on the page like ants. It was only six but it felt like midnight. His back hurt, his neck was stiff, his eyes burned, and his stomach roiled. He should go home, should make an early night of it. Maybe watch a comedy or a game show, something mindless. But the only thing his suburban home had to offer was emptiness and he carried enough of that around with him.

He leaned back and closed his eyes. He was a man of steely confidence, a man who saw arrogance as a virtue. Rare were the times when he felt the blues, but depression was settling on him as sure as darkness was blanketing the city outside.

"You ready?"

He opened his eyes with a start and forced himself to sit up straight. "Andrea. I thought you had left for the day."

"Nope. Still here. The perpetual bad penny and all that."

"You're no bad penny. I wouldn't get anything done without you around, but you should call it a day. You don't want to end up looking like me."

"No, but I don't mind looking at you." She gave a quick smile.

John blinked a few times. "Thanks. I think. Ready for what?"

"Dinner, of course. I made reservations at William Clarke's. If we leave now, we'll be right on time."

"I didn't agree to dinner. I have work to do."

She entered the office and walked to the side of his desk. "I know. That's why I didn't ask first. Let me get your coat."

She turned to a walnut coat rack in the corner—handcrafted at the Bureau of Prisons—and retrieved John's suit coat. "I was thinking of a shrimp appetizer and maybe a beer. They have great steak."

"I know, I've been there, but—"

"Here, stand up and I'll help you with this." She stepped to the side of his chair and held out his coat.

"Andrea . . ." A whiff of perfume graced his nose. There was a sweetness about it, a hint of rose and something he couldn't identify. The objective part of his brain said it was probably a synthetic scent created in a lab; the subjective part of his brain said to shut up and put his coat on. He caved to the subjective side. A steak sounded good.

"Andrea, I shouldn't. First, I have all this work to do, and second, there's a certain distance that should remain between employees."

"I couldn't agree more. Now turn around and let me see if this is hanging correctly." He did and she ran her hands on the coat, smoothing winkles and adjusting lapels. Having a woman's hands on him again felt good. "Hold still. Your tie needs a little work." She began to adjust the necktie. "Have I ever told you how much I like this tie? The dark blue with red narrow striping works well. Blue looks good on you."

"Andrea—"

"Hush. You've already lost this battle, you just don't know it."

"But—"

She retrieved his wallet, cell phone, and keys from the top side drawer of the desk and handed them to him. Fifty objections came to John's mind, but he couldn't give them voice. For once, it felt good to be led rather than to lead. He wondered how she knew that.

Andrea stepped back from the desk, giving John room to step out. She took his arm but only for a moment. He admired her situational awareness. Although forward and pushing the boundaries of their relationship, she showed she knew they were still in the work place and it would be inappropriate for others to see him walking with his secretary on his arm. There were also the security cameras to consider.

He walked to the door, and Andrea took her usual place two steps behind him. They walked from the office.

***

William Clarke's was an upscale eatery that catered to Washington's elite. Business execs, ranking government employees and lobbyist frequented the place. It was always crowded and noisy. It was trendy. It was expensive. It was one of the best places in town to eat. It was also a contradiction. Many assumed the establishment was named after the American explorer William Clark. Truth was, the placed was owned by one Bill Clarke of Tennessee. The interior had a western flavor that was a jarring contrast to the "quantum" style meals with unusual blends of spices and prepared in nontraditional manners. John had been told the kitchen included such things as liquid nitrogen, vacuum cookers, and other items stolen from Buck Roger's kitchen.

Jake, a tall man with a salt-and-pepper beard and a ponytail that hung to the middle of his back, greeted them. Judging by his face, the greeter spent a few years following the Grateful Dead around the country, but his manner, speech, and intelligent eyes said there was another side to him. He was refined and elegant, Grizzly Adams in a tuxedo. He led them to a dim corner in the back of the restaurant, to a booth with tall sides that gave a measure of privacy.

"I love this place," Andrea said as she slid into the booth. "It's filled with so much . . ."

"Ambiance?"

"Power."

John had to smile. He had worked with everyone of importance from the president on down and had grown used to powerful men and women. What he enjoyed most was being considered a man of power. It is what he worked for and something he would never relinquish. "You come here often?"

"A couple of times. It's beyond my normal budget, but not tonight. It's my treat."

"That might be a tad unseemly, Andrea."

"I don't care."

A waiter appeared and recited the menu. William Clarke's never printed menus. Every day was different than the day before. That was part of the adventure. John decided on wild mushroom soup with sour cream and a Sam Adams beer. Andrea went with tomato bisque and a glass of white wine.

"Okay, what's going on?"

Andrea raised a perfectly crafted eyebrow and spoke with an accent any Southern belle would admire, "Why, whatever do you mean, Mr. Knox?" She batted her eyes in comic fashion. It made John laugh, something he hadn't done in weeks.

"You've always been a little . . . what's the word?"

"Confident?"

"Assertive. You kidnapped me from my office."

"I believe they call that hyperbole, Boss. I did no such thing; I just casually invited you for a simple dinner."

"Ha. This is an abduction and they don't know how to serve a simple meal in this joint. You even made reservations. That shows premeditation so don't try to plead insanity."

"Drat. That was my fallback plan."

"Seriously, Andrea. What's going on?" Her expression tuned serious and for a moment, John thought he had offended the woman. "Look, I'm not trying to ruin the evening; I'm just suspicious by nature."

Andrea cocked her head to one side. "She filed, didn't she?"

"Who filed what?"

Andrea exhaled like an exasperated mother with a child who refused to listen. "Your wife, Cathy. She filed for divorce, didn't she?"

John pushed back in the booth as if trying to add a few more inches between them. "That's none of your business, Andrea. What makes you say that?"

She leaned her elbows on the table, reducing the distance John was trying to gain. "It is my belief you keep me around for a reason. I do good work and I'm smart. Am I wrong?"

"No, but—"

"It's common knowledge Cathy left you. She never could appreciate the destiny of a man like you. The tension between you two is well known, but when you were served papers, then immediately asked me to set up an appointment with Eddie Goodall, I suspected things had taken a turn. Mr. Goodall is a divorce attorney."

"He does other work."

"I'm sure he does, but he is primarily a divorce attorney. Okay, so what? Sixty percent of all marriages end in divorce. That number is something like eighty percent for men in powerful places, especially government. You're spending more and more time at the office, your clothing which used be immaculate, is not what it once was."

He looked down at his coat and shirt.

She shook her head. "You look wonderful. No one else would notice but me. That's because I notice everything about you. You've been unusually grumpy—"

"I'm not grumpy; I'm assertive."

"A rose by any other name . . . I can sense the difference."

His ire began to rise. "It's been a bad week, Andrea. I'm not in the mood for games."

"This isn't a game, John. I would never have done this if you and your wife were still together, but it seems that chapter is closing and I want to be in the next chapter."

He rubbed his eyes and started to speak, but stopped when the waiter appeared with their soup. He started to speak again when he saw a couple, a congresswoman and her husband, bow heads and pray. It turned John's stomach. He turned back to Andrea. "I don't know what to think of this. The Preston case is heating up with the Pope stirring the pot; the FBI agent on Matt's murder case treats me like a suspect; and an advisor I wanted to hire to handle the countess chick reads me out and implies I'm unethical. Now this. This is awkward."

"It doesn't have to be, John. You're a man; I'm a woman. It's normal, expected. It's what men and women do. All the stress you just mentioned is why you need someone like me in your life, and I don't mean merely as your administrative assistant."

Her boldness caught John off guard. He had long suspected she had some interest in him beyond the office. "Andrea, do you remember our trip to Europe—"

She raised a hand. "I knew you'd bring that up. Yes, of course I remember. For the most part, it was a wonderful trip."

John couldn't help smiling. "You had fun until we were leaving. Do you think of Julian Giordano often?" He referred to an Italian attorney who specialized in UN and EU judicial policy. Andrea and he had become an item while some of the DTED team were visiting an international law conference in Rome, a conference at which John read a legal paper.

"Not since I stepped on the plane home."

"Still . . ."

"I was not as interested in him as I pretended. Truth is, I knew he liked men more than women."

"It didn't seem that way when he admitted it. What was it he said? 'I'm Italian and you are a pretty woman.' I guess we should call him bisexual."

"You were under a lot of pressure then and very distracted. I was trying to get your attention."

"Well, you achieved that. Look, Andrea, we are coworkers. This wouldn't be wise."

She folded her hands. "Think about what you're saying, John. You have been fighting to put an end to hate speech spoken by those who want to peek into bedrooms and see who's sleeping with whom. What we do is our business and no one else's." She picked up her spoon but did nothing with it. "I've struggled with this, John. I'm taking a risk here. I love my job. It's more than a job." She pushed the soup around with the spoon.

John reached across the table and touched Andrea's arm. "No worries. I need you more than you need the job." He withdrew his hand. "I'm flattered."

"I want to be here for you, John, not just as your assistant. I want to be more. You need me to be more."

John couldn't think of a counter argument.

Chapter 19

Unofficial Report

———⟫◆⟪———

Greg Mayer felt a weariness he hadn't known since Air Force boot camp forty years before. It was the Air Force that started him on a career in aviation, first as an airman working in flight control centers, then, after showing an above average aptitude for all things flight related, helped him earn a BS degree in aerospace engineering. A commission as an officer followed and Mayer spent the next ten years as a pilot for various transport planes. He spent the next five years as a military crash investigator.

After receiving an honorable discharge, he was recruited by the FAA and the NTSB. He chose the latter and quickly rose through the ranks of investigators until he was the lead of one of the fast response teams. Now, with retirement looming ahead of him, he struggled with the crash that would define his career. Not that the dozens of other investigations he oversaw were meaningless, they just didn't have two associate Supreme Court justices on board.

"You still with me?"

Mayer looked down at the scrawny computer jockey with the pock marked face. "Of course."

"You seemed to drift off there for a moment. I suppose that's not unusual in a man your age." He grinned.

Mayer didn't. "Are you familiar with the phrase, 'Inappropriate humor directed at a man who can fire your worthless carcass without shedding a tear?'"

"Yes, sir. It seems I have heard that somewhere, sir."

"You see, you're not as socially awkward as everyone says. You have something new for me?"

"Yes . . . did you really run this on the simulator?"

"Yes."

"And you rode it to the ground?"

"Yes. Several times."

"I'm surprised you didn't spew." Warner Steiner looked up from the wide computer screen. His face was pale and the light from the monitor washed him out even more. The twenty-something-year-old seemed destined to set a record for the lowest vitamin D result in medical history. Mayer wondered when the man last spent any time in the sun.

"Who says I didn't?"

"Oh, gross."

"Can we get back to the computer program?"

"Sure, Boss." He turned his face back to the monitor. "As you know, we've reconstructed much of the material on the flash drive found in the airport. It had lots of info on the business jet and hidden program. You've already used the flight data to simulate the crash. We also know a program was loaded into the flight computer to screw with the information flow."

"The Pitot tubes."

"Exactly. As far as the on-board computer was concerned, the craft lost significant airspeed. The computer tried to fix a problem that wasn't there. Then things went bad."

"This I know."

"Understood, but this is what you don't know . . ."

Mayer was losing his grip on his patience. "I'm listening."

Warner fidgeted and rubbed his face. "Okay, here's the dealio: I'm in a bind. I'm about to tell you something you're not supposed to know. And if you aren't supposed to know, you can bet your last buck, I'm not supposed to know. You follow me?"

"I think so."

"I'm placing my job in your hands." He mumbled a curse. "Actually, I'm putting my life as a free man in your hands."

"You know you're being a drama queen, right?"

"Mr. Mayer. If I tell you this, you will have to make a choice: to be an accessory or a snitch. I'm hoping you'll choose the first."

Warner's discomfort spread to Mayer. Warner was considered a computer genius, but one with black hat hacker credentials. The only reason he wasn't in jail was his smart lawyer who arranged to "channel rare skills into something our country can use." The judge agreed. Warner could choose prison for hacking the FBI central computer or he could put his skills to use for one or more federal agency. Having been warned prison was not a good place for a young man and it came with a twenty year ban from using anything that connected to the Net or the cell system, made Warner decide to be a patriot.

"I'm just trying to be fair with you, man, er, sir."

"You found something the other computer jockeys missed? It's important."

"Most of those guys are light weights when it comes to off-road computing. No offense. Yeah, I've learned something uber-important."

"Okay, I'll risk it."

"Think about it, dude. You'll be putting a toe over the line into my world . . . former world."

"Let's hear it."

"One last thing. Should my brain fade and I happen to mention someone outside our close circle of friends, you can't ask who. This is one of the trust things. You follow me?"

Mayer didn't like having his hands tied and certainly didn't like flirting with anything illegal. He had spent his life being a straight arrow. Unfortunately, his only other choice was letting something important float past him. "Understood. Say it."

Warner took a deep breath. "Suppose there was a man—I'm just supposing here—suppose there was a man who, say, knew a lot about secret activities of some organizations; you know, one of those groups that love to use three initials?"

A string of government agencies ran through Mayer's head: FBI, FAA, CIA, DIA, NSA, ICE, and a dozen others. "Go on."

"Suppose the man, quite by accident, mind you, stumbled on a few activities the unnamed agency would be embarrassed to have made public."

"Would this be a felony accidental discovery?"

"Felony is such a harsh word, but yeah. Now suppose this man knew someone like me who might want to know about such a sweet nugget. And suppose some good looking former hacker obtained that information and wanted to share it with someone a little higher up the food chain."

"A lot higher up the food change."

"Fine. A lot higher." He took another deep breath. "In this story, the unnamed hacker learned and downloaded details of an attempt by the three-letter-organization's effort to bring down the private Gulfstream of some dastardly foreign leader type. You know, to save the lives of soldiers and innocent citizens."

It took a few moments for Mayer to realize he had stopped breathing. He closed his eyes, then slowly opened them. "Don't stop."

"Now, if I were writing a Hollywood movie, I'd have the unnamed hacker share that knowledge with a former friend. Not just the knowledge, but the program the organization used to kick the crap out of a flight computer. I'd also have that virus match, line-by-line, stroke-by-stroke, a program used to down a private jet carrying some really big wigs."

Mayer leaned forward and clutched his knees.

"You're not gonna spew, are you, man?" Warner bolted from the chair.

"No. I just need . . . I mean, you're describing . . . Oh, this is bad." He straightened. "In your obtuse way, you're telling me someone killed two Supreme Court associate justices by using a digital virus designed by the—"

"I didn't mention any organization. I'm just talking what-ifs. That's all."

"Does the virus match or not?"

"Yeah, man. The only differences I can find are those specific to the jet in question. You know what that means, right?"

"It means our killer is a skilled hacker or worse."

"China, North Korea, Libya, and even the Taliban have tried hacking our systems."

Mayer shook his head. "They wouldn't attack the justices. They would go after military or political leaders, not judicial." He thought for a moment. "I'm having unthinkable thoughts."

"Me too."

"Home grown terrorists. Someone with access to things only a handful of people know about."

Warner returned to his chair. "You know what this means, right? It means you can't trust anyone."

Mayer placed a hand on the young man's shoulder. "I know. Have you spoken to anyone else about this?"

"Are you kidding? I almost didn't tell you."

Mayer nodded. "Good. This stays between us. Others might not keep your secret."

"But you will, right? Right?"

"Yes. I didn't hear any of this from you."

"Thanks, man. Thanks. What now?"

"Now I think. You're not the only one with a network, you know."

***

The drive home through DC traffic was normally a grueling effort, only slightly less uncomfortable than going to the dentist. This evening the stop-and-go was therapeutic. Mayer wasn't in a mood to go home. Nothing awaited him there but a few old DVDs, mail he had made a point to ignore, and television that seldom played anything but documentaries. His wife had started retirement without him, traveling in South America with friends. His two children were away at college. He had lived in the home for a decade but knew none of the neighbors. Mayer was not a social butterfly who had many acquaintances but no friends. Fortunately, loneliness was more friend than enemy. He was not a man who feared his own thoughts. . .who *usually* didn't fear his thoughts.

Tonight was different. He had received disturbing information; information that could be interpreted a dozen different ways, and what interpretation he chose had ramifications beyond his imagination.

Clichés sprouted in his mind like weeds: Stuck between the devil and the deep blue sea; stuck between a rock and a hard place. Others tried to surface, but he closed them down. He needed to keep his thoughts streamlined, moving from Point A to Point B. Just like an old pilot. *Know where you are. Know where you want to go. Know what stands in your way.*

Warren's revelation had turned Mayer's insides to Jell-O quivering in a nine-point-oh earthquake. For the first time in his career, he wished he had taken early retirement as his wife had. He could be sailing up the Amazon or touring Mayan ruins . . . or was it something built by the Incas? He never could keep the pre-Columbian people groups straight.

A neon sign beckoned him as he crossed into Virginia. Mayer seldom visited bars, especially alone, but tonight he felt he deserved a couple of beers. He even told himself he needed one.

A thought occurred to him. He raised his cell phone and pressed it to his ear. He hated those Bluetooth devices that made people look like a Borg from Star Trek. A few moments later, he had a date.

***

Mac Adams once stood six-foot-four, but age had shaved off an inch or two. It had also put a slight bend in his back and a job sustained injury put a limp in his step. Still, the fifty-eight year old man had dark hair. Apparently his head was allergic to gray. His eyes were bright and reflected a thoughtful mind. He wore a tan pair of slacks, New Balance running shoes, and a navy blue shirt with gold initials: FBI.

Seeing Mayer seated in the back booth of the Boston Bean Bar and Grille, he waved and marched forward. Mayer hadn't seen the man in at least two years which was a shame. Of all the people he had worked with in the past, Mac was one of the truly good guys.

"How the heck are ya?" Mac said as he shook Mayer's hand, then slipped into the booth. "I see you're still ugly."

"Yeah, and you're still rude and self absorbed."

The men laughed.

"Been too long, Greg. You still working?"

"Yep, still got a few years left in me. Retiring scares me."

Mac sat back as if the words stunned him. "Why? Look at me. I'm retired."

"That's what scares me."

"Funny guy. Well, I'd still be working if the Emperor hadn't started forcing out the seasoned agents."

"Is that what you call the Assistant Attorney General now?"

Mac shrugged. "In polite company. Wanna know what we call him when we're not in polite company?"

"I think I know. Listen, I appreciate your coming here on short notice. I hope you cleared it with your wife."

"I don't need to clear things with my wife. I don't need her permission."

"Of course not, but you cleared it with her anyway."

"True. I don't pack a weapon anymore, so I'm greatly out gunned."

"Poor thing. Let me buy you a beer."

"No need, I can get it."

"You're doing me a favor, so I'm buying." Mayer waved at the cocktail waitress who delivered a pair of Killian's Red in glasses.

"Okay," Mac said after the first sip. "What makes you dredge up an old agent like me?"

"I need a referral and I can't tell you why."

"NTBS stuff?"

"Yeah, I'm working a case."

"The Supreme Court Justices?"

"I can't say."

"You just did. I didn't get to be an agent-in-charge by being dense. Tell me what you can and what you need."

"How much have things changed in the Bureau?"

"A lot. I still know people there, but most of us old guys were forced out with Knox's shenanigans."

"Shenanigans? It's good to know that word is making a comeback after being dead for so many decades." Mayer sipped his beer, set it on the table, turning the glass like it was the knob of a combination lock. "I need to talk to someone over there I can trust. Who can I trust?"

"No one. There's very few agents who are old enough to need to shave. Well, there are a few women . . ."

"I'm serious, Mac."

"So am I. Not about the women, but about who you can trust. Everyone is walking on pins and needles. The agents with half-a-brain and a shred of soul are having trouble doing what the DOJ is asking. Some are staying to hang on to pensions. Others, like me, were offered early retirement and are taking it. I wouldn't trust anyone over there now. Almost everyone is driven by a sense of self-preservation. Some can't get by on retirement pay and the private security market is choked with former agents from ATF, FBI, and Treasury. My wife makes good money selling real estate, so I'm okay, but some of the others . . . well, you get the idea."

"You said 'almost everyone is driven by a sense of self-preservation.' Does that mean there are a few noble souls left?"

"A few. A handful, maybe. At least among the people I know."

Meyer's looked around the dark bar. People, mostly couples, whispered in the gloom. It was a quiet bar. "So who swims upstream?"

"These days. No one. No one would dare . . ."

"What?"

"Well, there is one person. I'm pretty sure she's still there. Odd bird. Brilliant in her own way. A real loner. Old gal."

"Is she good?"

"I worked a few cases with her. The woman thinks like a cruise missile: one target in mind until it's destroyed, then it's off to the next thing. Warm and as cuddly as a startled porcupine. They offered her early retirement, too."

"Why didn't she take it?"

"Because they acted like she had no choice in the matter. It's was the wrong way to approach the woman. It'll take a bulldozer to move her out of the bureau. Ruby does as Ruby wants."

"Last or first name?"

"Special Agent Ruby Fay. Graduated top of her class. That was shortly after the dark ages."

"You trust her?"

"Well, it's not like we were dating. She was lead on a couple of cases. Nearly wore me out."

"Honest?"

"She'd arrest herself if she committed a crime." He shook his head. "The woman is a chain-smoking juggernaut who couldn't care less about what other people think. People used to say she was the evil twin sister of J. Edgar Hoover. I have to agree. I know several Mafia bosses that won't allow her name to be mentioned in their presence."

"Married?"

"I didn't know you were looking."

"Come on, Mac, I'm trying to get a feel for the woman. I'm sitting on a bomb here. I have to be careful who I trust."

"Okay, okay. She's your best bet in Washington. Don't mess with her. If she thinks you're taking her for a ride, she'll make your life miserable."

"It's already miserable, Mac. Can she swim against the tide?"

"Yes. I think she enjoys it."

"I want to talk to her tomorrow, but not at the FBI or the NTSB."

"She hates all that cloak and dagger stuff."

"So do I, so I guess we'll both be unhappy."

Chapter 20

Marcus Has Questions

————⟨⟐⟩————

"Any word on my family?" Pat Preston looked at the large guard who had just entered the cell.

"They are safe. That is all I know."

"You confuse me, Marcus." Preston sat on the edge of his bed while Marcus Aster undid the chain on Pat Preston's ankle. He also removed the cuff.

"Was it something I said?" He took the chain and cuff to the door, rapped on it, and handed the metal restraints to another guard.

"What are you doing?" Preston stood, stretching his back.

"I've convinced my supervisor the shackles are unnecessary. It's not like you can go anywhere. They put them on you to make a point. I assume you got the point."

"I have."

"So why do I confuse you?" The guard outside the door handed a tray of food to Marcus who carried it to Pat.

"You're different than the others."

"Nice of you to say."

"There's something about you."

Marcus pointed at the food. "You only have a few minutes. Go ahead and give thanks, then eat before they come and take it away."

Pat prayed, then ate quickly, barely noticing what it was he was eating. He recognized white-meat turkey, gravy, potatoes, and rye bread. Before, he used to do his best to ignore the taste, but the last few meals delivered by Marcus had been tasty. Once done, he handed the tray back to his captor, who pushed it through the slot in the door. It disappeared almost immediately.

"I have a question for Dr. Preston." Marcus' voice sounded smooth and still carried an accent Pat couldn't identify.

"I'm not sure I have many answers these days."

"Are you out of answers or just out of answers you like?"

"Probably the latter. You don't mince words, do you?"

"Have I been rude?"

Preston laughed. The sound of it sounded forward to him. "You have to be the only prison guard in the world who worries about being rude. No, you haven't been rude, just straightforward. What is your question?"

"Why do Christians suffer?"

Preston's eyebrows rose. "Whew, I thought you were going to ask a tough question."

Marcus didn't respond.

"You might be asking the wrong man." Preston began to pace his cell, stretching his legs.

"Why? You are a Christian man and you are suffering. True?"

"Yes."

"Then you are the best man to ask."

"I suppose it's hard for a suffering person to have an intellectual conversation about his pain." He put his hands behind his back. "Back in my pulpit days, I used tell my congregation we are not exempt from suffering and trials. We live in a fallen world and therefore must deal with the results of that. It was easy to say back then."

"So you did not believe your own words?"

"It's not that. I believed them then, and I believe them now, but objectivity is elusive when you're in the middle of suffering."

"Doesn't your Bible teach that suffering comes with faith?"

"Well, not directly. Not as you just put it. Certainly it teaches that faith can lead to suffering. It certainly did for the early Christians."

"Like?"

"Peter, Paul, Silas, all the disciples and early Christians. The early church was born one day and persecuted the next."

"How do you mean?"

"The first waves of persecution began with other religious people persecuting the followers of Jesus. Forty days after Jesus ascended to Heaven, on the day of Pentecost, the Holy Spirit descended on the disciples and Peter preached a sermon, a very brave sermon, calling out those who crucified Jesus. Long story short, about three thousand men came to faith. Most scholars assume the total number of people numbered twice that. From a few hundred followers to thousands in just a few minutes. That couldn't be overlooked by those who wanted to see the whole Jesus movement ended. Peter and others would be arrested several times and beaten.

That first wave of persecution was composed of Jews persecuting Jews. Ironically, Rome protected the church. For awhile. Then the rumors started." Pat stopped as his brain churned up years of study. "Christians were law abiding citizens, but many had trouble paying tribute to Rome. It wasn't the money, but it was required of the giver to say, 'Caesar is Lord.' They would pay their taxes but refused to utter those words. The Romans who believed in the deity of Caesar began to think of Christians as atheists. How's that for irony?"

Marcus nodded but didn't speak.

"They also accused Christians of being sexually immoral. They based that on Love Feasts the church would have. The Romans were not especially moral, so they assumed 'Love' meant sexual activity, but the Christians used a different word: *agape*, not *eros*. Do you know the difference?"

"Tell me."

"Eros refers to sexual attraction. The English word *erotic* comes from the Greek eros. Agape refers to a love that begins with God and is shared with others." Pat felt like he was leading a Bible study and it gave him the first warm feeling he had experience since coming to this place. "They also accused Christians of being cannibals."

"Because they ate the body and drank the blood of Christ."

"Exactly. You know more than you're letting on. The Lord's Supper, or as some churches call it, the Eucharist, is a symbolic accepting of Christ's sacrifice on the cross, and to Anglicans and Catholics it is much more."

"I'm puzzled, Dr. Preston," Marcus said.

"Was I unclear?"

"No. I'm confused because you say that persecution began with the early church."

"Yes."

"Was not the arrest, torture, and crucifixion of Jesus persecution?"

"Well . . . technically . . ." Pat fell silent. "I can't argue with that. Jesus is the head of the church so, yes, persecution began before the forming of the church."

"Didn't Peter mention the prophets in his early sermons?"

Pat watched Marcus. He knew when he was being led. "Yes, he said the religious leaders persecuted the prophets of old."

"Another question, Dr. Preston. Who was the first martyr for the faith?"

"Well, a disciple named Stephen was stoned to death for preaching. That happened in Jerusalem and . . ."

Marcus was shaking his head. "The very first person to die for doing what God asked of him."

The question irritated Pat. He was used to being the teacher leading the student. Not the other way around. After all, he had four years of college, three years of seminary training and couple more years perusing his doctorate. Who did the guard think he was?

Still, the question was intriguing. He began pacing again. He thought of all the Old Testament prophets who suffered, then he let his mind go further back. Moses and the children of Israel suffered at the hands of Pharaoh.

"Who do you have in mind?" Pat asked.

"Abel."

"Abel! He was the first murder victim when he was killed by his brother, Cain"

"Why was he killed?"

"Because he brought a pleasing offering to God while Cain's offering was rejected . . . Okay, I concede your point. Cain killed Abel for religious reasons. Where are you headed with this?"

"If persecution began with Adam and Eve's first children and continued through the ages, then why are you surprised you are here? Persecutors only persecute those they fear."

The words rattled around in Pat's head. So much so, he barely noticed Marcus leaving the cell.

Chapter 21

Locked Horns

---⬧---

Paul Atoms walked through the corridors of the FBI's J. Edgar Hoover building like a man familiar with the place. After a dozen years as a special agent, four of which were spent in this building, the place has an "old home" feel. He nodded at old acquaintances, occasionally offering a snappy, casual, two-finger salute. Several times old work mates stopped him to ask how life at DTED was and did he miss the Bureau. He took the time to visit, slap backs, and poke his head in on his former supervisors, two of which he learned had left, unable to tolerate the DOJ's new tolerance duties. He even had time to kick it in the cafeteria, drinking coffee with his old buds.

"So what brings you to the old stomping ground?" asked one agent, a fairly young face and an expert in white-collar crime.

"I'm going to drop by and see Ruby Fay."

"Yeow! Really?"

"Sure. She's working a case for us and my boss wants an update." There was more to it than that, but the statement was all Atoms wanted to reveal.

"You packing? She's been in a mood for . . . what? Five years?"

Atoms patted the left breast of his suit coat. "Always prepared, but she won't be a problem. She's a good agent."

"There's a difference between being a good agent and a pleasant one."

Atoms left the table with the stride of a confident man. Truth was, he'd rather have a toe removed than spend time in the presence of the dragon. At one time, he had enjoyed a cordial relationship with the woman. Very polite. Very professional. Then he left the Bureau to join John Knox Smith's Diversity and Tolerance Enforcement Division team at the DOJ. He had limited exposure to her after that, but their paths had crossed and he regretted each encounter.

Atoms found Ruby Fay at her desk. She held a pen in one hand and an unlit cigarette in the other. "Ah, she walks in beauty as the night."

"I'm seated, Paul. Didn't they teach you how to be observant in the Academy?"

"Top of my class. Got a sec?"

"And if I said no?"

"Come on, Ruby, I'm not your enemy."

"You sure? You work for that weasel, Smith. I'm pretty sure he's my enemy."

Atoms pulled a chair from one of the empty cubicles and sat. The limited footprint of Ruby's cubicle meant he had to sit closer than he liked. "He is the Assistant Attorney General. The title alone demands a little respect."

"Spoken like a true lackey."

"I'm nobody's lackey."

"Oh, please, you're a spaniel. A lap dog." She turned back to her desk as if speaking to him and facing him was too much to bear. "Why are you here?"

"Fine, down to business then. Did you really accuse my boss of killing Matt Branson?"

"Nope. Did he say I did?"

"I prefer to ask the questions."

"I prefer you leave, yet here you sit." She turned to face him again. "No, I didn't accuse him, but I did let him know he has come up on my radar."

"Well, fix your radar. He and Branson were friends in college."

"I know about the relationship. It seems being Knox's friend is dangerous. He locked up another friend of his and then had him shipped out of country to be tried in a foreign court. Apparently he doesn't think much of our judiciary."

"That's not it."

"Then what is it?"

He started to snap at her, but chose a more professional approach. "It's complicated and not germane to your investigation."

"Now you see that? When you were a real agent, you knew the investigator gets to determine what is or isn't germane."

He snapped. "I am still a good agent."

"Oh, sorry. I didn't realize persecuting preachers was so unnerving."

"You are infuriating. You know that, don't you?"

Ruby smiled. "It kinda makes you want to get up and leave, doesn't it?"

"Ruby, you're digging a hole for yourself. You know John can call the director and get the case moved to another agent."

"Now you're teasing me with empty promises. In point of fact, he won't do that. It would make him look guilty."

"He's not guilty. You need to focus your attention elsewhere."

"I am. Some people multi task, I multi accuse. How about you, Paul? You've shown up on my radar, too."

"Why would I want to kill Matt Branson? I didn't know the guy. He was just one of thousands who worked at the DOJ."

"He put your boss in a bad spot. He was defending someone you helped arrest and build a case against."

"Criminals all have defenders."

"Not many have lawyers leave their jobs at the DOJ to do it. You see, that's the difference between Knox's idea of friendship and Branson's. Branson went to his friend's aid; Knox deprived Preston of due process and a trial by his peers. Your boss doesn't have much regard for the Constitution."

"Is that what's stuck in your craw?"

"The fact that he and guys like you are using the Constitution as a doormat? Yeah, that's a little hard to swallow."

"We are trying to protect the rights of all people and put an end to intolerance and hate speech. It is a noble goal."

"If you say so. Tell me what I can say to make you go away." She rolled the cigarette in her fingers and Atoms could tell she was dying to light the thing.

"Knox wants to make sure you understand he respects you and your investigation skills."

"I'm about to blush."

"And he wants to be kept up to date on everything. He means *everything*. Will you do that?"

"I will inform the Assistant Director in the usual and accepted manner. It is up to him whether or not he informs your boss."

"Knox's wants to hear from you."

"I will inform the Assistant Director in the usual and accepted—"

"Okay, I get it. I'll let the Assistant Attorney General know you refuse to cooperate."

Ruby's face hardened. "You can tell him to stop interfering with this investigation. It would be a shame if someone let it slip than an FBI agent talked to him about his involvement in the murder of a DOJ employee."

"*Former* employee. And you wouldn't dare."

"Well, that changes everything and yes, I would dare, if it aids in my investigation. Knox has had no problem trying people in the media. I figure he might like the attention."

"You're messing with fire, Ruby."

"Is that a threat? Did you just threaten an FBI agent? Because I believe that's a crime."

Atoms stood and stared down at the middle-aged woman. She stared back, showing no emotion.

"Good day, Special Agent Fay."

"Good day, former Special Agent Atoms."

Chapter 22

Band of Brothers

⟫⋅◆⋅⟪

S ir Alan Hodge settled into the thickly padded leather conference chair. He had arrived early as was his custom. He liked
the foot of the table and so made a point of being first in the ICJ
conference room. The president of justice would sit at the head of
the table; the other members of the panel would find places around
the long wood table.

Fifteen judges were too many. It was a conclusion Sir Alan had
come to after his first three cases. The US Supreme Court had only
nine members and they were seldom united. The Supreme Court
of the United Kingdom had eleven and that was close to impossible to manage. Fifteen! To make matters worse, these were fifteen
very different people. In the US and the UK there might be a mix
of gender and race, but the International Court of Justice contained
jurists from around the world. English and French were second languages to them which sometimes led to misunderstandings, especially in the finer points of law.

He opened a legal notebook and glanced down the list of names
and nationalities. He knew them by heart, but Sir Alan believed fre-
quent review was good for the mind, especially now that he was
sixty-two and still had six years of his nine-year term left. That
made him one of the junior members. One third of the group was in

their last three years; another third in the middle three; and a third, like Alan, were in their first three years.

The door opened and a stream of ten men and four women in business attire entered. Alan Hodges stood. Their chatter filled the large room and reminded Alan of a bunch of high school students, except the youngest member was over fifty.

They chose seats and all but Yoshiro Kurosawa of Japan sat. Once everyone was seated, Kurosawa, the court's president, bowed, then lowered himself in the chair. "I trust everyone had a restful night." His English was without fault. Of the group, Alan considered Kurosawa the brightest of the bright.

Alan's eyes looked around the table and saw judges from Slovakia, China, Sierra Leone, Jordan, the United States, Germany, France, New Zealand, Mexico, Morocco, Russia, Brazil, and Somalia. Such diversity was to be expected since each member was elected by the UN General Assembly and the UN Security Council.

"We have before us today the motion by Countess Isabella San Phillipa representing the Reverend Dr. Pat Preston of the United States and an American nonprofit religious legal firm, the Alliance. Has everyone read the motion?"

"I have." The words were laden with accent. Alexzandr Kuchar, the vice-president of the group, hailed from Slovakia. "I found it offensive. As did all those of us who welcome this court's expansion of jurisdiction into lowering the world's tensions created by hate crimes."

"Offensive?" Sir Christopher MacKinnon of New Zealand seemed stunned. "You cannot have served the rule of law for so long and still have a thin skin."

"I am not offended by the request, Sir Christopher, but by the accusation." Alexzandr had a head of white hair, brushed back and held in place by some kind of oil that smelled of musk.

Alan said nothing. He knew the offending lines. They had stung him as well, enough that he was tempted to pass judgment then and there, but he didn't. Decades of legal work had forced him to be slow to respond or take offense.

Balduindo Pairo of Mexico agreed with Alexzandr. "The countess lumps us in the same league as Third World dictators." He lifted the legal form and read from it, his dark eyes snapping back and forth. "Here it is: 'Continued confinement of Dr. Preston is cruel by the standards of every civil country. To keep a man who has committed no crime imprisoned on another continent and far from his wife and two children is the kind of cruelty civilized nations associate with countries like Iran." He threw the document to the table. "Iran! The woman compared us to Iran. That takes some nerve."

"Woman?" Josette Girard of France said. "Do you have a problem with women?"

"Of course not."

"It sounded to me as if you were using her gender to disparage her." Alan swallowed a smile. The short French woman began her legal career defending women from oppressive husbands who pleaded religious and cultural privilege over their wives and daughters. She spent fifteen years of her career getting new death threats every month. Her face was cherubic, her manner soft and measured, but she possessed a steely will that no one had been able to bend.

"Don't play that game with me," Pairo said. "I have a well documented history of supporting women's rights."

"We're missing the real issue here," Dana Eichel said, her German accent carried an attractive power. "The real problem is the American desire to use us to solve their problem. I don't see how this case made it to the ICJ. We deal in more important matters."

"More important than tolerance?" The question came from the only judge from the United States. Mr. Tracy Doyle had spent years trying criminal cases in New York and then teaching law at Yale. "The world is filled with hatred and the rule of law is all that keeps hate-filled people from slaughtering others in the streets. Do I need to remind the body that just recently a Pakistani father was acquitted of killing his daughter, an act he confessed to committing, but since it was an honor killing, he was allowed to walk away. The thirteen-year-old's crime was running away to avoid a forced marriage to a man twenty years older than she. Intolerance is the issue of the day, one we will be seeing more and more. My country is committed to putting an end to hate speech and the violence it breeds."

"That is a nice speech, but I suggest we leave the legal arguments to the courtroom." Haim Harrar was a Moroccan Jew and the most conservative of the panel. "We are not here to try the case in this room."

"Mr. Harrar is right," Kurosawa said, resuming control. "We have several issues to address and we would be wise to act on those before coming to conclusions about a case we haven't heard."

Alan looked down. Kurosawa's statement was noble, but Alan knew what every judge in every country knew, what few on the other side of the bench understood. Judges often decided cases based on preliminary written arguments before donning their legal robes. Most of the public would be surprised to hear the language and attitudes of some judges when not at the bench or in formal chambers.

"The first matter at hand is the formal request of dismissal." Kurosawa looked up from the folder he had, a folder like what each member of the ICJ judges panel had. "Opinions?"

"I say we grant it." Eichel seemed relieved to have said it. "Let the Americans deal with their own problems. They've been bragging about their legal system since the 1700s. Dismiss the case."

"So you would free the man, just because you don't want to be bothered with the case?" Jinjing said.

"I didn't say that. I am merely putting the burden of prosecution on the prosecution."

There was silence for a moment, then MacKinnon spoke up. "Let me talk about the elephant in the room. Part of the problem we're facing here is the American proclivity to walk away from any organization that doesn't support their wishes."

"Excuse me?" Doyle said. "Speaking for all Americans, I'm offended."

"And there it is," MacKinnon responded, "the 'you hurt my feelings' response. I suppose if we vote to grant the dismissal, your country will pull you from the ICJ, even though the world agreed to its expanded jurisdiction demands."

"That's ridiculous."

"After this court ruled against your country, ruling your invasion of Nicaragua was contrary to international law, you took a pick-and-choose approach to the court's decision, embracing the ones you like, turning up your nose at the ones you disagreed with."

"That was a long time ago. There have been several new administrations since the 1980s."

MacKinnon tapped the table with his index finger. "I just want to be clear, that of late the court has been so worried about offending the conscience of the American leaders that it can influence our decisions. Will that be the case today?"

"Just for the record," the Brazilian Socorro Barraso said, "this is a small matter but there are two Americas. Maybe we could be a little more specific."

"You know who I'm talking about," MacKinnon countered. "And for the record, I'm undecided at the moment about the dismissal."

Alan wondered how such a contentious case would play out in the courtroom. At the heart of the issue was religious freedom. When he first came to the court, he did his best to learn as much about the other members as possible. That information combined with observation caused him to realize how divided the court was, especially on religion. Almost every one present had a religious background, although only Haim Harrar practiced anything close to the faith he was reared in. Buddhists were Buddhist in name only. Several professed to be atheist; there were two judges from predominately Islamic countries, and several from predominately Christian ones, although he doubted any of them could give directions to the nearest mosque, church, synagogue, or prayer center. A second later he realized he was numbered in that group.

"It seems a vote is in order," Kurosawa said.

Alan raised a hand. "Excuse me, but I have a suggestion."

"Please share it, Sir Alan."

"The countess asks for a hearing should we be inclined to reject the request for dismissal."

"We have her written request," Alexzandr said.

"Yes, I know, but she requests a public hearing."

"That would be a waste of the court's time." Pairo looked irritated by the suggestion.

"With all due respect, I think we owe it to her. She still worked here when some of you first came to the court. I arrived too late to benefit from her orientation. She is not just any attorney. She is someone who labored within these walls."

"It's a bad precedent to set," Doyle said.

"I don't think it is. It does not hurt to hear a formal presentation of a dismissal request. We must not only be open in this case, we must appear open. It won't hurt us to listen."

"Do you make that as a motion?" Kurosawa asked.

"I do, Mr. President."

"Then I put it to the panel: Shall we listen to oral arguments on the merits of dismissal? If so, please raise your right hand." It took a moment, but eight hands rose; seven remained down including the hand of the judge from the United States.

Chapter 23

Denied

━━◆━━

"**W**hat should I expect?" Pat Preston asked. "What should I do?" He stood in a small ante room just outside the International Court of Justice. The small space was crowded. Two court guards stood in a room already made small by the presence of Isabella, Scott Freeman and Larry Jordan of the Alliance, and Pat.

"The court will ask nothing of you," Isabella said. "This is a hearing. I will present a very brief argument stating why the case should be dismissed. If that fails, I'll ask that you be released on your own recognizance or, at very least, released into my custody."

"Will they do that?"

Isabella's eyes softened. "No. If they don't dismiss the case, then there's very little chance they will release you from prison."

"Will this take long?" It took willpower to stand straight. It felt good to be out of his prison garb. Isabella had arranged for a suit, a real shower, and a shave with a clean razor. Pat felt close to normal.

"I don't think so."

Freeman spoke. "I understand the judges are free to ask questions?"

"Yes, it's like your Supreme Court. Judges may interrupt at any time, ask questions and even argue with counsel."

"Are you prepared for that?" Freeman asked.

"No one is prepared for that. This is an international court. The laws and practices of the United States have very little bearing here."

"At least you sound confident." Pat forced a smile.

"It's all an act. Inside, I'm shaking."

"Good," Pat said. "I don't want to be the only one."

Isabella adjusted her black robe, closed her eyes, and crossed herself. Pat watched her lips move. *I don't know what she's praying, Lord, but I say amen.*

Her head snapped up and she took a deep breath. A moment later she turned the knob on the door and stepped into the large courtroom. Pat followed, Scott Freeman and Larry Jordan followed behind. The floor was covered in a red, patterned carpet, the walls in dark wood paneling set in squares. The paneling rose many feet above the floor; above which were set wide arched, stained glass windows. Multi-bulb pendant light fixtures hung from chains attached to a ceiling that loomed thirty feet overhead. Pat was struck by the overwhelming, musty smell in the air...the odor of a room long closed and seldom used. Yet, this was the inside, public face of the Peace Palace which was being used while the new criminal court was under construction. Pat felt no peace.

Isabella led the legal team and Pat to a long table covered with a forest green cloth. In front of the table was a long wood rail that led to a dais. Four steps bridged the distance from the common floor to the wide platform and bench. Isabella and the others sat.

Pat looked around the room. The press was present, seated in the gallery. The balcony had a few spectators. Behind the public rose thick curtains, also of forest green. His eyes fell on a similar table to the one at which he sat. There were two men at the table, but Pat could only recognize one: John Knox Smith. He looked tired, worn. They made eye contact, but it lasted only a moment. John looked away without revealing a single emotion. Isabella had told him John had very little notice about the hearing and had been flown in just this morning. That must have left the man with extreme jet lag. For a moment, but only a moment, Pat felt sorry of him. Then he thought about his prison cell and decided a last minute flight across the Atlantic was better than any day he had spent in jail.

A line of people dressed in black robes, white shirts, and a neck piece of lacy-white cloth filed in. The way they filed in reminded Pat of a line of mourners at a funeral: dark, solemn, grave.

Isabella and the others in the room rose. Pat joined them, doing as Isabella had instructed, his head up his shoulders back, but not so much as to appear arrogant. He was to avoid looking repentant for something he didn't do nor was he to stare the judges in the eye as if daring them to confront him. The goal was to look like a simple man who is the victim of a misunderstanding. He had no idea how he was doing.

The panel of judges sat, each looking powerful in their judicial robes and seated above everyone in the room. *Emperors on their thrones*.

As they sat, so did everyone else. An Asian man with a kind face but firm jaw sat at the center of the line of judges, glancing up and down the bench to be sure everyone was set with papers in order. To the side were several nicely dressed court reporters typing on keyboards.

The Asian judge read the date, the time and a series of numbers which Pat took to be the case number. "We are to conduct a public hearing to hear arguments regarding a motion for dismissal of the *United States on behalf of the Reverend Dr. Pat Preston, a citizen of the United States*. Is counsel present?"

Isabella rose. "Yes your honors—Countess Isabella San Phillipa, Mr. Scott Freeman and Larry Jordan, for the defense."

Pat looked John's direction. He was on his feet. "Yes, your honors, John Knox Smith, Assistant Attorney General for the United States and Joel Thevis, lead attorney for the Diversity and Tolerance Enforcement Division, a division of the United States Department of Justice." There were two more men at the table, but John didn't introduce them.

A name plate sat in front of each judge. The Asian man's read: Yoshiro Kurosawa. During his prep time with Isabella, she had told him Kurosawa was the president of the judge's panel and was from Japan. "He's a good man, but hard as nails. He looks patient, but doesn't put up with anyone wasting the court's time."

Kurosawa looked at Isabella. "Since this is your motion, counselor, we'll begin with your remarks."

"Thank you, Your Honor."

He held up a finger. "Please confine yourself to the motion. This is not the time to try the case. Am I clear?"

"Yes, Your Honor." Isabella stepped from the table to a wood lectern, adjusted the microphone on its gooseneck stand, took a deep breath, looked up and took enough time to gaze at each judge in turn. Pat knew enough about public speaking to know that a moment or two of silence was the best way to seize the attention of any crowd.

"First, I thank the court for receiving my motion and then granting my request for a public hearing. To my right sits the Reverend Dr. Pat Preston, PhD, Oxford. He is an educated man dedicated to helping people through church work. He has a history of self-sacrifice in which he has put the good of others before his own. I have scores of affidavits from those who know him, testifying of the help, guidance, and counsel they have received from Dr. Preston. Yet, despite a lifetime of service, he has been snatched away from his family, his home, his church, and his country. He was held in the United States for weeks without benefit of trial, then when the prosecution felt their case slipping through their fingers due to evidence problems, they orchestrated Dr. Preston's transfer from the country of his birth to a foreign land."

"Objection," John said. "Counsel is demonizing the prosecution and attempting to sway the court with groundless emotionalism."

"Mr. Smith?" Kurosawa said. "You'll have your turn." He looked at Isabella. "Try to stay on track, Countess."

"With all due respect, You Honor, I am on track. Seated before you is a man who is being tried for exercising what is a basic right in the United States and in most of our countries: freedom of speech."

"You know as well as we do," Judge Alexzandr Kuchar said, "that no citizen in any country is free to say anything he or she chooses. The American Supreme Court dealt with the matter in 1919. I believe it was Oliver Wendell Holmes who said the law had a right to restrict speech when it was false, such as falsely yelling fire in a crowded theater."

Pat saw Isabella cock her head just an inch to the right. "Your Honor refers to *Schenck v. United States* in which that country's right of free speech—what they call their First Amendment right— could be limited. In that case, the limitation was directed at a group distributing fliers against the draft during World War I."

"That's the case I have in mind." Alexander seemed proud of the citation.

Isabella nodded. "It was an important case in US law. It was also overturned by a decision in *Brandenburg v. Ohio* in which the court clarified that speech could be limited by law when such speech was being used to incite lawless action such as a riot. Dr. Preston has never used his pulpit to call for lawless action."

"But the United States has new laws and has recognized the treaty criminalizing hate speech and you can't hope to argue the right and wrong of those laws in this court."

"I agree, Your Honor, which is why I believe the case against my client must be dismissed as not suitable for this court. Let the Americans try their own."

"Hate-speech is a global problem, Counselor." The female judge had a thick German accent. "This court and others like it are having to deal with such matters and the number of such cases is alarming."

"I would argue, Your Honor, that Dr. Preston is a victim of hate speech, not the source of it. He has been marched in front of the press and made to look like a mobster by the prosecution."

"Objection!"

Kurosawa pointed a finger at John, "Please don't make me warn you again. We will hear from you in due time."

John didn't reply.

"If the court please, as we argued at length and in detail in our motion, Dr. Preston is being used as a test case for the future prose- cution of those who hold religious views. Even if he did utter some- thing that someone somewhere took offense over, then he's guilty only of having an opinion. He does not deserve confinement. He does not deserve to be denied the support and love of his family. He has never been violent. This case is at best ill conceived and at worse contrived to promote a political agenda." She took a deep breath. "My client is not guilty of the charges leveled against him; if trial is required, it should be conducted in my client's own country; my client has already suffered irreparable damage to his image, his work, his family, and his future; further punishment—including the stress of a trial—is cruel; my client is being kept in a prison when he could be held on his own recognizance; he has no criminal record; none of the principle papers filed by the prosecution show criminal action beyond anything other than a misdemeanor. Based on these reasons and the others I listed in my formal request, I respectfully request this case be dismissed and that all charges brought against Dr. Preston be dropped. Please, Your Honors, let the man go home."

"Thank you, Countess," Kurosawa said. "Mr. Smith, your turn."

John took the spot at the lectern Isabella had just vacated. "I, too, wish to thank the court for addressing this matter. My comments will be short and to the point."

"Glad to hear it," Alexzandr said.

John held up his index finger. "One, we in the United States are committed to ending hate-speech and all forms of intolerance. It's time our country joined other countries in the twenty-first century." Another finger went up. "As the court will see in the trial, we have overwhelming evidence that Dr. Pat Preston did willfully and purposefully commit hate-speech as prohibited by international law in many of his sermons and Bible studies and caused such to be aired over public airways and the Internet—material that anyone in the world could access."

Another finger shot up. "Dr. Preston's hate speech was directed against a wide range of people: atheists, Buddhists, New Age adherents, those who practice Wiccan nature rites, homosexuals, cross-gender persons, and even other Christian organizations including Catholics, Pentecostals, Lutherans . . ." He looked at the German judge, " . . . and many more." A fourth finger joined the others. "Those messages went into the homes where children could hear them and be unfairly biased against others different than themselves." A fifth finger: "He has through speech and writing caused emotional harm to disenfranchised peoples by threatening an eternity burning in Hell."

John lowered his hand but quickly raised his other hand. "Dr. Preston has, over a period of many years, conducted psychological warfare against those who believe differently than he does." He glanced around the court, his arm and hand extended. "In this room—based on social statistics—are atheists. Christians, Hindus, lesbians, people of mixed ancestry, homosexuals, and much more. To that I say, 'Bravo.' I cannot imagine a world where a man like Dr. Preston can look with disdain at the members of this court and pass judgment on their value as humans and members of society. This case is important, not just to the United States, but to the world. Religious bigots like Dr. Preston should not be allowed to continue to inflict emotional harm on the innocents of the world.

"As to Dr. Preston being a gentle man, nonviolent, and only interested in helping others, I offer these simple statements, knowing you have the facts in front of you. Dr. Preston kept guns and ammunition in his home; he was a hunter and killed harmless creatures during his hunts; Dr. Preston resisted arrest to the point of physical violence while assisting his secretary who interfered with an officer of the law conducting his duties; that as recently as a few days ago, Dr. Preston had to be subdued in his own cell after an expression of fury and an attempt to disable surveillance equipment in his cell."

"I object!" Isabella was on her feet.

"Sit down, Countess," Kurosawa said. "I wouldn't allow Mr. Smith to interrupt and I won't allow you."

"He's describing the actions of a frightened man who had just learned of a threat against his family."

"I said, SIT DOWN."

Isabella did. She was shaking.

"Since the court's time is valuable and since I can't imagine any circumstance that would compel you to release such a threat to society, I will conclude with this: As the court has noted, more and more evidence of hate crimes and hate speech are making their way to your bench. This case will go a long way in instructing the world that it, too, can put an end to all forms of bigotry. I request the court to reject the motion to dismiss and allow us to bring to trial the full measure of evidence against Dr. Preston. It is a decision that will change the world and one that will be an educational model for my own country's actions. Thank you."

John returned to his seat.

Kurosawa turned to his fellow judges. "Does the panel have questions for either side?"

Fourteen heads swiveled in unison. "Very well, we will confer and make known our decision before close of court this evening."

The judges rose, as did Pat and the others. The judges walked out in single file. Pat looked to Isabella. "That didn't go well, did it?"

"I'm afraid not"

***

"Do you know the first thing I learned about trials?" Scott Freeman stood next to Pat. Isabella sat herself at the table. Larry Jordan took a place at the end of the defense desk.

"That quick is bad?" Isabella answered.

"Exactly." Scott Freeman rubbed the back of his tanned neck. He had taken to cutting his graying brown hair short. "In a jury case, when the jury is out for a short time, it doesn't bode well. I had hoped this would take at least the rest of the day. They reached a consensus in less than two hours."

Pat felt the pit of his stomach drop like a loose elevator.

Isabella pressed her lips into a thin line. She looked worried. "I've been praying about this since I first came on the defense team, but I don't have a good feeling about this. Still, maybe God worked a miracle."

"Here they come."

The side door opened and the line of judges reappeared. Again they walked in a way that reminded Pat of pallbearers. He stood as did everyone in the room. The judges sat, and the others followed.

Judge Kurosawa glanced first at the other members of the panel, then at the support staff to see that everyone was in there place. Satisfied, he said, "The motion to dismiss the case of *United States et. al. v Pat Preston* has been reviewed by the court and denied. As to the motion that Dr. Preston be released on his own recognizance, that is also denied. The court finds he is a flight risk. This ends the hearing."

Isabella sprang from her seat. "If it please the court, I would like to be heard."

"Denied." Kurosawa and the other judges stood and exited. Pat felt glued in place. He couldn't move. All he could see was the cell he was about to return to. A soft hand touched his arm.

"They haven't won yet." Isabella spoke in whispered tones.

"It sure feels like it," Pat said.

Chapter 24

Flying with Freeman

⟫⟩◆⟨⟪

Isabella's flight back to Rome was not as lonely as the flight to The Hague. The Cessna 525 Citation Jet bounced lightly through the air at 28,000 feet. Below, a low layer of clouds swollen with rain provided a carpet that shielded the scrolling earth from her view. She had been looking out the window for the last fifteen minutes. Larry Jordan and Scott Freeman sat in the rear facing seats of the luxury jet.

"You did an admirable job, Countess." Freeman's tone managed to be firm, fatherly, but still loaded with compassion.

Isabella looked at her guest. "Thank you, but I still feel like my approach was wrong."

"I don't think so," Larry said. "It seems to me that any approach you took would be dismissed. I was surprised they allowed a public hearing."

"They were doing it as a favor to me." Isabella leaned her head back and stared at the ceiling. "I provided orientation for several of the judges, but that connection goes only so far. That may have been my mistake. Maybe one of you should have argued the dismissal. I was hoping they would be more open to me, but now I think that may have been a tactical blunder. Perhaps they feared looking as if they were showing favoritism and so ruled against me."

"Can they be that concerned with their image?" Freeman asked.

She shrugged. "Is it different in the United States?"

Freeman rubbed his chin and glanced at Larry. "Not really. In most cases, judges are not in the public eye. Occasionally, a case comes along that draws a lot of attention and the judge becomes a personality, desired or not. But that's rare. However, I see your point. This case is going global."

Isabella lowered her gaze and looked at the two Americans. "My greatest fear is that the court has already made up its mind. They don't want to offend the US president. The ICJ has had trouble gaining American participation. They have a tendency to walk away when things don't go well. I mean no offense."

"None taken. American law and politics is very complicated and often resembles a car with no breaks speeding down a steep hill."

"With a cliff at the end of the road," Larry added.

"The European Union has similar faults. The ICJ wants America involved in its evolving, world-wide legal system. It's one reason, I think, that there's the new judge from the US. Of course, judges are selected with UN Security Council input and the US is a permanent member. If this were a case where another country brought Dr. Preston to the court, then I think they would have dismissed the case. But since the US is bringing the action, they are reluctant. Of course, I can't know that with a high degree of certainty, but I don't think I'm wrong."

"So we go to trial. We assumed trial would be required from the beginning." Freeman leaned toward the window.

Isabella let her eyes linger on Freeman, seeing evidence of a man pressed down by the weight of his work. "How are you holding up, Mr. Freeman?"

"Scott, please. People in the same foxhole should be on a first name basis."

Isabella nodded in assent. "Of course."

"I'm fine."

"Really? People stuck in the same foxhole should be honest with each other."

Freeman's grin was the first genuine smile she had seen from the man. He glanced at Larry who was doing his best to hide his own grin. "Not much gets by you, does it? Okay, I'm tired. The last two years have been grueling. I assume you've done your research on us."

"As you have done on me."

"True. Then you know we are fighting a war on several fronts. We focus on freedom of speech, equal access, and so much more.

"Some time ago, the IRS stopped by the office and took six years of files." He waved a dismissive hand. "Our records are so clean they won't be able to find anything to complain about. We spend a good bit of money on outside auditors to make sure we are compliant with all current laws governing nonprofits."

"That won't keep them from fabricating problems for us." Larry loosened his safety belt. "My first pro bono case involved a young architectural draftsman being sued for structural problems in a set of condos. The kicker was, his plans were stolen, he was fired, and didn't even know the project had been built. He could not be held liable, but the simple act of saying that costs a great deal of money. I got the case against him dismissed, but he was still out a fair amount of cash. The IRS could do the same to us. They might not win in court, but they could win in the bank."

Freeman nodded. "I won't deny it. We're in a tough spot. Our work depends on the courage and money of donors." He paused. "You know, I've never looked at it this way before, but in a sense, I suppose we are, with this case, fighting for the Alliance's survival." He stared out the window. "A few months ago I had to lay off some of our staff, people who had been with us for twenty years." The pain showed on the man's face. He took a deep breath. "But we are not beat. Not yet. God is still good and firmly on His throne. We fight on. I'll quit when I'm dead and buried."

"I'll be right by your side, Scott." Larry gently elbowed his boss.

The determination of the men bolstered Isabella's flagging spirit. "I don't think the usual trial course is going to work." She reached beneath her seat and removed a tablet computer.

"What would the normal course look like?" Larry asked.

"The first thing the court will do is decide if the entire panel will hear the case. There's no requirement for all fifteen judges to be seated. Sometimes they hear a case with a smaller number." She turned on the tablet and called up a word processing application.

"Would that be to our advantage?" Larry reached for his laptop.

"There's no way to say. We have no say in which judges sit on the panel. Not that any of the judges are on our side."

"How well do you know them, Isabella?" Freeman didn't bother with a computer. In doing background work on the other members of the defense panel, she learned the man was famous for his eidetic memory.

"Each judge serves for nine years and that period is divided in thirds. By that I mean, one-third of the judges are in their last three years; one-third in their middle three; and the remaining third in their first third. I know Yoshiro Kurosawa, Alexzandr Kuchar, and Jinjing Luo. I helped with their orientation six years ago. Kurosawa is a tough man with a giant intellect. Speaks six languages. He is highly respected in his homeland of Japan. If he sits on the panel, and I'm sure he will since it involves the American government, he will keep things on track. He is impatient by nature, but also fair. He is old school Japanese who believes in honor and dignity."

"Does he have a religious bent?" Larry laid his fingers on the keyboard.

"Buddhist, at least ostensibly. I don't think he practices his faith."

"And Kuchar?" Freeman leaned closer to Larry to see what he was typing.

"Alexzandr Kuchar is a sixty-two-year-old Slovakian with a mean streak. He is old enough to remember the old Soviet system. He's a hardliner and no fan of the United States."

"So he might swing our way?" Larry asked.

"No. He's unpredictable and an avowed atheist. Jinjing Luo of China is also an avowed atheist."

"Is there anyone who might be friendly?" Larry asked.

"Not on religious grounds. None of the panel is especially religious, at least as far as I can tell."

She had thought about these questions before. "There are four who might be sympathetic, but I can't be sure. Sir Alan Hodge of the United Kingdom has a grandfather who was an Anglican priest and a sister who is an evangelical missionary. There is a connection between him and Sir Christopher MacKinnon of New Zealand, both are subjects of the UK, both have been knighted, and both have some connection to Christianity, although neither practice the faith. Balduino Pairo of Mexico is a Catholic but probably a nominal one. The problem with him is the Mexicans think the Americans have been treating them unfairly over border issues."

"That problem has been around for two decades," Larry said.

"And it's gotten worse since 2015. We have troops stationed along the border to fight the drug lords," Freeman added.

"We might get some sympathy from Socorro Barroso of Brazil. Truth is, gentlemen, we don't know."

"I'm concerned about Pat's ability to endure the prison. His outburst hurt his chances for a dismissal."

Isabella glanced at Larry. "He wants to protect his family. He feels responsible for their problems. We need a way to speed up the start of trial. Things could stretch out for months, even years."

"We need some out of the box thinking."

The sound of jet engines filled the lull in the conversation.

"I have an idea," Freeman said.

"So do I." Isabella started typing on the tablet pc's virtual keyboard.

Chapter 25

Guarding the Guards

———⋙◆⋘———

"**I** don't want to walk." Pat refused to look at Marcus. Pat had been back in his cell for two hours staring at the walls and doing his best to squash every thought. Thinking made him feel worse. What he couldn't stop were the flashes of the court, the faces of the judges, the smug face of John Knox Smith, and the slumped shoulders of his attorneys. He didn't want to see what emotion Marcus had on his face.

"I'm afraid you have no choice." Marcus spoke softly but there was granite in the words. "Daily exercise is required of all prisoners not in the infirmary."

"I don't care."

"That is obvious." Marcus stood by the closed cell door. "We could spend time debating this, but in the end you will only bring more trouble upon yourself."

"What? Are you going to work me over?"

"Work you . . . No. Of course not. I'm suggesting that you not draw attention to yourself."

"I still don't want to walk."

"Because things did not go as you wish?"

"I think that's a pretty good reason."

"Did you expect it to go differently?"

"I prayed that it would. A lot of good that did."

187

"I see. God didn't read your memo."

"That's a ridiculous statement." Pat slumped back on the bed and closed his eyes. "I don't send memos to God. I asked for this nightmare to end today."

"And it didn't, so now you blame God?"

"Look. I don't expect you to understand."

Marcus cocked his head. "You think I'm too stupid to understand?"

"That's not what I meant. I meant . . . Never mind."

"Oh, I understand now. You think you're the only Christian in the room; maybe in the world. Is that it?"

Pat finally looked at Marcus. "You're telling me you're a believer?"

"I thought our last conversation indicated that."

Pat swung his legs over the edge of the bed. A pounding emanated from the door. Pat ignored it. "You just asked questions about persecution."

"Has any other guard done that?"

"If you're a Christian, then what are you doing here?"

"Where else would I be? You have your ministry, I have mine."

More pounding, followed by a muffled voice.

"Had a ministry," Pat said. "The past tense is the operative factor."

Marcus took a deep breath, then exhaled. "You have a very narrow definition of ministry, Dr. Preston."

The door to the cell opened and three guards entered. Jacques led the way. "Why isn't this prisoner on the exercise track?"

"He's coming." Marcus said.

Jacques sneered at Pat. "I heard you had a bad day in court. That doesn't matter to me. Get up."

Pat didn't move. Jacques motioned to the other two guards who started for Pat. One raised a truncheon and started it down. Pat turned his head to avoid the blow. There was no impact. He heard a grunt and turned to see Marcus holding the guards hand, stopping its downward swing.

"Let him go," Jacques snapped. "If you can't do your job, we will."

"I am doing my job." Marcus shoved the guard back.

Jacques sprung forward, leaving only an inch between himself and Marcus. "Don't make me physically move you." It was comical, in a way. Marcus stood six inches taller and fifty pounds heavier.

"A bold move, Jacques. It takes a special kind of courage to ruin your career with a hasty decision. You must be well off financially."

"I am your supervisor."

"Are you? Have you checked with the warden recently?"

The expression on Jacques face indicated he had. "This man is required to exercise every day."

"And he is. In fact, we were just getting ready to come out. Of course, you'll have to move out of the way. You can do that, can't you? Or do you need help?"

Jacques backed away, hesitated, then marched from the cell. Marcus looked at the other two guards and raised an eyebrow. Both left without a word; one rubbed his wrist where Marcus had held him.

"Pat?"

"Yes?"

"Do a favor for me, please."

"Get up?"

Marcus nodded.

Pat rose. "Thank you."

"It's my job to guard you."

"Thanks for that, too, but I was referring to your effort to keep me centered."

Marcus smiled. "Let's take a walk."

***

Word of the public hearing before the ICJ judges came suddenly to John. He had just returned home after spending the night at Andrea's. The encounter had surprised him. He wasn't sure why he gave in to her advances. He had been firm in his rejection, but somehow she sensed what he refused to allow himself to acknowledge: he was lonely and stressed. He needed the company of someone who understood him and Andrea was the only person on the planet who came close to that requirement.

She was waiting for him at the hotel she had booked in, The Hague, and joined him, Joel Thevis, and the others for dinner, taking notes of the conversation like a good personal assistant should. She had even been smart enough to avoid sitting next to him, then leaving early so she could send an e-mail. John knew she was playing the game like an expert. It was best others not know of the change in their relationship.

John and Thevis spent the next hour in the hotel bar, he drinking Crown Royal Scotch and Joel sucking down a beer. Both suffered from jet lag. Even though it was late in the Netherlands, it was early evening in DC. Since they would be flying home in the morning, it made no sense to adjust their sleep schedule.

"You did a super job, John. I expected a longer argument, but the whole ticking off points worked perfectly."

"I needed to show the judges I valued their time. They didn't want to be there. The whole idea of dismissal was just an exercise. The countess thought she might have more sway with the judges because she worked at the ICJ. That seldom works. Judges will swing the other way to show how impartial they are."

"Well, it worked like a charm."

"Thanks." John ran his finger along the rim of his glass. "I don't think we're home free on this yet, Joel. Did you watch the faces of the judges when the countess was making her argument?"

"Of course. Expressions ran from disgust to deep interest."

"We can't take anything for granted. Everything hinges on this case and it's taking turns I didn't expect."

"You can't predict everything." He sipped his beer.

"True, but we need to stay on the offensive. I want you to work with the team to stall things. I want the case to take as long as possible. Use whatever excuse you can come up with. The world is starting to swing to our way of thinking. I want the judges to be tired of the case."

"I'll get on that. We can have one of our local attorneys quit for some reason, requiring time for his replacement to catch up with the case. I'll come up some other ideas."

"If we can win a few more cases in the US, then that might influence the judges. We need more time to do that."

Thevis raised his glass of beer. "To success."

John lifted his glass. "To proving might makes right."

Chapter 26

The Court of the Media

———⟫◇⟪———

John Knox Smith did something he hadn't done in two years: he took a vacation. Not a long vacation. While others in position often took two to four weeks off to recharge their batteries, John had avoided such extravagances for two reasons: One, DTED was keeping him busy working ten to twelve hours a day and taking work home over the weekends; two, a vacation had meant spending time with his wife who had learned to take nagging to new levels. Now that she was gone and filing for divorce, John could take a week to be by himself.

He was losing sleep and dwelling on the fifty stressors in his life. He refused to take more than a week, but decided the week he did take would be as far away as possible. He needed alone time, something he explained to Andrea over dinner at her place. She agreed and gave him the name of a small hotel in the seaside town of Cambria in California. It was there, in a room with a balcony facing the rolling Pacific, John slept, ate, slept, read, and slept. He needed sleeping pills the first two nights. Something he had started taking with one form of alcohol or another.

He read two novels and the latest Malcolm Gladwell book. He avoided newspapers and news shows, forcing himself to let the world take care of itself. The first few days, he felt like a drug addict going cold turkey. He longed for a copy of the *Wall Street*

Journal, the *New York Times*, and the *Washington Post,* even if it was an e-version. Someone else would have used the time for soul searching, but John didn't believe in souls.

By the end of the vacation, he had relaxed enough to sleep without help. He extended his stay over the weekend, walking a wood walkway that fronted the beach. The sound of the surface, the cry of gulls, the smell of salt, and the leisurely pace of residents and tourist did what chemicals could not. He allowed a few moments to imagine himself living by the ocean, concerned only with choosing between fish tacos and clam chowder for dinner.

Such thoughts never lasted long. By the time he began his journey home, he was missing work. As difficult and tiring the grind, it gave him a sense of purpose and of value. To many, he was the savior of human dignity, dignity of all people of all persuasion of all habits. He was not hampered any more with a belief in God, but if there was a God, he was certain the Deity was proud of him.

He made it back to DC late Sunday night and immediately went to bed. He wanted to arrive at the office early.

The morning came too early on Monday. John's internal clock had reset to West coast time. Six in the morning was three a.m. in California. Still, he rose, showered, dressed, caught a little breakfast at a restaurant near his home and then, after notifying his driver not to pick him up, drove his old Mercedes E320 to the Department of Justice building on 10th and Constitution. The old car was a gift from his father and the only gift he wanted to keep. He passed through security and was welcomed by the guards and other DOJ employees he saw on the first floor. An elevator ride to the fifth floor put him in the compound of DTED offices. He poked his head into Andrea's office. As always, she was in the office before him. The woman was dedicated.

"I'm back."

She looked up and smiled in the way only intimates could. "And sporting a tan I see." He could tell she wanted a hug and a kiss but remained behind her desk. "Did you have a good time?"

"Nah, I did it all wrong. I may have to start the whole thing over next week."

Her smile disappeared. "You may be busy. The Reverend Lynn Barrett is in your office."

"So early?"

Andrea nodded.

"I'm not going to like this, am I?"

"I don't know the details, but she looked grim."

"Swell. Okay, hold my calls."

"Reverend Barrett, what a pleasant surprise." John breezed in, set his briefcase on the desk and removed his coat.

"Did you have a good vacation?"

"After not having a day off for two years, any vacation is good. I got to rest my mind."

"Feeling revived?"

"Yes, but you're going to try and spoil that, aren't you?"

She looked away. "That's not my goal. You'll have to choose your own response. Can we go to the conference room? I have video and other presentation material."

He groaned. "Okay, but I need a cup of coffee."

"Andrea said she put a pot and some cups in the meeting room."

"All right, let's do this."

Lynn Barrett had her computer tied into the wireless in less than a minute. While John poured coffee, Lynn had the wall monitor active. It was a slide with a small paragraph stating that the material was property of the US Government, the Department of Justice. There was a line that read: Prepared by Reverend Lynn Barrett, consultant.

John set a cup of coffee in front of the woman. She doctored the drink with artificial sweetener and powdered creamer. "Unfortunately, the world kept turning while you were away." She paused as if her words bothered her. "I don't mean to imply that things would be different if you hadn't taken a week off. Your presence wouldn't have changed anything."

"Thanks. I think." John sipped his coffee, set it on the conference table and faced the monitor.

"Go ahead, ruin my day."

"Two things, John. You remember our last conversation?"

"About the Pope's decree asking for prayer for Preston. What about it?"

"The prayer encyclical. Well, people are taking it seriously."

"By 'people', you mean Catholic priests."

Lynn seemed bothered by the comment. "John, you have a tendency to belittle things you don't understand."

He turned to face her, feeling his face turn red. "Excuse me?"

"I'm not trying to anger you, John, but it's a trend I've noticed. Maybe you do it because you're so passionate about your mission. I can understand that, but I think your knee jerk reactions are limiting your understanding of the situation."

"Oh, do you? Are you unhappy working for the team?"

She frowned. "Look, John, if you want to fire me for telling you the truth, then do so. When you recruited me, you did so because I agree with your principles, and I can't abide hate-speech directed at anyone. My point is that you're dismissing something significant because you believe your opponents are superstitious morons. Don't make that mistake. Some of the most intelligent people on the planet are religious. I happen to think most of them are taking advantage of others and I'm determined to do something about it."

"I don't want to fire you. I'm just surprised by your sudden defense of the Pope."

"I'm not defending him or the bigoted Roman Church. I'm telling you they are powerful and may be a bigger problem than you realize. To prove my point . . ." She tapped a key and a video began to play. A small digital image at the bottom right of the screen identified it as coming from a New York television station. "This is Saint Patrick's Cathedral, New York City. Last Wednesday, the church leadership held a special prayer vigil for Pat Preston."

"All of those people are waiting to get inside?"

"No. The church holds a little over two thousand people. What you're looking at is the overflow crowd. Estimates run close to five thousand. Factor all the other Roman Catholic churches in and the number reaches seventeen thousand." She tapped a key. "Boston, maybe twenty thousand all total; Chicago, eight thousand; Miami, at least seven thousand; Los Angeles, twelve thousand."

"That's . . . that's a lot."

"Remember, John, this was on a Wednesday during work hours. Another prayer vigil took place yesterday. I have someone tracking down the numbers. They're larger. It also appears Eastern Orthodox, Greek Orthodox, and others are doing the same. It's spreading from the Catholics to other high church denominations."

"It's like an infection."

"John!"

"I know, I know, I tend to belittle. Okay, so what. Prayer can't hurt us."

"Let me finish. This isn't a one week thing. I have word that several dioceses are planning vigils each week." She tapped the keys again. "This is a medley of video news from around the world. The same thing is happening in Rome, London, Paris, you name it, tens of thousands of Catholics have taken the Pope's encyclical to heart in a way I've never seen before. Soon the evangelicals will be onboard."

"I thought they hated the Catholics. Preston preached against them."

"Preston taught about the differences in their doctrine. It's not quite the same thing. Look at this." The image of a letter appeared on screen. "Recognize the signature?"

"Scott Freeman, the head of the Alliance." He swore. "That man really gets under my skin."

"This letter is an appeal—"

"He's good at raising money, although I hear they're having financial troubles. Laid a bunch of people off."

"He's not asking for money. Maybe because he thinks the post office will file charges under the new law governing raising money for hate-speech. He's asking his people—and he has a huge mailing list—to do two things: pray for Preston and freedom of speech, but that's not the worst of it. He's asking them to write about how Christ has changed their lives and send the letter to the—"

"ICJ!" John was on his feet. "He's asking them to interfere with the court!"

"No, John, he's not. I have a copy of the letter you can read at your leisure. When you do, you will see that all he's doing is asking a few million people to tell the justices why Jesus is important to them, how He's changed their lives."

"That's still trying to influence the court."

"So what? I'm no lawyer, but isn't that what attorneys do? Freeman's letter encourages the letter writers to be polite and to avoid sermons. 'Just tell them why your faith matters to you.' That was his line. No legal arguments. No rants. No name calling. No condemnation, just a testimony—to use their terminology."

"I doubt the judges will do any more than order the letters be destroyed."

"I hope you're right, because this isn't going to go away. Preston's case has brought Christian groups closer together. I have it on good authority that not only did Freeman send this to his massive database, but other nonprofit CEOs sent it to theirs. It numbers in the tens of millions."

John sat again. "Tell me this will blow over. How long can they keep this up?"

"They can make this battle last for a very long time and with the Pope onboard, it can only grow. Other religious leaders will do the same."

"Meaning?"

"Meaning that what started out as a single case to make a point has just become a worldwide phenomenon."

Lynn ended her presentation. "You're our leader, John. The team is going to look to you for direction. You need to think long and hard about the next few steps."

"You're the one who understands these people. I know, I know— you're not one of them, but you were part of their ranks before your enlightenment. What should I expect?"

She began to close down her computer. "One of two things will happen. It will run its course in one or two weeks. The Christian response will lead the news cycle for a couple of days, then the media and the viewers and readers will lose interest. It is, after all, an intellectual battle and the population prefers something more graphic, like crime, war, and corruption. My guess is— you know what?" She pointed at the conference speaker in the middle of the table. "May I?"

"Of course."

Lynn stood and hit the intercom button. Andrea answered. "Yes?"

"Andrea, this is Pastor Lynn. Has Mr. Knox received any media requests while he was gone?"

"Yes. About a dozen. I was going to meet with him after you left."

"Thank you, Andrea." Lynn switched off the device. "You know the media better than I, John, but it's been a slow news week, which means the talking heads are going to want info. It doesn't take much research to tie you to Preston."

"I've done these interviews before. I know how to handle them."

"Yes, you're very skilled with the press, but this time you're not talking about legal principles and general principles of tolerance. Preston will be—scratch that—Preston *is* the face of the opposition. Now, if things go our way, this will all die down quickly. It's up to you whether you talk to the media or not. My advice is to avoid it or do very little. Everything you say will be scrutinized and perhaps become fodder for the opposition. Especially if you lose your temper."

John knew she was talking about a blowout he had on a television debate not long after the new tolerance laws went into effect and arrests were being made. He had done his best to forget the event. "And the second thing that could happen?"

"Ground swell, John, ground swell. It won't be pretty. The thing to remember is that Christians are connected to each other, even across denominational lines. Guys like Freeman can stoke these fires. He has already called in favors from other large Christian ministries. Don't forget, some of these organizations still pull in millions, despite our best efforts to curtail that."

"It's criminal."

"Yes, but never say that in public, John. I make my living from the contributions of my parishioners. It's how honest clergy pay for our building and our social ministries. Contributions made to the charities and Christian causes are part of our country's history; part of our society's fabric."

"I still think it's wrong."

Lynn swore like a longshoreman stunning John. "You're not listening to me. It doesn't matter if *you* don't like it. People will fight and die for three things. Are you listening, John? Three things: family, faith, and freedom. The opposition is setting this up so it looks like we're persecuting Preston as the poster-child for these three concepts. Read Freeman's letter. He calls Preston a martyr for the faith, he mentions the danger and affliction that have come upon Preston's family—even calls the children by name; and highlights how Preston has lost his freedom, even the freedom to be tried by a jury of his peers."

She paced a few steps. "Here's what I would do if I were Freeman: I would keep the fires stoked. I would hammer away on the three pillars important to American Christians, their faith, freedom, family. It's 2018. . . anyone with a computer or cell phone can communicate with the world. You saw how the Internet, Twitter, and other social media brought the masses out in Egypt and other countries. Governments changed one-hundred-forty characters at a time. That was back in 2011. It's even easier now."

"You're depressing me, Lynn." John tried to sound light-hearted.

She ignored the comment. "If I were the Pope, I'd mention Preston by name during his weekly address at Saint Peter's square. I might even visit Preston in The Hague again, this time with the press. Wow, would that ever play!"

"That seems like a political move to me—"

"To many Christians, there is no difference between their political views and the spiritual ones. There should be, but most don't agree with me. Call it political if you want, but naming it won't change it. And, of course, there are the fringe groups."

"Fringe groups?"

She stopped and stared at the carpet as if her next words were stitched into the pile. "There's no gentle way of putting this, John, but there are less than mentally stable people who will take up the cause. They're really not part of historical Christianity, but they use the name, the same way white supremacists claimed to be Christian. I don't know a denomination in the world that would associate with them, but nonetheless, the group takes the label."

"Are you saying there might be violence directed at us?"

"Yes, that's what I'm saying. The reverse is true; those who hate Christians might become violent against Catholics because of the Pope's encyclical or against Baptists because Preston was a Baptist preacher. It's happened before."

"Would Christians do that?"

"I wouldn't classify them as Christians, and I have the most liberal definition of Christian you'll ever encounter. They are unbalanced people who think they're doing God a favor by killing someone. It's the difference between the Christian who lobbies against abortion and the nut job who breaks into a clinic and kills the doctors and staff."

"I like your first scenario better."

"Me too, but I'm afraid the second one may happen."

"So Freeman and the others are stirring up people to violence."

Lynn looked exasperated. "No, John, they're not. I don't want to defend these morons, but they do have a strong moral core that would keep them from doing such things. They will bring their influence to bear but not violence. The fringe groups can't tell the difference." She looked at John and he could see tears rising. "Frankly, I'm frightened. I'm really scared."

"We'll be fine, Lynn. We knew this would be difficult."

"I'm not talking about *we*; I'm talking about *me*."

Chapter 27

A Reporter Gets It

$\Longrightarrow\!\!\!\Diamond\!\!\!\Longleftarrow$

S tephen Sinclair leaned back in a well-worn desk chair at the *Los Angeles Times*, donned a pair of headphones and let his computer read the article he had just written, a practice he learned at San Diego State University where he studied journalism.

Catholics and Protestants Hand in Hand Over Freedom of Speech

Although well known in his hometown of Nashville, the Reverend Dr. Preston was little known except to a few thousand zealous evangelicals who attended his mega-church, and those who listened to his sermons and Bible studies over the radio, television or Internet. While it might seem tens of thousands of followers are a lot, it is a drop in the proverbial bucket compared to the millions who now know the Baptist preacher's name.

In what may be one of the great ironies of contemporary Christianity, Preston was not drawn into the limelight by his sermons or by his fellow Baptists, but by Pope John Paul Benedict I who has undertaken the cause of the beleaguered pastor. Two weeks ago, the pontiff issued a papal encyclical—a letter to cardinals, bishops, priests, and deacons of the Roman Catholic Church— calling upon the billion plus members to daily lift up Dr. Preston in prayer. The Catholic Church has come to the aid of a Protestant.

Preston is one of the first clergymen tried under the 2014 Respect for Diversity and Tolerance Act. Since the implementation of the law, scores of prosecutions have been brought against organizations deemed hateful in their actions and speech. Many of the early targets were obvious: racial hate groups, but quickly expanded to include charges leveled against those who discriminate in word and deed against sexual preference and lifestyle. At first, arrests were limited to obvious crimes of assault and intimidation, acts already illegal under decades old laws.

Unexpected to many was the shift to the prosecution—what some call persecution—of any organization that taught the sinfulness of homosexuality, transgendered persons, and organizations that claimed to be the exclusive track to heaven.

This made the Christian church a prime target for the Department of Justice in general and the Diversity and Tolerance Enforcement Division in particular. Several churches and many ministries have been forced to close their doors rather than face court for their beliefs. Dr. Preston refused to back down from what he considered a biblical mandate in his ministry and this led to his arrest. In what can only be described as an overreaction by the DOJ, Preston has been kept confined without bail. His church has dismissed him.

Such loss might seem enough for most, but the DTED team, led by Assistant Attorney General John Knox Smith, has chosen to make an example of the preacher. Dr. Preston is now kept in a solitary confinement prison in The Hague in the Netherlands, to be tried by the International Court of Justice in its expanded role to include hate speech crimes.

Smith has not responded to our requests for an interview. Attempts to gain access to Preston have been thwarted by prison officials. When asked why Preston was moved out of the country, Professor Ed Bateman of UCLA School of Law said, "The United States has lagged behind European countries in the granting of full rights to outlier groups. By taking this case to the international stage, the DOJ and the executive branch of the government are signaling the world that we take individual liberty as seriously as any other country."

Dean Ford of the University of San Diego Law School adds, "There has long been a movement toward a world court that can help unify diverse laws into a single canon. This is one very significant step."

While some see such a move as a benefit to the world, others see it as undermining the principles upon which our country was founded. Scott Freeman is the CEO of the Alliance, a Christian legal ministry that provides legal help for people like Preston. In a phone interview, Freeman said, "Every country has a unique set of events in their founding that influence their laws. England and the United States share many of the same principles of law, but their origins are different. The United States was founded on the idea that the government could not interfere with the free expression of religion and no church could control activities of the government. The first amendment is clear on the matter. Every citizen is free to exercise religion, a freedom of expression and speech, access to a free press and the right to peaceable assembly. The tolerance law of 2014 stripped away the First Amendment."

Freeman and his organization is part of an international defense team trying to free Preston.

It seems an odd assemblage: the Pope, shepherd of over a billion people, a jailed Baptist, and a former DOJ attorney. Odd as the pairing is, it has ignited a flurry of activity, first in the US and now we're receiving reports that outrage has spread to other countries. Although the numbers overseas seemed to be much smaller, something that can be attributed to the less religious society of the older countries, it is nonetheless worthy of note.

What will come of all this remains to be seen. A date for trial has not been set, according to a spokeswoman for the International Court of Justice. Freeman and his team believe the case is being pushed back because the case against Preston cannot be won even in an international setting. The DOJ has remained silent on that accusation, responding by e-mail with the terse, "Such a claim is ludicrous. The case against Dr. Preston is well-founded."

Only time will tell. While this paper has in the past been favorably disposed to err on behalf of the current administration, on this *one subject we must disagree. We ask, "At what point did we in the United States lose our ability to try our own cases?"*

Stephen Sinclair, Religion Editor

Sinclair was satisfied. He hit the send button.
The article appeared in the next day's paper.

***

The next morning, John Knox Smith sat at his desk reading clippings from newspapers, online news organizations, and blogs. He opened a copy of the *Los Angeles Times* and read an editorial by Stephen Sinclair When done, he carefully cut the article from the broadsheet, then read it again. With disturbing slowness and meticulous attention, he began to tear the article into narrow strips, listening to the sound of the paper as its fibers gave way to the gentle assault.

At the foot of his desk rested piles of similarly torn articles.

Chapter 28

Disquiet in the Palace of Peace

———⋙◆⋘———

"**M**ore?" Sir Alan Hodge looked at the sack of mail beside his desk.

His assistant, Janneka Mulder, was removing stacks of letters and putting them in neat piles on a table she had brought in when the missives first began to arrive. In her late forties, Janneka was as patient as the long Nordic summer days. Her reddish-brown hair was short, just touching the tops of her ears. A pair of stylish plastic-rimmed glasses hung low on her narrow nose.

"Da, this may be the biggest batch yet."

"How many so far?"

"Today or all total?"

"All of them." He moved to his desk where several small stacks of letters remained from last night's reading and set down his attaché case. Janneka had already turned on the digital player and the gentle sound of Sergei Rachmaninoff playing Nocturne Opus 9, Number 2 in E Flat filled the spacious chamber.

"All told, those addressed to you come to slightly over one thousand. Those sent over from the justices who don't want to read the material adds another eight hundred or so—so far."

"I don't like the sound of that."

"Most of the other judges are pushing their work off on to you. Somehow, they found out you were reading the letters instead of sending them to storage. In hindsight, a tactical mistake."

"I should have kept that secret." He looked around. "I'll never be able to read all of this. It's a lifetime's work. I hope these people aren't expecting replies."

"And you'd be just the chap to give answering every letter a go."

Alan looked up to see Christopher MacKinnon, although sight wasn't necessary; the man's mixture of New Zealand and Scottish accent made him easy to recognize even in a black out. Born to Scottish parents while they served in New Zealand, the man had his very own accent. "I wouldn't put any money on that, Sir Christopher."

The lanky man entered the office, his blue suit hanging limply on a near skeletal frame. Sixty-seven years of life had wrung out a lot of the man's physical strength, but had left his mind untouched. "Good morning, Sir Alan, Ms. Mulder." It was a game the men played. Every encounter required each man to use the honorific "Sir" once, after that, address was informal. "Might I have a moment?"

"Certainly." Alan looked at Janneka. "We can sort through some of this later. See if you can recruit some help from administration. Maybe we can get a few temporary clerks. It's a week's worth of work just opening the bloody things."

"Yes, sir. Tea for you and Sir Christopher?"

"Please." Alan motioned for Christopher to move to the seating area where a sofa and two wingback chairs waited. They chatted for a few moments, waiting for Janneka to bring a pot of Earl Grey and two cups. She set the tray on a mahogany coffee table and poured. Each man took a cup and saucer.

"So tell me. Chris, are you one of the judges who decided to share your rush of mail with me?"

"No, but thank you for offering. I'll have it sent right over."

"Clever, but you just hang on to them. I've more than I can handle."

"Pity. I'm afraid the fire warden will close my office down, should he learn how much combustible material surrounds my desk."

Alan chuckled. "It's a good thing you don't smoke. You could send the whole place up in flames."

"I've read a handful of the letters. There are a few people who would like to see that happen."

"I've discovered a few of those, but not as many as I expected. Most have been civil, although I find the constant mention of praying for me a tad annoying."

Chris nodded. "It does come across as condescending, doesn't it? They must think us base sinners."

"I don't think so. I believe they mean well. At least they're not praying against us."

"As far as you know."

That made Alan laugh. "True. So true. It wouldn't be the first time."

"May I ask why you're taking any time at all to read these things? Seems a complete waste of time. These people can make no legal arguments. They are simply trying to sway the court with their passion. I don't need to tell you how upset some of the others are." Christopher had a way of saying "others" that made Alan think it should be capitalized.

"I've heard from a few of them. I thought Dana would burst her spleen, not that we would be able to tell the difference. She always looks emotionally constipated."

"I can't argue with that, but I do understand the anger. Freeman and his cronies are making life difficult for us and that can't help his case."

Alan pushed out a doubtful lip. "I don't agree, Chris. In some ways, I think of it as a compliment." He saw Chris' eyebrow shoot up. "Most of the letters I've read have not called our position and authority into question. Oh to be sure, there is some vitriol present in a few, but not what I expected. I had Janneka run down the letter Freeman and the Alliance sent to its supporters. He made it clear they were just to send messages about how faith has affected them and nothing more. Ninety percent of what I've read has remained true to that."

"So what? Freeman only angered the court against him."

"Perhaps, but he has made one thing clear to me: This case is being tried in the global eye, not just our little legal world."

"That should not influence us, Alan."

"Of course not, and it won't. Freeman is too sharp an attorney to expect otherwise." He sipped his tea; it was hot and strong, just the way he liked it. "He must have studied us, and he has the countess on his side. Who knows more about this court than the countess? I ask you, who? I'm sure she coached him about our personalities and commitments."

"Meaning?"

"Meaning, my good friend, that Freeman knows that no matter how different our personalities, no matter how liberal our politics, this court does service to the law first and opinion second. He's counting on us to be what we already are, dedicated jurists."

"You think quite highly of this man."

Alan's shoulder's rose in a shrug. "I'm not sure I'd put it that way. I don't know him. First I saw of him was in court unless you count seeing his name on the court documents. Then I did some research. Did you know he tried many cases before the US Supreme Court? Did you know he won all but one case? Did you know he worked for the organization that now opposes him?"

"The Department of Justice?"

"The very same. He knows his way around American law and was wise enough to surrender the case lead to Countess Isabella when the case was brought before us."

"I can't share your admiration, Alan. To me and to the others, he is a thorn in our britches."

"Oh, I quite agree, and we haven't seen the last of him. My point is this: Let's not underestimate him or the countess—"

"Or the Pope."

"I still can't figure that one out. I don't know what the Pope hopes to gain by supporting a man who isn't even Catholic. I bet he has more people bending his ear than he cares for."

"I came here for another reason, Alan. I suppose you've guessed that."

"I suspected it. I bet I can even guess."

"Have at it."

"Some of the others have sent you to me because they want to know if my sister's work will have any bearing on my thinking. Am I right?"

"Close enough to call it right. Your sister is a missionary of sorts, true?"

"Yes. She works in the East End mostly. A few other places in London. She's a nurse. Works in the slums."

"It must be difficult work."

"I assume so. I've never been to her clinic. Why bring up my sister?"

"You are the only sitting member with a strong connection to any kind of Christian church. Some wonder if you should recuse yourself."

"What? Recuse myself, you say? What utter nonsense!" The tea cup rattled in the saucer he held. "Who says that? Let them come to me and tell me that to my face. Recuse myself indeed. Why? Because I share a genetic link with someone who is connected to the Church of England? What a load of . . . Who said that?"

"Easy, friend. I did not come to upset you, but I didn't want you to be blindsided, should it come up in chambers."

"We haven't even heard the case and they want to know my judgment of its merits?"

"I'm not one of them, Alan. I'm here as a friend."

Alan calmed. "Yes, of course. I know. Let's just leave my sister out of this, shall we?"

"That is fine by me." Christopher set his cup down and rose. "You sure you don't want me to send my share of the letters over to you? You could paper your walls with them. Come to think of it, you could paper all of Buckingham Palace."

Alan stood and laughed, but the chortle was an attempt at courtesy. Anger still roiled in him.

After Christopher left, Alan sat at his desk and opened another letter.

Chapter 29

A Favor Asked of the Fisherman

⟫•◈•⟪

"**I**'m nervous," Fredrico said. It had taken him an hour to choose which of his many suits to wear. When meeting the Pope, does one wear his best suit or does that appear ostentatious? Does one wear a cheaper suit in order to appear more humble? Isabella had watched him. He was more entertaining than television.

"Don't be. You look fine."

"I'm not worried about how I look I *am* worried I'll fall flat on my face, or shake the man's hand too hard, or start drooling, or . . ."

Isabella placed a hand on her husband's knee just as the car pulled into Vatican City. The driver was part of the Vatican staff and drove through the gates of the tiny city like a man well familiar with every turn. "You rub shoulders with billionaires on a daily basis. You have a den full of photos taken of you with heads of state. I've never know you to be this nervous."

"Those were just people, Izzy. He is the Pope. It's a sin not to be nervous."

"Is it? I wasn't aware."

"If it's not, it should be." He looked around. "It's fine that you've met him many times, but this is my first." He wiped his palms on his pants legs.

"Stop that. You'll ruin your suit."

"Can I wipe them on your outfit?"

"You are funny when you're scared." She straightened her black suit coat and picked a piece of lint from her calf-length black skirt.

"Did you tell me where we're meeting? I don't recall you telling me where we're meeting him. Where are we meeting?"

"Fredrico, my dear? You're drooling."

"I am not." He drew a hand across his mouth.

"This is an informal meeting, not an audience. We are meeting for a stroll in the Vatican Gardens."

"Sounds lovely. Stroll? Really? The Pope strolls."

"So long a Catholic and still so misguided. Shall I tell you what to expect?" The car moved slowly as if the driver were giving the couple time to converse. "We are meeting outside to avoid Vatican gossip and so the Holy Father can speak freely."

"It's just going to be the three of us?"

"No. The Pope is always accompanied except in the privacy of his chambers. You are here so as to avoid any suggestion of impropriety. There will be at least one other person with the Holy Father, Monsignor Ramone Erik. He is like the Pope's chief-of-staff. His Holiness may have others there."

"It must be horrible to so seldom be alone."

Fredrico's sensitivity was one of the many things she loved about the man. "So many think he lives in luxury, and in many ways he does, but it comes with a great price."

Isabella had been to the expansive garden several times, taking in the verdant surroundings: perpetually green lawns that spread over acres, full grown trees lining one side of the sinuous walkway, and statues which in their stillness told unforgettable stories, all spread over fifty-seven acres. She had been most taken with the recently erected statue of sixteenth century scientist Galileo.

The driver pulled along one of the paths, stopped and opened the back doors. Isabella and Fredrico exited. They then followed the short, olive skinned driver down one of the paths past a patch of forest. He led them to a large olive tree under which five seats had been set. Benedict and two men sat in the shade, chatting like old buddies on a picnic.

The moment they reached the seating area, the driver gave a small bow and excused himself. Panic flooded Isabella. She bowed before Benedict as did Fredrico. "My apologies, Holy Father. I did not realize we were late. I hope we have not kept you waiting long."

He grinned and the sun seemed to brighten. "You are not, my child. We are early. God has given us a beautiful day. You know Monsignor Ramone Erik. Let me introduce a very old friend and confidant: Cardinal Michael Mahoney. It was he, you'll recall, that read the encyclical. I believe he did a masterful job, no?"

"Yes, Your Holiness. May I present my husband, Fredrico?"

"Please sit," Benedict said. "We were just chatting about Dr. Preston. You may not know this, but my good friend here thinks I have lost my senses. Too much time in the African sun." He grinned again.

Isabella noticed Benedict had chosen to speak in the first person. The conversation would be casual, something she appreciated.

"Now, Holy Father, we said no such thing." The man's brogue played lightly on Isabella's ear. "Well, at least we didn't blame the African sun." Mahoney spoke as a longtime friend, managing to keep in mind the dignity of the office his friend occupied and familiarity of decades of loyal friendship. The monsignor looked to the ground as if the comment embarrassed him.

Two men appeared as if from nowhere, one carrying a tray of lemonade and the other a small folding table. They set up the table, poured a glass for each person, then disappeared as quickly as they arrived. Isabella watched them work their way up the path. That's when she noticed men spaced evenly around the area. Security was needed, even for a visit in the garden.

Benedict took a sip and savored it as if the drink were a fine wine. He was enjoying his time in the outdoors. The Vatican Gardens had existed for four centuries, a refuge for the men who were chained to daily responsibilities and to the pressures of an ever changing world. He raised his glass and motioned to the large olive tree. "Fredrico, do you know about this tree?"

It took three tries for Fredrico to utter, "No, sir, —Holy Father."

"It was a gift to the Church from the Nation of Israel. The olive tree is very symbolic in the world but especially to Christians. It was among such trees that our Lord suffered in the Garden of Gethsemane. Do you know that Gethsemane means 'olive press'?"

"Yes, Your Holiness. I have read the passage many times. It was where Jesus sweat great drops of blood in His agony before going to the cross."

"It is also where Peter cut off the ear of a servant and where Our Lord healed the man." Erik said.

"Do you think my support of Dr. Preston was an act as rash as Peter's, Monsignor?"

The priest seemed to shrink a size. "I meant no criticism, Your Holiness."

Benedict turned his eyes back to the tree. In its branches, shielded behind the canopy of leaves, a pair of birds quarreled and fluttered. "What happened to our Lord after that incident, Monsignor?"

"A mob of Jewish religious leaders, their servants, and a cohort of Roman guards arrested the Savior."

"How large a group do you estimate that to be?" the pontiff asked.

"The Scriptures do not tell us exactly, but a Roman cohort was six hundred men. We must add to that the religious leaders and their servants. It is likely there were others there so . . . eight hundred persons, maybe more."

Benedict nodded, his gaze distant, perhaps looking through time and seeing the brutal arrest of the One he had served all his life. It must have seemed as if the world had turned against Him who knew no sin and His followers." He paused. "I felt that fear as a boy hiding in a tree in Nigeria. I could do nothing then. I was too young, too frightened, too weak." He brought his gaze back to the present. "I am older but not so weak; not so impotent."

The others sat in silence. While the trauma that shaped the boy who would be Pope was well known, less known was the way the event motivated his decisions. He looked at Isabella. "Dr. Preston must feel the world has come to him with torches and weapons."

"He does. You know of the incident with his family? The threats?"

"Yes, I have read your memos with interest. I was just telling the others of the concern. Has our person arrived on scene?"

"Yes. She is in place and the family is fine."

He looked into his glass as if expecting information to rise to the top of the fluid. "And the case in The Hague. Does it go well?"

"No, Your Holiness. I made a formal motion for dismissal, followed by an appeal for release on personal recognizance but both were denied." Benedict was already aware of this. She sent communiqués immediately following the trial. She guessed the questions were for the benefit of Cardinal Mahoney and Monsignor Erik.

"I assume the news was discouraging to Dr. Preston."

"Very much so. He is better now."

"Perhaps another visit would help."

"Your Holiness, please." Erik set his drink on the table. "I believe that to be ill advised."

"My predecessor, John Paul II, visited Mehmet Ali Agca in prison."

"With all due respect, Your Holiness, His Holiness John Paul was setting an example about forgiveness by visiting the man who almost killed him with a gunshot."

"I wish to set an example, too. The world needs to know that Dr. Preston represents freedom of public profession of faith for all people, Catholic and Protestant alike."

"If I may, Holy Father," Isabella said. "Such a visit might make matters most difficult for Dr. Preston. While I am sure he would love to receive any grace you can offer him, the guards are not so happy about such things. They take the matter out on poor Dr. Preston."

"I see." He shook his head. "It is an evil world we labor in."

"The just have always suffered at the hands of the unjust," Mahoney said. "'Tis a sadness in the heart."

"I do have something the Holy Father can do." Isabella's words made Erik fidget.

"I am eager to hear it."

Isabella shifted to the edge of her seat and took a deep breath. She was having trouble mustering the courage. To buy time, she set her glass down on the table. "I know this is . . . unprecedented, but I must ask."

Benedict made a slight circling motion with his hand, encouraging her to speak.

She did.

Mahoney dropped his lemonade, Erik sputtered. Benedict said, "I agree. You will guide me?"

"Yes, Holy Father."

Erik popped to his feet. "Your Holiness, we should consider this first. We must consult with others. We should. . . should pray."

Benedict looked up at the man with sadness. "This comes as no surprise to me, Monsignor, and I have already consulted with God. I will do it."

Erik stood as unmoving as some of the statues in the garden, and he looked as white.

Chapter 30

The Lifted Up

⬛▻◆◅⬛

"Y ou seem down again, Dr. Preston." Marcus Aster, dressed in a uniform that never seemed to wrinkle, handed him a tray that held a carton of cold milk and two large cookies.

"What's this?"

"You've never seen milk and cookies?"

"I've never had anyone bring me cookies and milk, not since kindergarten anyway. This place is no kindergarten."

"I can take them away."

Pat took the tray. "It would be rude of me to turn them down." He studied the treasure. "I haven't had a treat since they tossed me in here; just the three meals each day. Always the same amount."

"They want to keep you healthy."

He bit into the cookie, the sweetness aroused comatose taste buds. "Oh, man, that's good." He sipped the milk from a waxed carton. It came up the straw, silky, smooth, soothing. "I never thought I'd see the day when something so simple would make me feel like I found a gold mine."

"The greatest riches are in the simple things. The most valuable thing in the world is water to a man dying of thirst. Humans always want what they can't have."

Pat took another bite and chewed it slowly, savoring even the crumbs on his lips. "How did you arrange this? It's not feeding time at the zoo."

"I have my ways." Marcus moved to the opposite side of the cell and leaned against the wall. Watching Pat eat made him smile.

"How did you know I was feeling down?" He looked at the camera, indicating his awareness of the never blinking eye.

"The way you lay on your bed. "In your better moments, you face away from the wall; when you're depressed, you face the wall."

"I'm always depressed."

"Excuse me: When you're less depressed, you face the cell and not the wall. In your more settled moments, you read your New Testament and C.S. Lewis compilation."

"They teach you to read body language in the prison guard school?"

"Such is the way with men. Highs are followed by lows. Men in your situation face the extremes of emotion: up one moment; in tears the next. Same is true for those told of a terminal illness."

Pat finished the first cookie. "That would be far better. I don't fear death."

"Of course you do. You're meant to."

"Not me. Death is freedom. I've started praying for it."

"How about the death of someone you love? Would you rejoice in their new freedom?"

Pat froze mid bite. "What? Is that a threat? You're threatening my family?"

"Don't be silly, Dr. Preston. Have I done anything to make you think I'm your enemy? I'm just saying you're not as comfortable with the idea of death as you think, nor should you be."

Pat started to get up, but Marcus waved him down. "Stay on your bed. The others are a little nervous about you these days. They're looking for an excuse to punish you."

He settled back on the thin mattress.

"You know, they listen into everything we say."

Marcus shrugged in a way Pat thought odd. "I am saying nothing or doing nothing against the rules."

"The cookies and milk might be pushing it."

Another awkward shrug, this one better than the last.

"May I ask a question?"

"Of course."

"You often refer to your fellow guards as 'they' not 'us' or 'we.' Why is that?"

"I hadn't noticed."

Pat set the tray on the bed. "It is almost like you consider yourself apart from them. They're of one tribe, you're of another."

"We do the same work, we just have different motivations."

"Such as?"

The guard pushed off the wall and began to pace. "For some, it is a job. They work here because it is either the only job they could get, or they need the benefit package, or because some are insecure and here they can have power over people."

"But not you."

"I choose to work here. My compulsion is different than most."

"Your compulsion, eh? And what might that be?"

"It is where I'm needed. Men like you need someone like me to remind them that the world is not as dark as they imagine it."

"It looks pretty dark from inside this cell."

"I didn't say it wasn't dark, just not as dark as you assume it to be."

"Spoken like a free man." Depression began to soak his soul again. "I can't imagine things being worse."

Marcus looked disappointed. "Are you finished with the cookies?"

"Yes. Thank you. Look, I know you mean well, and appreciate being visited by a guard who doesn't want to punch me, but the bottom line remains this: You'll walk out that door in a few minutes, but I won't."

Picking up the tray, Marcus started for the door. He paused, then turned. "Sometimes, Dr. Preston, the best thing a man can do is stop feeling and start thinking."

Before Marcus reached the door, it opened. Two guards entered, both ignored Marcus.

"Come on, Preston. Your lawyer wants to talk to you."

"She's here?"

"No. Video conference room. Let's go."

Pat rose and wiped the crumbs off his fingers. When he looked up, Marcus was gone. That saddened him.

***

The video conference room was next to the client conference room where Pat had met Pope Benedict and Isabella for the first time. The fact that he had been brought to this room instead of one of the small cubicles that contained only one chair, a shelf with a flat screen computer monitor on it shielded by a thick piece of plastic told Pat that his attorney was not in town.

"Hello, counselor."

"How are you, Dr. Preston?" Her voice sounded tinny. For a state-of-the-art facility, such things as comfortable communication was beyond them, that or it was just one more tiny torture for the inmates.

"I am healthy." He had ceased saying he was well.

"And your attitude?"

"Just peachy."

She frowned into the camera, not at him, he knew, but at what he was being forced to go through. More than once, she had expressed genuine sorrow.

"As your attorney, allow me to remind you we are on an open electronic system. What you say is probably being recorded. Understood?"

"Yes. Every conversation in this place is recorded. I understand."

"I made another motion, this time to have you released to me. My husband and I have a rented home in The Hague. I had hoped they would put you under house arrest where you could be electronically monitored."

"You mean with me wearing one of those electronic ankle bracelets?"

"Yes. You wouldn't be able to leave the house, but you would be more comfortable."

"It's a wonderful thought, but after the motion to dismiss and the one to release me on my own recognizance failed, there was no chance that would go through."

"I had to try for several reasons. First, John Knox Smith had already left for the United States, leaving the two local attorneys to handle things until the trial. It was a small hope, but I felt it worth a try. I also wanted to test the court again. I want to keep this case in front of them. I have become a nuisance. So have Scott Freeman and Larry Jordan. They've been busy."

"Doing what?"

She explained the letter writing campaign. "Some of my friends in the court tell me there's been a steady flow of letters from the United States and parts of Europe. So much so, they've had to designate a room in the Peace Palace just to hold all the letters."

"Letters, not e-mail?"

"That was the beauty of the idea, Pat. E-mail can be deleted quickly. Social media can be ignored, but letters are physical things. I know they can throw away the letters, but we've made sure the media is aware of the situation. Many reporters have broadcast stories about it. This means the judges can't just burn the correspondence."

"Do you think they'll read them?"

"Probably not. Maybe some will, but that's not the point. The point is that the world is now more aware of the situation and watching what the court is doing. This has led to something positive: your case has been moved up."

Pat's brain tried to process the statement. "Moved up? You mean we're going to court sooner than expected?"

"That's exactly what I mean. I think we've annoyed them into pushing us up in the calendar. My guess is they want to be free of us."

Pat just sat there.

"This is a good thing, Pat. These things can take two years. It looks like we'll be in court in two weeks."

He blinked and his vision blurred. "Things are not as bad as a man imagines." He whispered the words.

"Excuse me?"

"Just something someone said to me recently." He leaned closer to the camera in the monitor.

"What should I do?"

"Keep praying, Pat. We all are. Just keep praying."

Chapter 31

Letters, Letters

―――◇――――

S ir Alan Hodge settled onto the balcony of his room at Hotel Akersloot. When court business didn't demand his presence, Hodge preferred to escape the city and drive up the A9 to the hotel where he maintained a "get away" room, a place where he could feel like he had escaped the pressures of international law. Except this time he brought work: a briefcase full of letters, most from the United States. He ate a hearty dinner, rested, took a swim in the Olympic size indoor pool, then moved to the brown-tiled balcony.

Local farms sweetened the air and in the distance, through the evening's dimming light, he saw the slowly moving arms of a classic windmill. Hodge had often wondered if he had more farmer in him than solicitor. His grandfather had tilled the land near Yorkshire Dales. In his most stressful moments, Hodge thought of the summers he spent there, the smell of crops, the sounds of animals, the noises of farm equipment, the taste of fried eggs and sausage. Farming was a challenging life, especially in the difficult economy sweeping Europe again, for the second time in a decade. Still, it was a simple life; a satisfying life.

He opened a bottle of cognac, poured a small amount into a snifter and returned to the porch. A cool and gentle breeze graced his brow. Setting the snifter down, he pulled one of the letters from the case and glanced at the address: Omaha, Nebraska.

To whom it may concern,

You should be ashamed of locking up a good man like Dr. Pat Presley. How could you jail a woman of God?

Anonymous.

Hodge looked at the envelope again; the author's name and address were clearly printed in the upper left corner. "Pat Presley? Woman of God? Moron. At least you spelled *anonymous* correctly." He crammed the letter back into the envelope and opened another. This one was from Portland, Oregon. It was written in a woman's hand.

Greetings,

I hope this letter finds you well. I am writing to share with the court the importance of my faith. Although I have several earned graduate degrees and teach at the university level, I wish to share from the heart.

In our day, Christians have fallen on hard times. It is true that some, by their actions, have brought it on themselves and on the rest of us. I suppose this is because people are people, none perfect. I certainly know of my own imperfections.

I came to faith in an unusual way, not under a preacher's sermon, or from the example of godly parents. My father was an atheist and my mother just didn't care enough to have an opinion. They were great parents but there was no spirituality in my home. My conversion experience came while I was working on my PhD in microbiology. I won't bore you with the details other than to say this: the more I learned of the microscopic world, the less I could dismiss the need for a Creator.

My journey to faith was long and bumpy, but in time I learned of my need for God and the love of Jesus. I know that sounds like preacher talk, but I don't know how else to say it. At first, mine was a mental, academic assent to the reality of God but as time passed, my mind came along for the ride.

Today I cannot imagine myself without my faith.

How does this affect your case? I don't know, but please understand this: except for a few who are Christians in name only, we are not a hateful people. People of faith have served society well for centuries. As for me, it has made all the difference.

I am praying for you all.

Stephanie Beck, PhD

"Honest. To the point. Intelligent." What he didn't say was, *Unconvincing*. The third letter of the night caught him by surprise.

Dear Justices,

My name is Jason and I'll get right to the point. I am not a Christian. Just the opposite, in fact. I have not attended Dr. Preston's church, nor do I have any desire to do so. I haven't been to church since I was a child. I have no belief in God; I have no use for a god. I make no apologies to anyone, but I have chosen to respond to Scott Freeman and the Alliance's letter asking supporters to write to the member justices of the ICJ. No one would consider me a supporter of the Alliance, yet I am not its opponent. Confusing? Perhaps.

I read the request online after hearing about it through the news media. At first, I was furious. To be brutally honest, Christians annoy me. I am weary of the preaching and the church talk and I have said so publicly. It is the last part of that statement that has made me write this letter. I believe in freedom of speech. If some take away the right of people—even Christians—to speak, then they can take away my right to promote atheism.

When I call the logic of Christians into question, I did so believing I was exercising my right to free speech. Now, I'm not so sure. Could I be told that I am involved in hate speech? I don't know. This I do know: people must have the right to speak their beliefs or disbeliefs, even if I don't like what they say. I strongly disagree with the teachings of Dr. Preston and his ilk, but I do believe he has the right to express them, no matter how furious it makes me.

To criminalize the free speech of one group is to criminalize the free speech of every group.

Respectfully,
Jerry Mortimer

"Didn't expect that." He lifted the brandy snifter to his nose and inhaled. He took a sip of the strong drink, then set it down again.

Letter followed letter, most were respectful and articulate; some were incomprehensible rants. On a few letters, he saw tear stains. Some of the missives were obviously written by elderly, shaky hands; others were crisply lettered. Several were threats of harm. Ironically, a few threatened violence should Dr. Preston be found guilty; others threatened bloodshed if he was found innocent. Those would be turned over to security. Most, however, were heartfelt expressions of how the spiritual life had given a meaningless or wayward or empty life purpose.

Another brandy followed and a glass of water followed that. The thin darkness had thickened into blackness. A three-quarter moon climbed its nightly path. Hodge rubbed his eyes, then stared over the farm fields painted in ivory light. He left the balcony behind, undressed and crawled into bed. Sleep wouldn't come. Disquiet percolated in him and his tired mind wouldn't unknot.

His mind revisited the letters, then turned to the conversations he had had with the other justices. This should be a simple case, an easy decision. When he sat at the bench during the dismissal hearing, he had been confident how the case would go. He was still pretty sure how the others would rule. The one he doubted now was himself.

He rolled to his side and looked at the radio-alarm. The red numbers: 2:13.

He needed sleep. He wanted to be sharp the next time he was in the office. He took satisfaction in convincing the others to move the case up the docket. At the very least, they would be done with it sooner.

He wondered what the other thousand letters contained.

Chapter 32

God's First Mistake

What Countess Isabella asked was indeed unprecedented. It was too much, went against the advice of all his advisors, and would put a strain on him and the Church.

Benedict walked to the corner window of his apartment and gazed into the sun's first rays as they fell on Vatican Hill. The compound was quiet. Soon, priests would be offering morning prayers. So would he, and he wondered if he should begin with a private confession. Had he been too bold? Too quick to agree? Had he offended his friend, Michael Mahoney, and his chief aide, Ramone Erik? Was he, the Pope, being impetuous? Foolhardy? Cavalier? Was his motivation as true and noble as he allowed himself to believe?

Question after question flickered in his mind like a thousand votive candles lit by the faithful and continued throughout the night. Benedict doubted he slept more than a few moments at a time. Every tick of the clock was greeted with another concern. Between the encyclical and Freeman's mass mailing, the media had been whipped into a fury. The only television Benedict watched was news shows and very few of those. Most of the news was brought to him in digested form with stories that might have an impact on the Church at the top. It was the most depressing part of his day.

He stepped closer to the window and pulled his robe snug. He felt cold, an iciness that worked *out* from the marrow instead of *into* his bones. Despite being surrounded by people, aides, priests, and security, despite seeing tens of thousands who gathered in Saint Peter's Square when he conducted a Papal Mass, he was a lonely man. This was no surprise, but foreknowledge did nothing to dampen the effect. At the end of the day, he returned to his rooms alone. Over the years, he lost count of the number of times he held wistful memories of his days as a simple parish priest in Nigeria where he would play soccer with the children of the Catholic orphanage, or argue points of doctrine in seminary. He exchanged worn, dirty sneakers for the red shoes of the Pope.

Outside, birds took to the air to begin their day of foraging, many—especially the pigeons—had grown accustomed to bits of food provided by tourists. He felt a link with the pigeons. Others provided for his every need, too. All but the most private of human activities were watched or aided by others. The gray and white pigeons that populated the area had grown accustomed to being provided for.

Benedict did not want to be a pigeon except in one respect: they could still fly.

"Sometimes Lord, I think making me the earthly shepherd of your church might be Your first mistake."

He stretched his back, gazing out the window for a few more moments. Thin clouds, low and gray, formed the ceiling of the sky, diffusing the light of the rising sun. A small slit appeared and widened. A beam of gold light pressed through the opening illuminating Vatican Hill.

A tear formed in Benedict's eye.

"Thank you. I will stay the course."

The old Nigerian priest crossed himself.

Fredrico had been up before dawn as was his custom, to maintain a lifestyle habit passed down from his grandfather: "Up early, exercise, big breakfast, then grab the world by the throat." The last part was a bit of hyperbole that made Fredrico uncomfortable, but he got the point. Success travels with those who begin the day early. He adopted the habit as a teenager when most of his friends were sleeping until noon. Of course, Fredrico's father gave him no choice.

Isabella was not an early riser. Her habit was to work late, sometimes into the wee hours. Resting in her bed, she looked content and at peace. She also snored. He kissed his wife on the forehead. She returned a thin smile, but didn't open her eyes. She never did.

Walking softly from the room, he closed the door and padded down the steps of the mansion in his bare feet, moved into the large kitchen and started a pot of dark Italian roast. While the coffee brewed, Fredrico hit the pool. The water chilled his skin, driving away what little sleepiness remained. At first, he made slow laps, increasing the pace with every lap until his arms ached, his lungs burned, and his legs felt like concrete. He reached the shallow end, taking in great gulps of crisp morning air. He sat on the submerged steps, letting the water caress his bare chest, his chin just below the waterline, his lower lip just above. Ripples, driven by his exhalation, rolled away from him.

He let the rhythm of his breathing, the pounding of his heart, and the chirps of birds in the trees that populated the estate cover him in peace. This was his favorite moment of the day. He enjoyed his work, loved the challenges of shipping cargo around the world, the mental exercise of the finances, but being alone and immersed in the water satisfied his soul like nothing else. This was his chapel, his prayer closet, his meditation den. With a mind refreshed from a night's sleep and fueled by vigorous exercise, he could think of greater things, holy things.

Fredrico prayed, as he did every morning, that what he did today would be useful to the Kingdom of God. He prayed for his wife, he prayed for his employees, he prayed for his friends. And now he prayed for a man he had never met, an American named Pat Preston. Isabella had shared with him the legal challenges, but he understood only some of it. He had a head for business, but not for law. So he prayed God would grant strength to Isabella, to the Pope, and to Dr. Pat Preston. The fact that Isabella believed in the cause was good enough for him.

He rose and reached for a thick, white towel. A breeze conjured up chill bumps, but Fredrico didn't mind. It made him feel all the more alive and free. He seldom thought of his freedom, but knowing where Preston was made him all the more thankful. For a moment he wondered if he possessed the same kind of conviction to a cause that Preston did. He doubted it and the realization shamed him.

He poured coffee, fixed a breakfast of fruit and wholegrain toast, then trotted up the steps to shower and dress for the day. Forty-five minutes later, he exited the front door, rearming the home's security system. A slate-gray BMW 745Li luxury sedan waited for him at the front of the house. A light-skinned, redheaded man in a chauffeur's uniform opened the back door as Fredrico approached.

"Good morning, sir." The man was in his early forties but looked five years younger. His physique strained the seams of the uniform.

"Good morning, Leo. Is your family well?"

"Yes, sir. My teenage daughter is making me old."

"I hear that's their job."

"Well then, she is fulfilling her purpose in life."

Fredrico slipped into the backseat. The limo was, in his mind, an extravagance and he would prefer to drive to the Rome office. His board held a different opinion. There was always a danger of kidnapping. Few outside the boardrooms of major companies knew the danger to heads of businesses. There had been over four thousand kidnappings in Columbia alone. It wasn't just dangerous countries like Iran, Iraq, and Pakistan. Every country had executives snatched and held for ransom. It had become a growth industry. Many companies carried kidnap and ransom insurance. His did. Having a professional driver and body guard was no guarantee of safety, but it helped.

Leo slipped into the driver's seat and started down the long drive, activating the automatic gates. Moments later, they were headed from the hills outside Rome and into the city. Fredrico found, as he always did, newspapers from key business publishers. Most of his news came digitally, but he still loved the feel of paper and the smell of ink in the morning. He began to read as the sun tried to push through the low cloud layer.

He had been in the car for twenty minutes and was reading the *Barron's* when he heard Leo say, "Seatbelt."

"I always wear a seatbelt. You know—"

"Down, down, down." Leo jerked the wheel to the left and the car lurched to the side, then accelerated. The acceleration pressed Fredrico back in the seat.

"What's going on?"

"Get down. Make the call."

They had practiced this. In a "situation", Leo would be too busy driving to call the police. That meant Fredrico had to make the call. He reached for his cell phone as he dropped his head below the seat line. Cars race by the side window as Leo speed into the city.

He dialed 112, the emergency number in Italy. Before he could speak, something rammed the back of the BMW. Leo swore and swerved.

"Hold on!"

Another impact jarred the phone from Fredrico's hand. The luxury car made a hard right turn. He couldn't tell if Leo was making an evasive maneuver or if whoever was ramming them was pushing the vehicle that direction. Fredrico heard the roar of the mighty engine. "I dropped the phone—"

Another ram. The sound of tearing metal filled the car.

"Hang on." Leo's voice was strong but also ice cold. Fredrico had no idea if the man heard him say he dropped the phone.

Fredrico lifted his head in time to see Leo crank the wheel hard to the left. The back end of the car swung around. The painful sound of squealing tires pierced the air. He could hear the rattle of metal. They were dragging something. The BMW sped forward. Fredrico released his lap belt to better reach the phone which had slid under the front seat.

He reached into the dark space, fingers stretching, probing, longing for the feel of the familiar device. The car vibrated and a loud thumping came from the left rear. Leo swore in Italian.

Fredrico had to dial 112 again. The two seconds it took for the cell phone to connect passed like an hour.

"Policia."

"This is Fredrico San Philippa. My driver and I are being attacked by another car. We are traveling . . . Leo, where are we?"

"Viale Palmiro Togliatti just north of A22. We're northbound. The vehicle behind us an American Humvee—full size—"

Another tooth-jarring impact. Fredrico cried out and tried to reach for his lap belt and talk on the phone at the same time. Impossible. He relayed the information from Leo when he heard . . .

. . . a thump . . .

. . . the pounding of a burst tire beating its tread on the rear wheel-well . . .

. . . vehicle horns sounding . . .

. . . sheet metal dragging the pavement . . .

. . . the crash of impact . . .

. . . then . . .

The BMW tipped on its left side, slid for a moment, then began to flip side over side, becoming airborne with each twist. On the first flip, Fredrico caught a glimpse of a large military style vehicle; on the next tumble, he saw Leo's head hit the side window and bounced into the crushed ceiling, the same ceiling that closed in on him. He felt fire in his body; heard snapping he feared came from his body and not the car; felt the buckle of the seatbelt he had released while reaching for the fallen phone slap his hip.

The car stopped flipping and slid to a stop on its roof. Out the fractured passenger window, he saw the large tires of the Humvee.

Then he saw nothing.

The phone next to Isabella's bed jangled to life. She groaned, rolled to her side and placed the receiver to her ear.

"Yes?" She listened for a moment. "Speaking." Another moment. "Blessed Jesus." She dropped the phone.

Chapter 33

A Room with No View

―――◆―――

When Isabella arrived at the hospital, the sun had begun to dispel the clouds and painted Rome with hues of warm gold and white. The streets were buzzing with impatient drivers fighting to arrive at work on time and to work their way around tourists and retired residents who had no need to rush anywhere. She pulled into the parking lot of Azienda Ospedialiera Sant' Andrea Hospital, a ten-story sweeping structure on Via di Grottarossa. Even at that early hour, the parking lot was choked with compact cars. She decided against trying to find a space near the entrance. Less time would be spent if she took the first available stall and started walking.

The putty-colored building loomed over her and she wondered about the people confined there by illness, surgery, or, like her husband, auto accident. She prayed as she walked and each step came faster than the previous. Reason said her being in the building three minutes earlier would make no difference, but her heart wasn't in the mood to listen. The only man she ever loved, the man she grew to love more with each passing day, was "grievously injured." Those were the nurse's words: "grievously injured." The woman had been firm and controlled, like any emergency room nurse would be, but Isabella was certain she heard a mixture of pity and shock. "I recommend coming as soon as you can."

Isabella was dressed and out the door five minutes later. She gave no thought to her appearance. She wore a pair of jeans, slip-on shoes, and a simple, white pullover top. Normally meticulous about her hair and makeup, she gave neither a thought.

That had been twelve hours before. The sun that watched her flee her home and grab the family Toyota SUV was now calling it a day, moving its warmth and light to the other side of the world. Blessings or tragedies never affected the course of the orb.

She found the emergency room, which, thankfully, was only half full. Most of those people had come to the hospital after midnight. Isabella went to the counter in emergency. The nurse was stout but had kind eyes. "Excuse me. I am Countess Isabella San Philippa. My husband was brought in a short time ago."

"One moment, Countess." The woman typed the last name into a computer. "Yes, senora, he's here and being attended to."

"May I see him?"

"I'm afraid not. If you'll have a seat in the waiting room, I'll make a note you are here and we will let you know when we have more information."

"But I'm his wife."

"Yes, ma'am. I understand that, but the emergency room is extremely busy and hospital policy does not allow for any but medical staff in the back."

"Can you tell me his condition?" Tears flooded her eyes.

"I don't have specifics, but I will go back and ask—if you'll have a seat."

"Mrs. San Philippa?"

Isabella turned to see a police officer in a dark blue uniform standing at her side. "Yes . . . it's countess, actually."

"My apologies, Countess. My name is Dacio Bianchi. I'm sorry to bother you at such a frightening time, but I wonder if I might ask a few questions."

They moved to an empty hall but no so far that Isabella could not see the ER desk. "Were you at the accident scene?" Isabella pulled a tissue from her purse.

"I was not at the scene. I'm a criminal investigator. I arrived on the scene after your husband was removed from the vehicle and brought here."

"Criminal?"

"Yes, Countess. There are many witnesses to the accident—I should say attack. Another car ran your husband and his driver off the road."

"Leo. I forgot about Leo. He was hurt, too?"

Dacio looked away for a moment. "I'm sorry to bring you such sad news, Countess. The driver died at the scene."

"Oh, no. No!" She brought a hand to her mouth. "That can't be. He has a family, a wife and children."

"I'm afraid my work has taught me that death doesn't care about such things. Since the accident was intentional, this is now a homicide. Your husband is the best man to answer these questions, but he is not available at the moment."

"I know almost nothing, officer. The hospital called and said he had been injured in an auto accident. That is all I know." She turned to the front desk. Still no nurse. Her stomach felt full of acid.

"Has your husband ever received a death threat?"

"No. Not that I know of."

"Does he have enemies?"

She shook her head. "He runs a big shipping firm, so he has competition, but he's not your typical business man. He's been known to help his competitors during tough times."

"No unpleasant phone calls?"

She dabbed at her eyes. "No. None. Not at home. I work from home. I take most of the calls."

"What about at work?"

"Not that I know, but I wouldn't know. I can give you the names of his key executives and his assistants. They would know if something like that was going on."

"He wouldn't tell you?"

"It's never come up. He's been happy, carefree. I don't . . ." A dark thought began to spread through her mind like an oil slick.

"Can you think of any reason someone would try to hurt your husband?"

"To get a message to me." Isabella's words were barely audible.

"Excuse me?"

She lifted her head. "To get a message to me."

"I don't understand."

"Excuse me." She removed her cell phone from her purse.

"Countess, perhaps that can wait a few minutes?"

"It can't."

The officer looked angry. "Countess. Who are you calling?"

"The Vatican."

***

In less than an hour, Cardinal Mahoney entered the emergency room. Dressed in his red cassock, he reminded Isabella of a meteor streaking to the ground. Two men in dark suits followed Mahoney. Isabella guessed they were plainclothes officers of the Vatican police.

"Countess, His Holiness asked that I come right over."

"You are very kind, Your Eminence."

"Is there word?"

"No. They won't tell me anything."

"I see. Come with me."

They walked to the nurse. Mahoney gave a nod to Isabella. "Excuse me, nurse—"

The woman didn't look up. "Countess, I know of your concern, but there is nothing more I can-" The moment her eyes moved from the computer screen, she caught a glimpse of red and was on her feet in an instant. "Excuse me, Your Eminence. I didn't see you there."

"I'm easy to overlook, child." He smiled and motioned to his clothing. "Red is so hard to see."

Isabella noticed the man's Italian was as good as his English. "I wonder if you would be so kind as to let the head of your department know Cardinal Mahoney would be grateful for a moment of his time."

"Yes, Your Eminence. Right away." She disappeared through the door and into the bowels of the emergency room. Before the door fully closed, he heard a man say, "Here? Now?"

A few moments later, a dark-skinned, narrow man in a doctor's smock appeared. The name stitched on the coat read, "Dr. Gerolamo Ricci, MD."

Mahoney smiled as if seeing an old friend. "Thank you, doctor. I know you must be very busy, but one of your patients is the husband of Countess Isabella. He is also a friend of His Holiness himself. Might we have a word?"

"Yes, of course, Cardinal . . ."

"Mahoney, doctor. Michael Mahoney." Another blazing smile. "The sensitivity of this makes privacy something to be desired. Is there a room where we might talk?"

Dr. Ricci looked at Mahoney, Isabella, and the two serious looking men in suits. "All of you?"

"Why yes, that would be appreciated. Thank you."

"If you've come to give last rites—"

"A room if you don't mind, doctor. I would consider it a favor."

"Yes, Cardinal. This way, please." The doctor led the small group to what looked like a doctors' break room. Unlike the rest of the hospital, this room was dirty and in disarray. Once everyone was in, the doctor, who looked a little weak in the knees, offered the worn chairs and sofa.

"We don't mind standing, Doctor, and we don't want to keep you from your duties. Count San Phillipa, what is his condition?"

He nodded and switched into the monotone common to doctors worldwide. He looked at Isabella. "Your husband presented with multiple injuries sustained in an auto accident. He had lost a good deal of blood, has a broken clavicle, two fractured ribs, a concussion, and he also damaged his spleen. There is some damage to the eye socket, but our ophthalmologists believe the eye is safe. Of course, there are more tests to run."

"Where is he now?" Isabella pushed.

"In surgery. He's likely to be there for several more hours, depending how damaged the spleen is."

The room began to spin and a vise-like hand took her by the elbow. She looked into Mahoney's eyes. "Perhaps you should sit."

One of the Vatican policemen pulled a chair near and Isabella made use of it. "Is there more, Doctor?" She was surprised by the weakness of her voice.

"Not as yet, Countess. We'll keep him under observation for several days to monitor his recovery, especially his head injury. Early scans showed no bleeding into the brain. We have that to be thankful for."

"Indeed," Mahoney said. "Doctor, I will need to speak to your hospital administrator. Security arrangements will need to be made."

"Security?"

Mahoney seemed surprised. "The police did not speak to you?"

"Only that someone ran Mr. San Philippa off the road and his driver died at the scene."

Hearing those words again sent searing sorrow through Isabella.

The conversation continued a few moments longer, but Isabella heard none of it. Images of her husband on the operating table blocked out every other thought.

***

Twelve hours. From the time she arrived at the hospital to the moment Fredrico awoke twelve hours passed, each one seeming like a year. He lay in a hospital bed, an oxygen tube tucked under his nose and three IV bags filled with things Isabella didn't understand dripped fluid through clear, flexible tubes to large bore needles in his arm. A purple-black bruise covered half of his face. Matching bruises dotted his arms and legs. A thin, white sheet lay across his lap, the only modesty his injuries would allow. A heart monitor told Isabella her husband was alive. Every jagged peak on the monitor was a source of joy.

One eye opened. The other was too swollen for the lid to move. The eye moved back and forth.

"Fredrico?"

"Ouch."

"Are you in pain? You've been out for a long time."

"Where am I?" He reached for the oxygen line.

"You are in the hospital. You were in an . . . accident."

"Accident?"

"In the car."

"I don't remember."

She stood and stepped to the bedside. "They told me you might not remember. It's the trauma. There's no need to remember."

He blinked the one eye. "The office."

"I called. They know about the accident. Everything is taken care of. I'm here. I won't leave your side."

He looked away, staring up as if the events of the day were written somewhere above him. "We were run off the road. Big car. Rammed us. Leo tried . . . Leo? How is Leo?"

Isabella burst into tears.

***

Hours passed and with each one, Fredrico recalled a detail or two. Often, Isabella would have to answer a question several times because he would fall into a drug aided sleep, only to wake up in the middle of the same conversation.

"Cardinal Mahoney came to say prayers?"

"Yes, but not last rites." She smiled and took his hand. "He has been wonderful. While you were in recovery, he made hospital rounds praying for everyone who asked. He must have been here six hours."

She wiped at her eyes.

"Hey, no tears. I'm going to be fine." He closed his eye, then snapped the lid open again. "I am going to be fine, right?"

"Yes, of course. The doctors say you will be well soon, but you will be recovering for a while."

She listed his injuries, which he thought about for a moment. "So nothing serious, then." He chuckled, then groaned from the pain it caused. "I'm still pretty, right?"

"You will be. Right now your head is swollen like a pumpkin, a great big, blue pumpkin."

"Too ugly to kiss?"

"You could never be that ugly to me." She bent and kissed him softly on the lips. At least those weren't damaged. When she straightened, tears flowed like tiny rivers.

"I said no tears. I will recover and once again be a bother."

"I'm—I'm so sorry, my love. This is all my fault."

"I was attacked by a mad man in a big car. An American car at that. How can that be your fault?"

"I think this may have happened because of my involvement with Dr. Preston. You remember what I told you about Matt Branson."

"The murdered lawyer? You said that no one has connected that to the Preston case."

"But there has been a threat against his wife and family."

"Yes. I know. We're paying for the security . . . um . . . firm." He winced and Isabella could tell his thinking was slower than normal. The shock, trauma, and medication had dulled his mind. "Still . . ." He couldn't form the rest of the sentence. He closed his eye again.

"You rest, husband. I'll be here when you wake up again."

"You're not quitting."

He had read her mind. "I didn't say—"

"You were thinking it. Am I wrong?"

"No." The word was little more than a whisper. "The danger—"

"Those who stand up for truth always face danger. You know that."

"I don't think I'm strong enough to continue. Not after this."

"Yes, you are. You are the strongest person I know. You are the steel in my spine." His voice was fading. "Too . . . much . . . at stake."

"Preston has other attorneys."

He moved his head side to side. "You. It must be you. You are God's person for this. If you quit now, everything is lost."

"I'm frightened."

"So am I. For you, for me, but most of all for Dr. Preston and what he represents. This . . ." He exhaled in frustration at his muddled brain. "More important than me . . . than you. Don't let them take our voice away."

The tears flowed unabated.

"Promise me, wife. Promise . . ." He drifted back into a drug induced sleep.

"I promise. God help me, I promise."

Chapter 34

All things Beatrice

———◆———

B eatrice switched off her cell phone, leaned forward and buried her face in her hands.

"What?" Becky Preston was standing in the kitchen making stew for that evening's dinner. The open floor plan allowed her to see the living room, the dining room and the front door.

Beatrice rubbed her face, then brushed back her hair. "Nothing."

"Please don't lie to me, Beatrice. I need to know I can trust what you say."

The Vatican police officer made eye contact with the tutor working with the children at the dining room table. The woman was matronly, a veteran of thirty years in the local school system who made extra money tutoring children in home. She got the idea.

"Let's take a break, kids. Who wants to go in the bedroom and color for awhile?"

"Me, do," Phoebe said.

"I do," the tutor corrected.

"I know. I'm jus' teasin'."

"I want to play a video game." Luke had been pouting all morning. He didn't like being cooped up in the house.

"Okay, but only for awhile. You have arithmetic to do."

"Just kill me now."

The three moved to the bedroom and closed the door.

Beatrice walked into the kitchen. "Someone attacked Countess Isabella's husband."

Becky raised a hand to her mouth. "Is he . . ."

"Dead? No. He's in the hospital recovering from surgery. The countess said the doctors are very encouraging."

"What happened?"

Beatrice told the story in as few sentences as possible. "Don't assume this has anything to do with your husband. The countess' husband is a very wealthy and influential man. It may have been a kidnap attempt."

"Do you believe that? You don't, do you?"

Moving to the stove, Beatrice began to stir the stew meat. Becky knew evasive behavior when she saw it. "First, threats against my husband, the murder of Matt Branson, that wicked, evil doll on my doorstep, and now this." She rubbed her temples. "I don't think I can take much more of this. I'm losing my mind. Why did Pat have to be so stubborn? This is his fault."

Putting the lid back on the pot, Beatrice turned and leaned against the counter. "Look at me."

"What?"

"Becky, look at me. Look in my eyes."

"Why?"

She pushed off and approached Becky, leaving less than a foot between them. "Look me in the eyes."

"Are you going to hit me?"

"Of course not. Look me in the eyes and tell me again that all of this is your husband's fault."

Becky glanced away. "It is. I know it is."

"My eyes, Becky. You look me in the eyes and say that."

Fury heated Becky's cheeks. She snapped her head around and stared hard into the security agent's eyes. "It's all Pat's . . ." She looked away.

"You can't say it because you know it's not true and you're nothing if not a lover of the truth. You're scared. You should be. You should be terrified. You feel this is all unjust. It is. You feel persecuted. You are. You're concerned about your children. You're a good mother, so you should be. Now listen to me. None of this is your husband's fault. Don't make the victim the criminal, Becky. I understand your need to strike out at someone. Well, I'm here. You want to unload some anger, you direct it at me. Am I clear?"

"I guess."

"You guess? That's it?"

"I'm sorry. I've always been this way. Pat once said being married to me was like being wed to a roller coaster." Her voice grew soft. "Lots of ups and downs, but still a thrilling ride."

That made Beatrice smile. "Your husband has a way with words."

"You have no idea." Becky took a deep breath. "So, I guess this means the countess is leaving the case."

"Why?"

"I would."

"Come with me." Beatrice removed two bottles of iced tea from the refrigerator and walked to the dining room table. She set the glass bottles down. Becky retrieved two glasses and followed. They moved the children's school work and sat. Beatrice opened the bottles easily, giving one to Becky. Both poured. "As a rule, I don't talk about myself much, especially with a client but, I'm going to peel back a few layers."

She took a sip of the tea, then continued. "First, a confession: I'm frightened all the time. I mean all the time."

"I don't believe that."

"Believe it. I grew up in an abusive family. Abusive verbally and, at times physically. Fortunately, not sexually or I'd be more . . . what's the English word . . . whacky?"

"That says it. I'm so sorry."

"I was sorry too, for a very long time, but I've come out of it stronger. Do not misunderstand me. I'm not happy about what I had to endure, but I am proud I learned to endure it. Do you understand?"

"I think so."

"I wish the beatings never happened. I wish thousands of comments made about how worthless, useless, and ugly I am, were never said, at least never heard by me, but they were and I can't go back in time and change that."

"You poor thing."

Beatrice raised a hand. "No. Don't say that. I'm not poorer for the experience. I am mentally and emotionally scarred, but not weak." She moved closer to the table, resting her forearms on it. "One day, my father slapped my mother. I tried to stop him and he turned his anger on me. He knocked me to the floor. A neighbor had come to our door to borrow flour. She heard everything and called the police. They arrested my father and I was glad to see him go, but then something else happened. After the other officer left, a female office knelt in front of me. I was only ten at the time.

"She said something I repeat in my dark moments. She said, 'Little one, my papa treated me the same way. He told me he loved our dog more than he loved me, but you know what? I learned I had a super power. I can endure criticism from anyone. As I grew older, I learned that both the good and the bad shaped who I was. I stopped trying to forget the abuse and started using the memories to make me stronger. It is why I became a police officer.'"

Becky's eyes began to burn.

"I didn't understand it all then. I was just too hurt and scared. The older I grew, the more I understood. What I'm trying to say is the bad in my life still hurts me, but it also gives me my courage. I can't change it, so I embrace it. If I run from my past, I will never find my future."

Becky looked away.

"You are going through an ordeal. You know you can't change that. You can't wish it away. It is what it is, just like my abusive past. You can choose to be angry with your husband and with the world, but in the end, the only ones you will hurt are you and your children."

"I'm not as strong as you, Beatrice. You're a trained police officer."

"I came to grips with emotional injuries long before I put on a uniform, and I put on the uniform to help people like you. When I had an opportunity to transfer from the Italian Metropolitan police to the Vatican force, I realized I could do even more." Beatrice laid her hand on Becky's. It felt warm and firm. "There is no shame in fear. Face what is and spit in its eye."

"I don't have that kind of courage."

"Courage? Courage isn't what you feel, Becky, it is what you do. I don't trust people who have no fears." She tapped the side of her head with a finger. "Such people are not right in the head. I've served with very brave people and seen their hands shake. Still, they do their job. Feel whatever you wish, but always act with courage." A thin smile spread across her face. "End of sermon."

"Amen." Becky's smile was weak, but it was there.

Chapter 35

First Offer

><==>◦◆◦<==>

During the warm Tennessee summers, Pat would barbecue in the backyard of his home. When he did, he insisted on being in charge of the whole operation, frequently handling all of the cooking duties. He prepared the meat, often T-bone steaks for he and Becky and hot dogs for the children, made the salad dressing, barbecued ears of corn still in their husks, and prepared a fresh fruit salad for dessert, a concoction of Mandarin oranges, honeydew, cantaloupe, seedless grapes, and watermelon balls. He would use a "melon-baller" to make little spheres of the red, juicy fruit. When he was done, only two hollowed halves of a watermelon remained.

That was how he felt at the moment. Isabella had made a video conference call to the prison. She was home, but looked as if she hadn't slept for two days. She began with a terse statement: "As your attorney, it is my obligation to keep you informed." She then launched into an account of the assault on her husband. With Isabella drained and Pat stunned, the conversation became an exchange of short phrases.

"He's going to be okay?"

"Yes."

"Is he safe?"

"We have security around his room and around me."

"Good. He was the target?"

"We think so."

"Business related or because of me?"

"We can't be sure."

"Guess."

"Because of your case."

Pat had paused, then, "I relieve you of your duties and commitment. Take care of your husband."

"The same thought crossed my mind."

For a moment, it seemed to Pat that every internal organ shrank to the size of a walnut. "It would be the wise thing to do."

"Yes, it would, but you're stuck with me."

"I'm concerned for you."

"And I for you. I'm not quitting."

"What if I fire you?"

"You can't. I won't allow it."

"You can't stop me."

Her smile was forced. "I just did. Nothing else has changed. The case goes forward on the new schedule. Okay?"

"No."

"I knew you'd agree."

Pat lowered his head. "You are a formidable woman, Countess."

"I have one other bit of news, Pat. I'm obligated to share it with you. I received an e-mail from John Knox Smith. Please listen to the whole thing. Agreed?"

His heart quickened. "Okay."

"If you make a public apology for your crimes"—his words not mine—"and if you seek the forgiveness of the world, and if you sign a statement saying you will no longer preach or teach in any manner deemed as hate speech directed to or about people of other faiths, specifically claiming that Jesus Christ is the only 'true savior', and that you will be silent regarding your views on sexuality and family values, then he will ask the court to accept your guilty plea and release you for time served."

The flicker of hope that blazed so brightly a moment before went out like a ember falling on snow.

"I . . . I . . ."

"Dr. Preston, don't answer now. The offer has no time limit. Take a few days to think about it, to pray about it."

The only response he could offer was the nodding of his head.

"Shall I let your wife know of the offer?"

Several moments drifted past before he could speak. "No. Not yet. I have to think." He released a mirthless chuckle. "You know, Becky suggested apologizing months ago."

"Well, now it's an official offer."

"Do you have a suggestion?"

"I do, but it's not my place. I want you free and with your family, but you should know if you agree to this, they win. They win everything."

His guards walked him back to the cell in silence. The grip on his elbow was lighter and the cuffs on his wrists not as tight. Even they seemed bothered by the news.

***

"Do you think he'll take you up on your offer?" Andrea lay in her bed with the sheet pulled to her chin. A half empty glass of red wine rested on the night stand.

John was standing, fiddling with his tie. "He has to. By now, he must be so beaten down and worried about his family he'd volunteer to swim the Atlantic with cement shoes to get back to a normal life."

"I was surprised you made an offer at all."

"It was the team's idea. We need a moral victory more than a legal one. I believe it will bolster our right to prosecute verbal hate crimes, and one of the symbols of their cause will have gone down in flames, proving they love themselves more than their principles."

"Would you take the offer if the roles were reversed?" She sat up and finished the wine.

"I'm made of sterner stuff than Pat. I knew that in college and I believe it all the more now. I fight for what is right and nothing can keep me from pursuing that cause."

"You're a rock, Boss. Now I have another question. Have you ever thought about running for president?"

"President? No. I'd rather help someone get elected and sit in the AG's chair."

"You should think about it. Not this next election, of course, but maybe the one after that. You'll be in your late forties. That's a good age to enter the White House."

"You're a dreamer, Andrea."

"Is that all I am to you?"

He ignored her question and walked out the door.

Chapter 36

Wadi Cherith

With no window through which to watch the rising and the setting of the sun, Pat had no evidence of the passing of days. The best he could do was count his meals and how often he was allowed to exercise. The light in his cell never went off. At times, Pat had trouble knowing the difference between two a.m. and two p.m. He wasn't sure he cared about time. Not being able to sense the flow of time allowed him to think of other things. Most days, that was a problem. Pat had learned he preferred to be unhappy. It was a startling revelation and one he came to slowly, but the constant rehearsal of his problems was proof enough. He prayed frequently, but often his words had no depth. Most of the conversations were those of a whining child trying to convince a reluctant parent to buy a particular toy. Of course, more was at stake here than a toy.

The offer to settle the case with time served and an apology split his personality to a degree that would make Robert Louis Stevenson proud. Jekyll and Hyde had nothing on him—except Hyde was guilty of horrors and Pat was not. Half of Pat wanted to accept the offer.

Pat had eaten neither his dinner from the night before, his breakfast, or lunch. His refusal to eat stemmed from two causes: one, he had no appetite and the sight of food turned his stomach; two, he was fasting as part of his prayer. He couldn't remember the last time he had abstained from food for spiritual reasons. Fasting was certainly part of the biblical teaching, but he had given it little attention, assuming it was for extreme situations and his life had been one of leisure, compared to what others endured. That is until his arrest. His situation now qualified as extreme.

Another part of his brain spoke about the issue in the background of his thoughts. Fasting always seemed manipulative to him. "God, I won't eat until You answer my prayer." Of course, that thought was foreign to biblical teaching, but it nonetheless surfaced from time to time.

On deeper reflection, fasting wasn't done for God's benefit but for that of the petitioner, a way of focusing on prayer and little else. Prayer consumed nearly every thought. What was the right thing to do? What did God want? Pat was thirsty for direction.

When not directly addressing God, his mind played images like a projector in a movie theater. He saw himself wrestling with his children; snuggled in bed with his wife; watching 1950s science fiction movies; reading; consuming coffee at the local coffee house. Each image warmed him. He wanted nothing more than those things and the hundreds of other images about being home with his family.

So Pat prayed.

He prayed on his knees, not caring if the "eternal eye" in his ceiling sent the image to prison officials.

He prayed while reclined on his bed.

He prayed while he paced his cell.

He prayed during the required exercise period, keeping his head down and his petitions up.

When he dozed off, he dreamed of praying.

What was he to do? What answer should he give? Was an apology so much to ask? Maybe his sermons had offended some, although he had gone out of his way to be kind and loving in all matters, but the Bible could be offensive. The Apostle Paul even said so in 1 Corinthians 1, calling the Gospel foolishness to the Greeks and a stumbling block to the Jews. Pat had done nothing Paul hadn't done, but then Paul was beheaded for the faith, a fact Pat found neither comforting nor inspiring.

Then there was his family to consider. His children were living without a father. Someone had implied violence against his little Luke and Phoebe, a fact that ate at his gut like acid. He would do anything to protect them. He would die for them. All he had to do here was humble himself and apologize to people he had never met. He'd have to give up the ministry, but it might be refreshing to relate to God as a layman. One didn't have to be a pastor to be a servant to God's people. He no longer cared about titles and positions.

He had advanced degrees—an M.Div and a Ph.d—;maybe he could teach at the college level or seminary. He'd like that. Teaching had always been his greatest ministry joy. A professor's salary was small and they'd have to simplify their lives, but even that would be a joy.

Is that what You want, heavenly Father? I can serve You without being a professional minister. But what price would there be for denying who You are?

The prayer seemed to bounce back from the ceiling.

The lack of sleep and food was taking a toll on his already shredded emotions. One moment he'd be working on the phrasing of his apology; the next he was awash in guilt and failure. Pat again returned to his knees. Tears dripped to the mattress.

Oh God, source of my strength, my life, my being, my hope, my assurance . . .

Too formal. He tried again.

Father, I . . . I'm broken. My mind. My heart. Everything. I can't make sense of myself or my situation. Do You want me here? Is this you will? Do I deserve this place, this treatment? He ran a hand through his hair, pulling as he did. *I have failed you. I have failed my family. I have ruined my witness. I have lost control. I admit it. Sometimes I don't even know how to pray.*

He struggled for more words and found so few. He had always prided himself on his eloquence; now he felt like a child looking for words he had yet to learn. What approach should he take? What words did God want to hear? He didn't know. Only one phrase seemed right: *Forgive me*

The tears came unabated. His shoulders heaved with each sob. From deep within him, from a place he didn't know existed, a cry, a groan, a wail he didn't know he was capable of emitting. Waves of cold sorrow and hot regret pulsed through him. He wept for his failures, for his situation, and for his family. He wailed over his weakness and shaky faith. Again . . . the only words he could speak were, *"Forgive me."*

His mind fell silent. He waited, not knowing what he expected.

Warmth rose from the floor, like perfectly drawn bath water, surrounding him, caressing his heart and mind. Although his eyes were clamped shut, Pat could see a golden light in the cell. It made no sense, but he didn't question it. He accepted it.

Spiritual surgery was being done to his soul. Guilt was being excised. The boils of self-hatred were being lanced.

Pat shuddered, not like the heaving that came with sobs, but a gentle, pleasant tremor. This was forgiveness. This was acceptance. This was the healing of brokenness.

Exhaustion took hold. Pat fell from his knees, no longer able to kneel on the concrete, no longer able to muster the strength to lean against the bed. He became a heap of flesh and bone.

Forgiveness had taxed what remained of his strength, but he didn't care. The sense of relief made it all worthwhile. He opened his eyes and first saw the floor, then his bare feet, the opposite wall. Then he saw Marcus Aster, attired in his uniform, a tray of food in his hand.

"I didn't hear you come in." Pat struggled to his feet, but only managed long enough to turn and sit on his bed.

"You were preoccupied."

"I was praying."

Marcus nodded. "So I see." He tilted his head to one side as if reading Pat's mind. "Wadi Cherith."

What? "Excuse me?"

"Wadi Cherith. Do you know the name?"

Pat thought for a moment. "You mean the spot where the prophet Elijah hid from King Ahab and Jezebel? *That* Wadi Cherith?"

"Do you know of another?"

Pat didn't.

"Tell me the story."

"Of Elijah?"

"Just the Wadi Cherith part."

It took effort for Pat to reorder his mind. "Well, Elijah stood up to King Ahab and his Phoenician wife, Jezebel. She had introduced pagan worship into Israel. Elijah challenged the practice and tried to call the people back to a true faith.

"And, long story short, he held a showdown with the prophets of Baal. Two altars were created, one for Baal and one for the God of Israel. Each side would pray to their God and whichever answered with fire from heaven would be declared the God of Israel. The prophets of Baal did their best to get their god to respond, even to the point of mutilating themselves. Nothing happened."

"And when Elijah prayed?"

"It's clear you know this account."

"Humor me, Dr. Preston."

Pat sighed but continued. "Elijah ordered a moat dug around his altar, then had enough water poured over the offering and altar that it filled the moat. Elijah offered a simple prayer and God sent fire from heaven that consumed the offering, the altar, and all the water, proving he was the one and true God. Then he had all the prophets of Baal put to death. About five hundred of them."

"What about Ahab and Jezebel?"

"They were furious and Jezebel promised to kill Elijah the same way her prophets had been executed."

"And after this great display of power from God, what did Elijah do?"

"He ran. He ran a long distance, stopping by a river, the Wadi Cherith."

"His emotions?"

Pat shrugged. "He was tired, naturally. He was depressed. He felt he was the last faithful person in the country."

"How did God minister to him?"

"By miracle. Ravens brought him food. Elijah spent a good deal of time sleeping and eating."

Marcus nodded. "I've been gone a couple of days and I come back to learn you've stopped eating."

"I've been fasting."

"While you were greatly stressed and depressed." Marcus stepped to the bed and held out the tray of food. "Here. Eat. I'm your raven." He then moved to the opposite side of the cell, leaned against the wall and crossed his arms. "Eat up, Elijah."

"I'm no Elijah."

"No, you're not."

Pat ate, forcing himself to do so slowly. He told himself he wanted to avoid shocking his system with food, but the nagging truth came forward: he liked having Marcus around. Before he finished, Marcus crossed the cell again and removed the paperback New Testament and began leafing through the pages.

"I assume the other guards told you of the offer my attorney told me about."

"They did. You're one apology away from freedom."

"What do you think I should do?"

Marcus looked up from the pages. "I am not allowed an opinion. It would be deemed an interference with your relationship to your attorneys. I'm just a simple guard. You'll have to make up your own mind."

"Somehow, I think you're more than a simple guard."

"I am what you see."

When Pat finished his meal, he set the tray on the bed. The food sat heavy in his stomach, but it made him feel better.

Marcus returned to the bed, set the New Testament down, still open to the last page he had been reading and picked up the tray. "You should rest." He moved to the door, but stopped before opening it. He turned to face Pat. "By the way, we're all unworthy of God's grace." He exited.

It took a few moments for Pat to make the connection. A few moments before he had, in prayer, confessed his lack of worthiness to receive God's grace. How had Marcus known? Pat didn't think he was praying out loud.

He turned his attention to the New Testament, picked it up, intending to return it to its shelf, but before he did, he looked at what the guard had been reading. The book was open to the twentieth chapter of the Book of Acts. He read the two pages facing him, but his eyes hung on one line: "But none of these things move me, neither do I count my life dear unto myself, so that I might finish my course with joy, and the ministry, which I have received of the Lord Jesus, to testify the gospel of the grace of God." The line was from the Apostle Paul's farewell speech to the church at Ephesus.

The verse shone in his mind like a neon sight. "None of these things move me. Neither do I count my life dear to myself. Finish the course with joy."

A new warmth flood the Reverend Dr. Pat Preston.

Chapter 37

Cloakroom Talk

⟹◆⟸

"**S**o, how goes the letter reading?"

Sir Alan Hodge turned from the mirror where he had been adjusting the white band at his neck, making sure the front piece hung properly from the neck and faced Alexzandr Kuchar. "I'm reading a novel, a history of the British navy during the nineteenth century. Or perhaps you're referring to one of the many periodicals I receive."

"I believe you know what I'm referring to: the letters. Why would I care about what you read at home?"

"Sorry, 'ol boy, you weren't quite clear, were you?"

"Why do you Brits insult someone, then ask them to agree with it?"

"We are a supremely confident people." Alan brushed the front of his robe. "The reading goes well but slowly. How about you?"

Alexzandr shook the sleeves of his robe so they hung straight. "You know good and well I haven't read any. I don't plan to. I don't want to be swayed by outside influences."

"It would be a shame to have to waste a preconceived judgment."

"Ah, sarcasm, the last resort of the losing party in an argument."

"I wouldn't know, Alexzandr. I've never been on that side of an argument. Why don't you tell the rest of us what it's like?"

Several other judges in the "staging" area chuckled. Such banter was not new to the group. Fifteen judges meant blending fifteen very strong personalities.

"I chose not to waste my time, Alan."

"I don't believe such a letter writing campaign has ever been waged against an international court. At least history will record that one judge took the time to read what was sent his way."

"Careful now," Haim Harrar said. "Never let it be said that the jurist from Morocco failed to exercise due diligence."

"Not you, too?" Alexzandr shook his head.

"I find them entertaining. A couple have even been informative. Most are from Christians of course, but this Moroccan Jew doesn't let that bother him.

"I suppose you two are going to split the court on this." For a moment, Alexzandr flashed real anger, then softened it with a smirk.

"I will admit the countess's brief was compelling—"

"Oh, please," Jinjing said. "These kinds of cases would never come up in China."

"That's because this is a civil rights case, Jinjing. Civil rights cases never come up in China."

The American judge added enough edge to the words to make it uncomfortable.

"Show some courtesy, Mr. Doyle, or my country will call in all the money you owe us." Jinjing stiffened his spine as if trying to look taller than his five-feet-nine inches.

"Good luck collecting," Socorro Barroso said through her Portuguese accent. The Brazilian was one of the most popular judges in the group, mostly for her quick humor. "None of this really matters. The case will be over in short order."

"Should we be talking like this before the first day of trial?"

Alan let his eyes fall on Ernest Bankole of Sierra Leone. An experienced judge in his own country, he was new to the ICJ, having filled a vacancy created by the untimely death of one of the judges. Per custom, the vacancy was filled from the same country. He was the youngest member on panel. The more seasoned judges looked at each other and snickered. Only Kurosawa kept his emotion to himself, a practice he undertook when elected president of the body.

"I would have thought that by now, you'd know what we say here doesn't matter." The American Tracy Doyle looked like an impatient father. "There are no rules in chambers. What is said here never gets repeated." He frowned at the man. "Only the naive would raise such a question. We are judges, but we still have a right to private opinion. I once knew a politician who said that if a man couldn't drink a lobbyist's wine, accept his gifts, then vote against him on the floor, he shouldn't be in politics. The same is true about judges. If we can't exchange opinions about a case, then try a case with impartiality, we have no right wearing these robes. You weren't suggesting we can't be impartial, were you, Ernest?"

"No, of course not. I hold all of you in high regard."

"Way to backpedal, Ernest," Sir Christopher said. "Way to backpedal."

"Is everyone ready?" Kurosawa's voice cut through the chatter. "If so, we have a different case to try at the moment. Let's see if we can focus on that for now and deal with the Preston case when it comes before the bench."

They lined up and walked from the room into the court.

Chapter 38

The Letter

Alan Hodge had made his way back to his out-of-city hotel. The physical distance wasn't much, but the psychological gap was enormous. Although alone and missing his wife who carried on her career as economics professor in London, Alan felt most relaxed here.

As before, he brought a case full of letters with him. Some he read over a beef and potato dinner, the rest he read with Chopin playing in the background of his hotel room. The night was warm enough to leave the door open. With a glass of his favorite cognac in hand, he settled down on the balcony overlooking verdant farmland and allowed himself a few moments to unwind and take in the combined smells of the North Sea and rich fields.

He moved through a half dozen letters, most very similar to those he had already read. There were letters from men and women, young and old. The ratio of rational to insane remained the same.

One drew his attention. While most of the letters had come from the US and Canada, a few came from various places in the European Union. This particular correspondence was from London. He removed the missive and opened the page. The paper was common ruled-line like that used in school. The note was handwritten in pencil, the strokes becoming wider toward the end of the page as the pencil lead dulled. Some of the lines were smudged, the obvious result of a damp hand being dragged over the letter. The last line of the paragraph became difficult to read, as if the penman lost the strength to finish the strokes.

More surprising than anything, this letter was addressed to him.

Dear Alan Hodge,

I write to you on behalf of Dr. Pat Preston who is incarcerated in The Hague and due to be tried by you and your fellow members in the weeks and months ahead. I doubt I will hear of the outcome since I am soon to leave this life. A hardscrabble life has come to collect my debt. Cancer has invaded my liver and soon it will take what little remains of me. I am not a candidate for a transplant. I doubt I'd take one if I were.

Please understand, I do not begin this way to gain your sympathy. I have received enough sympathy in my life. No more is needed. Nor do I wish to use my illness to sway you. That is not my intent. In truth, Sir Alan, we are all dying, I just happened to know the cause of my death.

Why bring it up then? To help you understand my sincerity. The very writing of this letter taxes me more than I can say. I have friends who would take dictation, but I want to keep this personal. I thank you for taking the time to read this—if you do read it.

As you know, there is a move flooding your chambers with letters sharing personal experiences with faith. I am happy to do so. Perhaps because, well, I'm unique. You see, Jesus turned me into an honest man. I don't say that lightly. I mean it quite literally. I was a thief, a crook,who, until I heard the Gospel, never did anyone a bit of good, but did many a load of harm . . .

Alan couldn't read the next line. The penmanship was too shaky. He turned the letter to make better use of the balcony light.

Five years ago I stole a car, and a nice one at that. It wasn't the auto I was interested in. I just needed untraceable transportation. I wouldn't be using it long. You see, Sir Alan, I woke up that morning with one intent. I was planning on killing a man. I started out life in the slums by working my way free. I started a business, then another. When I wrote that I was a thief I meant it, but perhaps you imagined a man rolling victims in the park. I conducted my thievery through shady business transactions. I made money on the backs of others, often paying less than promised. By the time I was forty, I had earned millions. By the time I was forty-five, I was a billionaire.

All of that changed. For every thief in the corporate world, there are three others. I went from victimizer to victim. My money disappeared faster than beer at an Irish wake.

Alan smiled. At least the man still had a sense of humor.

I had been swindled by a crook smarter than I. The day I became a Christian, I had set out to kill a man. I had lost all reason. I not only planned to shoot him, but to do so in front of his family. I imagined the act over and over until it was branded in my brain. I hadn't decided what to do with the family, but I'm pretty sure that one pull of the trigger would be followed by three others: one for his wife, two for his children. I know that makes no sense. That's the way it is with madmen.

The car I stole from an employee had the radio on. I was so lost in my hatred I didn't notice for several minutes. Over the airwaves came a sermon by some preacher. His name was Dr. Pat Preston. The research I conducted later revealed that a Christian radio station was playing sermons from pastors who led large churches.

I tried to turn the radio off, but couldn't bring myself to do it. Dr. Preston spoke with such conviction but also with such love I was enthralled. He spoke about man's greatest enemy being himself. That was me. I know now he preached that sermon long before I heard it, but it changed me. I drove past my enemy's house without slowing. I returned the car and locked away the gun I had planned to use.

What his accusers call hate speech was speech that saved the life of a family—and my life.

Sir Alan, I know business. I know the white-collar crime world. I don't know American or international law. This I do know. Once I was a hateful, greedy man; now I am a man who spent the last few years trying to make recompense. I am a man who may be dead by the time you read this, but that is fine with me. Finally, at long last, I am at peace and I owe that to Dr. Preston and to the freedom of speech God used to bring that message to me. I wonder what would have happened if a message like Dr. Preston's was prevented from airing in England, or anywhere.

A gentle ache pestered Alan's heart. As he began folding the letter to return it to the envelope, he noticed a small note on the back, written in black ink and delicate hand.

To whom it may concern. Mr. O'Shay died shortly after signing this letter. I am sorry to tell you in this fashion.

Nurse Cindy Holden.

That night, Alan struggled with sleep. His legal mind seemed to be losing a battle with his heart.

The next morning, he called his sister.

Chapter 39

A Quick Trip

—◆—

Alan Hodge was dressed casually, wearing a pair of khaki pants, a blue t-shirt, and a pair of brown loafers. It was Saturday and he had flown from Rotterdam The Hague Airport on a CityJet shuttle to Heathrow. The flight was short but long enough to allow a short nap. He hadn't been sleeping well of late. The throttle of his mind seemed to be stuck.

The British Aerospace 146 had sailed through smooth, quiet air, making the flight more pleasurable than usual and set down only ten minutes late. As an experienced traveler, Alan considered ten minutes late as right on time, especially on a weekend.

He carried no luggage, just a computer bag with a laptop and some reading material. He kept two well stocked closets, one in his hometown of London, and one in The Hague, something that made the weekend commute much easier. This weekend, however, would be different: his wife, Lily, had already made plans to attend a seminar in France and would be gone all weekend. Just as well he had made plans himself.

Mia, his thirty-eight-year-old sister, met him at baggage claim. She was thin with black hair that always looked as if she washed it with motor oil. Her face was round and pleasant, her smile wide, and her eyes bright. She wore jeans, low-rise, canvas sneakers—*bright pink* sneakers. She sprinted to Alan and threw her arms around his neck, hugging hard enough to hurt. It was one of his regrets that he spent so little time with her. They lived in the same city and only a few miles apart. It wasn't the physical distance that kept them apart; it was their philosophy.

"Alan, it's so good to see you. It's been too long."

"It has, Mia. I've missed you." The last sentence felt like a lie. He loved his sister, but they held so little in common beyond growing up in the same mansion. Mia had always been the thoughtful, emotional one, and more than once she had proven to be the smarter of the two, something she would deny. Self-deprecation was her habit.

"I must admit," she said, "your call caught me by surprise." Her voice was half an octave higher than most expected.

"I haven't been that distant, have I?"

"We both live busy lives, Alan." She started toward the front of the airport. "I'm parked out front."

"I would have arranged for a driver."

She flashed a smile. "Ashamed to be seen with your sister?"

"Of course not. I'm afraid of your driving."

She punched him in the arm. "Ow! You know, assaulting a judge can land you in jail."

"Just about everything can land one in jail." A frown accompanied the statement.

They pushed through a throng of patrons, hearing a dozen different languages. There was a time when the weekend crowds at Heathrow were smaller than those of weekdays. Not anymore.

They worked their way through the masses like salmon swimming upstream. Five minutes later, Alan slipped into the front passenger seat of a battered, white Ford van that surely looked old in the 90s. The inside had a faint smell of body odor, cigarette smoke, and old diapers. On the side of the van, hand-painted letters read: INNER LONDON CHRISTIAN MISSION. Slipping into something overtly Christian made Alan uncomfortable. He wondered what the other justices at the ICJ would think. Then he decided he didn't care. All he was doing was visiting his sister. A tiny wave of guilt rolled through him. He was doing more than that. He had questions.Mia pulled the big vehicle from the parking stall and started for the exit.

"What did you mean?" Alan watched the other cars that passed the old van, the drivers taking a second look. A few frowned. Some shook their heads. At first, he thought they were responding to the lettering on the side of the vehicle, something that was very possible, but then decided their disgust was aimed at Mia's slow and sometimes erratic driving.

"Mean? About what?"

"When you said, 'Just about everything can land one in jail.'"

"Oh, sorry. You know me, no opinion goes unsaid."

"You're avoiding my question." The air of London seemed thicker than elsewhere.

"The world is changing. Well, the western world. It's becoming more intolerant."

"More intolerant? Many countries are working hard to pass laws making tolerance available to all."

Mia pursed her lips and Alan saw her knuckles whiten as she squeezed the steering wheel. "If you say so, brother."

"You don't agree?"

"No, I don't, but then I have a different life experience than you."

"We grew up in the same home, went to the same schools, except after university I went to law school and you went off to Bible school. Other than that, I don't see how our life experiences can be all that different."

She didn't respond, keeping her head and eyes straight ahead. Her mouth became a thin line and her eyes narrowed.

"Am I wrong?" Alan pressed.

"Yes. You are wrong." She pulled from the freeway and headed down surface streets. Suburban gave way to urban; individual homes and business morphed into row housing with peeling paint and dirty streets. Cliques of youth hung around on street corners, troubled and looking for trouble. Graffiti marred walls and signs. A few blocks deeper into the old city's bowels revealed men and women sleeping on the walkway.

In a frightfully sudden move, Mia pulled to the side of the road, forcing the large vehicle into a space meant for a much smaller car.

"What are you doing?"

"Come with me."

"Is this it? Are we at your mission?" He slipped from the front seat.

"If you mean the building, then no; if you mean the work, then yes." She walked back in the direction they had just come from. "Did you see them?"

"See whom?"

"I'll take that as a no." She picked up her pace. Alan had to jog a few steps to catch up. "Let me handle this. You keep your mouth shut. Got it?"

"Excuse me. That's a little harsh."

Mia ignored him. Alan looked down the street. A dozen meters ahead, a woman lay on the sidewalk, her back pressed against the wall of a vacant store front. In front of the woman, two toddlers played hopscotch. The oldest looked to be five years old. The other, a year younger. Both were girls. Three young men, early college age, dressed in torn clothing and smoking small cigarettes Alan was pretty sure were illegal were watching the children. Two of the men seemed to be prodding the young man with shaggy blond hair. They laughed in a way that made Alan uncomfortable. The blond kid looked at the unconscious woman on the sidewalk and then at the kids. Even though he was still some distance away, Alan could see the teenager leer.

He stepped to the children, interrupted their game, and leaned toward them. His buddies behind him laughed. "Do it!" One of them shouted.

Mia quickened her pace.

"Mia? Mia!"

She gave no indication of hearing Alan. He broke into a jog, reaching for his sister's arm, but she shook him off in a single motion. Two steps later she was sprinting.

"Hey, girls? Wanna do something fun?" The teenager had a grating, squeaky voice. He reached for one of the girls, beaming a smile of dirty, crooked teeth, too absorbed with the images in his mind to notice Mia's approach.

She arrived before the blonde's hand could touch the girls. She didn't slow. She mowed between the children, planted her left foot on the concrete and brought her right knee to the young man's face.

Alan saw blood splatter the sidewalk. The blonde rocked back and raised his hands to his face. Mia shot a hand out and between his upraised arms seizing the man by the throat. In the same motion, she lowered her hips and drove forward like the star player on a rugby team. The teenager backpedaled until he hit the glass front of the empty shop. Alan could hear him gasping for air. Mia pulled the kid forward and slammed him back, making the widow rattle, something she did three times.

"I got me some questions, Danny-boy. Real serious questions. You hear me?" When he didn't respond, she slammed him against the glass again. Alan was certain one more such impact would bring a rain of glass. He was too stunned to do anything but pull the children close to his side.

Mia's speed, strength, fury and bizarre change in speech pattern baffled him. "I asked you a question, Danny. You deaf?" She put her face near his ear and shouted. "You DEAF?"

"No, ma'am, I hear ya. I hear ya."

She slapped him with her free hand. "Who was it picked you from the street when you were face down in your own puke? Who was it?"

"It was you, ma'am."

"Who was it gave you food when no one would do anything but show you the rubbish pail? Huh? Who was it?"

"It was you, ma'am. It was you."

Danny was having trouble getting words past the vise that was Mia's hand.

"When you OD'd last month, who carried your sorry carcass to hospital? Was it your mates? Eh? Was it?"

"No, it was you, ma'am."

"I know your name, don't I, Danny-boy? I know where you shack up, don't I? I know how to find you, I know everyone who knows you, and every one of them owes me—jus' like you owe me. Tell me you understand what I'm saying."

"I understand, ma'am."

"Where are your mates?"

Danny cut his eyes to the side. "I-I don't know."

"I do. They're gone. They left you. Abandoned you. What's that tell you about them?"

"That they're no friends?"

"You got it. Who is your friend?"

"You are, ma'am."

"Bottom line, you don't want me coming after you."

"Yes, ma'am."

"Last thing. I had better see you in church Sunday. If you die between now and then, I wanna see your corpse."

"Yes, ma'am. Church Sunday. Yes, ma'am."

She released him. "Leave."

Now free of her grasp, he gave her an icy stare, something that melted under the heat of her gaze. He jogged away.

Mia went to the woman lying nearby and set two fingers on the woman's carotid artery. The woman's pale complexion told Alan what Mia was verifying. The woman was dead. Mia pulled a cheap cell phone from her pocket and punched in a number. She gave the address, her name and said, "Woman down . . ." she glanced at the girls, ". . . deceased." When she switched off, she moved to the children and knelt. "Is that your mum?"

"No, ma'am. That's our auntie."

"I see."

Sirens filled the air.

"Bloody—"

She pointed a finger at him that appeared as fast as the business end of a switchblade. "Watch it, brother. You know I don't tolerate swearing."

"Yes, ma'am."

***

"I am fully and thoroughly stunned." Alan was back in the passenger seat. "I have no words for what I just saw."

"I'm sorry you had to see that."

"I didn't even notice the dead woman or the children, but you did."

Mia pulled onto the street. "You learn to see such things after a few years down here. I saw the dead woman and the children. I know the boys who were causing the problem. They're troubled in so many ways and the only thing they respond to is a strong hand." Her hands began to shake. She tried to conceal it, but it was too late.

"Are you okay?"

"Yes. It's just adrenaline. Once the anger is gone, the left over adrenaline needs something to do. So I shake."

"I take it you've had such confrontations before."

"A few. It's a tough neighborhood." Mia pulled the van to the back parking lot of an old church that looked as if it hadn't been painted since the Second World War. She parked and exited. Alan followed. A few moments later, she was seated in an antiquated kitchen filled with pots and pans, every one scratched, dented, and baring the black marks of many hours spent over an open flame.

"Tea?" she asked.

"Got anything stronger?"

"I assume you mean coffee or you're joking about having booze in a church."

"I was teasing. Tea is fine." He watched her put water on to boil. He started to offer help, then realized she was trying to work off some of the residual energy from the confrontation. They passed the minutes in silence until the water began to boil. With a precision and a speed that came from decades of preparing the drink, Mia had the pot on the table steeping and two chipped cups, each showing stains from years of use.

"Listen Alan, I don't want you to get the idea I roam the streets grabbing people by the throat and threatening them. What you saw was . . ." She searched for the right word. ". . . rare."

"You're worried I'll get the wrong idea about Christians?"

"In a word, yes."

"I'll admit, I didn't think missionaries were so physical."

"It's this place, Alan. You go on the streets and see buildings, people, cars, and it all looks normal. Poor, but normal. It's not. It's a different planet. The language is different, the people are different, their world view is something I couldn't imagine. Yet, they're people."

"Who need help." Alan poured the tea.

"We all need help, Alan. Everyone you see needs help. Everyone is injured, worried, frightened. The tough guys are the worst. Guys like Danny. The kid has had a tough life, if you can call it a life at all."

"Why?"

"He grew up in an abusive family—"

"Not him. You. Why are you here, Mia?"

"You've come to rescue me?"

"No. You're a big girl; you can make your own decisions. Why here?"

"It's where I'm needed." She tapped the cup with her short fingernails. "I feel called."

"Called? As in a call from God?" He studied the table.

"I'm happy here, Alan. I have purpose and I'm making an eternal difference."

"It's hard for me to comprehend how two people who grew up in the same home, to the same wealthy parents, studied at the best schools, trafficked in the best social circles ended up so different from one another."

"I wasn't happy, Alan. I didn't know happiness until I gave my life to Christ."

"You see there? I don't understand that. You had everything. So did I."

"I was incomplete." Mia pushed the cup away and rested her folded hand on the table as if she were about to pray. "I first sensed it when I was thirteen."

"The teenage years are difficult—"

"Stop it, Alan. It had nothing to do with my being a teenager. I said I first noticed it when I was thirteen. It persisted for years. I'm surprised you didn't notice. I was pretty miserable. It continued through college."

"So what changed?"

"A friend took me to a small church just outside the city. I immediately felt at home."

"You'd gone to church all your life, Mia."

"On Easter and Christmas. I need something more. That little independent church gave meaning to the message. It was there, when I was twenty-one, that I gave my life to Christ."

"What does that mean? You were baptized into the Anglican church."

She shook her head. "It's not about the denomination, Alan; it's about the message of Christ. The label doesn't matter. This church is independent of any denomination. That doesn't make it better; it doesn't make it worse. The church—the true church—has nothing to do with buildings or denominations. I admire the work done by different denominations, but the one thing everyone needs is a personal relationship with Jesus. Had that church not been there, I don't know where I'd be right now, or *what* I'd be. My life was changed because I could hear the message of Christ, hear about the forgiveness of my sin, about how to live a life that is spiritual."

"I don't want to be offensive, Mia. You know I love you, but that sounds like brainwashing."

"Brainwashing? Really? Is that what it sounds like?" She scratched at a spot just above her left ear. "Do you think I'm that shallow? I may not be as intelligent as you, brother, but I'm neither stupid nor gullible."

Alan grinned. "I don't know if you know this, Mia, but I've always been intimidated by your intelligence." He paused. "It would be inappropriate of me to reveal details, but I'm sitting for a case—"

"Dr. Pat Preston."

"So you know?"

"Every serious church person knows, Alan. What happens to him happens to all Christians." She thought for a second. "And people of other faiths."

"I think you misunderstand. The case is about hate speech and the propagation of intolerance."

"You can't believe that, Alan. I became a Christian because someone was free to tell me of the Gospel."

"That won't change."

"But his ability to teach from the Bible will and the Bible is the source of authority for all Christians."

"People will still be able to read from their Bibles—"

"But not teach from it. The people discriminating against Christians want to silence us, to dictate what can be taught."

"'Discrimination' is too strong a word, Mia."

"Is it? You lawyers are big on the legal meaning of words; all I know is that governments are trying to muzzle us. If that's not discrimination, then I don't know what is." She poured more tea in her cup which she had barely touched.

Alan was taking in more than her words; he was hearing her heart. For the first time. He had known about her conversion, of course, but every family had a member who was slightly off center. For the first time in years, Mia seemed more centered than Alan thought possible.

Chapter 40

Round 1

 ━━◆━━

I sabella noticed she was having to work harder than normal to breathe. The condition reminded her of an unwise decision she once made to wear a too-tight dress to a party. Although only there two hours, the inability to draw a full breath made it seem like a week. She had never worn the dress again. This time, however, the inability to breathe normally had nothing to do with her clothing. Fear constricted her, a fear she couldn't show to her Alliance co-counsel, Scott Freeman and Larry Jordan, her client Pat Preston, her opponent John Knox Smith, and certainly couldn't show the panel of fifteen judges.

Behind her, the court's balcony was filled with press. The Pope's encyclical and Freeman's mass mailing had been the buzz of the media for two weeks. Major news sources like CNN, the BBC, and even Al Jazeera were present, as were reporters from every Western European state.

The court was slow in starting, something to do with the computer system that fed monitors in front of every judge. Court president Yoshiro Kurosawa sat patiently while the matter was resolved. Isabella stole a glance at Pat. He seemed more comfortable and relaxed than she had seen him in some time, something she considered odd since he had recently said no to John's offer to drop the case in exchange for a full apology to the American people and a commitment to abandon the ministry. She had been a bit surprised by his refusal to accept the offer but pleased.

The more she thought about the offer, the more she came to believe John Knox Smith knew her client would refuse, and even if he accepted the offer, Smith would look like the victor without the risk of losing in a trial.

Kurosawa tapped the bench with a knuckle. "I apologize for the delay. I am told our technical difficulties have been resolved." He looked around the court, making sure support staff were in their places and ready for work. "This morning, we will hear opening remarks. Is counsel present?"

John rose first. "Thank you, Mr. President. John Knox Smith for the prosecution and the people of the United States and its offended global citizens. Prosecution is ready." He was entirely too smug for Isabella's liking.

Isabella stood. "Mr. President, Countess Isabella San Phillipa representing one of the afore mentioned people of the United States." Several in the gallery snickered. She glanced at John who seemed unfazed. "Defense is ready, Mr. President."

"Let's keep the sniping to a minimum, please." Kurosawa's eyes narrowed like a father questioning the veracity of teenager's explanation for returning home late. "Mr. Smith, if you will, please confine your statement to opening remarks."

John stood again. He looked more rested than last time he had sat in that chair. He stepped to the central podium and took a moment to look each justice in the eye. He carried no notes, but Isabella had no doubt he had a full outline in his mind.

"Members of the panel. On behalf of the American people, I thank you for giving your very busy time. The prosecution will present an ironclad case showing Dr. Pat Preston did willfully and constantly break the laws of the United States, specifically the Respect for Diversity and Tolerance Act of 2014 and subsequent international legislation related to it and evolving standards of international law and decency. What is being tried here is of great importance, not just to the United States, but all of Europe and the rest of the world. This case matters to any country that holds human dignity in high regard.

"We will further show that Dr. Preston's crimes, although verbal in nature, did target with the intent to do emotional and potential physical harm to select groups of people; did so with the intent of ostracizing large segments of the world's population depriving them of their right to seek happiness and fulfillment as they see fit; that such discrimination was done under color of spiritual authority; and that Dr. Preston's intent was to foster intolerance, and hinder the common acceptance of diversity.

"We will show that Dr. Preston did benefit from such activities through the financial growth of his church and through the publicity it brought. We will further prove that Dr. Preston used various multimedia venues such as but not limited to public speeches, printed material, digital audio recordings, digital video recordings, the Internet, television, radio, and other means of mass communications across the globe.

"It will become clear to the court that Dr. Preston's actions were not only a violation of US law but did, in practical effect, harm innocent people, calling into question their value as human beings and threatening eternal punishment of those who hold differing opinions or spiritual heritage. Such a threat seems laughable to us, but it has harmed countless thousands, perhaps millions, over the history of Christianity. In short, your honors, the prosecution will present a case that will show beyond all doubt that Dr. Preston is an emotional and spiritual terrorist who delights in minimizing and marginalizing those within and without the walls of the church. That such actions were aimed at not only adults, but youth and children as well.

"Our case will demonstrate the need for laws such as Respect for Diversity and Tolerance Act of 2014 and the intent of the United States government and the people it represents who desire to join the rest of the world in granting full human rights to all people, regardless of race, creed, gender or sexual orientation."

John returned to his seat.

Kurosawa motioned to Isabella. "Countess, if you please."

A knot the size of a grapefruit formed in her gut.

"Countess?"

Isabella sprang to her feet. "My apologies, Mr. President and to the full panel. I'm afraid I was stunned by what I just heard." She shook her head like a disappointed teacher. "The defense believes this case is the fruit of legal misrepresentation and that Dr. Preston, a man who has given his life to helping others make sense of this life, has become the target of people like Mr. Smith who wish to use my client as a foot bridge along the path to their own philosophy and, dare I say it, enrollment in history.

"We will demonstrate that Dr. Preston has committed no crime, done no harm, has never shown bigotry, or done anything but be faithful to his religion, a faith that extends back two thousand years, and some would argue much longer than that. We will further show that Dr. Preston is the victim, not the perpetrator of the very crimes his country lays at his feet.

"We will demonstrate that the 2014 law to which Mr. Smith alludes is universally accepted by the good people of the United States in fact violates the constitution of the United States, accepted norms of international law, and that it is itself a cause of discrimination, marginalization and now persecution.

"We will show that Dr. Preston has been the target for trial to serve as an example to others Mr. Smith wishes to intimidate. We will also demonstrate that this case was not tried in the United States because it was mishandled and, because of its very nature, cannot be won in a higher court.

"We will also show that Dr. Preston has suffered untold torment at the hands of his accusers, being unjustly arrested, held, deported, separated from his wife and two young children who, along with him, suffered ridicule, intimidation, loss of income and position and emotional stress beyond description. It is our intent to show that Mr. Smith and the United States Department of Justice are attempting to use this court and their own gross misunderstanding of law as a tool in their own attempts to discriminate against people who hold views which they do not approve.

"In the end, your honors, we will show that the prosecution's case was planted in ego, grown in the soils of injustice, and that it is an attempt to control what men and women are allowed to believe. They wish to be the arbitrators of thought and they wish to become so by sacrificing my client and making this court party to their efforts."

Isabella moved back to her seat.

Kurosawa grunted. "Thank you, counsel. We will hear from the prosecution on Wednesday of this week. This court is adjourned."

Everyone stood and waited as the justices filed from the room. Isabella watched as Pat was handcuffed and led from the courtroom. Her heart ached.

"Countess?"

She turned to see a smiling John Knox Smith. "Yes?"

"I wonder if I might have a word with you. Perhaps over dinner."

"Over dinner? I'm sorry; I'm dining alone while I call my husband."

"Of course. I heard about the accident."

"It wasn't an accident; it was an attack."

He lowered his gaze for a moment. "Either way, I'm sorry to hear of his injuries. How is he doing?"

"He will survive." Her words were tense.

"Countess, you can't possibly think I had anything to do with it."

"One of Dr. Preston's early defense attorneys was gunned down before he could do much for the case. My client has received death threats. Someone left a pair of dolls on the doorstep of his family's home with knitting needles shoved into their eyes. My husband was almost killed—"

"Let me stop you there, Countess. Matt Branson was a friend and I mourn his death. I have called for and monitor the investigation into his death. I know nothing about dolls, and I had nothing to do with the attack on your husband. I only mention dinner because a nice restaurant is good neutral ground, nothing more."

"Dr. Preston was your friend, too, and look at where he is now. I have nothing to say to you."

"But I have something to say to you and as the lead defense attorney, you owe it to your client. Do you want to hear my offer or not?"

She turned to Freeman and Jordan. Freeman nodded. "All right, but I insist co-counsel be present."

"I have no problem with that. Your place or mine?"

"Excuse me?" Isabella's jaw stiffened.

"Your hotel or mine?"

Freeman spoke up. "There's a restaurant on the coast. American owned. It's called Millie's."

"I know it," Isabella said. "They have a back room we can use."

"So be it." John nodded and walked way, meeting his co-counsel at the back of the courtroom.

Chapter 41

Unexpected Meeting

⇒·◇·⇐

Millie's was a small restaurant in a line of such places lining the North Sea beachfront. The sun was making a leisurely approach to the horizon. Tourists and locals mingled along the concrete boardwalk that separated the business establishments from the beach. It looked like many seaside communities Isabella had visited. When she and Scott Freeman arrived, they found John Knox Smith already seated in the back room. A youngish blonde woman sat next to him, a professional distance between them.

They entered the back and the owner, a stout man with a balding head, approached. He spoke with a southern accent. Freeman had explained he'd eaten in the eatery a few days before. He had been staying in a nearby hotel and the front desk made the recommendation. Americans like American food. Freeman had told Isabella the owner was from somewhere in Georgia where he owned a small cafe. He had saved enough money to pay for a trip to the Netherlands, the homeland of his wife's grandmother. They fell in love with the place and managed to open a down home restaurant. It did well and they were able to open the beachfront eatery. "He'll tell you the story," Freeman had said. "The man loves to talk."

John stood and introduced the blonde as Andrea, his personal assistant. "Where is Mr. Jordan?"

"He's working on the case. The conversation will be easier with fewer people." Isabella shook Andrea's hand and fought off the urge to wash. Freeman said hello and then slid back a chair for Isabella. A few moments later, the owner brought a plate of fried pickles. She looked at them with suspicion.

"They taste better than they look. It's a Deep South delicacy. She decided against the adventure. She wanted this bit of business over as soon as possible."

"I will confess," John said, "that you two have made my life difficult. The gag with the Pope was brilliant but useless."

Isabella looked at Freeman. "Gag?"

"What the esteemed Assistant Attorney General is trying to say is that the Pope's encyclical was a disingenuous bit of trickery."

"Oh." She looked at Smith. "You think the Pope is an ignorant man? That someone like me can trick him into doing something he thinks is wrong?"

"I'm afraid Freeman misrepresents me. I meant it was an excellent bit of showmanship." John looked at Freeman, his gaze as friendly as a rusty knife blade. "And that stunt with the mailings. Just so you know, I'm having postal inspectors decide if you've misused the US mail service."

"I'm not surprised, John, nor am I intimidated. You have my address. You know where to find me." Freeman pulled one of the deep fried, battered appetizers onto a smaller plate. "Is that why you wanted to talk to me, John? You want to insult and intimidate us?"

"No. I want to talk some sense into you. You can't win."

"How kind of you to let us know ahead of time." Isabella showed no emotion.

"Listen, lady," Andrea began.

"Stay out of this, Andrea," Smith snapped. "I wanted to meet because we're about to get into the rough and tumble of the trial. Things are only going to get worse for Pat."

"Dr. Preston," Isabella corrected.

"Countess, I've known the man a lot longer than you. We went to college together—"

"I know all about that. It was one of the reasons I hold you in such high disregard."

279

It took a second for John to recognize the jab. "I'm extending my offer."

"The offer? Oh, you mean the opportunity for my client to confess to a crime that is no crime; to admit fault when there is none; apologize to people who don't deserve an apology; give up his life's calling; embarrass himself and his family; demean church work; insult the millions of people who believe as he does? That offer? It is puzzling why he didn't leap at that."

"I'm trying to help an old friend, Countess."

Isabella's face warmed and the muscles in her neck and jaw tightened. "You don't get to stab a friend in the back, make a name for yourself while he lays bleeding to death, then offer to wipe the knife clean."

"You're obligated to repeat the offer to him."

"I will, but I can tell you right now what he'll say: No. Here's what I suggest. You drop the case. Dr. Preston goes free. Your government pays him damages for the pain and suffering you've caused. You do all this with no conditions. I'm sure I can talk him into accepting that offer."

"I'm trying to help your client out."

"Then free him."

"I can't. It's too complicated."

Freeman couldn't let that go. "No, it's not, John. It's not complicated at all. First, the case is bogus. Always has been, then your team botched the evidence so it couldn't be used in US court. That means you had to take it somewhere else so you wouldn't lose momentum in your systematic shredding of the Constitution."

"Don't start with me, Freeman. I know constitutional law better that you." A glass of beer was before him, which he almost knocked over with a sweep of his hand. Andrea removed it from the playing field. "The Constitution was designed to be changed. That's why the first one was ratified, then amended with the Bill of Rights, the first ten amendments. There are twenty-seven amendments now and over ten thousand amendments have been proposed in Congress since 1789. Ten thousand, man. What's that tell us? It tells us the Constitution has always been subject to change."

John's voice rose until Andrea laid a hand on his arm. He quieted the volume, but not the intensity. "Those amendments came about because society changed. Think of the Thirteenth that abolished slavery and enforced prohibition. I'm pretty sure you think that's an improvement over classifying Africans as three-fifths of a man. The Nineteenth allowed women the right to vote. Christians tried to stop that. Would you argue against that?" He didn't let Freeman answer. "The document is designed to be revised, Freeman. That was what the founding fathers intended."

"Last I looked, John, the First Amendment is still in place, although I can see your boot prints all over it." Freeman took another bite of the appetizer as if no conversation was going on. He pointed with his fork: "Freedom of religion, in which the government is pro-hibited from starting a state church and ensures the free practice of religion; freedom of speech; freedom of the press, freedom of assembly and—"

"And freedom to petition the government. I know what it says."

"And there's the difference, John. I not only know what it says, I *respect* what it says."

"I know what I'm doing, Freeman. You're focused on your little religious groups, while I'm focused on the country as a whole and everyone who lives in it. I'm the one trying to take our country to the world stage and make it part of the bigger picture."

"Wow, that must have been one costly room addition."

John shook his head, then looked at Andrea. "What does that mean?"

"You must have expanded your house to make room for that ego."

"That's unprofessional."

Isabella couldn't sit quietly. "And accurate. Let my client go."

"Only under my terms." He crossed his arms.

"Has he always been this way?" Isabella asked Andrea.

"As long as I've known him, he has been a man of high convictions."

"High convictions, is it?" Isabella's eyes fixed on John like a scope on a hunter's rifle. "When was the last time you saw your son?"

"That's none of your business." John's face resembled a beet.

"Your wife?"

Andrea stood. "That's none of your business, either."

Isabella stood, opened her purse and removed a twenty Euro bill and tossed it on the table. She then made eye contact with Andrea. "You're right, it is none of my business, but I want your employer to know I do my homework. You know the problem with people who have no morals? They can hurt whomever they want and somehow justify it. If you're the replacement, Andrea, then bear in mind that Mr. Smith has turned on his friends, his family, his country's heritage. From where I sit, you're next." She closed her hand bag. "Now, if you'll excuse me, I promised to have a telephone date with my husband in Rome."

As Isabella left, she thought she heard teeth grinding.

Chapter 42

Negative Response

⟫◈⟪

It had taken John Knox Smith two hours to cool the heat of his anger and to settle his nerves. He was not a man of violence, but he really wanted to punch someone. Hard. Several times. To her credit, Andrea stayed out of the way, choosing to sit close to the window of his hotel room. Also to her credit, she stayed in his room rather than escape to her own during his diatribe. She offered no soothing words. That would have only inflamed him. She didn't join the cursing. That would only deprive him of free expression. This was his fight, not hers. So she sat, gazing at him, nodding at the appropriate time.

When the flood of expletives eased to a trickle, Andrea rose from her chair, approached John, and wrapped her arms around his neck, gently running her fingers along the back of his neck. He allowed it. It felt good to be held. The boy inside the man fought to the surface.

He was tired. So very tired. He had risen to such a level of power and prominence in such a short time, ramrodded several pieces of controversial legislation through Congress, something President Blaine had been happy to help with. He had done more in a few years as Assistant Attorney General than most do in decades of service, but that came with a price. A heavy emotional toll. There were days when he felt like life was a giant shredder, slowly pulling him into its metal teeth. It was a feeling he didn't know how to handle.

He had the kind of confidence that would intimidate Alexander the Great, but lately, cracks were appearing. It made no sense. He loved his work. He *lived* for his work. It was his exercise, his hobby, his entertainment; it was his reason to crawl out of bed. Why was he feeling shaky now?

"Everything you said was right, John. I wanted to rip the woman's eyes out, but that wouldn't have been good for your reputation. Would you like a drink?"

"I don't want to go out." He pulled away and moved to the window.

"I can pour something from the mini-bar. You're off duty for the rest of the day."

"I'm never off duty, Andrea." A moment later: "Beer." He heard the small refrigerator open and close. When he turned, he saw Andrea opening two bottles of Grolsch beer. She handed him one.

"I got a text from Mr. Thevis. He wants a few minutes of your time. I put him off since it came while you were, um, depressurizing."

"What's he want?"

"All the text said was that he wanted to update you."

John nodded. "Good. It'll get my mind off things."

"I think you should take the evening off, John. You've been working day and night since your short vacation."

"Call the front desk and book a small conference room for us."

"We could sit in the bar."

He took a drink of the rich beer. "I'm getting paranoid, so I don't want to meet in public. That *woman* knew about my pending divorce and my estranged son. How did she know that? She's been checking up on me."

"She's not all that powerful." Andrea moved to the sofa.

"She arranged for security for Preston's family at her own expense. She's rich. She's smart. She has the Alliance behind her and that's saying a lot. She's well connected—"

"Hey!"

"Business and legal connections, Andrea. Don't be a school girl." He returned to gazing out the window. "She knows the Pope, for Pete's sake. I wouldn't be surprised if she has this place bugged." He set the beer down and put his hands behind his back. "If I were her, I'd do everything I could to understand my opponent. I know about her."

"I see your point."

"Andrea? Set the beer down and get us a place to meet."

She was on her feet and at the phone in a moment. "How soon do you want to meet?"

"ASAP."

***

Joel Thevis, John's lead litigator and co-counsel on the Preston case, was in the hotel conference room waiting when John and Andrea arrived. He was dressed in a button-down, white shirt and black slacks. A pot of coffee sat in the center of an oval, golden oak desk. He had already poured a cup for himself. He had bags under his eyes. International travel was not his strong suit, although he never complained. Next to the coffee cup sat a laptop, on, running and ready for action.

Joel stood when John entered. "John."

"What have you got for me, Joel?" He waved off Andrea's offer for coffee. He had enough things interfering with his sleep.

"You're familiar with Sir Isaac Newton's third law of motion."

"I'm not," Andrea confessed.

John filled her in. "For every action, there is an opposite and equal reaction."

"Oh."

"That observation carries over into realms other than physics," Joel said. "Except in matters involving people, the reaction can be greater than the action, and that's just what we're seeing."

He tapped a key and a wall-mounted monitor glowed to life. "At my request, Paul Atoms has been monitoring the reaction to the Pope's encyclical and Freeman's letter. The news media has been keeping the issue alive. I can't help but wonder if Freeman and his team are keeping things alive. If he is, it's starting to back fire."

"How?" John watched the monitor.

"Like this, Boss." Another key tap. The image of a church on fire appeared. A dour looking newscaster was saying something in

German. Joel lowered the volume. "This is a Lutheran church in Germany. As you probably know, Lutherans are big in Germany. They arrested three men who set the fire. They confessed and said their motivation was the church's attempt to control their lives."

"They're part of a disenfranchised group?"

"I asked the same question of Paul. He said he checked into that and the men had no affiliation with the gay or transgendered community or any non-protestant group. In fact, they're not part of any group. They're steelworkers. They burned the church because they hate the Pope."

"But Lutherans aren't Catholic. They broke off from the Roman Church. Martin Luther and all that."

"You're right, John, and that's the concern. This was an act of violence just for the sake of violence. Maybe they just hate churches."

"Who doesn't?" Andrea said. "It's just a building."

The corners of Joel's mouth dipped toward his shoulders. "The pastor was trapped inside. He burned to death."

"Oh, I didn't know." John felt his anger rising again, this time at Andrea.

"This next footage happened last Sunday." A new bit of news footage played on the screen. "Orange County in Southern California." The video showed a crowd of several hundred people with signs walking in an unbroken line around a large church building. "OC is an island of conservatism in California, so a number of picketers probably came from outside the county and successfully kept worshippers out of the building. The pastor came close to conducting the service in the street, but the police talked him out of it. Instead, the church made sandwiches and served bottled water to the group. It didn't do much good, but it did keep people from passing out on an unseasonably hot day.

"This is a news report from Grand Rapids, Michigan."

John saw the front of a small, white chapel with a well kept lawn and flower garden. In the middle of the lawn, a sheet of plastic covered an uneven form. A body. "A murder?"

"Yes. A sixty-eight year old pastor was beaten to death in front of his church. The perps are still at large. One more. This next clip shows a pastor leaving a hospital. As you can see, he's been badly beaten. This account, however, is a little different. That pastor's name is Clifford Harper. He's what the evangelicals call a liberal pastor. In fact, he has gone on record as supporting DTED."

"But someone still beat him?" Andrea looked uncomfortable with the visual evidence of violence.

"To some people, a pastor is a pastor. I have a dozen more of these, John, but I think you get the idea."

"Has there been a reaction to the reaction?"

"You mean have Christians and other religious groups returned the favor?" He shook his head. "There have been a couple of cases, but all of them minor and conducted by fringe groups already known for picketing funerals and the like. They're not taken seriously and most church leaders consider them an embarrassment."

John rubbed his face. One more problem; one more issue to tax already frayed nerves. "What's your suggestion, Joel?"

"You need to make a statement condemning the violence. If you don't, people will assume you agree with it, at least tacitly."

"That's ridiculous," Andrea said.

"No, it's not," John said. "Joel is right, but it has to be done right. We have to strike the right balance. Can't appear too soft; can't appear to condone lawbreaking." John stood. "Andrea, let's get someone to draft a press release saying something like DTED and the DOJ are committed to ending all hate crimes, no matter the philosophy behind it."

"Yes, sir."

"I want to see it before it goes out."

Chapter 43

The Question

<<=>◆<=>>

The phone in Becky Preston's home rang, startling everyone in the house except the children who were already in bed. Wilma had come to visit Becky. They were drinking tea and chatting when the old style ring rebounded off the walls. Becky let out a gasp and even Beatrice was startled. Becky looked at her watch: almost ten in the evening. That made her heart speed.

"Who could be calling this time of night?" Then she thought of Pat. It would early morning on that side of the world. The phone rang again, and Becky snatched up the receiver. "He-hello?" She looked up and found Beatrice by her side.

"Mrs. Preston, this is Isabella San Phillipa. I'm sorry to be calling so late."

"Hello, Countess. Is Pat okay?"

"Yes, he's fine. He seems stronger of late."

"That's good. I've been worried. The trial has started, right?"

"Yes, but only opening arguments. The trial portion begins on Wednesday. That's why I'm calling. I have a favor to ask. I want you to come to the Netherlands."

"I don't understand."

"Having you in court will be a help. I want the judges to see you and the children. I want them to have to look in your face. Right now, Pat is just a prisoner accused of a crime. I want the judges to see him as a husband and father."

"When? How do I get there?"

"Do the children have passports?"

"Yes. We got them before Pat went to Oxford. Pat made us keep them up to date. He was hoping to take the kids overseas someday."

"Good. I will take care of the travel, but you have to leave soon. Can you get to the airport tonight?"

"Tonight? Wait. This is too fast."

"Is Beatrice there?"

"Yes. She's always here." She handed the phone to the security agent and moved to Wilma. "It's Pat's lawyer. She wants me and the kids to fly to the Netherlands."

Wilma moved a strand of gray hair. "Will you get to see Pat?"

"I don't know. I don't know what's going on. She says I should bring the kids."

Beatrice said, "Yes, ma'am. We'll be online in a minute." She hung up, retrieved her laptop and set it on the dining room table.

"What's going on?" Becky asked.

"Isabella wants to video conference. I'll be online in a second, then . . ." She worked the keyboard and soon the image of a weary looking Isabella appeared on the screen. She turned the laptop so the camera above the monitor was facing Becky.

"How is your husband?" Becky asked.

"He's home and we have the home secured. It will be a few months before he's back to normal, but God saw fit to spare him."

"Praise God."

"I do every time I see him." Becky saw the countess lean into the camera as if leaning forward to whisper in her ear, even though separated by thousands of miles. "I'm doing the video conference so Beatrice can listen in. I want you to come to The Hague. I've made arrangements for you to see Pat again. I think he needs to see you again. More than that, the judges need to see you. John Knox Smith needs to know you're there staring holes in his back. We need to make the case more human and less about international law. Can you do that?"

"I want to, but I don't know."

"I'll pay for everything. I am one phone call from making it all happen."

"Can you guarantee our safety?"

Isabella hesitated. "No. I can provide the best in security. You will be as safe here as you are there."

"That's not very safe."

"I can't argue with that, Becky. Beatrice will travel with you. Will you come?"

Becky said nothing. Her mind twisted like a tornado.

"You should go." Wilma touched Becky's arm.

"Who is that?" Isabella looked worried.

Beatrice answered. "Wilma, a family friend."

"Becky, I don't want to manipulate you into doing this. It has to be your decision."

"But you think it will help."

Isabella nodded. "I do. I don't know how much it will help, but it will help. Will you come?"

Seconds oozed by. "Yes."

Chapter 44

Agent Fay

—⬩—

"There's some guy in the conference room who wants to see you." The announcement came from a young female agent. "What do you mean 'some guy'? What's he want?"

"I have no idea what he wants. He's with NTSB."

That figured. Getting into the Hoover Building wasn't something just anyone could do. It took credentials. Ruby rose, tucked the ever-present unlit cigarette behind her ear. The young agent looked disgusted. "Oh, I'm sorry. Did you want a smoke?"

"No. Ma'am." The ma'am followed a little later than Ruby liked but she let it go, too curious about the man without an appointment.

She moved from her cubicle to the hall and to the meeting room identified by the other agent. She found the man in the room. He was seated and leaning back as if he were on break. His face was lined with years and spoke of determination seldom seen. "I'm Special Agent Ruby Fay. Who are you?"

"Well, Mac Adams said you were curt and impatient."

"I think he meant cute and unforgettable. Again, who are you?"

"Greg Mayer, NTSB."

"I promise, I didn't steal any aircraft. You know Mac?"

"Yeah, we worked a case a long time ago. We were both young then."

Ruby huffed. "I don't remember being young. What can I do for the NTSB?"

"I'm told you can be trusted. Is that true?"

"Unless it's illegal. I'm a stickler about such things."

"Do you know Paul Atoms?"

Ruby fought the urge to spit on the floor. "You a friend of his?"

"Nope. Don't like the man. Talking to him is like having a root canal done by a blind dentist."

One corner of her mouth lifted. "I sense wisdom. Are we off the record? This is just between us?"

"Yes." She started to say something then stopped and looked at the ceiling. Mayer got the message. There might be electronic ears. She waited for him to make the next move.

"Well, Mac said I should look you up when I was in the neighborhood. Said you were the kinda gal who liked to shake things up." He stood, reaching into his suit coat pocket.

"I'm a real party animal."

Mayer set an envelope on the table. "Here's my number. Let's take in the sights sometime."

She pulled the envelope close. "My dance card is pretty full."

"I imagine it is. Thanks for your time."

Mayer exited. Ruby opened the envelope and found an unsigned letter.

She read.

She swore.

***

They met in a Starbucks near L'Enfant Plaza. It was early evening and only a few patrons populated the place. Something that would change when the after dinner crowd looking for a way to extend the evening began arriving.

Ruby found Mayer nursing some sugary, iced concoction. "That stuff will shut your pancreas down."

"You say that like it's a bad thing. Have a seat. Can I get you anything?"

"Coffee. Black."

"Decaf?"

"Despite my appearance, I'm not all that delicate."

He returned a moment later with a paper cup in cardboard sleeve. "I suddenly feel less masculine."

"It's the twenty-first century; you can drink your girlie beverages."

"I feel better now. Thanks."

"I detect sarcasm." She removed the lid of the coffee. "Let's get down to it."

"I need the help of the FBI on this accident investigation. Paul Atoms is overseeing things while John Knox Smith is overseas. Truth is, I don't trust him. I'm turning to you because Mac says you're the last honest agent."

"Not true. There are others, but they've been stationed in places like Salt Lake City. The point is taken."

"What I'm about to do isn't found in the procedural manuals, yours or mine, but I think it's the only way to solve this case."

"It's that important to you?"

"I've been at this for a long time. I've solved every case I've touched."

"Except this one."

"I know the cause of the accident, but that's not enough. Something stinks." He reached into his pocket and removed a plastic bag. "I'm showing this to you, hoping that some judge doesn't consider it a breach in chain of evidence. After the plane went down, a janitor at THE departure airport found this in the trash. As you can see, it's been worked over pretty good, but the data remained good. Our techs found documents and engineering plans for the Gulfstream. We believe there's a program that tweaked the onboard computer. The flight data reenactment shows that the computer lost its silicon mind. I'll skip the details, but I will say the program changed the reading coming from the Pitot sensors."

"The what?"

"You ever see those little, bent metal tubes on the outside of a commercial jet?"

"Yeah."

"Those are hollow tubes with sensors used to measure airspeed. That information flows into an onboard flight computer. Higher end business jets have them now. The computer adjusts the flight angle, speed, flaps, and a dozen other things. Give it bad info and there's a problem."

"GIGO."

That brought a smile. "I haven't heard that in years. Yes, garbage-in-garbage-out. Bad sensor info equals bad flight."

"Why didn't the pilots just turn off the computer?"

"They should have, but the computer refused to disengage."

"That had to be horrible."

"I've flown the simulator fifty times and it scares me to death every time I do."

"So what do you want me to do?"

"Two things. First, see if you can learn anything more. We're good with the flight stuff, but my senses tell me there's more. Second, keep it out of the hands of Paul Atoms.

Ruby studied the thumb drive for a moment. "I know a guy."

Chapter 45

A Stroll in the Park

——>◇<——

"J ust walk with me for a bit."

Greg Mayer stepped to Ruby Fay's side as they walked along one of the paths of Founders Park. They paused by a set of stairs bracketed by a bit of abstract sculpture, a set of four "pieces" of sculpture, blocks of white stone: a left eye, a right eye, and a pair of mouths, all separated by a few yards.

"I've felt like that a few mornings," Mayer said.

Ruby smiled. She looked a decade younger when she smiled. "You must lead an exciting life."

"Nah, just going for the obvious joke."

"You like baseball?"

"You called me down to the park to talk baseball?"

"Humor me."

"I like it okay. It's the only sport slow enough that I can read at the same time."

"I like the Red Sox myself. You?"

Mayer shrugged and wondered what the woman was doing. "I spent a little time in LA, so I acquired a Dodger habit."

"Why is it so many people in DC don't cheer for the Nationals?"

"Nationals? Who are they?"

"Cute." Her cell phone chimed and Ruby looked at the text message. Mayer caught sight of it: PIZZA IS READY. "We're clear to talk."

"You're acting more CIA than FBI."

Ruby shrugged. "I do what I have to do. I have a few people making sure no one is listening to us. Did you know that Paul Atoms has a pilot's license? He flew in the military. Navy. Became a police pilot while he waited for acceptance into the FBI. Bright guy. Got a law degree but liked law enforcement better."

"So? There are over six hundred thousand people in the US with private pilot's licenses. I have a pilot's license, too."

She nodded. "Okay, did you ever fly corporate CEOs around the country? Atoms did that part time, when he wasn't patrolling from the air. Worked a ton of hours. He flew an earlier model of the same kinda craft these justices died in."

"You're not suggesting . . ."

"I've started investigating him. Be careful what you say around the man."

"There are over one hundred thousand commercial pilots in the US. I know I said I didn't like the man—"

"I don't like him either, but that's not why I did a little research. And stop with the numbers, will you? What set me off was your comment that Atoms has been riding you about the case and wanting to take the flash drive. Why didn't you give it to him?"

"It's not a very good reason."

"Try me." They walked by a stand of trees.

"I have a bad feeling about the guy."

"Me, too. Do you know where we are?"

"Founders Park."

She looked around. "I've been here a lot lately. You heard about the DOJ lawyer that was killed?"

"Yeah—that's right, it happened here."

She led him to a park bench. They watched an old couple walk by hand in hand. "He's been bugging me about the investigation. I know he works for the DOJ now as part of the DTED team. Maybe his boss is making him be a pest, but he's showing a tad too much interest."

"Instinct is fine, Ruby, I depend on it. Sometimes my unconscious sees more than my conscious mind, but you can only go so far without evidence."

"I know. I know, but just listen for a moment. Do you know that when Matt Branson was killed, he was no longer DOJ?"

"To be honest, there are so many murders I can't keep up with them. If they don't involve an aircraft, I just don't pay much attention."

"Branson was DOJ, working in the department that investigates complaints leveled against DOJ attorneys: Office of Professional Responsibility. He went to school with John Knox Smith. Both ended up at Justice, although their work was very different. You've been following the Dr. Preston case."

"The preacher? Some. He's in the Netherlands, right?"

"Branson left the DOJ to join Preston's legal team. They go back to college days. You see, Branson, Smith, and Preston were all buds in college."

"But it's Smith's DTED team that is prosecuting the case. Hang on. You're saying that Branson might have been killed because of Preston and that since Preston is being prosecuted by the team Atoms works for there might be a connection?"

"Right."

"What's that got to do with my investigation? I'm not involved with . . . You know, Smith has been putting the pressure on me, too."

"Now you're getting it."

"No. I agree that there are some connections, but it's too much like the six degrees of Kevin Bacon. Everyone in the world is somehow connected to other people who form a chain to Kevin Bacon. It's a statistical magic trick. This is just—You can't be serious."

"I am. I can't prove anything yet, but I wanted to bring you into the loop on this. It might be nothing but coincidence . . . but something reeks."

"How do you connect that to the flash drive?"

"Paul Atoms flew the same kind of jet. He is familiar with the Gulfstream operations."

"That's not enough."

"Would the fact that Atoms was out of town at the time of the accident help? Wanna guess where he was?"

"Houston?"

"He flew into town the day before the justices did. How he could get access to the plane is unknown, but I can come up with a dozen ways it could be done, especially for a guy who carries a badge and a gun, if you know what I mean."

"But why?"

"We have the most liberal Supreme Court the nation has ever seen. Justices are appointed for life. President Blain has an agenda for social reform. Someone like John Knox Smith might see the justices as a problem, but you can't just fire a Supreme Court Justice. A justice dies or retires. That's it. Now don't get me wrong. I'm not saying the president did anything wrong or that Smith did. I'm just saying that someone near them might be willing to go where a higher thinking man wouldn't. Or a higher thinking chimp."

Mayer leaned forward, resting his arms on his legs.

"You okay?"

"This is almost too much to hear. How sure of this are you?"

"I'm not positive. I can't take it up the ladder yet, but it feels right."

"What now?"

"I'm working on that."

Chapter 46

Down

<hr/>

Andrea knocked on John's door. No answer. She knocked again. Still nothing. Odd. He had summoned her to his room, something he wouldn't have had to do if they just shared a hotel room, but that was out of the question while he was still married and while he and other DOJ personnel were in The Hague trying Preston.

She put her ear to the door and heard nothing. No television. No radio. No talking as if he were on the phone or in a meeting. Raising delicate knuckles, she rapped on the door again. Maybe he was in the bathroom. That could make door answering difficult, but he had just called a few minutes ago. The conversation worried her. His tone was empty of emotion, like a man in shock. His words were short, "Andrea, I need you." Then he hung up.

Looking up and down the hall and seeing she was alone, Andrea removed a spare smart key to her boss's room and inserted it in the lock. A tiny, green LED light shone and she heard the lock disengage. She turned the handle and entered the room slowly, as if some carnivorous beast with dripping fangs awaited her entry.

"John?"

No response.

She entered the small foyer of the suite and glanced through the open door of the bathroom. It was empty. The door closed behind her. The room was a mess. Apparently, the maids had yet to come by. The bedding was rumpled and hanging from the side of the bed as if kicked off mid-nightmare. The television was off. John's brief-case sat on the rosewood workstation, the screensaver showing the DOJ emblem slowly moving around the monitor.

A salty breeze pushed through the space, fluttering loose papers on the coffee table in front of the suite's sofa held in place by a card-board FedEx envelope. Several tiny bottles of hard liquor from the in-room locker lay empty on their sides, one on the table and one on the floor, dripping the last drop of golden-brown booze on the carpet. Andrea's heart fluttered. Clutter was not John's way.

Another gust of breeze drew her eyes to the open sliding door leading to the balcony. The pathos in John's voice took on a new meaning. "Andrea, I need you."

"John?" A slow step. "Are you out there?"

No answer. A faster step. "John?" She plunged onto the balcony. The afternoon sun washed from overhead, spotlighting the wide balcony stage. The sound of children playing in the pool several stories down drifted up on warm currents. The smell of the nearby sea flooded her nostrils. Any other time she would have called this a "beautiful day," but worry made the colors garish, the sounds sharp and annoying.

John stood to the side, at the corner of the balcony, leaning against the curved rail. His arms hung to his sides. In one hand, he held a glass nearly drained of its cargo.

"John? What's wrong?" She approached carefully. He didn't move. "Here, let me take that." She took the nearly empty glass from his hand. His fingers felt cold, corpse like. He didn't speak. He didn't turn. He didn't acknowledge her. He just stared in the dis-tance, seeing something she couldn't imagine. "John, are you ill?"

He answered with silence. Then she saw something that sent rivers of ice water through her veins: a tear. "John, look at me." She took his arm and pulled, drawing him around. He looked into her eyes and did something she never thought she'd experience: he took her in his arms. On his own initiative. There was no lust in the embrace. He wasn't taking something he felt he deserved; he was asking for something he needed: comfort.

She held him for a few moments, then, as if suddenly coming to his senses, he pulled away and turned his gaze back to the distant ocean.

"What's wrong, John?"

"The table. Coffee table. Two documents."

She spent a moment wondering if it was safe to leave him alone on the balcony, then reentered the room and retrieved two letters. She stepped back to the open door, but not exiting, stopped by a brief vision of the wind ripping sensitive and private material from her hands and scattering them over the city.

The first was from a law firm. She recognized the name: Goodall, Crowe, and Banks. She scanned the document. "Your wife's attorney is asking for a complete summary of your finances and legal holdings." She looked up. "That's normal, isn't it?"

"Yes, it just came on the heels of the other." He hadn't bothered to turn around when he spoke.

Andrea shuffled through the other pages and found a letter from another legal firm, one with just a single name: George Platt, LLP, Attorney at Law. The letterhead was simple and dignified. There were initials beneath the signature, indicating a typist. The man had typed his own letter. She read it aloud in whispered tones.

Dear Mr. Smith,

It is my sad duty to inform you of the recent passing of your father, Mr. Chester Smith, after a short illness. He passed quietly and in his sleep, the victim of a stroke. As the trustee of your father's estate, it is my duty to seek his heirs. Your son, Jack, is staying with a family from your father's church. It was he who found your father on the kitchen floor after he returned from school. He was quick to call emergency services, but too much time had passed. The paramedics declared your father dead on arrival. Your son, at my urging, has contacted your wife. It is my understanding that the family is estranged. I encouraged him to reach out to you during this difficult time, but he has been reluctant.

Some legal matters exist regarding your father's real and personal property as well as final instruction for the body. I have spoken to your father's pastor and he has offered to conduct services, should you so desire. Please contact me as soon as you are able.

Please accept my sincere condolences over your loss.

"Oh, John. I'm so sorry."

"Don't be. We weren't close."

He said the words with conviction, but his reaction told a different story.

"Still, it's so sudden." She set the documents down and joined him on the balcony. She took his hand, but he didn't respond in kind. Holding his hand was like grasping a dead cod. The ice man had returned.

"At times, it seems the world is fighting me, turning every good thing I do to trash." He looked down and shook his head. "I don't need this now, Andrea. My plate is full. I don't need to be fighting a divorce and dealing with the death of my old man."

"You will succeed, John."

"There are moments when I'm not so certain."

"You will, John. You always do. That's your superpower. When others would collapse under the criticism and the load, you march ahead." A moment later. "How can I help?"

He lifted her chin and kissed her lips.

***

"I'm heartbroken for you, John." Joel Thevis looked and sounded sincere. He had been quick to say the expected things.

John stayed on his feet while the others sat in the same conference room they had used the night before. "Thanks, Joel, but I can't let this sidetrack things. We have too much at stake. We've come too far."

"I can prosecute the case, if you want. Just give me the word."

"I can't leave you alone on this."

"We can bring over one of the other lawyers on the team."

The idea had crossed his mind but for a different reason. If he were called back to the States on a family emergency and then lost the case—a one-in-a-million chance—,he could say that Joel bungled it. A tempting thought, but John's pride wouldn't allow it. "I've communicated with my father's attorney and let him know that I'm overseas. I followed that with a registered letter giving my instruction to go ahead with the memorial service and put the house up for sale. We move ahead as planned."

***

That night, alone in the silence of his room, John removed a manila envelope he had kept hidden from Andrea. With the clock moving close to midnight, John sat at his workstation, a bourbon in hand. The envelope read, "To my son." The handwriting was shaky but recognizable. The words had been inked by his father.

He took a long sip of his drink and felt the fire of it. He had been staring at the unopened envelope for an hour. His first urge was to take it down to the business center and shred it, but he couldn't make himself do it. He raised his glass. "To Chester Smith, a good man, a stable man, a caring man, a fine upstanding man. Not much on achievement. No ambition but upstanding. A community man. A church man." He knocked back the drink.

He couldn't complain about his upbringing. It hadn't been tough. The only abuse he had received at the hand of his father was being forced to go to Cottonwood Church every Sunday. In a sense, John had to admit, his father was ambitious. He had formed and grew a construction company from one person to over two hundred employees, building schools, government and business buildings. He also built a lot of church structures—for cost. He might have left a large inheritance, had John's mother not suffered a long, taxing, expensive illness like emphysema. John had been fourteen at the time.

Members of the Cottonwood Church had been kind. Like Joel, they said all the right things, at least things they thought were right. "You're mother is in a better place." "You'll get to see her again sometime." "God only takes the ones He loves." The last angered him the most. God took everyone. More accurately, God had nothing to do with it: people just died.

He wanted to ask the hard questions. "If God loved my mom so much, then why did he let her suffer?" That's what bothered him the most. Even at fourteen, he knew everyone was headed to the same fate, but did they have to suffer along the way? The meaningless platitudes. The artificial understanding. The cooing and soothing only made him burn more.

His dad, however . . . Oh, his dad ate it up, agreeing with each smoothly offered bit of nonsense. Each tasty dilution.

Then came Rose, John's stepmother. A nice enough woman, but by the time she came a long, John had moved on. Not physically. He was still years away from college, but mentally he had left the family at his mother's funeral. Dad continued on, building churches and retirement housing. He began to shy away from government work, focusing, rather, on "buildings that could make a difference in this tired ol' world." Well, the world was still old and tired.

"Never did make much of a difference, did you, dad? Lots of work and sacrifice, but for all the wrong reasons. At least you taught me the power of hard work, even if it meant you were gone most of the time." The last phrase was a self inflicted wound. The initial divorce documents listed him as an absent husband and father. The acorn had produced an identical tree, at least in that regard.

He picked up the sealed envelope and turned it over in his fingers. What could the old man have written? What final words had he penned for John's benefit? John was having trouble cranking up enough reason to care. The emotion he felt earlier had soured. Sure there was some sorrow. The man had shared his DNA with John and provided a comfortable home, but they could not have been more different.

He tossed the letter into his briefcase unopened.

Chapter 47

Ruby is a Gem

T he house was a simple bungalow that needed a paint job five years ago. Ruby Fay was as accustomed to the look of the place as she was nonchalant about the opinion of her neighbors. She opened the door which never locked. She owned nothing worth stealing, unless she counted the packs of cigarettes she kept in the pantry. If a thief did break in while she was gone, the guy might be moved with compassion and leave valuables rather than take them. If a thief broke in while she was there, she'd reward him with a nine millimeter round in the chest. She was just that generous.

The room looked untouched, undusted, un-everything. A two-decade old television rested across from a sofa that looked fresh from a 1980s sitcom. On the stained coffee table sat several paperback novels, each one a romance. If anyone else saw them, she'd say they belonged to someone else.

She removed her coat and hung it in the closest. It was part of her uniform; otherwise, she would have tossed in on the growing pile of clothing in her bedroom. She removed the clip-on holster from her belt and set it on the kitchen counter.

A few more steps put her in front of the refrigerator, standing in front of its open door. Inside: tiny cheese wheels, a half gallon of whole milk, the leftovers from her last three trips to the fast food joints, a tub of pretend butter, week-old pizza, and twenty or more cans of beer. She removed the pizza and set it next to the vintage microwave which still worked fine, if one doubled the cook time.

Then she grabbed a can of beer, popped the top and laid her nose over the opening. She inhaled and smiled. Rich, pungent. She took another long sniff, then poured the contents down the drain. She turned to a small dry marker board mounted to the wall near the stove. The letters D.O.S. graced the top of the board in black. "Days of Sobriety," she said to the empty room. A number, also in black, had been written below the initials: 585. Taking a paper towel, she scrubbed off the last letter and replaced it with a 6—586. She then studied another set of initials and did as she did every time she come home, recited their meaning. B.Y.P.B.Y.F. "Beat your past; beat your future."

She removed three slices of sausage, pepperoni, and black olive pizza, placed them on a paper plate, set it in the microwave and punched in a carelessly calculated cook time.

In the living room, attached to a wall was a shelf that held the only things she valued: A shoulder patch she wore as a DC cop, a diploma showing her graduation from the FBI academy at Quantico, and two photos: one of her dead husband; one of her murdered brother. The former was the reason she lived alone; the later the reason she went into law enforcement. She stared out her rear window at a black night, but didn't see the overgrown grass, the weeds, or the unkempt flower bed. In her mind, she saw the lights of DC.

"I'm coming for you, you piece of scum. I'm coming for you."

Ruby lit a cigarette.

The microwave beeped.

***

The next morning, Ruby found a young man who looked like he should be in a high school history class, sitting in her cubicle. His hair was too long to make old FBI folk comfortable. A black soul patch decorated his narrow chin. It contrasted with his yellow-blond hair. He wasn't an agent, so not subject to appearance codes. Oliver "Ollie" Anderson was one of those individuals she liked to call a genius. Like many geniuses, he was awkward in many ways, especially social ways, but when it came to electronic forensics, he was untouchable.

"Hey, Einstein. You're up bright and early." Ruby tossed her purse in a drawer of her desk.

"Up early? Oh, no, I see. I've been up all night."

"You party types. I don't know how you do it."

He looked nervous. Close to a breakdown kind of nervous. "I wasn't it at a party. I don't do well at parties."

"You okay? You look a little too amped to have been up all night." She sat in her desk chair. "No. Don't tell me you've been juicing."

"Of course not. I like my job and I want to keep it. Can we talk somewhere? You know, somewhere private."

"How about the ladies room?"

"I'm serious."

"Okay, the men's room."

"Agent Fay, please."

She looked into his eyes. He was onto something and it had him scared. "Sure. Let's go to the lobby. It's busy and noisy."

"Too many people. I should go to the AD with this, but you're the AIC so I want to stay within protocol."

"Okay, you've got my interest. Is this about the flash drive and the copy I gave you?"

"I don't want to talk about here."

"Okay, I have an idea. Anything to calm you down."

An elevator ride and a short walk later, they were in a small eatery that served bagels and little else. Ruby felt obligated to order and carried two blueberry bagels, cream cheese in individually-sized, sealed plastic containers, and two coffees to a table in the rear corner of restaurant, near the bathroom. "This cost me close to ten bucks, kid, so you better have something good for me."

"I do. I do. I just. I'm confused."

"Here, have some coffee. It'll settle your nerves." She smiled at the quip, but the line went over the guy's head.

"I did an analysis of the flash drive. It was beat up pretty, bad but the coding was still intact. It was really complex and the data I found was sweet. That's what got me thinking. First, the data: Everything you told me is spot on. There was a lot of information on the drive. Some had to do with the engineering specs of a Gulfstream 550. Easy enough to get and harmless. My guess is that the owner used the drive to transfer information from a source computer to his own. It's more information than the guy on the street needs. Engineers, pilots, safety personnel, sure, but not many others. Here's thing one: It's just basic information. Nothing more. Plain vanilla."

"I like plain vanilla."

"You know what I mean. There were no devious plane-busting viruses in it."

"But my guy at NTSB said it had a program on it that messed with the flight computer."

"It did. I'm just giving you the whole picture. That and I'm afraid to tell you the rest."

Ruby spread cream cheese on half of her bagel. "But you're going to, so get to it. Make it faster and funnier."

"I can't do funny, but here's the skinny: there was a digital virus, just as NTSB said. I found nothing else in the software."

"You'd better have more than that, Ollie. I spent good money on that coffee you're ignoring. If you found nothing new on the device, then why are you in such a tizzy?"

"It's a titanium case. It's made by Hummingbird digital. They've carved a place in an overcrowded accessories market by building storage devices that are nearly indestructible. Some people carry around important data and they don't want to lose it if the thing gets dropped or accidentally run over by a city bus."

Ruby started to comment on the statement, but let go. "And?"

"And only a few stores carry the item. So, I did a little checking. Only a handful have been sold in this area over the last few months."

"We don't know how old the device is."

"We know the age of the data on it. We can check that. All the data is new. Nonetheless, I went with the assumption that the perp bought the device in a big box store like Best Buy or something. Okay, they've sold a few thousand of these things over the last few months, so I checked sales in Houston—"

"Because that's where the plane took off from right before the accident."

"Of course, why else would I look there? Then I checked sales in the DC area because . . ."

Ruby took the prompt. "Because the Supreme Court Justices flew out of the area and were heading back to it."

"Exactly, but I know what you're thinking: that's not enough. Well, you're right."

"Of course I'm right." She took another sip of coffee, but her mind was spinning so much she didn't taste it.

"Next, I went to the director of data security for the Bureau. You know, hackers are always trying to mess with us. Anyway, I told him a little about the program that brought the plane down and asked if he knew any black hats."

"Wait. Black hats?"

"Hackers who break into the computer systems of governments and large business. Some countries hire hackers to bring our systems down. Some are just homegrown data cowboys who like messing with other people's data. The guy went real quiet, then said he'd talk to me later. He did, just as I was heading out the building. Now I'm going to simplify this because I don't fully understand it and some identities are being hidden. You catching my drift?"

"You don't want me to ask questions."

He nodded. "It wouldn't do you any good, because I don't think I have the full story, or the story has been altered, but I did get the straight scoop on a couple of things. Someone asked someone else in the know for the name of a black hat who might know something about flying. A connection was made and a program—what I believe the program on the flash drive to be—was delivered and some money was paid."

"So you don't know who wrote it, who brokered it, who sold it, or who bought it?"

"That's right. Agent Fay, I'm telling you the truth. I don't run in those circles, but I do know those guys are beyond paranoid. So I began working with the little I had. The program was sent through several fake Internet addresses, but ultimately ended up in the DC area, in a library. From there, I speculate that our bad guy downloaded the info onto the flash drive. With me so far?"

Ruby had stopped eating. "I think so."

"Okay, so now I have a few tidbits, see. I've got the fact that the virus was delivered to the DC area, probably this library I mentioned. You can get a subpoena and check it out when I'm done. Now, since the virus was delivered to DC, I made the bold assumption that the flash drive was bought in the DC area. I tracked the unit sales to a few distributers and limited the data field to the four weeks before the accident."

"Why four weeks?"

"It was just a guess. Nothing more, but I had to start somewhere. Now here's where I got lucky. You'll remember that in 2015 they passed a law requiring all video surveillance in stores and government buildings had to be saved for six months and made available to law enforcement. I got my whole team on it. I had six techs scanning store videos for those times when someone bought a Hummingbird titanium case. The people at Hummingbird keep track of when and where sales take place to track sales trends. There's no such thing as privacy anymore . . . Anyway . . ." He reached into his back pocket and removed a folded sheet of paper. "Guess who bought one special flash drive?" He pushed the paper her way.

Ruby unfolded it and saw a still image clipped from a security camera. "You know who this is?"

"Sure, I did some work for him when he was an agent with the Bureau. It's Paul Atoms."

"I was right?"

"You already knew?"

"No, no, but I had suspicions." She reached across the table, seized Ollie by the back of the neck and pulled him forward. Then she kissed him on the mouth before standing.

"Yuck. Smokers breath."

"You loved it. Ollie, you da best, man. I mean it. I owe you a steak dinner."

***

Ruby had never been so glad to be a "sensible shoe kind of girl" since her pace was just shy of a jog. She covered the distance from the bagel shop to the Hoover building in short order. She stopped at her desk, snatched up the phone and called the office of the Assistant Director.

"This is Special Agent Ruby Fay. I need to see Assistant Director Sleeth ASAP."

"I understand, Agent Fay," the AD's administrative assistant said. "He's busy this morning but I might be able to fit you in shortly after lunch."

"Great. I'll be right in."

"No, that's not what I said—"

Ruby rolled into the AD's office like a boulder roles down a steep hill. "Hi, Maggie." She waved at the woman she had been talking to less than sixty seconds before. "Don't get up. I know my way in."

"Agent Fay, you can't just barge in." The thirty-something brunette shot to her feet.

"Of course not. I wouldn't think of it." Ruby walked into her director's office and closed the door behind her.

Chapter 48

First Arguments

"Please state your name for the record." John reminded himself to stand straight and to breathe evenly. The man in the witness box was an over fifty but fit looking man with graying hair.

"Henry Hume."

"Where do you live, Mr. Hume?"

"Tennessee, sir. Nashville, Tennessee." He looked at the panel of judges. "In the United States of America."

John grinned. "I believe the esteemed judges know where Tennessee is, Mr. Hume." He put his hands behind his back. Pat recognized the motion. He had seen it when debating John at Princeton. John was the best member of the debate team. The thought terrified him. "How long have you lived there, Mr. Hume?"

"All my life."

"What is your line of work?"

Hume seemed to swell with pride. "I'm a landscape architect."

"Ah, a very creative profession."

"I like it."

"Mr. Hume, do you know the defendant?"

"I attended his church . . . for awhile."

"Awhile? Was he not a good preacher?"

"He's the best. Always interesting, and you can tell he did his home work. I never fell asleep in his sermons." Despite the compliment, the man wouldn't make eye contact with Pat.

"Yet you left the church a few years ago. Is that correct?"

"It is. His preaching became offensive. My partner and I could no longer go to the church and be comfortable."

"Your partner?"

"Lewis Bowers. He owned a nursery. You know, plants, not kids. I used to buy a lot of my plants from him when I was doing a yard. That's how we met."

"Lewis Bowers is a male?"

"Yes."

"When you say, 'partner', what do you mean?"

Although obvious, Pat knew that John had to establish certain information for the court so he could build on it later.

"My life partner. We were a couple."

"A gay couple?"

"Yes."

"How long were you in this relationship?"

"Twelve years, sir."

"Over a decade. Most marriages don't last that long."

Isabella's head popped up. "Objection. Counsel is editorializing."

Kurosawa agreed. "Please stay on track, Mr. Smith."

"My apologies." John looked back at Hume. "Is your life partner here with you today?"

Hume's head lowered. "No, sir. He's dead."

"Dead. I'm sorry to have to ask this, but how did Mr. Bowers die?"

"He . . . he killed himself."

"Suicide?"

"Yes. Pills."

"Why would he do that?"

"Because of Dr. Preston."

"Objection," shouted Isabella.

"Overruled," Kurosawa said.

John raised a hand. "Thank you. I want to make sure I understand. You're saying that Dr. Preston somehow influenced Mr. Bowers to take his own life?"

"Yes, sir. Everything was fine until he started targeting homosexuals. He would stand in the pulpit and say homosexuals would all go to hell. He seemed glad about it. He even used verses from the Bible. It began to eat at Lewis. First, he pulled away from me. You know . . . he was less intimate and when he was, he felt bad afterward. I'd see him crying all alone. I tried to talk to him, but he became more and more depressed."

"I'm sure you know that you're making a serious claim, Mr. Hume."

"I know what the truth is. I was there. He didn't even come to the funeral. He never reached out to us. Since he's the one that caused it all."

"When you listened to those sermons you mentioned, the ones about homosexuals going to hell, how did it make you feel?"

"Horrible. Worthless. I'll admit it. I've considered taking my own life."

"Did you feel that his words were hateful?"

"Objection," Isabella said. "Leading the witness."

"I'll rephrase. What emotion did you sense during that sermon series?"

"Hate."

John smiled at the defense team. "That is all."

Kurosawa nodded at Isabella. "Do you have anything for this witness, Countess?"

She stood. "I do." She moved to the podium. "Mr. Hume, I want to thank you for sharing your loss with the court. Most of us in this room have lost a loved one or watched one suffer. We can be sympathetic, even empathetic. However, I do need to ask some questions."

"I understand."

"Mr. Hume, you said you thought Dr. Preston was a fine preacher. What did you like about his preaching?"

"He was entertaining."

"He made you laugh?"

"Sometimes."

"What else?"

"He was systematic. He preached through a book in the Bible."

"He did not jump around? In the text, I mean."

"No, ma'am. He'd start at chapter one, verse one, and preach the stuffing out of each verse, then move on to the next."

"There are several passages about homosexual behavior in the Bible. Do you recall which one Mr. Bowers found most troubling?"

"I don't recall the exact verse."

"Well, was it Old Testament or from the New Testament?"

"I don't remember."

Isabella scratched her eyebrow. "Mr. Hume, I have no desire to belittle the loss of someone so special to you. Truth is, I grieve for you, but I'm confused. Your testimony is that that sermon profoundly affected Mr. Bowers and ultimately led to his suicide."

"It did."

"But you don't recall what sermon started it all or what passage of Scripture was used."

"It was too long ago."

"Were you there when the sermon was preached?"

"Well, no. I was behind on a project and had to work for a few weekends. It happens a lot."

"A lot. So you only occasionally attended the church."

"That depends on what you mean by 'occasionally.'" He shifted in his seat.

"You testified just a short time ago—with the help of Mr. Smith, I might add—that you felt hate. By that, you mean hatred from Dr. Preston."

"Yes."

"Directed at you?"

"At all homosexuals."

"But you weren't there to hear the hatred. You said Dr. Preston preached verse by verse through the Bible. That means that once he was through that passage, he'd be onto something else, isn't that right?"

"Well, yeah, I guess so."

"So this perceived hatred wasn't consistent? It wasn't an every Sunday thing?"

"No."

"Were you ever in church when he preached about love, forgiveness, grace, those sorts of things?"

"I guess so."

Isabella frowned. "You guess so? Did you not say earlier that you never fell asleep in one of Dr. Preston's sermons?"

"Yes, but . . ." Hume never finished the sentence.

"You felt hate from a sermon you didn't hear. So I can't ask you about Dr. Preston's tone since you admit to not being in the church when the sermon in question was preached. Still, there is good news, Mr. Hume. All of Dr. Preston's sermons are digitally recorded. We can listen to hundreds of his Bible studies and Sunday sermons. Dr. Preston keeps very good records of his speaking. We can listen to the very same sermon you mentioned. Do you know what? I have. In fact, I can introduce in evidence from a research firm that analyzes speech patterns for European police that the sermon you mention has nothing hateful in tone."

"Objection. Counsel is referencing information not entered into evidence."

"I will be happy to do that."

Kurosawa waved John off. "This is not a court in the United States, Mr. Smith. We will hear evidence as we wish and the court will allow the countess' reference."

"Thank you. All right, Mr. Hume. I know this is difficult for you. You've lost someone you love, you been asked to fly to the Netherlands to testify against a man whose church you chose to attend, you were coached by Mr. Smith in how to answer—"

"Objection." John was on his feet.

"I'll withdraw the statement and offer the court my apology."

"What about me?" John tried to look hurt, but Pat wasn't buying it.

Isabella moved on. "You complained that Dr. Preston didn't attend the funeral of Mr. Bower."

"That's right."

"Please tell the court by what means you notified Dr. Preston of Mr. Bower's death."

"I don't recall."

"E-mail? Phone call? Personal visit to home or office?"

"No, none of those things."

"Mail?"

"No."

Isabella sighed. She stepped back to the desk and picked up a file. She studied it. "The funeral home that handled Mr. Bower's remains was . . ." She looked at the file. "Green Hills Mortuary. Is that correct?"

"Yes."

"And you made the arrangements?"

"Of course."

"In making those arrangements, did you ask the mortuary personnel to contact Dr. Preston?"

"Why would I do that? His hateful preaching is what put Lewis over the edge."

"Did you not testify a short time ago that Dr. Preston didn't even attend the funeral?"

There was a long pause. "Well, yeah, I guess I did. But I didn't want him there."

"Yet you're angry with him for not attending."

"You're twisting my words."

"Am I? Mr. Hume, you blame Dr. Preston for the suicide death of your partner. Could there have been other reasons?"

"No."

"Did you two fight? You and Lewis, I mean."

"All couples fight."

"I'm sure that's not true, but I'll concede the point. Were you ever . . . Just a moment." Again, she moved to the table and pulled another file folder from the stack on the table. Returning to the podium, she opened the file and ran her finger down one page. Silence rippled through the full gallery.

Kurosawa cleared his throat. "Countess. The court is waiting."

"Yes, Mr. President, of course. My apologies. I just wanted to make sure I use the correct American term." She studied Hume like a person studied a painting. "Mr. Hume, have the Nashville police ever been called to your home?" She lifted the folder from the podium and looked at its contents.

"I object." John stood.

"This goes to the witnesses previous statements about his part-ner's suicide," Isabella interjected quickly.

Kurosawa pressed his lips together. "I'll allow it, but walk care-fully, Countess. The witness may answer."

"Do I need to repeat the question, Mr. Hume?" Isabella's tone was kind but firm.

"I'm not sure what that has to do—"

"What is appropriate for the case is determined by this panel of judges, not by you and not by me. I ask again. Have the police ever been called to your home?"

He looked down at his lap. "Yes."

"How many times?" She closed the folder.

"Three."

"Why were they called?"

"Lewis and I had been arguing. A neighbor called them."

"All three times."

"Yes."

"Let me get to the heart of the matter, Mr. Hume. You were arrested multiple times and charged with domestic violence."

"That's because police hate gays."

"Do they? Usually police take photos of the victim in such cases." Again she opened the file.

"Did the police cause the bruising on Mr. Bowers' body?"

No answer.

"Mr. Hume, did the police cause the bruising on Mr. Bowers' body or was that you?"

"It wasn't the police. But heterosexuals are arrested for spousal abuse all the time."

"I agree, Mr. Hume. I agree completely, but one's choice in sexual partners is the issue here, it is your testimony. You would have the court believe that Dr. Preston spewed hateful sermons meant to degrade those involved in homosexual behavior and to foster hate, but we can produce those very sermons for the court and the media to hear, and not one person would be able to detect hatred. Sadness, yes; hatred, no. You would further have this court believe that your partner took his own life because Dr. Preston said in a sermon that all who engage in homosexual acts will go to Hell, a sermon you admit having never heard. The reality is that Lewis Hume may have taken his life because of many reasons, not the least of which was your physical abuse."

Without missing a beat, she asked another question. "What did his suicide note say?"

"There wasn't one."

"You mean to tell this court that Lewis Hume did not list Dr. Preston or one of his sermons as the reason for taking an overdose of pills?"

"He was distraught. I could see it."

"What kind of help did you get for him?"

"I tried to be there for him."

"I didn't know Mr. Bowers, but I have to wonder if that was a comfort."

John stood, but not as fast as before. "Objection. Counsel is—"

"I was out of line," Isabella said. "I apologize to Mr. Hume and to the court."

Pat saw John staring at Isabella, waiting for her to include him in the apology.

She didn't.

***

John introduced several more witnesses, each with a heart-wrenching tale. Each witness had been well rehearsed. Some wept. Some held back anger, but in the end they could do little more than state they had heard "anti-gay" rhetoric from Pat over various broadcast mediums.

When the day's court session was called to a close, Isabella stood and spoke before the judges could rise from their chairs. "I beg the court's pardon. I have a simple request before your honors leave."

Several judges frowned as if the act had been rehearsed. Kurosawa spoke for the group. "What is it, Countess?"

"Dr. Preston has been separated from his family for many months. His wife has only been able to see him over a video monitor. Becky Preston and their two young children are with us today.

319

Would the court grant a few minutes for my client to see his wife—in the flesh?"

Pat's heart pounded with hope. He looked at Kurosawa, not caring if he looked pitiful.

Kurosawa looked at the faces of court visitors. The countess had put him in a bind. "The request is granted."

Pat was on his feet and turned to the galley. Becky, Phoebe, and Luke made their way forward, the crowded viewing area parting before them. On their heels was a woman Pat didn't recognize, but had been told was the Vatican police officer assigned to protect his family.

A rail separated them, but Pat managed to enfold all three of his family in his arms.

The weeping began.

And spread through the gallery.

Chapter 49

Another Big Decision

The small room seemed crowded, filled as it was with one defendant and three attorneys. They had arrived thirty minutes before the next segment of the trial was to begin.

"Thank you for that, Isabella." There were still tears in Pat's eyes.

"I wish I could do more. Asking for permission in front of a full courtroom seemed the only way to force the panel to allow a brief time with your wife."

Scott Freeman sat at the end of the table. The room was provided for attorney and client conferences. "Isabella, you were amazing. You dismantled John's case plank by plank."

She didn't feel confident. "The judges on the panel are some of the best legal minds in the world. They know I was playing old legal tricks on the witnesses, getting them to admit to things we might not be able to introduce otherwise. I'd feel better if this was a jury trial. I don't think we can sway judges the way we can one of your American juries."

"Are things that bleak?" Pat asked.

Larry Jordan answered. "We've done in-depth research on the judges. Their past decisions show an inclination to rule against people like us and to favor new limited-speech laws. Several are from countries where free speech has been undermined or eliminated. A couple, like the Somali judge, come from a country were freedom of expression isn't a value."

"You're saying the deck is stacked against me."

"Yes," Larry said. "Isabella is doing a great job, but even though we might win in the legal journals, we might lose in court."

"But you're tearing down every accusation and witness."

"We have an underlying problem, Pat." Isabella stood at the other end of the table, too agitated to sit. "The court is supposed to be impartial, but as you know, humans have trouble with impartiality. The judges have other pressure on them from their countries. No matter how apolitical they seem, their decision will impact laws in fifteen different countries. They can be seen as undermining the progress to eradicate intolerance. I use the word 'progress' lightly."

The room was silent for a moment, then Freeman spoke. "What Isabella is saying is that we are not going to get a fair trial. It's impossible."

"Then what do we do?"

"Isabella has already started the process and we'll see the real impact tomorrow, but the plan is to change the game, to give the judges the unexpected, and apply pressure of our own. We have to make it about more than you and recast the meaning of intolerance."

"How do you plan to do that?"

"We endure a few more of John's witnesses and specialists, only one of which concerns me, then we put you on the stand." Freeman seemed hesitant to make the statement, as if the words tasted bad in his mouth.

"Me? I thought putting a defendant on the stand was bad trial practice."

"It usually is, but you're not a typical defendant." Isabella finally sat. "You're smart, articulate, and kind. That's what the world needs to see."

"But then John will be able to cross examine me."

"Yes," Isabella said. "Yes, he will. Scott will do the examination."

"Shouldn't we prep for this?"

Freeman said no. "I don't want this to seem staged."

***

"Mr. Pasternack, are you an anti-Semite?"

"Of course not!"

"Objection!" John shouted the word which overlapped Dr. Brian Pasternack's reply.

Kurosawa's face darkened. "Don't make me warn you, Countess."

"It's a question, Mr. President, not an accusation and the answer is important to my cross examination." Before Kurosawa could speak, Isabella addressed the academic. "So you're not an anti-Semite."

"I'll fight anyone who says I am."

"That's very noble of you, Dr. Pasternack. Are you anti-Arab?"

"No."

"Objection!"

"Anti-Hindu?"

"No!"

"Yet, you are anti-Christian."

No response.

"Dr. Pasternack, are you anti-Christian?"

"I wouldn't put it that way."

"Your dissertation seems to indicate otherwise." She drummed her fingers on the podium. "What was the title of your PhD dissertation?"

John rose. "That was introduced in my initial examination."

"I want to hear it again." Isabella drummed her fingers again. "Well, Dr. Pasternack?"

"A Quantitative Analysis of Christian Influence on Hate Crimes in the United States from 2005 to 2015. I defended the dissertation at the University of Chicago and received my PhD."

"A great accomplishment. You testified that the influence of contemporary Christianity has led to the segmentation of society, fostered a hatred of science, prejudiced the minds of the young, and created a growing prejudice against anyone other than fellow Christians."

"And that they even turn on themselves."

"Of course. Families sometimes have spats."

"It's more than that. I contend that the basic doctrine of Christianity creates an atmosphere of distrust that results in the belittling of others, hindering social advancement, and the marginalizing of groups Christians consider sinful."

Isabella let the portly young man stew for a moment. "It is your opinion then that Christians are a detriment to society."

"Yes. Oh, I'm sure there are many good people who call themselves Christian."

Isabella smiled. "I would imagine so. There are even a few good lawyers. Or so I hear."

The observers laughed, and half the judges smiled.

"Dr. Pasternack, when were you last in a church?"

"It's been awhile."

"A year or more."

"Probably."

"More than five years?"

"I can't be sure. I was probably a child."

"Child? Preteen? Elementary school?"

"Maybe."

"A toddler?"

"Maybe."

Isabella pinched the bridge of her nose. "So you haven't been in a Christian church that you can remember."

"I guess."

"Dr. Pasternack, my client's freedom is on the line here." She turned to the audience. "His wife and two children are here, praying for his release. He's lost everything. Maybe, if it's not too much trouble, you can stop guessing and give us honest answers."

"I was taken to church by an aunt. I was five years old."

"And since then?"

"I've never been back."

"How many books are there in the Bible?"

"Objection. I don't see how this pertains—"

"Sit down, John." Isabella didn't look at the judges, she kept plowing forward. "How many books in the Bible?"

"I don't recall."

"Sixty-six in the Protestant Bible, the Catholic canon has a few more, often called the Apocrypha. How many authors?"

"Well, several, of course."

"Of course. Over forty authors written over fifteen hundred years in three languages on three continents. This is new to you, isn't it, Dr. Pasternack?"

"I don't see how it is germane."

"You haven't been to a Christian church except once as a toddler; you know nothing about the book Christians hold dear, and yet you present yourself as an expert on Christian action and intention."

"Well, there's more to social research that just that."

"Than just the basics? How many practicing Christians do you know?"

"Many."

"Name ten . . . no, name one."

"Well . . ."

"Dr. Pasternack, I'm afraid your testimony is just a regurgitation of other peoples' opinions. You might not be an anti-Semite, but it appears from your testimony and your dissertation that you are anti-Christian." She walked from the podium. "I'm finished with the witness."

Kurosawa let a moment pass before telling the witness he could step down. "Prosecution will continue later, defense may now call a witness."

"I call Derrick Rimbaud."

A pale, thin, well-dressed man came forward and took the stand.

Isabella took a seat, and Scott Freeman rose. "Mr. Rimbaud. Please state your name, place of residence, and occupation for the court."

"I am Derrick Rimbaud. I reside in Glasgow, Scotland. I am by training a solicitor in the UK legal system and for a time, served as a Member of Parliament. These days, I lead a small nonprofit that monitors intolerance aimed at Christians."

"The name of that organization, if you don't mind, Mr. Rimbaud."

"The Center for Christian Protection."

"Protection, Mr. Rimbaud. Are you saying that Christians need protection?"

"More and more every day."

"What is it your organization does?" Freeman struck a casual, comfortable pose, resting his hands on the podium.

"We monitor incidents of intolerance directed at Christians. We do this by monitoring news reports, reports from other Christian organizations, and from direct reports made to us."

"Are you a large organization?" Freeman asked.

"We have a few employees and a goodly number of volunteers around the world."

"So you defend Christians who are victims of intolerance?"

"No, sir. Organizations like yours, the Alliance, provide the legal defense. We focus on gathering information we use to brief international governmental organizations, governments themselves, NGOs, journalists and individuals who might be interested in the problem. For example, we have advised the European Union's Fundamental Rights Agency, the OSCE—Organization for Security and Cooperation in Europe in Vienna."

"Then what?"

"We use the information to raise awareness about the subject and encourage victims."

Freeman scratched his chin as if in deep thought. "Are you saying that Christians are victims of intolerance?"

"Yes, sir. On a daily basis. Every year, the rate at which Christians are selected for marginalization grows. It has moved beyond those who have a different spiritual or moral philosophy disagreeing with Christians to outright infringement of their rights."

Freeman furrowed his brow. "Now wait a minute. Many would suggest that Christian's cannot be marginalized since they represent the majority in most countries, at least in the Western world. You don't agree?"

"No, sir, I don't agree. First, I would challenge the basic assumption that Christians form a majority in these countries. True, many people claim the name of Christ, but are in no way active in traditional church activities, calling upon the church only when they need a baptism, a wedding or a funeral."

Isabella had been watching John. She saw a slight flinch at the word funeral.

Rimbaud continued. "I once had an uncle who thought he was an avocado, but the family was quite sure he was mistaken." Titters rolled through the court. "Let us think of South Africa. Black Africans compose the majority of the population, but for many years they were the victims of apartheid. Being in the majority was of no help to them until the laws changed in the late twentieth century. Now the laws are changing in a way that has brought discrimination and intolerance. Christians have always been victims of discrimination. During the first century, for a Christian to work for a secular guild, he would be asked to swear allegiance to the guild god, usually a Roman deity. Christians and Jews could not do this and consequently were kept from practicing their trade in many cities. Of course, there were waves of physical persecution that led to the martyrdom of tens of thousands. People back then suffered from Christophobia."

"Christophobia?" Freeman leaned over the podium as if eager to here the next few comments. "Did I hear that right?"

"Yes, sir. Phobia is a Greek word that describes an irrational fear. Like some people are afraid of spiders or heights or dogs—you get the idea. We're seeing a new wave of people and government leaders who have an irrational fear of Christ and Christians. This is leading to persecution as it did in the early years of the church and when this fear becomes law, it leads to the systematic abuse of Christian rights. And there is the irony: nations who pride themselves on tolerance are becoming the most intolerant of all."

"Objection!"

"Overruled."

"Why do you suppose this is going on?"

"The Christian message is one that demands repentance and a change in behavior. Some accept this willingly, others fight against it. The Christian life often makes others feel uncomfortable. This is why there is a move to make religious expression allowable only behind closed doors."

"How is this being played out in society?"

"In so many ways. There are so many attacks on Christian symbols that a catalogue of such occurrences would take the size of a phonebook for a major city. Almost everywhere a Christian symbol appears in public, there is a group who calls for its removal: crèches at Christmas time, crosses on the exterior of church buildings, Ten Commandment displays, denial of public buildings for church services or programs, the removal of crosses on, or in view of public property. The Italian crucifix case. We are very close to seeing a day when equality, openness, and fairness apply only to non-Christians. This case is a classic example."

"How so?"

"Dr. Preston is on trial for preaching a biblical message. Those who preach a contrary message are allowed to do so freely. There is some irony in all of this."

"How do you mean?"

"One of the greatest disparagers of the Christian faith was Voltaire. He said, 'Christianity is the most ridiculous, the most absurd and bloody religion that ever infected the world.' He also said, 'I disapprove of what you say, but I will die defending your right to say it.' One doesn't have to agree with Christianity to know that even Christians have a right to speak."

"Thank you, Mr. Rimbaud." Freeman turned to John. "The witness is yours."

John rose to the podium, but he seemed to Isabella to stand a inch or two smaller. Something was wrong.

"Mr. Rimbaud, as an attorney, I assume you know that the role of law, at least in a democratic society, is to protect the innocent and foster neutrality with regard to the intangible matters of faith. Do you agree?"

"No. Of course not."

John seemed genuinely stunned. "Why is that?"

"Because the assertion is nonsense. Tripe. You've offered two falsehoods in hope of making a single truth. In math, two negatives might make for a positive, but it does not carry to the laws of a civil society. The growing efforts by men like you does not bring neutrality, just the opposite; it marks off a large segment of the population and removes from them rights others use freely, such as voicing an opinion. Second, there is nothing intangible about faith."

"Many would argue that the new laws in the UK, Spain, the United States, and many others create a canvas of neutrality for all."

"If only that were true, Mr. Smith. Neutrality is a nice word, but there is no such thing. No one in this room is neutral. A blank wall makes a statement, especially if a religious picture is forcibly removed to make the wall blank. Is your organization neutral, Mr. Smith?"

"I'm not on the witness stand."

"Perhaps you should be." Rimbaud maintained a steady expression.

"One of my key advisors is a pastor."

"The pastor of a Christian church?" A few in the audience chuckled. Kurosawa silenced them with a glare.

Clearly, John didn't like having the tables turned. "Do I need to ask the court to remind you of your responsibilities as a witness?"

"No need, sir. I'm just trying to be open and honest with my answers. I can be less open if you like." The audience responded again.

Kurosawa cleared his throat. "The witness will refrain from attempting humor and answer the questions. Understood?"

"Yes, sir."

John stared at the witness for a moment. "So it is your contention that people of all faiths should not have the same rights."

"I believe that's your position. My position is that the rise of radical secularism is depriving religious groups of basic human rights. The first target has been the Christian. What is at stake here is *equal* rights for Christians. Over one hundred million people are the victims of persecution, seventy-five million of those are Christians."

"Persecution is a harsh word."

"Persecution is a harsh affliction. Let me be clear; persecution comes in many degrees. The worst is physical persecution, but there are other forms which include social discrimination, restriction of historic freedoms. Pope John Paul II called this a form of 'civil death.'"

"I assume you're a Catholic, Mr. Rimbaud."

"Presbyterian, but we make no distinction in our work."

"Isn't it true that there are Christian groups that marched against homosexual gatherings, who carried signs that read 'Fags will burn in Hell'?"

"Yes, there are, but their percentage is microscopic and we strongly disagree with their approach. If it were not for the media's focus, no one would have ever heard of them."

"Do you think they have a right to do such things?"

Rimbaud lowered his head and looked embarrassed. "Yes. I detest such things, but I am aware that there exists such groups and do not defend their behavior. To be honest, it sickens me, but some outrage is the price one pays for the freedom of expression."

John started to ask another question, then pulled up. "I'm finished with the witness."

Chapter 50

Ruby Uninvited

──◈──

R uby marched into the DOJ with three male agents in her wake. As she approached the security check point, all four flashed FBI badges and IDs. She paused long enough to call the security people working the metal detectors and X-ray machines for a five-second meeting: "Anyone who calls upstairs gets to spend a great deal of time in a federal prison. Questions?" There were none. She left one man behind to make sure the others got the point and to monitor the lobby.

She had another question: "Who's the supervisor?"

An overly tanned man with a wrinkled face raised a hand.

"Come with me."

"I don't understand—"

She took him by the arm and marched him to the elevator. Once inside, she motioned to the security card system. "Take me to the DTED offices." He hesitated. "Now!"

The man complied and the elevator started up. She had been to the floor before, most recently to report to and suggest that John Knox Smith might be involved in Matt Branson's murder. That was still up in the air, but not Paul Atoms.

When the doors parted, several people were waiting to get on the lift. A glance told her none was Atoms. "Make a hole." They did.

She moved into the DTED office area. A young attorney poked her head up. "May I help you?"

Her question was cut short by Ruby's badge. "Paul Atoms. Where is he?"

"Paul Atoms?"

Ruby turned to fully face the woman. Her scowl was incendiary.

"Um, he left about an hour ago."

Ruby swore in a way that would embarrass a Navy chief. "Did he say where he was going?"

"No, ma'am. I'm just a junior attorney. He doesn't clear things with me."

Ruby looked at her FBI escorts. "Ninety minutes. That's how long it took to get the search warrants. He's been tipped off. Search the floor. You have three minutes. Go."

The search proved the young attorney's point. Moments later, they were back on the elevator for the ride down.

***

Ruby got a break with the DC traffic. Something that happened once a decade. The two black FBI cars pushed slower traffic aside with their emergency lights. Ruby sat in the passenger seat while one of the other agents drove. Her mind raced like an Indy car. She used the radio to dispatch agents and muni police to the airport, train and bus stations. She also called in a BOLO. The Be On the Look Out message went out to all police agencies. Photos were sent to any agency that could receive them electronically.

Paul Atoms lived in an upscale townhouse in Arlington. She pounded on the front door as one agent went around back to check for possible escape routes. Several uniformed police officers took positions at the back, freeing the agent to join Ruby.

Ruby knocked on the door again. "Paul Atoms. FBI. Search warrant. Open the door." No response. "Paul Atoms. FBI. We have a search warrant; open the door."

The door had a thin stylish window running vertically near the door handle. It looked good. Looked expensive. A touch of class. She turned to one of the uniformed officers who carried a metal, collapsible baton. "Let me see that." He handed it over and she snapped it open with an authoritative snap of the wrist. Then, with the same authority, smashed the window, reached through the opening and unlocked the deadbolt.

Ruby took a step back, drew her sidearm and raised the business end at the middle of the door. "Open it."

One of the agents, his weapon already drawn, turned the knob and pushed open the door.

"Federal agents! Show yourself." She led the team in. To the left was an opening to the kitchen. She oozed around the corner of the opening. "Clear." She moved by a stair case toward the living room. A voice from upstairs cried, "Clear."

It took only a few more moments for Ruby to realize she had missed her man again.

"Agent Fay, you need to see this." The voice came from upstairs. She moved up the steps and looked in the master bedroom which had the kind of locks installed that are normally found on front doors. The closet was half empty. There were hangers for twice the clothing that was there. She saw no luggage. "In here."

Ruby moved to the second of three bedrooms. "This is disturbing." She took inventory of a wall upon which hung close to twenty weapons, including an AK-47; MIA2, MP5, a half dozen high powered pistols and more. "He's displaying them. Showing his manhood. This guy has some deep-seated issues." Then she noticed something even more disturbing: there were empty spaces on the wall—places where other weapons had been displayed. "He's packing big time."

"Can't tell what was hanging there," one of the agents said, "but I'm guessing it was nasty."

Ruby agreed. "Better get word out that our man is heavily armed and should be considered dangerous." The agent activated his radio and made the call. "Help me find his store of ammo. I bet he's got boxes of it."

"What will that tell us?"

"I'm looking for something in particular." She and the others searched the room. They found a small trap door beneath a leather chair near the window. The space was filled with various kinds of ammunition, from shotgun shells, to nine millimeter, to rounds used in various automatic weapons.

Then she saw it: A small cardboard box, aged and rough around the corners. She slipped on a pair of latex gloves and removed the box. "Bingo."

"What is it?"

"Treasury load hollow point."

The agent looked puzzled. "I thought those were extinct."

"They should be." She held up one bullet. "It was one of these that killed Matt Branson." She replaced the round in the segmented box and stood, then looked to one of the uniformed officers. He had threes stripes on his sleeve. "Sergeant, I want this place secured. No one in. I mean no one. Can you make that happen?"

"Yes, ma'am. I'll make it happen."

Ruby glanced around the room and mumbled. "He's packing significant hardware. He's a killer. He knows the system; knows our tactics. He might even be listening in to our radio conversations. I know I would." As her concentration increased, everything in the room disappeared. "He can't get on a plane with more than one side arm, even if he flashes his DOJ badge. He might even have his old FBI ID. But we have the airports on alert. Anyone not an air marshal carrying a gun will be stopped."

"He could just drive away."

The agent's voice brought her around. "True. Since flying is out . . ." She slapped her head. "I'm an idiot. Let's go."

"Where?"

"To the airport."

"But you said—"

"Private airport. The guy's a pilot. He won't go to a place with lots of security. He'll go to one with next to none." She called dispatch. "I need a list of private airports in the DC area and I need them yesterday."

***

Ruby listened to a caller on her cell phone, then rang off. "Leesburg Executive Airport. It's north of Dulles. Step on it." She started to punch in a number. "Atoms is in a cooperative that owns a plane there. A two-engine something or other. I should have thought of this earlier. If he gets away, I'm going to shoot you in the foot."

The driver glanced at her. "Me? Why me?"

"Because I'm planning a dancing career after I retire." She raised the phone to her ear. A few moments later. "That's odd. No answer."

"It's a small airport, right? Maybe whoever runs it is taking a break."

"I hope so. The alternative frightens me." She tried again. This time a winded, male voice answered. "This is Special Agent Ruby Fay, FBI. Whom am I speaking to?"

"Bill Pressman. I'm . . . I manage the place. How did you know?"

"Know what?"

"That someone held us at gun point, then locked us in a closet. I managed to work myself free of the duct tape he used to bind us."

"Is anyone hurt, Bill?"

"No, just shaken up."

"Okay, get everyone back in the office and lock the door. Do you know who did this?"

"Some guy. Yeah. His name is Paul Atoms. He's part of a cooperative that has a plane here. I've met him several times."

"Where is he now?"

"I think he's getting ready to take off."

"He's still on the ground?"

"Yeah, but . . ." Hang on. "I can see him he's headed to his plane."

"How long will it take him to get airborne?" Ruby gritted her teeth.

"Not long. I'm sure it's fueled, but he has to release the tie downs and taxi to the runway. Maybe ten minutes."

"We're almost there." She thought for a moment. "I need your help, Bill."

"Name it."

"I need to get on the runway."

"Okay, come in off Sycolin Road, make a right through the front parking area. You'll come to another side road. Turn left. There's a gate for emergency vehicles. I'll make sure it's open."

"You're the man. Just stay out of Atom's sight."

"You don't have to tell me twice." Bill hung up.

Ruby bounced in her seat, trying to make the car go faster.

***

Everything was just as Bill said. Ruby and her team barreled into the parking area with sirens blaring and lights flashing behind the front grill of the large sedan.

"Take me onto the runway." Ruby released her seat belt.

"That's dangerous."

"So's your driving. Do it."

A moment later, the sedan screeched to a stop at the edge of the runway. Ruby's door was open before the vehicle came to a full stop. She looked south and saw nothing, then turned her eyes north. At the end of the taxiway, a twin-engine prop aircraft pulled onto the runway. She motioned for the second car to head in that direction. Maybe Atoms would come to his senses, but she wouldn't wager a nickel on it.

The sound of powerful engines filled the air and the aircraft started down the runway, its wings biting the oncoming wind.

"They're not going to get there in time." She looked at her fellow agent. "See if we can't get a chopper or plane over here to follow him."

"Good idea."

As her team member made the call, a blaze of anger flared in Ruby. She wasn't going to let that plane get airborne. She grabbed an M-4 carbine from the car's visor rack, walked to the middle of the runway and started north.

Ruby Fay confidently snapped the weapon to her shoulder..."I'm coming for you, Atoms."

The sound of the aircraft engines filled the air. A glance to the side showed a man by the gate. Bill? She waved him back. With agents behind him, Atoms had only one way out: over Ruby—just the way she liked it.

The plane picked up speed, its propellers shredding the warm afternoon air. She leveled her gun. "Wait for it. Wait for it. Front sight, trigger."

Closer. She could feel the vibration of the engines. The speed of the craft grew with each second, making Atoms' intention clear. In this game of chicken, he would not veer off.

Ruby's first three-round burst hit the windscreen opposite Atoms, sending spider cracks throughout the glass. He was undeterred.

Ruby refused to move. She coolly dropped her sight down and to the left, emptying the magazine from her carbine into the plane's right engine. Bullet fragments and shards of fan blades sprayed through the intake and compressor, oil mixed with fuel, and the engine burst into flame. The disabled craft veered sharply to her left. As Ruby moved doggedly toward the crippled plane, the door popped open and Paul Atoms leaped to the ground. In his hand was an H & K MP5/10.

Ruby dropped the spent mag and quickly reached to top off her M4 with a fresh 30 rounds. But Atoms had already brought his muzzle to bear on Ruby, ready to punch 10mm Silver Tips through her chest. Ruby could see he had her beat. There was no way she could get her shot off before Atoms. But there was no fear. She remained focused, determinedly moving forward, raising her M4 and bracing for the rounds to hit her.

Atoms' rounds never came. Just as her front sight pulled up on his chest, a red mist sprayed the fuselage of the plane. Atoms' legs went limp, his arms flailed. His body and his carbine dropped heavily to the ground.

Three FBI agents advanced on Atoms, their freshly fired Glocks drawn, yelling unnecessary commands. Blood pooled around Atom's body as a senior agent calmly keyed his radio, no doubt calling for paramedics and alerting their ASAC.

Two hours later, Ruby received the news.

Paul Atoms would live.

Chapter 51

Bad News

The call to the Netherlands came late in the night. Not that it mattered. John was still up thinking about the next step in the trial. The cell phone chimed with unusual sharpness. He answered, expecting to hear Andrea's voice.

"Hello, Mr. Assistant Attorney General. I hope I haven't called too late or at an inconvenient time."

The voice was familiar. "Special Agent Fay?"

"Yes, sir."

"How did you get this number?"

"It wasn't hard. The Attorney General was happy to share it with the Director of the FBI. We're all one big happy family, you know."

"What do you want?" He did nothing to mitigate the anger in his voice.

"You asked me to keep you posted on the Branson case. I have good news. We've made an arrest."

"Outstanding, Agent."

"Well, there's bad news, too. The killer is your own Paul Atoms."

"What!"

"Yes, sir. I had trouble believing it at first, since I thought *you* were my guy, At least I thought that for awhile. I have more good news. Maybe it's bad news. Depends on your perspective. He fled, tried to leave the state in his private plane, and then resisted arrest.

He even threatened an FBI agent with a deadly weapon. I was that agent, by the way. My team had to open fire on him, but he'll live."

"You shot him?"

"Not me. I just shot his aircraft—a lot."

"But he's alive?"

"Came out of surgery a few hours ago. He's lucky to be alive. Then again, maybe not so lucky. Anyway, he's offering to talk for a lighter sentence, but that's up to your boss. Of course, I also can prove that he's responsible for the death of the two Supreme Court justices. Ironic, isn't it? The guy who assassinated two justices and killed your ol' college chum was working right under your nose."

"I don't appreciate your inference. How can you connect him to the justices?"

She told him how the evidence led to Paul and the arsenal he kept in his home, an arsenal that included difficult to find Treasury load hollow points. "When ballistics is done testing his stock of weapons, at least ones that can accommodate those kinds of round, I'm pretty sure we'll get a match."

"Why would he do that?"

"He's a believer, Mr. Smith, not in the spiritual, but in the ideas you've been promoting. He's your biggest fan. Until I get a full confession, I can't say for sure but I see it this way. You needed fresh, more liberal justices on the court. How often does a justice leave the Supreme Court? Not often. These guys were good to hang in there another decade. To get judicial support for your new laws, a friendlier court is required. President Blaine is on your side, as is the Vice President, the Attorney General, and most of congress. The Court, however, well, they're a different ballgame. They're not elected; they're appointed for life. Either they retire or die. They weren't going to do the former, so Mr. Atoms provided the latter. I'm guessing that Atoms thought he was doing you and the country a favor. You know what else we found in his home, Mr. Smith?"

He could hear the smile in her voice. "I'm afraid to ask."

"That's okay. I'm not afraid to say. He had a wall in a bedroom he used for an office. On the walls were his college diploma, a few awards and citations, and a whole bunch of news-clippings of you. Yep, it was a regular shrine."

John groaned. "Paul? I can't believe it. It's too much."

"Yeah, kinda makes the head spin, doesn't it? Well, I thought you should know your team will be missing a member for, well, the rest of his life."

"Um, thanks for letting me know, Agent Fay."

"My pleasure, Mr. Smith. I mean that. It is my *pleasure*. I just hope everything else in your life is going well. Oh one last thing. This whole thing stinks of conspiracy. I don't think he acted alone. I hope your legal laundry is clean. Let's chat when you get back, shall we?"

John Knox Smith hung up and stared at the wall until dawn.

Chapter 52

Pope on the Stand

⟫◇⟪

"Your honors, I call to the stand, Pope John Paul Benedict I."
Whispers erupted through the crowd but not the judges
or the prosecution. Isabella had to tell them of the plan. A side door
opened and an entourage of clerics and suited men entered. Benedict
walked straight to the witness stand. Half the audience stood at
his entrance. He smiled and made the sign of the cross in the air,
blessing the group.

Isabella had never felt so uncertain and unsure of herself. By
calling the Pope in secular court and his agreement to respond, they
had made history. She just didn't know what kind of history.

Kurosawa had to call the court back to order. When silence
returned, Isabella began. "Thank you, Your Holiness, for helping in
this matter."

"It is my pleasure, child."

First person. She hoped he would avoid the formal third person.
"Would His Holiness please state his name and—I know this seems
silly—your occupation and place of residence."

A light laughter filled the room.

"I am John Paul Benedict I. That is my ecclesiastical name. My
given name is Judah Chweng of Nigeria. I live in Vatican City. I am
a priest."

"A priest. Some would consider that an understatement."

"Many titles have been applied to my position, but I am first and foremost, a simple priest in service to the Lord Jesus Christ and His Church."

"Holy Father, you are here at my request, is that correct?"

"It is, Countess. It is my honor."

"But this is an unusual event for a man in your position."

"Yes. I'm sorry to say that my movement involves the work of many others. There are security issues as well. It is unfortunate."

"You have followed this case closely, have you not?"

He nodded. "I have. I believe it is important, pivotal in the history of the Church and the world."

"This is not your first participation in this case, is it?"

"No, Countess. You are trying to make clear my earlier involvement?"

"I am."

Benedict turned to face the judges. They seemed unsettled by his gaze. "Countess Isabella and I know each other from her work at the Vatican. She has provided valuable counsel in the many legal matters with which the Church must deal. I became aware of Dr. Preston's plight and asked the countess to craft a report for me which she did. The more I learned and the more I prayed about the matter, the more I felt God's leading to lend whatever help I could. I met with Dr. Preston at the prison and he agreed to allow the countess to help with his representation."

"Thank you, Your Holiness. Why is the case so important to you?"

"Not just to me, but to every person of faith. Dr. Preston is not a Catholic, but he is still a man of great faith. If a man can be jailed for preaching from the Bible, then every priest and preacher will be a criminal."

"Including you."

"Yes, including me."

"Do you feel this is a form of persecution?" Isabella began to relax. The pontiff was casual, his voice even and smooth.

"A form of persecution, yes. There are hundreds of believers who suffer great physical persecution and death. This is a different form of persecution, but a persecution nonetheless. Just ask Dr. Preston."

"We have had many witnesses who have talked about the importance of free speech, freedom of worship, freedom of expression."

"Yes, the court was kind enough to set up a room with a closed-circuit television so I could watch some of the testimony. Very enlightening."

Isabella paused. She pointed at John, then asked. "Holy Father, if this man were to tell you that you can't celebrate Mass or preach on various topics, would you comply?"

"No. Never. I would continue as I have, and pray for his soul."

"And if you were arrested?"

"I'd preach to the guards and other prisoners and argue theology with Dr. Preston." The comment raised more laughter.

Isabella grinned. "I'm sure he'd love that. Do you think you are alone in your commitment?"

"No, by no means. Our missionaries have given their lives to take the Gospel to every part of the world. I would not insult our Lord and their memories by turning my back on the Gospel."

"Thank you, Your Holiness." She looked at John. He looked grayer than a few moments before.

John stood. "Might I have a few moments to confer, Mr. President?"

Kurosawa nodded. "A few, but let's not keep the court . . . and Pope Benedict waiting."

***

John leaned toward Joel Thevis. "I have a bad feeling about this."

"Why, he's just a man . . . and he wears red shoes."

"No, he's much more. He's a figurehead to a billion people. I don't even know how to address him. If I call him 'Holy Father,' I bolster his position. If I call him 'Your Holiness,' I give credence to the idea of holiness."

"Then call him something else."

"Like what? 'Hey, Pope Dude?' Here's another problem. I've been thinking about this all night. If I go after his position or his argument, it might look like I'm beating up the Pope. Not only that,

that *woman* has asked so few questions that I have nothing to build on."

"You want me to take this?"

"And do what?"

"Ask him why he hates homosexuals."

John ground his teeth. "Then he'll say he doesn't hate them. That we're all sinners in need of the saving grace of Jesus, yada yada yada."

"Okay, ask why the Bible hates gays."

"The Bible's not on trial, not directly. Besides, it's an inanimate object and not capable of emotion. The guy is the perfect witness. If I come across too strong, then we could lose a lot of support in Congress. I'll be branded the Catholic hater who verbally attacked the Pope. When congress-members come up for reelection, they'll have to distance themselves from my programs."

"So what are you going to do?"

"Mr. Smith?" Kurosawa hiked an eyebrow.

John pushed himself to his feet. "No questions."

***

"Dr. Preston," Scott Freeman began, "why are you here?" The usual recitation of name, occupation, and residence had been established. To Pat's surprise and those in the court, Pope Benedict decided to stay. He took a seat in the back of the gallery.

"I have been accused of hate-speech and disseminating intolerance through my messages, studies, and church activities."

"Hate speech directed at whom?"

"Those involved in homosexual and bisexual behavior, non-Christian belief systems like Wiccan, Hinduism, and others." John's stomach was in a knot as hard as a baseball.

"So you hate people who engage in homosexual acts?"

"I do not."

Freeman rocked on his heels. "You hate people who claim to be bisexual?"

"No."

"Wiccans? Hindus? Muslims?"

"No. Hatred is not part of Christ's teaching."

"But you believe they are sinners?"

"All people are sinners."

"Does that include you?" Freeman asked.

"Yes."

"Me?"

"Yes."

"Pope Benedict?"

"Him, too. Everyone."

"What is sin?"

"The common answer is that sin means to miss the mark. Preachers often speak of an archer who fires at a target, but the arrow falls short. The idea is that people fall short of righteousness. They do so through acts of commission or omission—doing things we know we shouldn't and purposely avoiding doing those things we should."

"So those who practice homosexual behavior are sinners?"

"As is the heterosexual. Sin is not confined to sexual sin."

"What if I don't accept your definition?"

Pat shrugged. "You are free to do so We all have freewill. My job as a preacher is to teach biblical principles and encourage people in their walk with God."

"What if I think you're a bigoted idiot who hates me because of my life choices?"

Pat smiled. "You wouldn't be the first." Laughter came from the crowd. "You'd also be wrong. I'm not a bigot. I don't hate others. The idiot part is a judgment call. I'll leave that up to you."

More laughter.

Freeman's face turned serious. "If I engaged in homosexual acts, could I attend your church?"

"Yes. Of course—if I still had a church."

"How can that be?" Freeman said. "You just said homosexual behavior is a sin."

"The greatest myth about the church, a belief held by many in the pew as well as those who never cross the threshold of the church is that the church is some kind of country club. It's not. It's a hospital. The church isn't filled with perfect people. There are no perfect people, just those trying to do right by God. Every Christian has a story. It is a place for those who want to make spiritual and life changes that come through Christ. When I stood in the pulpit, I looked over a sea of sinners and they were looking at a sinner in the pulpit."

"Dr. Preston, you heard the testimony of Mr. Hume whose male partner committed suicide. How did that make you feel?"

Pat looked away. He could feel his energy drain away. "Regretful." He took another moment to gather his words. "I wish I knew of his depression. I wish I had been told of his passing."

"He attended your church. How could you not know?"

Pat looked at Freeman. He knew these questions were coming. Freeman was attempting to anticipate John's cross examination and ask the hard questions, first allowing Pat the opportunity to answer fully before being forced to the next question. "This will sound like an excuse. I don't mean it to." He took a breath. "I was the senior pastor of a church that saw ten thousand people every Sunday. That's the size of a small city. You add tens of thousands more from the radio, television, and Internet broadcasts. My secretary once did a little math and shared it with me. I was feeling overwhelmed and a little sad that there were so many people I couldn't call by name. If I spent one minute with each person who showed up at our morning services, it would take nine days, twenty-four hours a day, to accomplish the task. And that's just the number who show up on a Sunday. The number of people who called the church home was double that."

He turned his eyes to Freeman. "I received on average two hundred e-mails a day. We try to keep people connected using small groups, but many don't participate. The truth is, I knew nothing of the men or the events." He swallowed bile-tasting regret. "I wish I had. I don't know if I could have helped, but I would have tried."

"You've been very forthcoming, Pastor Preston. If asked, would you have performed the funeral for Mr. Bowers?"

"Yes."

"In spite of what you would describe as his sinful choices?"

"Yes, of course. I would not refuse the request."

"Not every Christian minister would agree with you. Why would you do that?"

"It wouldn't be the first time. Why? I can't help people at a distance. I would not condone his life choices. I would not change my doctrine, but I would offer whatever comfort I could to those who knew him."

"Pastor Preston, you were offered the opportunity to avoid this trial. The prosecution extended an olive branch of sorts. You could have walked away a free man for just a few concessions. What were those concessions?"

"I was told that if I apologized for my hate-speech and promised to give up the claims of Christ from my ministry, Mr. Smith would drop the case."

"But you refused. Why?"

"I have not been involved in hate-speech. Jesus is Lord. To say otherwise is contrary to my Christian principles and I won't . . . I can't give up the ministry, so I declined his offer."

"You chose to remain in confinement rather than walk away from your principles, even if it meant continued separation from your family?" Freeman had not prepped him for this. He felt sucker punched.

Pat's eyes began to burn. He couldn't look at his wife and kids. He lowered his head and looked at the floor.

"Take your time, Pastor."

Time compressed, then dissolved. Pat had no idea how much time passed. Mucus filled his nose. He heard soft, familiar weeping. Becky's weeping. "Yes."

"Don't you love your family?" Freeman's voice cracked.

"More than I can say."

"Yet, still, here you are. You chose incarceration in a foreign country over time in your wife's arms; over time spent playing with your children. Why, Pastor? Why would a man do that? Why would you choose to breathe the air of a prison instead of the air of freedom?"

"Because . . . because I'm innocent of any crimes. Because men like John—Mr. Smith—are stripping away the rights of people to spread the Gospel. Because . . . I must stand for Christ, no matter what the . . . cost." He broke into tears.

Pat heard Freeman speak. "Your witness."

***

John was furious. Isabella and Freeman had out maneuvered him, first with the Pope and now with a weeping Pat Preston. He couldn't go after the Pope, knowing how bad it would look to the world and how it might alienate elected leaders he needed to further his agenda. Now he was being asked to pound on a man he had separated from his family, a family that sat in the court. As a young prosecutor, he had many times been forced to cross examine weeping defendants but this was different. Pat wasn't weeping because he was frightened or remorseful. In fact, he showed no remorse at all.

At the podium, John stood in silence waiting for the sniffling to stop. He stood, giving Pat all the time he needed but grew impatient. John wondered what else could go wrong with this case and with his life. A full five minutes later, Pat looked up, drew a shuddering breath, then faced his accuser.

"Jesus loves me, this I know," John began, "for the Bible tells me so. Do you know that song, Dr. Preston?"

"Yes. It's from an old children's hymn."

"Jesus loves me, this I know . . . unless I'm gay, bisexual, lesbian, transgendered, Wiccan, Hindu, living together without benefit of marriage, or chosen a different definition of marriage, or believe in open sexuality, or don't fit the mold and model of evangelical Christians. That's accurate, isn't it?"

Isabella rose. "Objection. Compound question."

Pat didn't wait for the judge to rule. "I've never said anything like that."

"But the Bible does. 'No homosexual shall ever see the Kingdom of God.' Isn't that what the Apostle Paul said to the Corinthians?"

"You're proof texting. Taking things out of context."

"Am I? I grew up going to church. I clearly recall reading that verse."

"Objection. Argumentative." Isabella was on her feet again.

John waved her off. "I'll rephrase. Doesn't the Apostle Paul say that no homosexual will see the Kingdom of God?"

"You have to read the rest of the text. Paul says, 'And such were some of you.' The passage reads, 'Don't you know that the unrighteous will not inherit God's kingdom? Do not be deceived: No sexually immoral people, idolaters, adulterers, or anyone practicing homosexuality, no thieves, greedy people, drunkards, verbally abusive people, or swindlers will inherit God's kingdom. And some of you used to be like this. But you were washed, you were sanctified, you were justified in the name of the Lord Jesus Christ and by the Spirit of our God.'"

"Very impressive memory, Dr. Preston. Why is God so interested in my sex life?"

"He's interested in you, John, because He loves you."

"Does He? Yet, He will punish those who don't conform to His arbitrary list of sins."

"They're not arbitrary, John. Every sin has a consequence and repenting of them opens the door to life. God's concern is the result of sin."

"You know this from a book written thousands of years ago?"

"Yes."

"Were there cars back then?"

"Of course not."

"Airplanes?"

"No."

"Aspirin? Higher education? Mass transit?"

"No."

"So the world has changed since then, am I correct?"

"Yes."

"But the Bible remains the same as it's always been. Nothing new has been added over the last two thousand years. Is that correct?"

"Though some translators have tried otherwise, its truth is timeless."

"But its application, Dr. Preston—its application has altered. Is that also true?"

"Human needs remain the same."

"Do they? Surely some parts of the Bible are great literature—"

"It's more than that."

Kurosawa tapped the bench. "Dr. Preston, please don't interrupt the questioner. I will make sure you get your say."

"Yes, Your Honor."

"Why should any educated twenty-first century man limit his life to a box drawn by a book that was out of date a hundred years after it was written?"

"The same reason traffic laws dictate the way you may drive. Your actions have an impact on others, not just yourself."

"Dr. Preston, the Bible dictates who should be ostracized, who should be declared unclean and cast out of the camp. True?"

"Interesting, John, those are all Bible metaphors. You learned something in your Sunday School days."

"I learned the meaning of prejudice and discrimination. I learned the meaning of hate. You and those like you want to press down those who disagree with you. Have you not, by your preaching, caused emotional and spiritual harm to innocents?"

"I live my life in an effort to help hurting people find God's love."

"By ridiculing them? By making them feel worthless? By calling them sinners from the pulpit and over the open airwaves? You don't care to admit it, but it's abundantly clear that Christians are a cruel bunch, willing to tread others under foot so they can feel righteous and exalted."

"Your father is a Christian, John. Was he cruel? He built many churches. He used to take you to church."

"I'm the one asking the questions, Mr. Preston. Leave my father's memory out of this."

Pat blinked several times. "John, what do you mean 'his memory'?"

John felt himself flush. *What a bonehead slip.*

"Has something happened to your father?"

Kurosawa tapped the bench with a knuckle. "Dr. Preston, please confine yourself to the questions asked."

Before Pat could answer, John said, "That is not pertinent to this case."

"It's pertinent to you, John. What happened?"

Kurosawa tapped the judge's bench again. "Dr. Preston—"

"He died, Pat! He's dead!" John's veneer crumbled. He was making mistake after mistake. He was an excellent prosecutor, but he could not contain himself. Too much. Too much grief. Too much guilt. Too much fear.

Several in the audience gasped.

"When did he die, John?"

"Let's not waste the court's time."

"You and the court have stolen months of my life; I have the right to a few minutes. When did he die?"

John didn't answer.

Kurosawa addressed John. "Do you need a recess, Mr. Smith?"

Pat didn't let up. "We were friends once. I know you've forced those days from your mind, but I haven't. When did he die?"

"Dr. Preston, I am warning you." Kurosawa's words came with force. John didn't seem to hear him.

"Just a few days ago."

"And you're here?"

The ground beneath John shook. He seized the podium. "I couldn't put this trial off."

Joel Thevis shot up. "I would like to request a short recess."

"John," Pat spoke softly but firmly. He was in full pastor mode. "John, listen to me. Go home. Take a week. If I have to spend another week in that cell so you can take care of your father's estate, your son's grandfather's remains, then I will."

Joel raised his voice. "Mr. President, please. A recess is in order."

"No," John said softly. His heart slowed as if winding down to a stop. His guts trembled. "I have no more questions."

John stood at the podium looking down.

Chapter 53

Alone, All Alone

John Knox Smith sat in the passenger seat as Joel Thevis drove him and Andrea back to the hotel. No one spoke. A kind word would have been nice; a friendly hand laid on a shoulder would provide a little encouragement; a caress from Andrea might sweep away a little of the pain.

None of those things came.

The traffic on the streets of The Hague disappeared by degrees: first the sound, then the sight of the cars and trucks. Buildings followed suit. Soon, John could only see images of his wife now divorcing him; his son who would no longer speak to him; his father who was dead and very nearly in the ground; of Matt Branson lying murdered in a Washington, DC park; Paul Atoms in FBI custody; Ruby Fay briefing the FBI director and Attorney General Alton Stamper. Images of recent violence against churches strobed on his brain. He pictured Pat in his cell, laughing at John's misfortune. No, that wasn't right. He would never do that. That realization burned him with guilt.

John had been cored out by events. "Joel?"

"What?" Joel had made no secret of his anger.

"I want you to call the AG and bring him up to date."

"That's your job, man, not mine." It was the first time he had ever heard a harsh word from his lead attorney.

"You're more detached. You'll be more . . . accurate."

"Accurate yes. You can bet on it, but don't count on my being detached. You've chewed me up one end and down the other over this case and now you flush it in a single meltdown."

"I'm sorry."

"That can be taken two ways, pal."

"Shut up, Joel," Andrea said from the backseat. "You're not helping."

"This case was as important to me as it was to John. I'm sorry about your old man, John, I truly am, but you should have brought me in, let me know. I could have handled the questioning. I could have handled the rest of the case, but no, you have to be preeminent in all things. You have to be upfront, visible. I'm a good prosecutor. I am a *great* prosecutor. Your ego has doomed this case. You want to fire me? Go ahead. I'd consider it a favor."

"The case is still good. We chose this court for a reason. The justices have a track record of international laws and liberal decisions. Besides, they don't want to send the wrong signal to the US. For the ICJ to have any real power in the world, they need our country."

"Yeah? Well, I don't have your confidence."

"You do the closing, Joel. I may have undercut my own authority."

"Ya think!"

Joel pulled the car into the hotel parking structure, slammed the automatic transmission into park, yanked the keys from the ignition, and exited slamming the door. He took two steps away, then came back. "You are a joke, John. A colossal joke."

Andrea opened the rear door. "Um, listen, John. I know you need some time, so I'm going to go shopping or something, but if you need me, just call my cell. Okay? It'll be okay, John, It always is."

There was something dismissive in her voice.

John spent the next hour sitting alone in the car, wondering at what point he lost his mind.

Chapter 54

Final Word

———⟫·◆·⟪———

O nce again, Sir Alan Hodge sat in the large room used as chambers for the full panel alone. He liked the silence, a quiet that would soon be broken. The trial had ended with Joel Thevis presenting a mediocre closing of the prosecution's case. The countess presented a more logical set of reasons why Dr. Pat Preston should be found innocent. Still, the best both sides could do was rehash the case. In a jury trial, they might have put on a more dramatic summary, but jurists frowned on television-style closings.

He pulled the letter from the dying man he had read shortly before going to visit his sister. He thought of the man who used the last dregs of his dying strength to pen the missive. The subject had been that important to the man. Sir Alan still didn't understand the depths of Christian belief, but he could admire their commitment. He thought of Mia dealing with hookers, drug addicts, and the poor and forgotten. He thought of the children playing in front of their dead auntie and of the kid Mia had manhandled. She cared for both. How could a person do that? It wasn't natural.

And maybe that was the answer. It was supernatural.

The other judges entered and got down to business.

"Does anyone need more time to weigh the testimony and evidence?" Kurosawa asked. "No? Well, let us see where we stand, then we can debate. Those in favor of rendering a guilty verdict, raise your hand—"

"I have something to say," Sir Alan said. "I've been thinking . . .

***

"So we're finally down to it." Pat felt ill. "Thank you for all you've done." He shook hands with Scott Freeman and Larry Jordan, then kissed Isabella on both cheeks in true European style.

"I wish we could do more," she said.

"You provided the best legal defense a man could ask for, you provided for my family's security and even came close to losing your husband. I could ask for no more."

"I do have a bit of news," Freeman said. "I don't know if this is the time and place for it though."

"Is it bad news?" Pat asked.

"No."

"Then tell it; I need something else to think about other than what's about to happen."

"Okay. The FBI has made an arrest in the Matt Branson murder and the man will be offered a plea bargain, if he cooperates."

"Praise God." Pat lowered his head. "That is good news."

"There is more. We have a few friends in the DOJ and FBI. They can't talk about the case, but they did give me some information. The murderer was one of John's DTED team members: Paul Atoms.

"You're kidding," Jordan said.

"Let's pray he confesses to the murder *and* to bringing down the plane that killed our two Supreme Court Justices."

"He would never admit to that without a deal. I wonder what the FBI will offer."

"Life in prison, I assume. Maybe a choice of prisons. A former FBI agent doesn't fare very well in a federal prison."

"Matt Branson and the justices." Pat shook his head. "So much pain caused by one man."

"The FBI is also trying to link him to the doll incident and the attack on Isabella's husband. They might not be related. We may never know."

The door to the courtroom opened and Isabella led the legal team and Pat into the room. John and Joel Thevis sat at the prosecution table. Neither man looked up. John looked frail.

Pat glanced to his left and saw the court was full. His family was in the first row. He smiled. Phoebe waved at him, causing his heart to deflate like a balloon. He waved back.

Dear God, let me be strong.

Pat had been seated for only a moment when the entrance of the ICJ judge's panel entered, requiring him to stand again. They took their places quickly. As always, Kurosawa glanced at the court support staff and satisfied all was ready, called the court to order. He opened a file folder.

"The court will make no statement at this time beyond the announcing of the verdict. Those in the majority will file a brief, stating the majority's view of the case; those in the minority will voice their opinion in the same manner." He took a breath. The accused will stand."

Pat stood, along with his entire team. He heard a slight noise behind him, turned and saw his son stand.

Kurosawa lowered his eyes to the page in front of him. "In the matter of the *United States of America vs. Dr. Pat Preston*, the court finds the defendant guilty of general hate speech. However, this case will be filed in a category called "unpublished," which means it cannot be used or cited as precedent for any other court or judicial decision. No finding is made on what the defendant has said about the controversial religious figure commonly called Jesus."

Pat heard Becky gasp. Others made the same noise, but Pat could only hear his wife. He looked at John who remained seated and staring at the table in front of him. Joel Thevis looked as if he just won the lottery.

Kurosawa continued. "The court further decides that a penalty phase is unnecessary. Penalty shall be time served. The defendant is free to go." Kurosawa stood as did the others and exited.

The shaking began in Pat's chest, moved to his arms and hands, then to his legs. "I-I can go? I'm free?"

"Yes," Isabella said and threw her arms about Pat's neck. They hugged for a second, then she stepped back and motioned for the family to come forward.

Pat took his children in his arms.

After a few moments with his family, he turned to Isabella and the Alliance legal team. "I'm free, but what does this mean about our freedom to proclaim Jesus as *the* way, *the* Truth, and *the* life?"

Scott Freeman replied, "The battle will continue. But with God's grace, we will defend and we will win—if God's people stay on their knees. As long as God gives us the means, we will persevere."

Epilogue

Pat played "sock wars" in the hallway of the small Nashville rental, a game he once described as an intellectual pursuit in which a father pelted his children with rolled up socks and where children gleefully returned the favor.

Two weeks had passed since his return to the States and to the love of his family. The first week, he couldn't stand being apart from them for more time than it took to take a shower. When the children went to bed, he would sit on the floor and listen to the music of their breathing.

Police caught the man who left the mutilated doll on the doorstep. He had come around the house again shortly after Becky and the children had left for The Hague. Although Beatrice had left with the family, the security team she left behind was happy to detain the man until police arrived. He carried two more dolls. Pat learned the man was a schizophrenic with authority issues and unconnected to Paul Atom's crimes.

Puzzles remained. The Rome police recovered the Humvee that attempted to kill Fredrico San Philippa, Isabella's husband. The driver had yet to be found. Pat had a feeling that mystery would remain unsolved.

The doorbell rang. Pat called a truce in the sock wars and went to the door. He had yet to become comfortable with Becky answering the door alone. Wilma Benson stood on the step, wearing a three hundred watt smile. "Hello, Pastor. It's good to see you."

"Come in. Come in. It's good to be seen. That used to be a joke, but after so much time in a cell being watched 'round the clock… well, you get the idea."

Becky gave the woman a kiss on the cheek and led her to the sofa. Pat remained standing.

"Pastor, I have a question for you."

He listened, then said, "Yes?"

A rolled up sock hit him in the side of the head.

***

John Knox Smith had spent the last two weeks trying to get his life back in order. He called his estranged wife. She refused to take the call. He wrote his son. The letter was returned with the words, "Leave me alone," written on the back.

Multiple meetings and interviews were held with Attorney General Alton Stamper. The last meeting ended with the removal of the DTED team from John's leadership and handed over to Joel Thevis as interim Assistant Attorney General. Some in Congress called for hearings.

Andrea quit. Suddenly.

The FBI, in the form of Ruby Fay whom he started calling "that woman," still had questions about his activities on the night of Matt Branson's murder. Why couldn't they be happy with Paul Atoms who still hadn't opened up?

The funeral for his father was held before John could make it back to Colorado. He didn't try very hard.

He had won the case, but it seemed he'd lost. The Sunday following Pat's release, Pope Benedict celebrated a Mass in Saint Peter's Basilica in which he addressed the need for freedom of speech in religious matters. He then preached a sermon that John knew had been written deliberately to test the new tolerance laws. He wasn't alone. The news media was reporting that hundreds of pastors of every denomination were doing the same. These preachers were saying that no government agency, no court, no ruler, only a church's leadership, could decide what words would be spoken from their pulpits in their sermons. It was a spiritual revolution and John knew he couldn't arrest them all. They were out of control.

John walked into the National Gallery of the Arts and entered the East Building. He paused in the atrium, beneath the angled skylights and beneath the seventy-six-foot long red and black hanging mobile by Alexander Calder. He paused to admire its freedom of shape, its gentle motion, its ability to be without concern with any passerby below. He had long loved this 1977 work of art.

So beautiful. So free.

John reached beneath his coat and removed a handgun with a suppressor attached, loaned to him by Paul Atoms. He raised it to his temple and in full view of art lovers and security cameras, put a round into his head—a rare Smith & Wesson, jacketed hollow-point, Treasury load round…only the second round ever fired from that gun.

***

The Reverend Dr. Pat Preston stepped into the pulpit of the tiny Chapel Street Church and looked at the forty elderly faces looking back at him. The church buildings were rundown, the bank balance hovered near zero, and it was situated in a declining community. It was very different than Rogers Memorial Baptist church with its massive building and the buzzing of ten thousand worshippers. Still, Pat never felt more needed or more at home. He grinned at Wilma whose husband had occupied the pulpit for so many decades until his tragic killing in the pastor's study.

"God is the God of second chances," Pat said. "Thank you for this second chance."

***

It had taken two weeks before the medical examiner and police in Washington would allow the release of the body. Pat stood at a simple graveside in a small cemetery. It had been awhile since he had performed a graveside funeral. There were only three other people present: Becky, Wilma, and a deacon from Pat's new church.

In death, John Knox Smith was alone: no wife present, no son, no member of Congress, no one from the Department of Justice, not one person from the DTED team John had created and led.

"We gather at this somber time to put to rest the remains of John Knox Smith. He was a friend of mine . . ."

***

The letter on the worn desk in Chapel Street Church bore several international stamps and the return address of the prison in which he had spent agonizing months. The sight of it at first tore at his stomach, despite reminding himself that he initiated the correspondence.

He picked up the envelope and a plastic letter opener and removed the letter inside.

Dear, Dr. Preston,

I am sorry to inform you that the person addressed in your letter, the guard Marcus Aster, is no longer in the employ of our facility. He left shortly after your release and gave no forwarding address. We will keep your letter, in case he should make contact sometime in the future.

The letter bore the warden's signature.

Pat had wondered about the strange guard and at times likened him to the angel who came to Peter in prison. He pulled his Bible to the center of the desk and turned to the book of Acts. Finding Chapter 5, he read verses 19-20: "But an angel of the Lord during the night opened the gates of the prison, and taking them out, he said, 'Go your way, stand and speak to the people in the temple the whole message of this Life.'"

An angel of God or just a man? It didn't matter. Marcus was the messenger he needed and Pat was thankful for him. Now it was his job to stand as never before and boldly proclaim the "whole message of this Life."

You know, that text would make a good sermon for next Sunday. Pat sat at the desk and started making notes.

The End

A Note from the Author

"Today's fiction is tomorrow's truth."

————⟫◆⟪————

While nonfiction has been a staple in my legal training, law practice, ministry, and general reading, I have found a certain liberty in fiction. Things can be said in a novel, events shown in fiction that cannot be done in typical books. And with activist courts pushed to find new ways to reinterpret the nation's laws and Constitution, accompanied by demands the courts redefine American sovereignty, all too often we see things once considered as wild, improbable fiction become unpleasant reality.

Fiction also allows a degree of latitude not present in other areas of the written arts. In this book, I took our project model, "Today's fiction is tomorrow's truth," to heart. As with all fiction, certain liberties were taken with regard to locations and "future" news.

For example, as some of you sharp-eyed readers may have noticed, I used as the final stage for Dr. Pat Preston's drama the International Court of Justice (ICJ) and not its cousin, the International Criminal Court. Some might assume the ICC would be the natural court body to rule in a situation like Dr. Preston's, but such is not the case. The ICC exercises jurisdiction over extreme crimes in three areas: genocide, crimes against humanity, and war crimes. Pastor Pat's "example" case used in this book does not fit such categories as currently construed. As explained in the text, Preston's "Hate Speech" case is being tried at the request of the United States (technically, the United States of the near future) in an

ICJ with expanded and personal jurisdiction. The trial is being conducted to appease a very powerful member nation wanting to shape the International Tribunal.

Could such a case be tried in the near future? Yes. Ask Pastor Ake Green of Sweden (whom ADF helped represent at the Swedish Supreme Court), who was sentenced to jail by a lower court for preaching from God's word on sexual morality. With the help of ADF, his conviction was overturned. Or, ask The Reverend Stephen Boissoin of Canada, who was facing a lifetime ban from writing on certain moral issues in Canada. His legal defense was provided by an ADF-allied attorney and he was ultimately exonerated.

In my travels around the world, meeting with lawyers, government and religious figures, I have witnessed the rapid and continuous decline in legal protections for Christians, many of whom are deprived of basic legal and human rights. Increasingly, people of sincere faith are being treated as if they possessed a disease that hinders the progression of the human race. In what strikes me as an ironic twist, those of the highest moral character are being considered *immoral* people who should be avoided, silenced, punished, and deprived of rights once considered universal in Western society.

On a recent trip to Den Haag, the Netherlands, this attitude was pointed out to me in a startling way. While researching some of the elements in this book, I paid a visit to the sweeping grounds of the Peace Palace where the ICJ meets and, with several others, received a VIP guided tour.

The building is a magnificent structure designed in a Neo-Renaissance style by French architect Louis Cordonnier. On one end of the building, a tall bell tower looks over the city. Inside, one gets the feeling of entering a world-class museum that befits the name "palace." Blue and white tiles cover the floor on the ICJ wing. Stairways are wide and grand. Sweeping structural arches give an old world feeling. Gifts of art and material are used throughout the structure, including contributions from Russia, Indonesia, Switzerland, and the United States.

The structure also houses the Permanent Court of Arbitration, the Peace Palace Library, and The Hague Academy of International Law.

On my visit, our small group was led by a knowledgeable tour guide who spoke with unmitigated awe about what the building represented and about Andrew Carnegie who, through his friendship with Tsar Nicholas II and their common dreams for peace, was led to provide the funds for its construction and to attract the impressive collection of art within. Clearly, our guide was a woman in love with the concept and the conduct of all that goes on in the Peace Palace.

I saw many unforgettable things, including the massive female figure reliefs of Veritas and Justitia (*Truth* and *Justice*) overlooking the ICJ courtroom, but the most memorable event came after we ascended the wide central staircase, a staircase designed in the fashion of the Paris Opera House.

We saw several magnificent pieces of art, were shown one of the largest oriental rugs in the world, and magnificent silk wall coverings. But atop the stairway was a statue that I never expected: a depiction of Jesus Christ, holding a cross. No one has accused me of being shy and retiring, so I asked the tour guide, "Isn't that Jesus?"

She seemed stunned by the question. The Peace Palace is a purely secular site and operates in a purely secular fashion. Talking about Jesus clearly made her uncomfortable. She passed on the question and said we would talk about it after the tour of another room.

One thing I should mention is the limitation on photography. We were told that taking photos inside the Peace Palace is strictly forbidden. In fact, at the time of this writing, a determined "computer nerd" found it almost impossible to find an authorized photo of the Jesus statue.

Once the tour was over, but before the group scattered, I asked the guide again about the statue. Her first response? An apology.

"I apologize that you had to see an image that reminded you of a religious personality. This is a place of peace, not a place for religion or division. That is not a statue of Jesus as you may think."

She was never able to tell me whom the statue represented. She did, however, tell us that the artwork was a replica of one in the Andes Mountains, sculpted there to remind the world of the peace between Chile and Argentina brokered over many years, but in part by the Permanent Court of Arbitration. She explained that to show their commitment to a new peace, the two countries had commissioned a peace statue and had it made in part from the metal of melted weapons. A replica was made later and given for display in the Peace Palace, so therefore the statue had no meaning except to celebrate the success in finding peace.

What amazed me was the true embarrassment this guide expressed that a guest would think the statue to be Jesus the Christ, and the denial of the statue's likeness. One might argue that I was inserting Jesus into the robed figure, but the presence of a large Christian cross sealed the deal for me. An easier explanation would have been for her to say, "Chile and Argentina have a strong Catholic heritage, so an image of Christ is to be expected. Neither the ICJ nor the PCA advocate any religion." That's an explanation I can understand. Not agree with, but understand.

Upon my return from the Netherlands, I did some research to see if I could confirm my assumption regarding the statue. I wasn't disappointed. I discovered that the original sculpture located on the border of Argentina and Chile is, in fact, called, "Christ in the Andes". And at its base is the following powerful inscription, *"Sooner shall these mountain crags crumble to dust than Chile and Argentina shall break this peace which at the feet of Christ the Redeemer they have sworn to maintain."*

Though I was pleased to affirm what seemed obvious, what will stick with me for a long time is the guide's frustration over my identifying the statue as a likeness of "Jesus". It reminds me how the world has changed in its view of Christianity. It makes one recall Pope John Paul II's 2003 call that the European Union's new Constitution acknowledge Europe's Christian heritage. His plea was rejected.

This growing mindset is chilling. Every day, I deal with people who must battle for simple religious liberty and their freedom of speech. Just a few decades ago, this was unusual, but now these battles are pervasive throughout the world, East and West.

The Church has endured – and continues to endure – many persecutions. What is fairly new are the current forms of "legal persecution," and the rise of laws that deprive individuals of freedoms they have enjoyed for centuries, freedoms granted not by governments but by God Himself.

This book is an attempt to show some of that frightening change and the threat to religious freedom that we at ADF face daily, across America and all over the world.

The battle is far from over, but attitudes are quickly changing in ways that must be met and challenged. These times call for many new alliances and common efforts within the Body – some of them uncomfortable, but without which we will fail. If the Lord delays His return and we hold back the legal tides, we will have plenty of time to argue about the countless issues that divide rather than unite the Body of Christ. In the meantime, my colleagues and I at ADF and allies around the world are committed to protecting religious liberty and the right to freely speak, hear, and live the Good News (James 4:15).

There are many people like Pat Preston out there, and we are doing our best to help them and to confine the scenario presented in this book to the pages of fiction.

The outcome of this legal and moral struggle will determine what tomorrow looks like in America and across the globe. Much of how this turns out depends on what people of good will and faith do or fail to do.. . . And in the midst of it all, we must first and foremost recognize the simple but foundational truth found in John 15:5, ". . .without me [Christ], you can do nothing."

Alan Sears, Esquire
www.telladf.org
September, 2011

ALLIANCE DEFENSE FUND

Defending Our First Liberty

The Alliance Defense Fund is a *legal alliance* defending the right to hear and speak the Truth. ADF protects and promotes religious freedom through a unique combination of *strategic coordination* with other like-minded organizations; *training* practicing Christian attorneys and law students in Constitutional law and Christian worldview; *funding* key, precedent-setting cases; and, when needed, engaging in direct *litigation* through our in-house team of Christ-centered attorneys.

For more information on ADF, please visit www.telladf.org

Trial & Error is the sequel to Alan Sears first novel, *In Justice*. To request a copy of *In Justice*, visit www.telladf.org